The

Jonathan Izard is
the theatre as both an actor
presenter on Melody Radio and lives in London.

CW00449242

JONATHAN IZARD

THE BIGGER THE BETTER

HarperCollins*Publishers*

HarperCollins*Publishers*
77–85 Fulham Palace Road,
Hammersmith, London W6 8JB

A Paperback Original 1994
1 3 5 7 9 8 6 4 2

Copyright © Jonathan Izard 1994

The Author asserts the moral right to
be identified as the author of this work

A catalogue record for this book
is available from the British Library

ISBN 0 00 647335 0

Set in Linotron Meridien by
Rowland Phototypesetting Ltd
Bury St Edmunds, Suffolk

Printed in Great Britain by
HarperCollinsManufacturing Glasgow

All rights reserved. No part of this publication may be
reproduced, stored in a retrieval system, or transmitted,
in any form or by any means, electronic, mechanical,
photocopying, recording or otherwise, without the prior
permission of the publishers.

This book is sold subject to the condition that it shall not,
by way of trade or otherwise, be lent, re-sold, hired out or
otherwise circulated without the publisher's prior consent
in any form of binding or cover other than that in which it
is published and without a similar condition including this
condition being imposed on the subsequent purchaser.

For my parents
Joan and Don James
who have always encouraged me
in everything I've done

Thanks to

My agent, Mark Lucas, at Peters Fraser & Dunlop and my editor, Nick Sayers, at HarperCollins for their belief and advice. Rena Valeh for research and an invaluable critical eye. Also to Marian M, Angie K, Vicki M, Vicki H, Laura C, Elizabeth Z, Becca N, Sarah G, Ken Evans and Sister Wallace and her nursing team at the Intensive Care Unit, Queen Mary's Hospital, Roehampton.

PROLOGUE

'Look, Christopher. Look at the pretty patterns.'

The summer breeze gently ruffled the floppy fringe of hair that hung over the little boy's eyes as he stood by the pond with his baby brother, proud that he'd been left in charge for a few minutes. Well, he was four now and that was quite grown up. Daddy was in charge really, but he'd gone to answer the door.

The two young faces watched as the late afternoon sunshine dappled the shallow water, making sparkles of light dance around like diamonds across the rippling surface.

'Look at the fairies on the water,' he said and saw the baby laugh with delight and point his stubby finger at the magic picture before them. The world was full of so many exciting things; as they grew up they were going to explore them together.

'Daddy said we mustn't get too close to the edge. Here, hold tight.'

But just then he thought he heard a cry and turned to look behind him.

The windows of the big old house were in shadow and they gazed over the rambling garden dark and unseeing like the eyes of a blind man. There was another sound from inside, something odd and not quite clear. Was it his father calling him? He let his brother's hand go and walked importantly up the garden path; perhaps he was needed.

He climbed on to a stone pot on the terrace, pushing the spidery fingers of honeysuckle aside to look through the window. He pressed his soft nose to the cold glass and calmly watched the scene inside.

Daddy and the babysitter were playing a game on the

settee. He couldn't see her face but he knew it was her because of her school uniform, the grey skirt with the yellow shirt and socks and the straw hat she let him play with. The hat had a blue and yellow ribbon and it was lying on the floor. Daddy was on top of her but with his hands on her shoulders and his arms straight so she couldn't get up. He seemed to be trying to squash her and the game was for her to push him off.

He laughed at their game, it looked fun. But it wasn't fair; Daddy was much too strong.

Then he saw that her shirt was open and she had lumps on her chest like Mummy only not nearly so big and squashy. Daddy bent down and tried to eat one but she squirmed her body away as if he was tickling.

He felt excited now in a different way. In a minute he'd go and fetch Christopher; they could watch together, another secret shared experience.

He couldn't hear properly and the window was misting up where he was breathing on it, but knowing that he shouldn't be watching made it even more exciting. He was hidden by the tendrils of the honeysuckle that wrapped around his neck and face, threatening to envelop him completely if he stayed still too long. The sticky-sweet odour was thick and heavy like a throbbing pain in his head.

She was really trying hard now to get him off her, but Daddy was being pretty rough. She tried to shout something, but Daddy suddenly brought his hand across her face with a loud smack that he could hear really clearly. She looked so surprised, her face had a funny look. He saw a trickle of red come from her mouth and now she didn't want to play any more. She started to cry but Daddy had her tie – more blue and yellow stripes – and was tying it round her wrists and then pulling her arms back over her head. He went on bouncing on her with his whole body, talking to her all the time and looking cross as if she'd spoilt the game.

He was sure now that Daddy would be cross if he knew

10

he was watching. He felt odd now; not excited but a bit afraid. He climbed down from the window to return to his baby brother.

But Christopher would never see Daddy's game. He must have liked the pretty patterns on the water so much he tried to catch them in his hand. His tiny body was floating calmly in the still water, bobbing gently up and down. His face was under the water, as if he was looking for something on the bottom of the pond.

The sunlight still danced all around him as if it was laughing at his foolishness.

1

Kate Fitch took her customary three deep breaths, sucking the air right down to the bottom of her lungs, feeling the satisfying movement of the diaphragm. As she exhaled for the third time she felt George's hand taking hers and she smiled encouragingly across at him. Or rather, down at him; even in his shoes with lifts he was a good three inches shorter than her.

Hal Brand, the new young host of the programme, had started their intro.

'Well, what can you say about today's special birthday guest? He is to British television what Thermos is to vacuum flasks: synonymous. He's done it all from tea boy via arts programmes like "Viewpoint" and political interviews in his series "Factfinder" to arrive at the very pinnacle of the shaky tree: his own live nationwide show is consistently the most watched programme of the week. He's the man I want to be when I grow up! And with this megastar of the media his lovely wife, actress and beauty ... ladies and gentlemen, please give a very special "Lunchtime Live" welcome to Kate Fitch and George "Mister Television" King!'

Kate licked her lips and gums to make sure her smile didn't become fixed and, to the sound of ecstatic applause from the studio audience, George led her out through the wooden archway, down the steps and across the studio floor. They waved and smiled like politicians with small majorities and even after the floor manager had signalled for the noise to die down it continued spontaneously for almost thirty seconds – an age on live television.

Hal Brand couldn't get a word in and he could obviously

see from the monitor that the director had chosen a giant close-up of his face, waiting, waiting for the applause to die away. His black skin was already damp with perspiration, Kate noticed as she turned to him with her 'Queen Mother' expression. Poor love, he was a new boy at this game. Having to interview her husband in his first week must be like taking your driving test around Brands Hatch. Still, good old George would make sure it was all right; he was the ultimate old pro. He knew all the tricks. And then some.

'Welcome to the programme,' Hal was saying. 'Nice of you both to fit us into your busy schedule. George, it's an unusual position for you, to be the interviewee for once. Now, I said you were our birthday guest; it's fifty not out this week, isn't it?'

'It is indeed and I feel rather alarmed at the thought, but very privileged too, to be doing a job I enjoy so much.'

'Well, congratulations on the birthday.' More applause spattered around the studio. Kate joined in, gently patting her fingertips together so as not to give the sound boys any problems, and beamed her admiration at George. He acknowledged this with a modest inclination of the head. His hair reflected a healthy shine under the strong lights and his complexion was exactly the right tone, darker than pale but not so tanned as to inspire envy in the punters of Purley.

Kate looked at them now, row upon row of lumpy mums of a certain age who worshipped everything her husband said and did. He could have drowned kittens on his show, they would have understood and defended his right to do it.

She wondered what they felt about her position. They must hate her, being closer to him than anyone, able to touch and kiss him whenever she wanted, spending endless days and never-to-be-forgotten nights with him in his strong arms, listening to his romantic, silver-tongued flattery that would charm the very stars from the skies. Was that what they thought?

14

'Well, "George King Now!" has been peak viewing ever since it first began over a year ago, hasn't it? What is it that makes it so special?'

Dear, oh dear, thought Kate, what a cliché. He's a sweet young man, but his interviewing technique is zero.

'Ah, well, now we do have some excellent guests on the programme and they always give good value for money.'

'Oh come on, what about you, George? People don't watch for your guests, they watch it for you. Don't you?' Hal turned to the audience. Enthusiastically they called 'yes' and clapped again. George, in his well-practised style, crinkled his eyes and made his eyebrows into a comical expression that said 'I just can't help being so cute', aware all the time which camera was on him.

'Kate,' Hal said, his own gaze coming up from the notes on the sofa between them. 'What's it like living with this legend? Is he a megastar at home as well?'

'Oh no, Hal. When we're back at the ranch George is just my old man. Aren't you, love?' He goofed at the rows of shopping bags beyond the cameras and got his laugh. 'We're Mr and Mrs K. up the road and we get on with ordinary family life – when we have the time, of course!'

'Yes, there can't be much free time. What sort of things do you enjoy doing together? George?'

'Oh, you know, we go to the supermarket at the week-end, we're involved in the local community –'

'Hampstead, right?'

'Yes. And we do the odd spot of gardening. Sometimes we even watch the telly together!'

'And does he help you with your lines, Kate, when you're doing a play?'

'Oh yes, if he's not too busy with his own projects.'

Hal had discreetly wiped the wetness from his upper lip with a finger. He looked uncomfortable, terrified of the two of them. Perhaps the director had told him something through the earpiece that had upset his plans.

'Now, fifty is a fine age. You've achieved just about everything there is to be achieved in British television. Where do you go from here?'

'Oh, I don't plan anything, I never have. I've just been lucky and enjoyed what I've done. I don't even map out the interviews, you know. I mean, I give them some thought, of course, but I like to sit down and just have a good old natter with my guests. I think they appreciate that. Even the big ones, Streisand, Newman, Reagan . . .'

'Yes, you've done them all, haven't you? Tell me, which was the best interview ever of all the hundreds? The most interesting?'

George considered it for a moment, as if he'd never been asked it before. Something passed over those famous striking features, a change of mood, a shift of emphasis.

'Of all the hundreds, the thousands in fact, I think the most . . . satisfying to do was with that little eight-year-old girl Sinead who'd lost her sight, her two sisters, her mum and dad in that bomb explosion in Belfast last year. Do you remember that?' The audience murmured that they did. 'I think the sheer courage and matter-of-factness of her attitude was what almost made me cry. The humanity of that child, the fact that she could forgive the . . . I'm sorry, the bastards who did that terrible thing and talk optimistically about the future of her country took my breath away. It really puts your own rather shallow life into perspective. It makes you re-evaluate things when you come across the display of such magnanimity in a mere child . . .'

There was a stillness in the warm studio, every eye on George's pensive expression. Hal let the moment speak for itself, nodding in silent agreement, unsure perhaps how long to let it ride. Finally, when he realized George wasn't going on, he took up the baton again.

'And in fact you're putting your weight behind a similar project that you believe in very strongly, aren't you?'

'That's right, Hal.' George bent forward and picked up

the book from the glass table where Becca, his amazingly efficient PA, had made sure it would be. 'It's about the terrible situation in East Africa. Everyone knows about it but we don't seem to be doing enough. It's heartbreaking what those poor people are going through, not only civil war but famine and now flooding too, so that what few crops were growing have now been completely ruined. As I say, things like that really make you feel very humble, don't they? And make you wonder how you can help.'

'And this book is part of that, is it?'

'Yes. I suppose I've been in a privileged position for quite a few years, nattering with some jolly famous people that not everyone gets the chance to meet, and I thought I could jot down some little stories and it might make an interesting collection. And here it is. I've called it *From the Horse's Mouth*, because I like to let people tell their own stories.'

He held the glossy hardback up to camera two, careful not to obscure the large photograph of himself or the full title: *From the Horse's Mouth: George King and other Stars*.

'All the profits from this book will go to George King's FEAR. The Fund for East African Relief. So, you get a good read, some lovely piccies of me with the likes of Hoffman and Connery and Madonna and you do a lot of people a lot of good. So,' – straight to camera one with his famous twinkle – 'get out there and buy it, okay? All right, Hal, enough plugging. Sorry about that.'

The audience laughed. Kate smiled too, dutifully. She knew what was coming next.

'No, George, that's fine,' said the young interviewer, still in awe of the Great Man of Television. 'For something like that, feel free to plug all you like.'

'You think it's a good idea, do you?' George had his most sincere face on.

'I certainly do. I hope it does very well.'

'You know, the hardback costs less than twenty quid. One penny less, in fact. Got your wallet on you?'

17

Hal laughed with the audience but there was a frightened look in his eyes. This interview was getting away from him. 'Actually, no . . . I, er . . .'

'Look, I'll even sign this one for you.' George opened the book and flourished his Mont Blanc pen dramatically across the page, his usual scrawl with the little crown over the 'K'.

'There, that's probably just about doubled its value. What d'you reckon?'

Poor Hal Brand was out of his depth. He looked to Kate for support, but that's exactly what she was: merely the support act. George was away on his own here, in his element, manipulating a live television audience with the renowned King charm and wit.

'What shall we do, auction it?' George called to the rows of eager faces gazing at their heart-throb hero. Someone called out, 'I'll give you thirty quid', then another, 'Forty', then 'Fifty'.

Hal put his finger to his ear to help him catch the instructions from his director. 'Well, we will auction the book later on, so don't you worry.'

'Ah good, and there are plenty of copies for all of you,' George added conspiratorially and heard a satisfied mutter in reply.

'For now, though, let's get back to the birthday. How will you celebrate?'

'Oh, nothing special. Perhaps we'll go out together for a quiet meal somewhere. Nothing flash.'

'Just the two of you?'

'Oh yes, me and the old lady.' He smiled at Kate, took her hand in his and held it on his lap. The biddies sighed with envy.

'And, Kate, just before we finish, what about you? Are you busy these days?'

'Oh yes, very busy. Not only looking after the old man here but considering various scripts at the moment.'

'Anything you can talk about?'

18

'Well, I'm hoping to be involved in a new series on the other side but nothing's settled yet.'

'We haven't seen you on our screens for a while, have we? Are you avoiding telly in favour of the stage?'

'No, not especially. I like to ring the changes. It just depends which way things go at certain times, you know.' She smiled wildly at him; he looked alarmed.

'Of course all the talk at the moment is about the casting for the London production of the next smash hit musical from Broadway, isn't it?'

'You mean *O Jackie*? Yes, it certainly seems to be on everyone's lips.'

'And the exciting thing is that if British Equity agree to JFK himself being played by an American actor they're going to insist that Jackie is played by someone British.'

'Or vice versa. An American Jackie and a British Jack. I certainly think that would be the right compromise otherwise we'll have the *Miss Saigon* situation again but in reverse, with the producers refusing to bring their show over here. And that would be a huge loss for West End audiences.'

'And who do you think would make a good Jackie?'

'Oh well, there are so many fine actresses of the right age. Dear Judi would be excellent. Or Maggie. Or even Vanessa.'

'Glenda would be good for box office, wouldn't she? Especially now she's in the Cabinet.'

'Well, I'm not sure about the singing and dancing. And then Jackie was a very . . . glamorous lady.'

The audience tittered at her gentle put-down. Hal didn't seem to understand it. He was probably listening to a countdown in his ear.

'Of course, there's someone else who would be very good for the part,' Kate smiled coyly.

'Who's that?'

'Well, modesty forbids . . .'

Hal looked miles away. Was he being very stupid or very cruel? Whichever, it was unforgivable.

19

'Oh! You? Really? But . . . well, yes, of course. You'd be
. . . excellent. Er, George, tell me, how exactly did you get
your big break in television . . . ?'

Kate could feel the blush rise in her elegant cheeks.
She'd been made to look a total fool, out of her depth in
the company of the Dames of British theatre. Why would
no one take her seriously any more? She pointed her
listening face at George while he settled into a familiar
anecdote on his favourite subject: himself.

2

'*A sooty! A goddam sooty!*' George fumed as soon as the dressing-room door was closed and he was alone with Kate and his PA.

'George, please. Hal is not . . . what you said. He is black.' Kate braced herself for the inevitable onslaught of her husband's ire.

'He's a coon, for Christ's sake! Becca! Why didn't you tell me I was going to be grilled by a jungle-bunny?'

'Oh George, really!'

'I'm sorry, Mr King. I wasn't told until the programme was already on the air. I was as shocked as you were that the plans were changed. Apparently the original interviewer, Belinda Sinclair –'

'That's the tall tart with knockers like netballs, yeh?'

'She was taken rather ill during the transmission with some stomach bug and had to leave the set, so Hal Brand inherited her pieces, as it were.'

'Stomach bug? Morning sickness probably. She's fucking the director, isn't she?' George lit one of his favourite giant cigars and inhaled the bitter fumes.

'I really wouldn't know.'

'Well, she's screwed everyone else to get where she is now.'

Kate opened a window and looked at the dreary vista of car park, rubbish skips and bottle bank. So much for the glamour of showbiz.

'I'm very sorry, Mr King.' Becca sounded genuinely contrite. Kate wondered not for the first time just how much she was really in his thrall and how much secret venom she felt for the way he treated her. It was impossible to

21

tell; Becca played her cards so close to her chest they'd have served as a novelty bra.

'Obviously I've demanded a written apology from the producer and the Head of Daytime Television for this change in agreed arrangements for the interview and some kind of compensatory appearance for you. For you both.' Becca suddenly remembered Kate had been part of the deal.

'Oh, don't worry about me. I don't do many live chat shows any more.' Kate didn't even try to keep the bitterness from her voice.

'It's out-fucking-rageous,' George chuntered, puffing away. 'That brat was doing children's continuity until about three weeks ago with his hand up some puppet's arsehole. Sooty and Sooty probably. Jesus! I'd never have agreed to do the spot with a coon.'

'George! Please, can we drop it?' Kate glared at him and then glanced towards Becca who was checking details on the lap-top computer that was the beating heart of George's — and therefore also her own — life.

'She knows what I mean. It lowers the whole tone of the thing. Drags me down to his level. It makes it so . . . sordid. So downmarket.'

'Well, we can only hope the fans of Mister Television don't have quite such narrow minds as their hero.' Kate wafted the foul fug of smoke towards the window.

'Mr King, your next appointment today is a meeting with Derek Kettle and the research team for this week's "George King Now!". There'll also be someone from *Famous Faces* there to do a quick interview, they're doing a profile. I have a list of the questions; we can go over them on the way. Later on there's a voice-over for Citroën UK and a photo-call at St Mary's Hospital. They've named a children's ward after you because of your fund-raising on their behalf.'

'What fund-raising?'

'Oh, don't worry about that. I've written your ad-libs. I suggest we make a move in the next . . . four minutes.'

George was excavating deep inside a nostril with the

nail of his index finger. 'You've got notes for me on that fiasco just now, I take it?' He always needed her objective comments and criticisms to ensure the King image was up to scratch.

'One or two little suggestions. I actually thought it went very well. Considering.'

'Huh. No thanks to your incompetence.' He examined the booty under his nail and rubbed it to nothing between finger and thumb as if making a stagey gesture about money. Suddenly he rounded on Kate, jutting his ruddy face at her. 'And what's all this crap about "the old man", eh? We do not refer to age, right?'

She looked at him as she would at a spoilt child.

'Right?' he barked.

'Whatever you say, George.'

He pushed past her and slammed the window closed. His proximity caused her to flinch slightly and shrink away from him. Turning to Becca he bowed his head almost religiously, seeking blessing, and then with a well-practised gesture peeled his toupee off from back to front, letting it fall into his cupped palm where it nestled like a moribund rodent scraped up off a busy road. Becca quickly checked there were no members of that dreaded species the General Public outside who might glimpse him less than complete, and although they were safe she steered him gently with a hand on his shoulder across to the other side of the room. Here she took the mop of perfect hair from him and began to brush it meticulously. George scratched his shiny scalp with stubby fingers; tiny flakes of dry skin showered into the air around him.

'And touting for work! All that shit about some play and who's going to get the part. Who fucking cares?'

'Every actor in England cares, George,' she snapped. Kate would defend her thespian corner with the fury of a mother fox protecting injured young. He might be the great star of television but he knew nothing of her world, the real world of talent and craft: the stage.

23

'It's not just any production, it's *O Jackie*, the biggest thing since the stage version of *Dances with Wolves*. And who gets to play Jackie matters to every actress between thirty and sixty. This is an Evita of a part. It's made a star of the woman on Broadway, that Dyane Schotts. It'll do the same over here. So don't belittle it.'

'My, my, we are touchy, aren't we? Just because that little milk chocolate bar kid didn't think you were leading lady material. Ha! Perhaps his granny hasn't told him about the days when you were a starlet.'

That hurt. Anything did that rubbed in the differences between their careers, his riding the crest of an apparently never-ending wave and hers in terminal slump after that early promise. The events that had mysteriously changed both their professional lives – and so much else – would be with them, even if unacknowledged, always.

Kate tightened her lips and determined yet again not to sink to his level. Not in front of a third party, at least.

She took a sly, sideways look at Becca. There was something unnerving about her, the way she watched and never spoke out of turn. As if she had no thoughts or feelings of her own, no personality at all, other than what was necessary for looking after a Major Media Commodity. Everything about her was perfect. Perfect hair, dark brown and scraped back off the face, held in a gold clip. Perfect manners and an appropriate pleasantry always ready to oil the wheels of communication or calm a potentially volatile situation. Perfectly polite and perfectly correct. Perfect clothes. Unexciting and conservative, but always immaculate. Today she was in a tailored cream jacket over a pale blue silk blouse with a classic navy skirt. Not a crease or piece of fabric fluff marred the effect.

There had been a time when Kate thought George was having an affair with Becca, especially when she was rapidly promoted from typist to researcher to PA and began to assume more and more responsibility for running his daily life. But that thought had passed; no, she was just bloody good at her job. And so patient. She never protested at his foul-mouthed invective or his attitude to the public – 'the Scum' he called them.

'Hello, Alec?' Becca was speaking into her mobile. 'Would you bring the car round, please? Mr King will be leaving in three minutes. Thank you.'

There was a knock at the door. Becca called 'Just a moment', and motioned for him to lower his head. Obediently he did so, allowing her to fit the toupee on to his bald crown again swiftly and professionally. She checked the effect, teasing a few stray hairs into place, the better to convince, then she nodded at him that all was well and answered the door.

It was Hal Brand, collar loose and holding a glass of wine. He came in and shook Kate's hand.

'Thank you both so much for the interview. I expect you know by now, Belinda was taken ill while we were on the air, so I'm afraid it wasn't as smooth as it might have been. I hadn't mugged up on . . . well, prepared for the two of you. Belinda would've done you a much better job. But you were both marvellous.' He smiled at them. He had an easy, boyish grin which would have helped the interview no end if he'd been able to show it then. He was actually quite charming, Kate thought. She found him refreshing. But then, after living with George for thirty years, a rabid hyena would have been a relief.

'Great! Great interview, Hal,' said George, pumping the younger man's hand enthusiastically, now all charm himself. 'You did very well, you've got a lot of talent. I shall have to watch out!'

'Oh, I don't know about that, Mr King.' Hal laughed at the flattery.

'George, please. We're colleagues, after all. Listen, send my very best wishes to . . .'

'Belinda,' Becca prompted.

'Belinda. I hope she makes a speedy recovery. We both do, don't we, dear?'

25

'Yes, of course, dear.' Kate stepped dutifully to his side and slipped her arm through George's. He stank of that foul cigar. From this angle she could just detect the discreet 'fishskins', sticky things like stamp hinges that, cleverly positioned, could lift loose skin with the rejuvenating effects of a temporary facelift. He was all sham. Bullshit and sham. It was so unfair that he continued to get away with it. She beamed at Hal, playing her part to perfection, the little woman in her place.

'Well done, you,' she said. 'I enjoyed the interview very much.'

'Really? Well, you both made it much easier for me. I'm sorry I messed up that thing about the play. The director was talking to me at the time and I didn't catch what you said.' He was a very poor liar, but she could forgive him for that. He was a sweet man. He'd probably been very good on kids' telly.

The director called round as well to thank them and apologize. George and Kate were equally charming to him. It had become second nature now. It was Becca's role to iron out problems and prepare the way for his coming; George was the front man, the charmer, Mister Nice Guy. And he was the best.

They left the building together, George and Kate arm in arm, ever the happy couple. A small crowd of about twenty surged towards them as they pushed through the glass doors of Television Centre. Eager bodies pressed up to them, holding out gifts or scraps of paper and articles of clothing for George to sign. He did, throwing naughty, flirtatious comments to the women — and they were all women — as he signed and kept walking. He knew he had a tight schedule, Becca saw there was never a moment wasted, and he had no desire to stop and talk with these pathetic, working-class crones. He had a busy life to run, for Christ's sake.

Nobody wanted Kate's signature, of course; she was used to the role of also-ran by now. Although it never ceased

pressing — and pecking — the flesh, making sure no stray hands got too near the hairpiece. 'Thank you so much for coming to see me. Bless you all. Now, don't stand about here and get cold, your varicose veins will give you hell!' They giggled and simpered at the same time, clutching their mementoes of this special occasion to their heaving bosoms. Kate climbed into the Rolls and George backed in next to her, still smiling and waving, blowing kisses like a teenage rock star. It really was pathetic.

Once they had pulled away and the tinted windows had made their world private once again, Kate let her fixed smile collapse; George slumped down into the soft leather seat and let out a fruity, reverberating fart.

'Oh, thank Christ for that. I've been hanging on to that for too long. That biddy with the lipstick from nostril to chin nearly squeezed it out of me just now.' He sniffed the air. 'Phwaaw! That could kill at fifty feet!' He opened the window again to share the perfume with the good burghers of Shepherds Bush.

They drove as far as the NCP car park where Kate left them to their business and transferred to her own car, a bright red Mercedes 500SL. One of the benefits of being married to George was the calibre of toys she got to play with.

She drove fast, as fast as London afternoon traffic would allow, to Robin's office. One or two heads turned as she passed but she knew they were impressed by her wheels, not her.

Robin had recently set up his new stall in Chelsea Harbour. Others said he was mad to move out of 'The Garden', as they called that special theatrical corner of WC2, but he said with his usual aplomb, 'I'm exclusive. They beat a path to my door.' And it was true, he was perfectly at home in this bright, shiny, soulless environment, looking down his long, slender nose at the incongruous mixture of ersatz glamour and dereliction with an air of patrician disdain from his eyrie on the seventh floor.

The brass plaque on the door of his half of the building said simply 'Robin Quick'. No 'Limited' or 'Enterprises' or 'Associates' or even explanation of what he did. If you didn't know, you didn't need to know.

Robin Quick had been her agent for more years than either of them would admit in public. Since she had been a star, at any rate. That long. They had courted each other, professionally speaking, when she was doing a season at the Old Vic. He was the new kid on the block, the hottest young agent in town and she had recently come down from Cambridge trailing glorious clouds and a string of reviews in the national papers that were to die for. They grew together, feeding off each other's contacts and helping to make one another's reputations. When her star waned, his continued to grow from strength to strength. He'd taken on the top people: Hopkins, Finney, Bates, Dench and a whole brood of Redgraves. He hadn't made the mistake of taking time off for 'personal reasons'. His own marriage, to a rather brassy girl from Caerphilly, had quickly fizzled out and he'd channelled all his energies into the agency. He described himself now as a 'triffid', more sexually interested in plants than people. Sometimes Kate wondered if he was a closet case, but in their profession he would have had more to gain by coming out than staying in so she doubted it. There was something of an up-market Kenneth Williams about him; arch, ascetic and acerbic. Outwardly warm, he was quicker than anyone with a 'thank you' card or a phone call of condolence, but under the surface was a distant froideur. He gave nothing of himself away. His spindly body could have belonged to a youth in mid-puberty but served him well enough, a fastidiously precise and elegant man of fifty-something.

'Kate, darling, what a joy to see you. How kind of you to pop in. You look marvellous. Mwa, mwa!' They kissed on both cheeks without touching. 'Will you have a tea with me? I was about to anyway.'

'I'd love a coffee, Robin.'

'Do you think you should? It can be very harsh on the stomach, you know. How about a Barley Cup?'

'Yuk. No thanks. Tea will do fine, the same as yours.'

'Marcia, my poppet, would you make it two of the rosehips? Thanks,' he said to one of his 'angels' in the outer office and then gave her his total concentration. 'Loved you on "Lunchtime Live" just now. So dignified, so cool. George doesn't appreciate you, does he?'

'Tell me about it.' She sighed. Robin knew what George was really like, of course. He was one of the few people who did. He had known the Great Man from university days. Robin had advised her to drop him, he was a dead weight around her neck, annoying people on newspapers and in television by telling them constantly, 'I'm Kate Fitch's boyfriend, you know.' 'So what?', was their usual response. 'What can you do?' He could hustle, he knew how to talk his way through closed doors and make it easier for the top brass to say 'yes' to him straight away than 'no' another dozen times. 'That irritating little runt, Kate Fitch's boyfriend' had grown up to be the top banana. Now Kate was 'George King's wife'.

'Without you at his side that nauseating Housewives' Choice image wouldn't count for half as much, you know. But he won't realize that until the day you leave him.'

'Oh no, it won't come to that, Robin. Not now.' Kate was used to this from him. He felt she was never taken seriously in her own profession because of always appearing in George's shade. 'There was a time . . . But we've come through too much together to be split apart by . . .' she smiled sadly at what she had to admit, 'by the fact that our marriage is now a hollow sham.'

'Quite.'

Marcia brought in the tea and a plate of various strange objects.

'Thanks, my dear. Katyushka, have a carob cookie. Or a piece of dried rhubarb? How about some sunflower seeds?'

'I'll pass, thanks, it's too healthy for me.' She was looking

31

forward to something really gooey later on. 'Look, about the thing on "Lunchtime Live". I really meant what I said. I think they should see me for the part of Jackie. It's often been said there's a certain similarity in the bone structure. The squarish jaw, wide mouth, hair colouring. She's got to age from teens to death at sixty-four, right? Well, that's no problem, especially if the actual assassination takes place behind a gauze in a strobe, like it does on Broadway.'

'You saw it, didn't you?'

'Yes, last year when George did that White House special. They gave it to a nobody out there. Now, I may be an ex-somebody but I'm not a nobody.'

She leaned forward over the desk, her strong features showing passion as if it were a pain. 'I know everyone wants the chance to play it but I have a right to be considered, Robin. I know I could do it! For the sake of our friendship, you've got to get them to see me. Just let me prove to them that it's my part. Please, Robin, do it for me?'

He sipped his rosehip tea impassively as she spoke. Having replaced the china cup silently in the saucer and turned it so the handle was exactly parallel with the edge of the desk he gave a thin, sad smile and spoke.

'Everything, and I mean everything you've just said to me I said to the producer yesterday afternoon. Barney was very polite, he listened to what I had to say. I've sent some of your tapes over to his London office and he said he'd look at them. I've no reason to disbelieve him. But I have to be honest, my love, and say it's going to be an uphill struggle.'

'But Robin —'

'I know, and I agree. You could do that part standing on George's head, but it's not me you have to convince. Barney Jungsheimer is one tough cashew nut, as they say. The good thing is that it's early days. For heaven's sake, the production isn't even definite yet; there's all the hassle over cross-casting to be settled with Equity first. It could be that they'll go for an American Jackie and a British JFK.'

32

'Oh, God, Kenneth Bragger.'

'We can only pray not.'

'There were all those ridiculous stories about Madonna when the thing opened. Is it true she only pulled out over a row about the costumes?'

'So I've heard. They wouldn't let her wear her bra made out of enamel funnels.'

'No!'

'That's not the worst; there was a *canard* on the loose about a certain . . .' Robin looked around theatrically and leaned towards her. 'Whoopi Goldberg.'

Kate's face was immobile with shock for a second.

'Robin! You're winding me up.'

'You're right. But remember these are not sane, rational people we're talking about; they are Americans.'

'True. But even so . . .'

'Even so. I know you want to be seen for that part and I'll do everything I can to make it happen. But . . . don't, *comme on dit*, hold your breath.' He gave her the look of a kindly uncle to an eager child to make sure she understood. 'However, it's not all *doomski-und-gloomski*.'

'Oh?' Kate paused in mid-sniff of rosehip.

'No, no. We're waiting to hear about the two telly jobs, of course; the market-gardeners and the disabled thingummy. Nice part that; you'd look fab in a wheelchair. But there's something else that might tickle your fanny. Bryan Harvey-Jones is casting for a pre-London tour of a rather entertaining new play. It could be just up your *Strasse*. It's called *Murder in Triplicate*. I've told him you just might be interested.'

'Oh, Robin, no. Touring a thriller? I'm worth better than that. Aren't I? After all my years in the biz? No, I won't do it. Absolutely not.'

'Never say *jamais*, my dear. Now then, you're not drinking your tea. Would you prefer blackcurrant?'

3

Suzi Sparks carefully applied her favourite mango and kumquat face pack and soaked herself in her pink, circular bath laced with a generous quantity of lemon and thyme scented gel which formed a heaving mass of bubbles. She took one of the many glossy magazines from the gilt table by the tub and flipped through the stories, the menus, the dress patterns, pausing to read only the article on 'How Princess Diana Keeps in Tip-Top Shape' and her horoscope. 'Virgo: you will be finding the world a dark place these days. You have every right to feel rejected but your patience will be rewarded in the end. Bide your time a little longer before making any decisive moves. Lucky colour: magenta.'

When the bubbles had all died and her body was visible through the cooling water again she cracked the white chalky mask off her face with a thorough repertoire of alarming grimaces. Then she showered and washed her hair with kiwi and coconut cream shampoo, which eased her conscience by not having been tested on animals. Those poor, furry little creatures. Not that she would ever have anything as unhygienic as a pet in her home and veal and pâté passed her pouty pink lips frequently, but the fluffiness of bunnies and pussy cats touched her little girl's heart.

With a delicate motion she dusted the rounded lumps and gentle damp hollows of her generous body with an expensive new powder by Nina Ricci and dabbed Chanel Number Five between her breasts and thighs and buttocks. Her body was, if not her fortune, her very comfortable income, so it deserved a little pampering.

In her bedroom Suzi stood naked in front of the wall of floor-to-ceiling mirrors which would reveal at the gentlest touch vast wardrobes crammed full with costly clothes that gave her almost more pleasure to look at than to wear. She hated the fact that they invariably looked better in the shop or even hanging on her rails than they did on her.

She observed her body now and tried to be as objective about it as she could. Well, within reason; there was no point in being too critical. In fact these examination sessions served as excuses for a little much needed ego-boosting before a session with her man.

Her breasts were full and, she liked to think, hung 'like delicious ripe fruit'. She'd read the phrase in one of those thin mauve books bought for a train journey once. Wasn't that what men wanted — something to remind them of their first suckling encounters, their mothers' nourishing teats? Not that she entertained more than one gentleman caller these days. He was adamant about that and made sure she didn't need to financially, but their company would be nice from time to time. She sometimes missed the giggles she'd had with the girls making blue movies or 'renting out her vajjie' in King's Cross.

Her hips were broad, certainly, but that's what her clients had always liked. Much better for business than those skinny-arsed little madams with no lumps or bumps, just straight lines like boys. 'Pear-shaped' was not an expression with which Suzi associated any insult. Pears were delicious.

Maybe, yes maybe her tummy was beginning to progress beyond the rounded towards the — well — plump, but that was no bad thing. Wasn't the Rubenesque figure highly praised and, more to the point, desired in the nineteenth century? Or was it the eighteenth? Anyway, 'comely wenches' were definitely in favour then; what about Nell Gwyn and all that?

Perhaps, though, it was time to make a trip to the swimming pool again. Half an hour's gentle breaststroke was supposed to be an excellent general muscle toner according to some doctor or other she'd heard on the radio.

35

She stepped closer to the mirror — peach-tinted to flatter — to examine her face. It spoke evidence of the money spent on it. On the facials, depilatories, massage, tinting, creaming, cleansing and bleaching, the perming, primping, crimping and cutting, the filling, capping and bridging. Not one of her visible teeth was real; she'd had them all done in one marathon session against the advice of her dentist and now she was delighted with what she called her 'American smile'. Anything too natural disturbed her.

She turned her back to the mirrors and, resting her hands on her chubby knees, wiggled what a certain Law Lord used to call her 'twin orbs', peering over her shoulder at the image as her evenly browned buttocks wobbled from side to side. Standing again she stroked a palm over the rolling landscape of a journey from throat to knee and smiled at her own soft, pink reflection.

Yes, she'd settle for that. She'd never see thirty again but still, she was in pretty good nick.

She dressed exotically in a see-through négligée, phoned the florist to order a delivery of flowers, anything pink — she liked having flowers around, preferably silk or paper ones but in extremis real blooms — and posed herself theatrically on one of the soft white leather settees to watch the television. She'd recorded 'Lunchtime Live' when she was in the bath. Now she saw George King telling the viewing millions about *From the Horse's Mouth*, tapping the famine relief badge on his sweater with a finger carefully positioned so as not to obscure the all-important knitwear logo. As she watched the images on the screen she let her hand stray beneath the flimsy gown and explore the soft moistness between her thighs. And she whispered words that she knew were taboo.

'Oh, Georgie, my darling. I love you. I do love you . . .'

As George talked about famine relief, Suzi took the matter of her personal relief into her own hands.

* * *

36

After George's session at the Back-Track Studios in Dean Street, spending fifteen minutes to earn a cool fifteen grand buy-out for some product that Becca had approved, he told her he had 'private business with an old school-friend' so she and Alec the chauffeur, their straight faces never betraying a hint of scepticism, dropped him at the entrance to a row of over-prettified mews cottages in South Kensington. Checking that the street was empty before he left the safety of the darkened interior of the Rolls, George took the mobile phone from Becca, checked his watch, said 'Be here in thirty minutes', and slunk out of sight.

Hunching and holding the collar of his coat up around his ears, he hugged the pink and cream walls to his left like some cartoon portrayal of a private eye expecting the ping of a bullet by his head at any moment.

At number nine he gave the special knock and the door was buzzed open.

'Oh, Georgie, honey, come in,' oozed Suzi. She gave him a little kiss on the mouth with coyly puckered lips. It reminded him uncomfortably of the way Kate kissed him on the rare occasions she felt she had to. 'You looked lovely on the telly just now.'

'Did you see me being interviewed by that niggerwimp Brand? God, what a cretin he is. Still, I was good. Bloody good.'

'Oh yes, you were, I thought you were –'

'Did they bring the package?'

'Yes, Georgie. It's here.' She showed him the cardboard box by the television.

'Thank fuck for corruption in Customs and Excise. Have you looked at them?'

'No. Just made sure they were all there.'

'And?'

'They are. One hundred and fifty. They're labelled "Playschool" and "Mister Floppy goes Shopping".'

'Ha-ha. Mister Stiffy, more like! Let's put one on.' He

37

took one of the cassettes from the box and pressed it into the jaws of the video machine. With the remote control he found the channel and watched as a young black girl, who looked no more than fourteen, was approached by two white men.

'Yeh,' breathed George. 'Take it, baby. Look at that, both ends at once. What a slut. Christ, I feel randy!'

'Ooh, so do I, Georgie.' Suzi looked away from the screen. 'I want to play with your peenie. But first I've got a special treat for you. Look, I made them myself.'

He looked where she was pointing. On the table was an old-fashioned cake stand piled high with tiny sponge cakes. They were iced in different colours — bright pink, white and an alarming electric blue — and each one was encased in a frilly paper cup. They were even decorated with glacé cherries, silver balls and pieces of shiny, plastic-looking angelica.

'Yeh, great.'

'They're fairy cakes,' Suzi explained. 'I made them this morning. From a recipe.'

'Right.'

'Especially for you.'

'Oh.' She never cooked. Never. Even toast confused her. George once said if she'd lived before the age of the microwave she'd have starved to death. 'Why?'

'Why?' She looked hurt. 'I thought we could have tea together. There are sandwiches in the kitchen, too. Would you like that, Georgie?'

'What?'

'Sandwiches. Salmon and cucumber.' Then she added proudly, 'I cut the crusts off.'

'Sod that, I haven't come here for fucking fairy cakes. Get your clothes off, woman.' What the hell was she up to? Getting all domestic, playing at being his wife. Was that it? He'd soon thrash that out of her. What he felt for her was impure and simple: lust.

She stood there, dressed ready for him in black

38

suspenders and stockings, without pants, very high heels and a see-through baby-doll négligée, beaming with a childish pride, as obvious and sickly as an iced cake herself. He loved it. He could smell her perfume; she'd used too much as usual. Her bleached hair was piled up on her head, ready for him to mess up in the frenzy of sex. The négligée was virtually transparent and her heavy breasts were thrust forward, inviting his touch, the large, dark nipples clearly visible.

'Christ,' he muttered. 'Look at your tits. They're so . . . so . . . what's the word? Big.' He was not at his most eloquent without his writers and the autocue. 'They're bloody fantastic.'

'Oh, Georgie, you sweet-talker.' She fluttered her blue-mascaraed eyelashes at him. 'Honestly, you're so forceful sometimes. I don't know why I let you get away with it.'

Suzi cupped her breasts together in her hands as if about to detach them and present them to him. He lowered his gaze to the fuzz between her legs and unconsciously licked his lips. His stumpy prick was rock hard, ready for action. He knew he could do whatever he wanted with her. Well, setting her up here with the allowance cost him enough, so why not?

'What did you have for lunch?' he asked, a look of real concern on his face.

'I had a three-bean casserole from M and S.'

'Magic! Come on, then.'

George took off his jacket and stepped out of his shoes.

'Don't you want a cakey first?' she pouted. 'Likkle Suzi made dem speshy for Georgie . . .'

'Sod that, bimbo. All I want to taste is your fucking pussy.' He began to paw at her, pulling at the flimsy négligée and tearing it.

'Oh Georgie –!'

'Come on!' He ran his fingers roughly over her nipples. They were hard and reminded him of the glacé cherries on the cakes.

39

Suzi loved it. He couldn't wait another second to have her; that proved he really cared. She let him maul her and press her clumsily down on to her back on the thick off-white carpet. Coyly she covered the mound of dyed blond hair between her thighs but he pulled her hands away unceremoniously, rolled her over and pushed his face up between her warm, cushiony buttocks.

'Ooh . . . wonderful,' he muttered, his voice muffled and tickling her. 'Go on now, fart in my face. Go on.'

With difficulty she managed it. He moaned with rapture. 'Mmm . . . that's so good.'

Then he had an idea.

'Mind you, it would be a shame to let your cakes go to waste.' He took one from the table, a gaudy pink one, and flipped her over on to her back. Without preamble he parted her legs wide, then pushed the cake up inside her, paper cup and all.

Suzi gasped at the roughness of the crinkled paper, then moaned with pleasure as she felt his nails dig into her soft backside and he pushed his face between her thighs, attacking her as a hungry dog devours a meal, his tongue probing towards the cake.

He was fully clothed still. With one hand he struggled to release his sweaty little cock into her mouth.

'Oh Georgie,' she thought, but not daring to say it aloud, 'I do love you so much.'

As Suzi wrapped her plump white legs around his head the delicately-posed toupee slid slowly to the floor.

4

'Well, he's asked me to do it.'

'Hm?'

'Bryan has asked me to do it. What do you think?'

'Yes.'

'You think I should do it?'

'Do what?'

'The show!'

'Hm?'

'Oh, for Christ's sake, George, will you put those bloody papers down for five seconds and talk to me!'

'This is important, it's Friday's show.'

'I want to discuss my career with you; that's important too.'

'Oh yeh? Important to who?'

'Whom,' Kate corrected him. 'To me.'

'Exactly. To nobody. Big deal.' He lowered his head to the papers again.

When he was in this mood he knew just how to light her fuse and watch her smoulder. Try as she did Kate could never rise above it; he always touched the nerve. They both knew exactly the buttons to push for each desired reaction in the other. Once, in those heady post-Cambridge days of her startling success, that reaction had been laughter and love. Now they goaded each other in ever cheaper efforts to put the other down.

'It may surprise you, George, but I'd like your advice.'

'Hm.' He reluctantly put the papers down among the remains of breakfast on the big oak dining-table, took off his gold-rimmed glasses and reached for his first fat cigar of the day.

41

'Bryan Harvey-Jones, the producer, has asked me to play the lead in this new play. It's called,' she paused, bracing herself for his scornful reaction. 'It's called *Murder in Triplicate*. It's going to tour for six weeks and then come into town. Almost certainly. We just met for a brief chat and he asked me straight out, did I want to do it. Oh, it was just like the old days, before I had to audition for things in competition with a lot of other actresses. I said I'd have to discuss it, of course, and that Robin would get back to him. What do you think?'

'I think it sounds like a load of horse crap.'

'I don't mean what do you think of the play; I mean do you think I should take the part?'

He tried to blow a smoke ring but it came out in a grey lump. 'No.'

'It's not a bad part. Angela. She's a rather grand lady who . . . whose marriage . . . is going through a bad patch,' Kate said quickly without looking at him. 'She takes a young lover, or rather, we think she's going to but her integrity overcomes her desire for the young researcher her husband has hired. But when his body – the husband, not the young man – is discovered in the greenhouse with fourteen stab wounds in it, she's the prime suspect. She gets some terrific scenes, especially in Act Two with the young researcher; lots of angst.'

'Yeh, sounds like crap.'

'It's a classy thriller, George. Written by that man who does the telly thing, "Rich Pickings". You know, Alistair Greene.'

'No, I don't watch crap.'

'George! It is not crap! It's highly regarded. It's won awards.'

'So has Benny Hill.'

'Oh, honestly!'

'And appearing in this . . . *crap*,' he savoured the word, his thin lips curling with amusement, 'is going to do you some good, is it? In your . . . "career".'

42

'I might get my name above the title.'

'Gee whizz! You must be close to getting your full Equity card.'

'It's exposure. It'll get me seen.'

'In Harrogate and Hartlepool. Tomorrow the world!' He tried another smoke ring. This time it looked briefly like a soggy doughnut before tumbling apart.

'Tomorrow the West End so I'll have a showcase when they're casting *O Jackie*. It'll tour to Plymouth, Cardiff and Brighton. Number One dates. And it opens in Norwich. So at least I shall get a chance to visit Ben.'

'Lazy fucking slob,' he muttered, as expected.

'If you'd been a better father to him he might be happier now. You never made any effort with him, did you?'

'Me? You were the one who relinquished your responsibilities, madam! You were too busy being the starlet to get involved. That's why he's such a waste of space now.'

They had slipped easily into one of the ritual arguments. They knew their lines, their cues and could play the scene in a hundred different ways. All so predictable and all so pointless.

'I, at least, think he's still worth spending time on. He needs us, George.'

'He needs a kick up the bloody backside. If he got out and worked like everyone else he might start getting somewhere. What's he spend his time doing now? Scratching his balls and writing crappy poems!'

'Everything you don't understand is just crap, isn't it? God, you're so self-centred. If your beloved fans could hear you now they'd soon defect to some other chat-show celebrity.'

'There's no one else in my league, lady. No one! Mister Television, that's me!'

He dabbed his half-smoked cigar into the ashtray. It lay there, crushed but still burning, neither alive nor dead.

Just how I feel, thought Kate. Neither independent, free to live my life in my own way, nor happily semi-detached to a loving husband. Just caught in this limbo of a moribund marriage. If she could get herself cast as Jackie O then she could really start to be someone again. A star. As she had been years before. Before it all went wrong.

She sipped her coffee; it was cold and bitter. She watched George, his head bowed again over Becca's notes.

How far they'd both come since that first night they'd made love under the wide East Anglian sky. Then he'd been handsome and strong, the leading light of Cambridge varsity life. Witty, larger than life, full of his own importance, able to cope effortlessly with any challenge. When she'd first been aware of him – 'That's George King! *The* George King!' someone whispered in awe as they spotted him in, appropriately, King's Parade – he'd been going out with Annabel Combes-Howard, the Most Beautiful Woman in Cambridge. She was actually Lady Annabel but in that chic, modest fashion never used the title herself. She was strong too, in the down-to-earth way only the upper class are; all vowels and no inhibitions. The pair of them were seen at the smartest parties, loud and bright, impossible to ignore, while Kate observed from the sidelines.

She wanted him. She set her mind to it and began to arrange to bump into him in people's rooms, at the library, punting on the river, at the theatre, anywhere. Each time she'd flirt just a little with him, showing him a glimpse of what could be his. She may not have been as striking as Lady Annabel but she had a delicate beauty and knew how to use it. She was subtle and suggestive, cat-like and crafty in the way she worked on George. She rose through the ranks of the university actors until she was a regular leading lady at the ADC Theatre and by the end of her second year she was, by common consent, the Most Talented Actress in Cambridge.

Then, the night after he'd seen her Juliet and come backstage with his little entourage to congratulate her, they'd met again at the Trinity May Ball. They danced for hours,

44

drank cheap champagne and talked as if time was about to run out. They kissed tentatively at first and laughed because it seemed inevitable. Kate knew they were being watched and wanted to shout, 'Look, I've got him! I've got George King for myself!'

As she seduced him in the dawn mist in a punt moored on the Cam, she made sure they were seen by the dregs of the glitterati, stumbling over the Bridge of Sighs towards tea and toast and tired sleep. He took her drunkenly, clumsily messing her hair and slurring words into her ear as they made the little boat bob and waves slapped its sides in a crude echo of their sounds of passion.

He didn't come but she had arrived.

When Annabel Combes-Howard didn't turn up for her final year Kate claimed a consummate victory.

She and George became an item. They were the Golden Couple. Seen at every occasion that aspired to be fashionable. Admired, envied and emulated but never, never outclassed. She was the fiery actress with a mercurial talent; he was the wit, charmer and man of fierce intellect. Together they were invincible.

Although snaring George had initially been a cynical ploy to raise her profile, Kate was surprised to find she was falling in love with him.

When they were alone, she reading, he writing, Kate would look up and find him watching her, the expression on his face one of pride and admiration. They could sit on the banks of the Cam as the sun went down, sharing the moment in silence as if some secret pulse were beating between them, tying them eternally together. The touch of his finger on hers thrilled her as much as the most intense orgasm. Their love-making could be energetic and eager, a piece of chamber music by the young Mozart, or it might embody the passionate power of some late Mahler, profound and disturbing in its force.

They were both picked for the series 'Young Mavericks' in the *Sunday Times* and sixties icon Klaus Zeschin had done that now famous spread of nude shots of them for *Vogue*. Its shock value had pushed them from Cambridge into the bigger world.

'Those were the days,' thought Kate. She looked at him now, running to fat, balding, bleary early-morning eyes screwed up behind his specs to focus. His jaw hanging open, shoulders sagging forward. Getting him ready for the show must take longer and longer as the weeks went by. Contact lenses, hairpiece, corset, fishskins, jackets strategically padded to give him a manly build again, the shoes with lifts. We have the technology . . .

He had his hairpiece on even though the two of them were alone in the vast house in Hampstead safely protected from the 'scum' by a fence, a wall, and a Japanese infra-red burglar alarm system linked to closed-circuit television. Or had they drifted so far apart since their private disaster that he had to keep up his image even to her? Kate felt a familiar chill of loneliness. They simply didn't communicate any more. Both their lives had been diminished by the same event.

Hers had been the first star to rise. Gossip columnists loved her; fashion editors fêted her. Journalists clamoured at her door for a picture, a pose, a quote. And she never denied them. She knew about the oxygen of publicity even then, and thrived on it. Her cream, thigh-length silk wedding dress had been copied by a thousand brides that summer.

George's qualities had been ignored for a while. While she went from one leading role to another just as easily as she had at university, expanding her repertoire and garnering reviews to die for, he had trailed in her wake, at first cheerfully and then more sullenly playing the role of consort.

Of course the moment that changed everything, the day the sun stopped shining for ever was the summer's day – it was July the eighteenth – that Kate came home to find the pair of them, her husband and her elder son,

46

sitting silently in the kitchen, the still wet body of little Christopher lying between them on the table making a stain on the wood that would never be removed.

'Coffee.'

'Hm?'

George had pushed his cup across the table to her. Obediently she topped it up. White, three sugars.

'Well, Derek reckons it's in the bag. I'm about to sign the big one. What d'you think, eh?'

'Amazing.' Considering what a talentless little shit you are, she thought.

'Right. What about last night's show?'

'You assume I saw it.'

'Of course.'

'I've been busy myself this week, you know.'

'Doing what? Being a mediocrity?'

Kate sighed, weary of the game.

'Yes, I saw it,' she confessed.

'And?'

Kate had thought his performance was, as ever, slick and professional, a clever mix of smug pride with apparent humility. And completely unimportant.

'I thought you were . . . great.'

'Yeh. And?'

It wasn't enough. He wanted details of his greatness.

'You were very good with Lord Barker. You didn't let him get away with any flannel.'

'What about after the break, with Sonia Scott?'

'Well, she's good value, isn't she? She knows what's required and delivers the goods.'

'She's no pushover to interview, you know.' George obviously sensed that his skills were being belittled. 'In fact she's a toughie because she doesn't do anything any more. She's just a clever little bitch who's gone up in the world by going down on some very big knobs!'

'She's about to play Hedda at the Old Vic.' A sore point.

'Very appropriate – Hedda Gobbler!' George shouted as

if in triumph and then began to bark his dreadful staccato laugh. 'Har-har-har-har!'

Kate calmly turned her head away from his ugly glee and looked out into the pleasantly unkempt garden. She saw the brown bushes and green ferns struggling to drink in the weak sunlight and wanted to run out and trample them underfoot, slash at them and tear them with her bare hands. Only a slight tension around the mouth betrayed her pent-up anger. She wouldn't let him bait her, this time she wouldn't.

She turned back and watched impassively as George gasped and croaked, trying to shift whatever had stuck in his throat. He'd gone a deep purplish red and the veins in his neck throbbed thick and dark like angry snakes. He bent low over the table, his tongue lolling out fat and long. A thin dribble of saliva dropped slowly on to the varnished oak. Water on wood. A cruel parody of the stain Christopher's little body had made two decades before. Twenty years on she could see the picture as clearly as ever.

She observed George's coughing fit and for a moment felt a rush of excitement as it occurred to her that this might be literally his last gasp.

Then there was a ghastly retching motion, some throat-cleaning and he sloshed cold coffee into his mouth. Wiping the back of his hand across his lips he muttered, 'Hedda Gobbler. Ha!' And he returned to his precious papers.

What had happened to Kate Fitch, Star? she wondered, gazing out into the grey, wintry drizzle. She was on the periphery now, clinging on and struggling. Clamouring for some sort of sense of completion and fulfilment. But instead she was adrift in a sea of regret and guilt, trying to maintain a lust for work while constantly aware that she had compromised her integrity.

She got up from the table, picked up a glossy magazine from a nearby shelf and took it to her favourite chair. She flicked the pages over noisily, making no attempt to read.

After a few minutes of this, getting no reaction, she got

up, unable to contain her anger, rolled the magazine in her hands and prodded the air with it as she spoke. 'Nothing gets through to you, does it? Unless it plays a part in the Great Plan to flood the media with the face, the voice, the thoughts of George King. Well, I'm not interested any more! I've had enough of . . . of living with a media monster!'

I'm being ridiculous, she told herself even as she ranted.

'Oh, sod it!' she spat. 'Sod it all!'

She threw the magazine towards him. After an initial streamlined flight it spread its pages open and fluttered pathetically to the floor, a giant moth sacrificing itself at his feet.

George watched in silence. After a beat he pushed a plate out of the way and leaned forward on the table.

'Oh, you've had enough, have you?' His voice was cold and ironic. It had a timbre the public never heard; not the fake jollity of the genial Friday evening host but the tones of deadly efficiency reserved for talking fees, percentages, billing. 'Enough of a Georgian mansion in Hampstead worth two and a half million pounds with its own indoor tennis court, a villa in Provence, an apartment in New York, a Roller, a Merc with your own personalized number plate, cupboards full of furs and silk, priceless jewellery, two racehorses, invitations to Downing Street and one of the finest wine cellars in the country. And you've had enough? You fucking hypocrite! I'd like to see you give any of this up.'

'George, I didn't ask for any of those things. They're the trappings you have bought because they're tax efficient. They're not mine, I don't want them. I haven't worn a fur coat for ten years. I don't want a tennis court; I haven't even got a racket. Wine and jewels aren't going to make me respected in my own right.'

'Oh, you want respect, do you? Respect for what? What have you ever achieved?'

'I used to be a star.'

'Used to be. I *am* a star!'

'Well, granted my career has –'

'Your career?' He sneered with glee. 'You haven't had a career for twenty years. You're stuck in the past. You can't let it go, can you? Everything you do is dictated by what happened two fucking decades ago. You stopped functioning then, didn't you? That's why you're a nobody now. Your only career is being married to me!'

'You bastard!' she screamed.

'You failure,' he said simply. She gasped with shock at the accuracy of his blow. There was no defence against the truth.

She could see in his bloodshot eyes the pleasure he took in hurting her. He turned slowly from her and trod on the magazine as he stood up from the table.

'I'll show you, I'll show you!' she screamed at his retreating back as he shuffled down the long hall. 'I'll do this tour and I'll get the lead in the Jackie musical and I'll be a star again. *I'll show you, George King!*'

She didn't believe it any more than he did.

5

Gina Howard shook four paracetamol tablets into her palm and knocked back a slug of whisky from the bottle to wash them down. She put some Chopin études on her new Aiwa compact disc player, lit a cheroot and began to flick through the pages of the trade press: *Broadcast*, *Radio Report*, *Transmission* and *Mediaweek*.

Her eyes scanned the pages swiftly, efficiently, for anything that might be fuel to her ambition.

There was a story about some new projects at Channel Four which she decided she could follow up and an article mentioned a new consumer unit being set up at Carlton. Yes, that might be just the thing to launch her on the next phase of her plan to get herself out of the current rut.

It had been a rotten month. She'd charged too much to AmEx, drunk too much vodka and failed to excite her bosses at the BBC with her radio features. They'd been underwhelmed by her series on Aids, accusing her of going over old ground, and now her stint on the new magazine programme 'Talkabout' was definitely not lighting any fires. The highlight of her batch of shows was meant to have been the great scoop about the Royal 'outing', but at the last minute it had fizzled to nothing. It was, as a transvestite acquaintance of hers would say, 'not all it was up the crack to be'.

She parted the slats of the black venetian blind and peered out into the street. Chelsea on a Sunday morning. Why did she feel so uninspired?

And so alone.

She'd just got rid of her last boyfriend, Paul, an obstetrician, because he'd started talking about living together and having babies. Stuff that, she'd said, and broken it off the same evening.

People always wanted to get paired off. Even at last night's party, at a designer's studio in Limehouse, most of the straight men had wanted to chat to her, then take her home and screw her just because they were male and she was female. That was pathetic. Besides, none of them was important enough to put out for and Gina certainly couldn't be bothered with sex for its own sake or because it might lead to friendship. She felt more efficient alone.

Not that her efficiency was getting her very far at the moment. She had been a radio producer now for nearly two years and didn't seem to be able to move on.

'Christ, I'm twenty-nine and the world has never heard of me,' she said aloud and stubbed her cheroot out violently in the Philippe Starck ashtray. Her headache was getting worse. She took off her glasses and pinched the bridge of her nose.

The flat was decorated self-consciously in black and gold; it was a shrine to the post-Conran eighties when 'Design' was synonymous with 'Success' and Queen Margaret was on the throne. Ah, the good old days.

The flat looked upmarket and stylish but anonymous; more like a set than a home. There wasn't a comfortable chair in the place.

Gina rang an acquaintance in the casting department at Euston Films. She got an answering machine.

'Nessa, it's Gina Howard. Hi. I need some info. Give me a buzz as soon as poss. OK? Ciao.'

Damn. Why had she said 'Ciao' for Christ's sake? She hated people who said 'Ciao'. And her headache was turning into a bloody migraine. She jabbed at the remote control and aborted the Chopin. She zapped through a few stations on the radio; nothing appealed. Television? Bound to be rubbish, but she gave it a whirl.

The phone chirped at her. She snatched it up, expecting it to be Vanessa ringing back.

'Hi?' she said eagerly.

'Hello, darling, it's Annabel.'

'Oh, hello, Mother. What do you want?' She made no effort to disguise her disappointment.

'Just calling to see how you are, dear. Everything all right?'

'No. I've got a lousy head and it's pissing with rain.'

'Ah. It's quite bright in Sussex. We've been lucky with the weather so far this autumn. Any job prospects on the horizon?'

'No. Zilch. It's a dead loss.'

'Ah well, maybe it's a sign. Perhaps you should stay where you are for the time being.'

'I want more clout. A higher profile. You wouldn't understand, Mother.'

'No, dear. Well, I'm sure something will turn up.'

Gina's mother, Lady Annabel Combes-Howard, had apparently retired from all chance of a public high profile many years ago to bring up her only child single-handed. She'd never been exactly conventional, but being a single mother and a member of the minor aristocracy hadn't exactly endeared her to her peers. She had, though, inherited Combes Hall in West Sussex from her father. It was a crumbling eighteenth-century pile of dubious architectural merit that squatted like an ageing, bloated bullfrog in a damp valley near Haslemere. Unfortunately Annabel's father had drunk or gambled away in middle age the wealth he'd amassed through his tradings with the Far East as a young man. Consequently he'd not been able to pass on any cash to pay for the upkeep of the family home, let alone any modernization or repair. Gina's childhood memories were of long, dark corridors never penetrated by daylight, of wallpaper hanging off damp plaster, buckets on the floor to catch drips from above, holes in walls and ceilings roughly boarded up with planks.

And the cold. Always the cold. Even in summer when the roses made the air by the kitchen door heady with their rich, old-fashioned aroma the Hall inside had been cool and damp. In winter she'd stayed in the same double-thickness underclothes for a week at a time; the thought of stripping to wash or change was unbearable. Since most of the time there had been only her and her mother in the vast house they had agreed not to get too picky about personal hygiene.

After a variety of menial jobs and a series of unfortunate father-substitutes for Gina, Annabel had finally found her own feet in the last five years in a big way through her series of Auntie Annabel's Country Kitchen Cookbooks. Begun as one-off recipes in women's magazines to pay a few bills, their potential had been spotted by a young publisher she'd been sleeping with at the time, marketed imaginatively and now the books and inevitable spin-off products – aprons, place mats, jams, stationery – made her a very welcome annual income of around half a million pounds.

But Annabel Combes-Howard still lived the simple life in her Sussex home, which was now gradually being restored to something approaching its original splendour. While teams of carpenters, masons and plumbers laboured on rotting pipes, wood and stone, Annabel cycled off to the local shops for ingredients to try in her latest recipes and occasionally invited to share her house a younger man who took her fancy. She lived in chaotic but comfortable style and although she enjoyed the benefits of her fame no longer sought public acclamation. If anyone ever recognized her or approached her for an autograph she blushed bright pink and failed completely to hide her embarrassment.

Now, in her early fifties, Annabel Combes-Howard had apparently learned the rare art of being able to relax. Something her own daughter was a long way from achieving.

'Oh, one thing, dear; I know it's a while off yet,' she said, pronouncing 'off' 'orf' in the way that had always been totally natural to her. 'Would you like to come skiing in the new year? I thought we could go together. What d'you think?'

'Oh, Mother, please.'

'Is that a "yes, please", or a "no, please"?'

'Skiing with my own mother? Do me a favour.'

'Another?'

'What?'

'Never mind. Well, I'd better go. I have some chestnuts soaking. Goodbye, dear. Be nice to yourself.'

Gina slammed the receiver down and lit another cheroot, knowing that her mother thought it a 'self-destructive habit'.

'Oh shit.'

God, that woman made her angry. Or rather brought out the rage that was always pent up inside her. So long as it was contained and seething within her, Gina felt it was a source of physical energy, but once it escaped its potency was dissipated. She'd been aware of an anger and a hungry ambition inside her as long as she could remember. There had always been a need to fight her way up to the top of the pile, a reason to kick at the world for the roughness of her deal. She didn't question it, only continued fighting and kicking and hoping that one day it would all prove to have been worthwhile.

'Oh, bollocks.'

Her mother's confident calm had done nothing to ease Gina's headache. Her whole skull was pounding and it hurt to look anywhere other than straight ahead. Nothing was ever simple for Gina Howard. She would have been suspicious if it had been. But right now she wanted just a little peace of mind or even the possibility of something good in her life, and it seemed impossible to find.

She piled her thick auburn hair on the top of her head and looked at the effect in a triangular mirror framed in matt black and gold. It had cost a fortune at a pretentious shop in the Fulham Road and she had regretted buying it ever since. 'It's a modern classic, madam; it'll never date.' Oh yeh, and the C5 will replace the 911.

She'd always considered herself striking rather than beautiful or pretty but with her myopic eyes screwed up with pain and no make-up on her pale skin after a very late night even 'striking' seemed a flattering description. 'Plain' was more apt. How about unattractive? How about dog?

'Oh shit,' she muttered and let her hair fall in a mess over her sour face. 'Life is such a hard shit.'

6

'Ladies and gentlemen of the *Murder in Triplicate* company, this is your half-hour call. Half an hour, please. Thank you.'

Kate was, as usual on an opening night, neurotically over-prepared for the show. She had all her make-up laid out on a towel. Not just any towel but her lucky towel. Tissues, cream, throat lozenges, toothbrush and toothpaste, nail varnish and bottled water all arranged in ordered rows. The script, heavily marked with comments and ideas from rehearsals, was to one side; it was the great security blanket. If it disappeared now she would have felt as if she'd lost a limb. Fellow actors were welcome to consult it in situ, but she wouldn't let it out of her dressing-room for anything. There were huge bunches of roses and carnations from Bryan, the producer, and Robin. He never let her down. He had many much bigger fish in his agency but there was something special in their relationship that went back years and would continue to bind them together, like family.

The mirror was stuck with good luck cards and telegrams from colleagues and friends. There was even one with George's scrawl across it, although she knew it was Becca's doing. Never mind. It all added to the ambiance, and if the look was right the rest would fall into place. And this was exactly what the leading lady's dressing-room — number one, of course — was meant to look like.

Kate repeated a few mouth and tongue routines just to make sure everything was loose but toned. Like any other muscle in the body, the tongue and the lips needed to be exercised regularly if they were going to be equal to the demands of live performance without letting her down.

'Fuck-Peggy-Babcock, bugger-Peggy-Babcock, fuck-Peggy-Babcock, bugger-Peggy-Babcock,' she repeated faster and faster until it became a blur. Then she pushed her tongue into each cheek hard until it hurt and pasted it up and down the roof of her mouth as if painting a ceiling. Good, it all felt strong and in control.

Her make-up was simple for this role. Angela was a middle-class woman of about her own age, so no special design was required. But there was no point not looking her best, so with judicial shading and highlighting she emphasized her good cheekbones, brought out the green of her eyes and filled out her slightly thin top lip with her brushes. Her hair was thick and dark but it did benefit from the merest touch of backcombing, although she had a fear of looking like Miriam Stoppard or Gloria Hunniford or some other big-haired babe.

When her ministrations were complete she opened the door and called down the corridor for her dresser.

Beate was a sweet girl although none too bright. Still, she meant well and thought the world of Kate so that was one major blessing as far as going on tour was concerned. She would need to pick up Kate's idiosyncrasies and treat them as gospel; that was a dresser's job, after all. She'd soon know that Kate liked to do her make-up in private and then be dressed so as to be ready by the five-minute call, that she liked to hear the company gossip and chat about inconsequential things until the last minute and then have a few seconds to clear her brain before going on stage. Beate would need to remember, too, that she expected to be called 'Miss Fitch' at all times. Never, ever 'Kate'.

But she'd do. Bryan Harvey-Jones said he'd pinched her from the number one dressing-room of the Albery Theatre where a Very Famous Dame was performing her one-woman show about Mother Theresa. That made Kate feel a lot better about opening in Norwich on a bleak winter's night. '*Murder in Triplicate* starring Kate Fitch'. Robin hadn't even managed to get her name above the title. She'd have willingly agreed to a lower fee for that kind of kudos but if Robin couldn't swing it, she knew it wasn't to be swung.

The tannoy was relaying the audience's anticipation. The sound was eager and lively, a crowd redefining itself as a single body, knitting together into a common mass, preparing to respond as one for the next couple of hours. Willingly sacrificing individuality for the pleasure of sharing the unique experience about to unfold. Kate loved to hear the mingling of voices, to eavesdrop on them, get their measure and test them in her mind like a hangman mentally weighing a prisoner condemned to his noose.

She'd made Robin promise as usual that he wouldn't come on the first night, but she knew Ben was out there in the auditorium. In seat B12. She knew too when she'd be able to check on him. On page four where she gave the stare into the middle distance on the line: 'Oh, how differently it might all have turned out if only . . .' She'd even practised searching for B12 in the final dress rehearsal that afternoon.

He'd said he would come. Not that he'd like to or love to, but that he would. He didn't sound exactly overjoyed on the phone at the thought of seeing the show or of meeting Kate but she'd left the ticket for him and Alex, the company manager, had already told her it had been collected. Just the one ticket he'd asked for. Not one for any girlfriend. Oh well, dinner afterwards would give them a chance for a proper chat.

'Ooh, listen to them,' Beate twittered while she helped Kate into her Act One costume, a rather splendid red Betty Jackson-style suit which she was looking forward to acquiring after the tour. They could get her something else for the subsequent West End run. 'It's proper exciting, isn't it, all them people waiting to see you!'

'Waiting to see us all,' Kate said humbly, realizing sadly that it was true.

'Well, yes, they'll know Mister McCone from his telly series, I suppose.'

'Mm. I'm told "The Beat" is very popular. I've never actually seen it myself.'

Beate brushed Kate's jacket and fussed unnecessarily over the precise position of the butterfly brooch.

'An' Miss Penny, an' all. They'll've seen her in that advert for ice cream, won't they?'

'Yes, I'm sure they will,' Kate agreed with some reluctance.

'What about Trevor Waterman? What's he in, then?'

'Well, he's doing a children's series at the moment.' For Christ's sake, was the silly girl going to go through everyone's CV just to remind Kate she hadn't done a decent telly part for years?

'Oh yeh.' Beate was quiet for a moment, perhaps tasting her mouthful of foot. Then she stepped back to look at Kate and gave a big beaming smile. 'But, I mean, you're the star, aren't you, Miss Fitch?'

'Oh, no, I wouldn't say that, Beate.' Kate stroked her hair modestly.

'Oh, yes. You're the one. You got the biggest part, anyway.'

'That's true.'

'And the nicest frocks. So you must be the top draw.'

'Well . . .'

The tannoy crackled and Stevie, the stage manager, spoke again. 'Ladies and gentlemen, this is your Act One beginners' call. Your calls please Miss Fitch, Miss Stiles and Mr McCone. Miss Fitch, Miss Stiles and Mr McCone, your calls please. Thank you.'

'Well, here we go.' Kate took her customary three slow, deep breaths, right down into the bottom of the lungs, ran through her first lines — 'God, what a miserable day for June. Donald will get soaked, poor thing' — checked the image in the full-length mirror, set her chin at a striking angle and left the safety of her room.

60

'Break a leg, old girl,' said Gordon in the corridor. 'It's going to be a corker, I can feel it.' He looked perfect for the part of Donald in his sloppy sweater and shapeless brown corduroy trousers. Mind you, that was what he wore anyway. Sometimes there wasn't much mystique to casting.

'Thanks, Gordon. Have a nice one.'

'How are your digs, by the way? Penny and I have landed on our feet. We're in the same place. Mrs Dillip. She lets us help ourselves to tea and biscuits from the kitchen. Not bad at all.'

'That's nice. I'm staying at the Imperial Hotel just down the road.'

'Ah well, it's different for the likes of you, isn't it?'

No, she thought. You're the one in the telly series. It's just a question of attitude. I wouldn't lower myself to tea and biscuits in seedy digs. Nylon sheets too, I expect. I'm more the five star type.

She popped her head around the doors of the other dressing-rooms to give a word of encouragement to Penny, Trevor and the others; that much was expected of a proper leading lady. It's what Edith Evans had done when Kate was the juve lead in the Old Vic tour of '65. This was a small company; that's all anyone could afford to tour these days. Still, that was no excuse for sloppiness; standards had to be maintained.

In the wings she breathed in the warmth and energy of the audience just the other side of the pros arch. Soon she'd be in her favourite place, in the bright pool of light surrounded by the dark that held the hundreds of eyes and ears that would drink in the sight and sound of her, the leading lady. Once she was there all the horrors that played daily in her head would be obliterated for the dur-ation of the show and she could float without care on the fantasy of being someone different, someone without the agonies of her own reality.

She'd show George how important her career was, not

just to her but to her public. They remembered her early days of success and they recognized her talent. The pendulum of stardom had swung dramatically away from her towards George over two decades ago; it was time to nudge it back in her own direction again. Fame wouldn't wipe out the horrors in her memory but this production, creaky as it was, could be the stepping stone to a whole new phase of her life. She had no doubt that if there was any justice – and you stood more chance of it if you were on Robin Quick's books – she would soon be playing Jackie Bouvier Kennedy Onassis to rave reviews in the West End.

The red standby light came on and Kate acknowledged it with a push of a button. She patted her hair and wiped the corners of her mouth. The house lights dimmed slowly, giving the audience time to settle with the usual coughs – they were nervous too, of course – and the taped music faded away. This was the worst moment; now it was too late to check or change anything. Come on . . . come on . . .

The red light went out and the green one came on. This was it.

The audience responded politely to her entrance with a reasonable spattering of applause. Kate counted it at twelve seconds. Not bad; she'd see what the others got. She was on good form, relaxed and comfortable and it seemed to go well. They got to page four. 'Oh, how differently it might all have turned out if only . . .' She checked B12. Yes, the seat was occupied. She wondered what Ben was thinking. Was he proud of her? It was so hard to tell with him.

She enjoyed the show. The audience enjoyed it too. They listened attentively, staying with the complex plot through all its clever-clever twists and turns, through the fake death and Gordon's reappearance as the Irish builder. They barely clapped him at all, five seconds at most. He milked everything mercilessly, of course, and Penny dithered delightfully. She registered no less than sixteen seconds' applause, the cow. She only had one performance, like a lot of character actors, but she knew just how to time the simplest line for the greatest effect; she was easy to play with. Trevor, as her potential toy-boy, was his usual wooden and unconvincing self. He was something of a box-office 'name' because of the kids' thing he was in on the television, but the mysteries of the stage baffled him utterly. He made no pretence to be any good, he said he hoped he'd be able to 'get away with it'. Frankly Kate wasn't sure that he did. She tried for passion and fury in their scenes together but what she got back was more like a British Rail announcement. It was impossible to sustain a love scene or an argument without the tension of a two-way struggle; she felt faintly embarrassed on stage with him, as if he was merely standing in until the real actor came back from a trip to the gents'.

Still, they fooled a lot of the audience a lot of the time. The shocks of act two hit home to gasps amid the rapt silence. The young ASMs, Zoe Something-or-Other, as the neighbour, and Jack Fever, handsome and proud in his policeman's uniform, both rose to the occasion in their first professional jobs despite their nerves. At the curtain the applause was strong and enthusiastic. It also rose several notches when Kate took her solo bow. Good, just as it should be.

The atmosphere backstage always put her in mind of pilots returning to Blighty after a successful raid.

'Well done, everyone!'

'Thank you, Gordon. You were great.'

'Sorry about the biz in the letter scene.'

'Well done, Miss Fitch. Nice show.'

'Well done, Penny. We showed 'em, eh?'

'Nice one, Jack, a star is born!'

'Ooh, super crowd, weren't they?'

'Keep it tight for tomorrow, don't let it sag.'

'I don't have much choice at my age, love!'

Kate left the cast to let off steam in the wings. She made a point of thanking the stage management team in the Corner and retreated to her dressing-room to prepare for her next performance, meeting the public in the bar.

When she walked in there were one or two pointed fingers and admiring gazes from the punters still doggedly making their schooners of sherry last, but no requests for autographs.

She couldn't see Ben at first and was sure he'd gone, having hated the play and her performance.

Then she realized that the creature right in front of her was her son.

She was shocked by his appearance. They hadn't seen each other for a while, since the big rows about his dropping out of university some months before. He had not blossomed in the meantime.

He was lucky enough to take after his mother in stature and colouring; he was tall and dark rather than small and auburn like George. He still retained that teenager's gaucheness, his limbs seeming too long to control. It gave him an endearing awkwardness, something girls couldn't help wanting to mother. But his face was pale and thin, as if he wasn't eating properly or sleeping well. Perhaps he was ill. His dark hair flopped over his eyes as it always did, but now it was more than a self-conscious 'artistic' fashion, it just looked a mess. His brown eyes burned brightly as ever, passing a cold and cynical view of the world back to his fine brain.

'Ben, darling, how are you?' She offered her cheek to him but, untrained in theatrical tradition, he wasn't sure what to do.

'Hello, Mother,' he said into her ear, as if she'd been hoping for the latest gossip.

'I saw you out there, you know, in B12. Nodding off, weren't you, in act two?' She laughed more than enough for both of them.

'Not at all, Mother. I was watching with unalloyed delight. I can honestly say I've never seen anything like that in my life.' His wicked eyes danced over her features and he left the interpretation of his remark to her.

'Oh, well, I shall want all your notes on my performance over dinner. Did you want a drink here first?'

'*Did* I? When?'

She sighed. He was in his bloody-minded mood.

'Do you want a drink here?'

'Oh, *do* I want a drink here? No, not especially. *Did* you want one?'

'Let's go to the restaurant, shall we?'

Kate was disappointed more than cross with him for looking half-alive and being so childish. All right, blame the parents for some of it but he was an intelligent young man of twenty-four, surely he had to take responsibility eventually for his own life. No, she decided, she mustn't be angry with him. He had a right to be whoever he was and she would love him regardless. Although, he could have made a bit of an effort . . .

She did her round of swift welldones and goodnights without Ben in tow and then collected him from where he was standing by the door, watching with an indulgent expression as if she was taking part in some harmless but faintly ludicrous hobby like morris dancing. As they left the bar she wondered how they looked together and what the wagging tongues were saying.

The restaurant where she'd booked a table was only a ten-minute walk away.

'I think I'll have the salmon, please.'

'Yes, madam.'

'What about you, darling?'

Ben ignored the menu and gave the waiter a cursory glance. 'What do you recommend?'

'The salmon is very good today, sir, or the braised kidneys in red wine.'

'In my experience that means you've got to get rid of them before they go off.'

'Ben.'

'I'll have the tuna bake. Should be safe enough.'

'Quite. And a selection of vegetables?'

'No,' said Ben. 'I want broccoli, mangetouts and cauli-flower. Mother?'

'Those will be fine, thank you.'

'Thank you, madam.'

When the waiter had gone Kate leaned over the table towards Ben. 'Really, that was rather rude.'

'Oh, gosh. How awful of me. Perhaps he'll poison my tuna bake.'

'Ben, please. I want this evening to be nice.'

'Nice? What does that mean? Nice? This isn't a story by Beatrix Potter, this is the real world, Mother.'

She took a slow breath and managed a smile.

'Do you remember those Beatrix Potter books you had when you were young? You used to love those. I'm sure they're still upstairs in the nursery somewhere. I'll look them out again.'

'I used to shit in my pants once too. Things move on, you know? Although maybe they don't move on quite enough.'

'Really, Ben, there's no need to be so . . . prickly.'

'No, there's no need. I just enjoy it sometimes. Don't you?'

Kate was grateful that they lapsed into silence for a while as they straightened their cutlery, nibbled at their bread rolls and avoided eye contact by taking in the décor of the place. It was dimly lit with bare wooden tables and a lot of maritime artefacts hanging from the walls and the ceiling. There was even a fishing net festooned over a couple of battered oars in one corner and quantities of little cork floats dotted about the place. It was probably called The Captain's Table but Kate couldn't be sure.

What she was sure about was Ben's disapproval. It was as if he was some kind of toy, something too loud and slightly embarrassing that could be set off by the merest breath. She could hardly believe it but she was nervous of him. Ridiculous!

'I'm sorry, Ben. I don't mean to fuss.'

'Don't you?' he said without looking at her, his finger

working vigorously away in his mouth to dislodge something from his teeth.

'It's just that, well, after the show and everything –'

'Yes?'

'– I'm still a bit . . .'

'What?' His eyes were more than curious, she saw anger there.

'Well . . . you know . . .' She couldn't think of a word which didn't sound pretentious so she just raised her eyebrows, shrugged her shoulders and smiled at him. He looked away.

Kate took her three deep breaths.

'We came here the other night after the tech. Sorry, the technical rehearsal. That's when . . . anyway. Gordon and Penny and, er . . . well, a few of us. Penny's husband too. It was nice. I had the skate then. It was . . . nice.'

'Right.'

'Well, this is . . . nice, isn't it? I mean, pleasant. We haven't had a chance to chat for ages, have we?' He said nothing. 'So, how are you? All right?'

'I'm surviving.'

'I mean, really, *all right?*'

'What?'

'How's everything?'

'Everything's all right.'

'The house is warm enough, is it? For you and your . . . friends?'

'Yes. We get cold, we light a fire, we warm up. That's how it works, you know?'

'Yes . . .' She smiled encouragingly at him, head slightly tilted to one side, Thatcher's caring look. 'And your . . . friend. Your girlfriend . . . She's . . . ?'

'She's what?'

Oh *really*, she thought. Why won't he meet me halfway? I only want to talk to him, have a conversation.

'Tell me about her, Ben. I don't know anything about her.'

67

'Well, I don't know much either. Her name's Sue. She's from the north somewhere. Derby, or Chester or Swansea.'

Kate laughed. Was he making a joke or not?

'Ben! Swansea's not in the north. It's in Wales, that's west! Really! Did you get your Geography "O" level?'

'Who knows, I don't remember. I don't live in the past.'

'What do you mean?'

'Let's order some wine. God, I could do with some.'

'What did you —? Yes, wine would be lovely. Just a glass.'

'Where's that ponce of a waiter?'

'Ben, you look jolly tired, you know. Or is it . . . ? Is there anything wrong? Anything you want to tell me? If there's something, anything at all . . . ?'

He looked down at his plate, picked up his empty glass and looked into it, then gazed across the restaurant, out of the window, anywhere but at her.

'All right, none of my business. But you can always come to me, you know.'

As if he'd been holding on for the right moment, the waiter arrived with the food. Kate gushed false brightness with a stock of conventional phrases substituting for conversation: 'Mmm, delicious; how's the tuna bake? More potatoes? Do you want to try this?' For what they received Kate was truly thankful.

Ben ordered the wine. When it came he knocked back a quick glassful and topped himself up again. Kate sipped delicately, studying him all the while over the rim.

She waited for him to ask her about herself, the play, her stay in Norwich; when it became clear he wasn't going to she decided to tell him anyway.

'The hotel I'm in is very nice. Just down the road from the theatre, which is handy. Most of the others are in digs but I couldn't bear that. Oh, your father sends his . . . says hello, by the way.'

'Great.'

'Now, now, I know he can be a bit of an old curmudgeon at times but he means well.'

Ben grunted and sloshed more wine down with his food. Kate wondered, not for the first time, when she'd lost him. She'd loved him once, and she was sure he'd loved her. But something had happened to tear them apart. She knew what that something was but it wasn't anything they could talk about. Even thinking about it was too painful.

'Norwich is very pleasant, what little I've seen. The cathedral's very fine and the market is rather jolly but it's all a bit . . . well, provincial, isn't it? Actually, Ben, some of us thought we might make a trip to the coast and I wondered if . . . if we might . . . They're very nice, there's Gordon, he played my husband, and Penny, well you saw them, didn't you, at the theatre?' She gave him one of her warm smiles; she wanted something from him. She needed his approval.

'So?'

'Well, darling, I suggested to the others that perhaps we could drive up to – um – Northstrand to see the sea and drop in to your little cottage for tea. Or –' she hurried on '– take you out for tea. Wouldn't that be nice?'

'Nice?' he echoed.

'Yes, Ben, nice! I haven't seen your new home yet, darling; I don't know where you're living.'

'I gave you the address.'

'Well yes, but I can't . . . picture it. It's like the difference between reading the script and making the words come off the page.' She made a large, dramatic gesture and saw Ben's eyes take in a head turning in their direction at a nearby table. A discreet comment was made and a second head turned to look. She hoped someone had the courage to sidle up and ask for her autograph; that would impress him.

'I did try phoning you yesterday but there was no reply.'

'No,' Ben admitted. 'Sometimes we don't pick it up.'

'What? Why?'

'It's always bad news.'

'Oh dear. Well, perhaps –'

'Is that the scarf I gave you for Christmas once?' He'd taken her by surprise. His eyes had a softer look; he really could still be a very handsome young man if he made some sort of effort. This Sue must be a terrible influence. Kate smiled sweetly at him.

'Yes. I wore it because I was going to see you.' She touched it, stroked it gently the way she would have liked to touch him. 'It's silk, isn't it? I've always loved it. It must have been frightfully expensive.'

'I wouldn't know. I stole it.'

'What?' She snatched her hand away as if scalded by the flimsy material.

'I pinched it from an Indian shop in Cambridge. It was so easy, you could ask for some weird kind of jossticks – sweetcorn and maple syrup or something – and they'd go out to the back to check so you could stuff any amount of things into your bag. Christ, they were so stupid. We used to steal hideous little brass statues and bedspreads and everything they had in there and then sell them on the market. We'd have starved without that shop.'

He poured himself another glass of wine, to the brim, and knocked half of it back in one swig.

'Sweet, madam?'

'Yes, profiteroles for me, please. Ben, are you having a pudding?'

'No, I can't justify it with the amount of poverty in the world.' Kate said nothing and gave the waiter a thin smile.

They both ate in silence, Kate waiting, waiting . . . Finally, as she put down her spoon and dabbed at the corners of her mouth with a napkin, she said, 'I can't bear it any longer. You haven't said a word about the play all evening. Darling, did you absolutely hate it? You can be honest, you know. Honestly.'

'No . . .'

'Yes, really, darling.'

70

'No,' he persisted, 'I didn't absolutely hate it.'

'Ah.'

'But I can't say I liked it much either. The play, it's . . . well, it's rubbish, really, isn't it?' His jaw hung insolently open.

'I'm sorry?' She wasn't sure if she'd misheard or mis-understood. Now she had the look of Thatcher when accused of being uncaring. Total incomprehension.

'I don't mean to be unnecessarily cruel. Let's keep things nice, after all. Actually, I thought you were . . . quite good.'

'Oh?'

'Yes. You had a bit of . . .'

Talent? she wondered. Style?

'. . . energy. Some of the others were really dragging it out. All that *acting* all over the place.' He made it sound like some particularly unsavoury bodily function. 'But you got on with it. You were . . . fast.'

'And loud?'

'Yeh.'

'And I didn't bump into the furniture once.'

'What?'

'Nothing. I should have known better than to ask.' Her voice was weary, full of regret. Does he love me? she thought. No, if he did he wouldn't behave this way, so distant, so dismissive. Does he hate me? It feels as if he does. Have I really been such a bad mother? Probably. Is it too late?

When they left the restaurant it was drizzling and the road shone like sweating flesh.

'God,' she said with a little laugh. 'By the time we get to the hotel I shall look like a drowned rat.'

The word *drowned* echoed through them both. Neither acknowledged it but each knew the other had registered it. Kate's first instinct was to apologize but she knew she'd be digging a deeper hole so she said nothing. But it was too late to wipe out the familiar images that had flashed into her mind.

'Well, I'm sorry you didn't enjoy this evening,' she said with undisguised bitterness. 'It was supposed to be a treat.'

'It was interesting. The meal was fine.'

'But the show . . . ?'

'The show was . . . well, your performance was good. I said that.'

'"... quite good ...",' she quoted accurately, his faint praise still haunting her.

He left it a beat.

'You don't think that play was any good, do you?'

No, of course she didn't; her silence acknowledged that. They walked on almost side by side but with Kate maintaining the merest advantage over her son; she would have breasted inches before Ben any finishing tape stretched between lampposts across the street.

Their footsteps rang out loud between the tall buildings. Ben's long legs struck a leisurely, steady rhythm; Kate's high heels pecked along the wet pavement with a light, nervous clicking. They were naturally out of step with each other as they had been for twenty years.

'Look, Mother, what I can't understand is what the hell you do it for. Touring in third-rate thrillers. What's the point? The objective correlative as you might say. Surely you don't need the money?'

'I'm touring in third-rate thrillers because that's all I'm being offered!' she snapped.

'But the whole thing – acting. Why do you bother? Is it a childish attempt to be somebody else because you don't like who you are? Is that it?'

'Christ!' Kate screamed suddenly, unable to maintain her polite exterior any longer, stopping outside the brightly lit window of an electrical shop. 'I don't believe this!'

If he'd made the slightest effort to match her poise and air of insouciance she'd have carried it off for the whole evening, as she did on countless occasions not just for herself but also to preserve George's precious bloody image. But if Ben was going to make no attempt at mutual self-preservation through the good old British route of 'manners', then Kate felt no compulsion to treat him gently either. If it was the brutal truth he wanted, and if he pushed her to it, then a lot of nasty facts could come spilling out.

'Christ!' she shouted again. 'You sound like him. Like father, like son! Why do I bother when I've got a villa in Provence, two racehorses and I can bath in champagne? Is that what you're saying? Well, what about me, eh? What about *me* — what I want. What I do. I'm an actress — Kate Fitch, that's who I am! Did you know that?'

Ben looked at her oddly as if she was speaking a language he didn't understand. Which of course she was.

Kate's up-front display of raw emotion was backlit by the shop display: novelty telephones, computer games and personal hi-fis; the rain had flattened her carefully styled hair and drops were running down her face like tears, taking a little mascara with them. My God, she realized, they were tears.

But she felt anything but sad. She was alive and vibrant. And she was going to play this scene for all it was worth.

She could see Ben's gaunt face showing a mixture of fascination and embarrassment. He had the look of a young Dirk Bogarde in a bad wig, his mouth open, his dark brows lowered as he stared at her. The street was empty and quiet apart from the rain; it could have been a scene from something by Visconti.

But she also felt afraid now; where was this improvisation going? Could she control it or would it damage them both more than heal past wounds? She'd challenged him; how would he react?

He stood his ground, his face alive with questions. They confronted each other, the rain drenching them both; she felt sure the irony of this was as obvious to him as it was to her. It poured on them, not cleansing but drowning.

Would he take up the fight or back out of confrontation?

Her body and face square on to him, Kate waited with a sense of dread for his response. Would he slug it out with her? Did she honestly want him to?

Yes, deep down she knew it all had to be dealt with. The whole hideous mess. For twenty years, almost Ben's whole life, the circumstances of Christopher's death had been half-acknowledged, the various versions of stories interwoven and left alone, as if that explained and excused the whole event. She knew that a half-truth was another kind of lie, that not to have tackled it properly at the time was a grave error and to have left it to fester only compounded the mistake. Nothing would heal by itself. George was right, she was stuck in the past. But she didn't know how to escape.

Was this the time? Was this the place? There was so much that needed to be said, to be clarified about the events of that summer's afternoon when Christopher's young lungs had filled with water and . . .

Horrified, she saw Ben's face register a look of withering scorn and with the slightest movement of his shoulders he registered his unwillingness to engage with her in the mending process.

'Oh, stop feeling so sorry for yourself,' he said, flicking his wet fringe out of his eyes. 'It's absurd, especially in a woman of your age.'

'God, how can you be so cruel?' Her face was ugly now, lumpy and distorted. 'I thought you might be the one person to understand the misery of being Mrs George King. Don't tell me it's a barrel of laughs being his son, I know it damn well isn't.'

'Oh, is that what this is about?' He wiped a bony hand languidly over his face. His damaged good looks as they emerged again shocked her anew. He would have made a great Heathcliff or a laid-back Hamlet if he'd followed her into the business. 'I think you have to work that one out by yourself. But if you'd like the name of a good therapist I've got a few contacts.'

'I don't need another therapist!'

He was suddenly and shockingly tender.

'I'm sorry, that wasn't meant to be patronizing. I care about you, you know.'

She didn't like his reading of the line. Instead of the verb he stressed the pronouns: '*I* care about *you*.' As if the opposite were not true.

'Don't, Ben.'

'Don't what, Mother?'

'We shouldn't be like this. We should be friends.'

He laughed. His mouth opened wide and showed his good teeth. But it wasn't a laugh of real amusement; he was doing it for effect. He was acting. He knew the power he wielded over her.

'It's rather too late to start redefining our relationship now, isn't it?'

'Look, Ben. This is so silly. Standing here in the rain and —'

'Yes. I think I'll leave you to make your own way from here. I'd better go.'

'No, come with me. You can get dry at the hotel. We can have a drink and a talk.'

'I think not. Thank you for a pleasant evening. Goodnight.'

He didn't even kiss her, just gave a slight gesture, as if making a discreet bid at an auction, turned and walked away up the street.

'Ben?' she called after him, but quietly, a forlorn plea for help.

He walked fast, his tall body loose and relaxed, his head not even bowed against the rain. Yet again he'd remained aloof from commitment to a real conversation with her about the things they both knew had one day to be resolved.

Her son. Her son Ben. Her only son.

She ran a hand through her wet hair, scraping it back off her face, then turned to lean both hands and her head against the shop window behind her as if studying the goods for sale. She felt old and very, very tired.

For a long time there was no sound but the hissing of the rain falling on Kate and on the pavement equally and unrelentingly. She stared at a price tag a few inches from her, through the glass in the dry, bright domain of the shop. 'Half-price. Shop-soiled.'

She let out a quiet sob. She tried to take a deep breath but it came in little gasps, out of her control. She seemed to be floating somewhere above herself, watching Kate Fitch perform and anticipating what was about to happen.

It was as if she did it for both of them. She clenched her right hand into a tight fist and slammed it hard against the glass. The window splintered from corner to corner with a sharp, squeaky crack, like the sound of a thick branch being snapped off a solid trunk, and where her fist had hit it there was an opaque area of a hundred tiny splinters.

She expected an alarm bell but none sounded. Nobody shouted or came running in response to the noise. No lights went on in the building. As the sound died away some shards of glass pattered around her feet on the wet paving slabs.

Kate felt the pain in her hand and saw a thin trickle of blood running down into the sleeve of her coat. The softly drumming rain watered it down, turning its redness pink.

7

Ben turned the radio on as he headed out of Norwich on the A140. They were playing 'Sailing By' on Radio Four so he guessed it was about twelve-thirty. He could look at his watch, but who cared what the time was anyway?

He twiddled the tuning knob on the radio, the sound slurred and whirred until it settled on music. Something bland would do just fine. It was the Carpenters' 'Top of the World'. Oh great. Just what he needed after a row with his mother. He snapped the switch to 'off', preferring silence. If only he could have quiet inside his head.

The battered old 2CV was going too fast and yet it was somehow out of his control to slow it down, so he clung on to the wheel as it bounced along.

The hitchhiker was standing at the junction with the by-pass and Ben stopped for her automatically as if she were a friend waiting for a lift.

'Thanks. Blimey, what a night, eh? I'm soaked. You going to Aylsham?'

'Yes. Get in.'

'Oh, ta. That's brill.'

'I'll turn the heater up. There.'

'Great. I'm wet through. To the skin.'

'I can imagine.'

He smiled at her, keeping eye contact for a significant and dangerously long time until she was the one to look back at the road. He thought she looked kind of cute, not pretty exactly but under different circumstances . . .

'It's a real *Walpurgisnacht*, isn't it?'

'Yeh. A what?'

' 'Twas a dark and stormy night . . .'

'Right.' She scrunched her hair and flung it back. 'You're not local, are you?' She spoke slowly.

'Is it that obvious?'

'I was just thinking, I'd remember if I'd seen you before.'

'Oh yeh?'

'Yeh,' she said. 'Someone as good-looking as you.'

'How kind.'

'Don't get me wrong, I'm not coming on to you.'

'That's a pity.'

'Ooh, don't get fresh.'

'Believe me, Deirdre, I feel quite the opposite; very stale indeed.'

''Ere, what d'you call me?'

'Deirdre. Isn't that your name?'

'No way. I'm Tamsin.'

'Oh. Well, you look like a Deirdre to me.'

She giggled. 'Well you look like a bit of a dish to me.'

'A dish? Well, thank you. Am I sweet or savoury?'

'Let's see. I reckon you're something la-di-da. Like scampi.'

'Oh dear. Not salmon?'

'No, not that classy.' She laughed at his crestfallen look. 'Unless you've got hidden depths what I can't see.'

'Would you like to find out, Deirdre?'

She giggled again and Ben liked the way her nose wrinkled up. He thought she must be about his age. Her body would be white and soft and it would smell of the rain. He'd like to lick the sweet drops off her warm skin.

'Tamsin,' she corrected him. 'What's your name, then?'

'Christopher.'

'Nice. I like that name.'

'Yes? What sort of person does that make me, then? If I'm called Christopher?'

'Nice and normal. Reliable. Friendly. Good at parties and that. Not screwed up.'

'Oh yes, that's me.'

They smiled. Ben wondered if their contract was made

yet, if she was offering and expecting the same as he was. Or would he have to force her to do it? That would be a bore, he'd feel even more guilt afterwards and tonight he didn't need it.

'Listen, Tamsin. I've had a bit of a rough evening.'

'Too many down the pub?'

'No, not that sort of rough. Had a row with someone.'

'Tch, tch. Your girlfriend, was it?'

'No. Yes, that's right.'

'She's a silly tart. She'll lose you if she's not careful.'

'The thing is, I feel . . . Look, do you want to fuck?'

She didn't reply for a moment but a wonderful, dirty look spread across her face.

'I thought you'd never ask.' She draped a hand over his thigh. He'd become hard already at the thought of it. 'Hell, boy, what you got in there?'

'It's not mine, I'm looking after it for a friend.'

'You can't come home, you know, I live with me mum and dad.'

'I don't want you at my house either.'

'Oh well, it won't be the first time I've been stuffed on the back seat. I'm used to better cars, mind. Still, take the next left by that phone box and then first right over the cattle grid. We can park in Davey Hewitt's top field.'

'You're more useful than an ordnance survey map, Deirdre.'

'I'm a better fuck, too.'

Ben stopped where she showed him and then switched off the engine. The sound of the rain on the flimsy roof pointed up the quiet inside the car.

'Well . . .'

'Right.'

There were no preliminaries. They clambered into the back of the car. She wriggled her damp jeans and knickers down to her ankles and placed his hand at her crutch. Straightaway Ben pushed his fingers into her, impatient for it, and she gasped as he explored clumsily inside her.

79

She fumbled incompetently with the buttons on his trousers but soon got what she wanted; it sprang upright as she released it from its restraining clothes. This was usually when the men Ben had been with got really excited, and the women had second thoughts. But he wasn't letting her off the hook now.

'Oh Jesus, it's enormous,' she said predictably. 'It's the biggest plonker I've ever seen. And I've seen some, I'm telling you.' So much for sweet talk, thought Ben. But there was more than a hint of anticipation in her voice and when he'd shoved his pants down to his knees he pressed his hand on the back of her neck, pulling her face towards his absurdly long cock and he felt minimal resistance.

What a filthy tramp! She was so easy. He felt nothing but disgust for her and was ashamed of himself for even going on with this.

He watched her with no sense of involvement. She was licking at him as if he'd given her an ice-cream cone. If only straight women would take blow-job lessons from gay men.

Brusquely he pushed her head away and tried to turn her around on the narrow seat. He pulled awkwardly at her, impatient to get it over with.

'Come on, hurry up.'

'Wait, what's the rush? Don't be so rough! Christopher, you're hurting me.'

'Tough!'

He pushed her legs wide, positioned his great battering ram at the brink and then gave one sudden thrust and entered her with a force that made her cry out loud.

'Ow! Wait, I'm in the wrong . . .' She wriggled about underneath him, like a butterfly pinned but still struggling for life. He looked down at her as if she was miles beneath him on the ground. He couldn't have been less bothered. This wasn't for her, it wasn't about her at all. He started to thrust in rhythm. Ready or not, here I come . . .

'Ooh, that's better. Now, let's have you.' She looked at him with real lust in her eyes. 'Come on, stick it right in.'

'Shut up. Just shut up!' He put his hands on her skinny shoulders and bore down on her, looking out of the window, the black of the night mirroring the darkness of his soul. Screwing his eyes up tight made it no better.

'Hey, what's your problem? Relax.'

Oh God, the little tart wanted to enjoy herself.

Wedging himself awkwardly between the seats, windows and doors like the giant Alice through the Looking Glass, arms and legs protruding from the house, he began to pump furiously, trying to get the thing done as soon as he could.

His backside bobbed up and down and he felt her legs wrap tightly around him as she tried to join him in his manic ride. She grabbed his face and pulled it towards her, planting her mouth on to his. Their tongues met in a muscular kiss, invaded by wet hair. She tasted of cigarettes and vinegar.

The car heaved and creaked on its springs as Ben worked away, shoving himself into her further and faster, one hand now under her sweater, kneading her small breasts with no thought of tenderness.

'Oh blimey, Christopher, you're gonna rip me apart, you are.' She moaned like someone in a tacky blue movie. 'You ought to be wearing something, you know; this isn't safe. Oh, God, can I trust you, are you clean?'

'Shut up, bitch!'

'Now, come on. That's not nice. What's up with you? Just 'cause you had a barney with your girlfriend. Ow, don't be so vicious. Slow down.'

He ignored her prattling and concentrated on chasing his orgasm.

'Look, this is serious. We shouldn't do it without a condom.' She pronounced it 'comdom'. 'You know what they say in the adverts, "If you don't know —"'

'Shut up, you stupid tart.' He redoubled his efforts, the

sweat trickling off his forehead into her thick, brown-blond hair and on to her startled face. He kissed her again to keep her silent.

The rutting continued, furious and loveless, the smell of wet clothes and lust filling the air, steaming up the windows.

'Oh yes, my lovely big boy. Hurt me. Ow! Here, you can't come inside me. You'll have to yank it out before you slime, okay? You will, won't you? Eh?'

'Yeh, yeh, sure. Call me by my name. Go on. Now, go on.'

'Do what?'

'Talk to me, use my name.'

'Go on, Christopher; that's it.'

'Again, keep saying my name!'

'Christopher, Christopher, Christopher, come on, Christopher, do it to me, Christopher!'

'Oh yes; *yeh . . .*'

He shoved his hips forward one last time. At his moment of climax Ben held his breath and his face was contorted in a silent scream. He felt himself teeter on the edge and then tumble helplessly over into the confusion of orgasm. As he plunged gratefully down into the maelstrom, waves of energy pulsed through his tense body, engulfing him totally for a few brief seconds.

'Oh no, don't slime inside me, you mustn't! You promised you wouldn't.' She wriggled half-heartedly beneath him. 'God, you're all the same, you men. Wait, look, I'm nowhere near yet. You could've waited for me. I told you to go slower. Talk about selfish. What am I supposed to do now?'

'Oh no . . . no . . .' Ben was moaning. 'Poor Christopher . . . he's gone . . .'

'What? Wait, keep going, I'm not there . . .'

He pumped himself once more into the soft flesh beneath him, then shuddered involuntarily, gave a deep sigh and collapsed on to her.

Even while his buttocks were still twitching with the final spasms the usual guilt began to seep through him.

'Hang on, I'll get there in a minute. Don't let it go soft.' She was moving against him, seeking her own pleasure, but he pulled out of her abruptly and tucked his swollen cock away, deliberately depriving her.

'Talk about wham-bam . . .'

'Get out.'

'What?'

'Just get out and fuck off, you little slut,' Ben said wearily. She wasn't worth any more of his energy.

'Who d'you think you are?' She looked ridiculous, standing on her dignity while lying on her back trying to give herself an orgasm, her torn knickers flapping round her legs.

He climbed into the front seat, threw her bag out into the wet field and coaxed the tinny engine to life.

'Oy!' She got out, clutching her clothes around her and scrabbling for her bag in the grass. It was still raining. 'You bastard. You fucking bastard! You think you're better'n me just 'cause you know long words an' stuff. Well, you've got a real problem, you have, you know that?'

'Yes,' he said, 'I know.'

Ben pulled the lever brutally into first gear, let the clutch out and with a dramatic lurch the car bounded off.

She'd got her lift. What was she complaining about?

8

It was noticed in the company that Kate was uptight about something. She snapped at Stevie when her act two dress split at the seam during the midweek matinée and she didn't socialize with the others after the show. She was withdrawn to the point of coldness where once she had made a conscious effort to join in.

Kate slipped easily into the old habit of hating herself, her world and everyone in it. She hated this stupid play, the director, the actors, the business for not making her a star. But most of all she hated Kate Fitch for making such a godawful mess of her life.

By Thursday she hadn't been able to get through to Ben on the phone and wondered whether she should drive out to see him the next day. However painful it was, they needed to talk.

She knew the real reason for their row, of course. What they couldn't bring themselves to discuss truthfully. The precise events on the summer's day when she'd rushed home to find her husband and eldest son sitting silent in the kitchen with the body of Christopher still wet on the table between them.

She didn't even think consciously about it any more. It was a constant pain in her heart and image in her mind. Sometimes it stabbed with a fresh ability to shock, sometimes it throbbed like a dull ache. She had almost learned to live with it now. She knew she would never find peace.

She'd left George in charge while she went to her matinee at the Theatre Royal. Gwendolen in *The Importance of Being Earnest*. That play had been poisoned for her for ever. George would hang on until the babysitter arrived, then he'd be leaving for some meeting about a series of articles he was going to write.

She didn't mind leaving the boys with the girl from up the road. They liked her, she was fun and very good at keeping them amused with her games and endlessly resourceful ideas. She was also totally reliable and although she could only have been about fifteen, had a real sense of responsibility.

The call to go home as soon as possible had come during the first half but they'd kept it from her until after the curtain was down. They didn't say what it was about but something inside her knew anyway. The sight of Christopher broke her heart. There he was even today, in her mind's eye, tiny and still wet, lying face down on the wood in his pale yellow fluffy suit, arms and legs spread out like a starfish. She picked him up, hugged him to her and in that moment her real life ended. The rest was merely a sham.

Between his own sobs George had explained. How the girl had been playing with the boys in the garden while he'd got his briefcase ready to go. That he'd heard a splash and a scream, looked from an upstairs window and seen her trying to fish the little body from the pond with a stick. He'd rushed to help, wading into the water and pulling poor Christopher out, how he'd tried to get the water out of his lungs and air in. But that he'd been too late. George had told her how he'd shouted at the babysitter, screaming that she'd let his son die; she had cried and said over and over again that she was sorry and it was all her fault, but in his anger he'd just gone on bawling at her and that she'd eventually run away in tears.

The police never found her. Her parents didn't know where she'd gone for ages until they had a phone call from Dover. After that nothing.

At four Ben was too young really to be involved. She hoped that the events of that day had faded quickly from his memory and not scarred him the way they had her.

85

She could remember George's voice, muffled as he held his head in his hands. 'Oh God, if only I could bring him back. That stupid, stupid girl. Oh Jesus, how could she be so bloody stupid?' Again and again he chanted it, like a mantra, but one that had no power to heal.

Kate could see it all in her head and hear the dialogue clearly as if on a video. She could fast forward to a particular moment – coming in through the door and seeing the three of them like a painting, two faces turned away, only Ben looking up at her, the dark stain on the table seen over Christopher's shoulder as she held him tightly to her sobbing chest – or she could repeat a sequence that gave her the most exquisite pain: the final sight of his sad little face, the burial. It was all there, not something that had happened to her, but part of her life without which she could not function.

She blamed herself. She blamed George. She blamed the babysitter. She blamed Ben too, of course. And yet she didn't blame anyone. Blame didn't help. She didn't know who to believe. She'd heard too many different truths, too many different lies. She knew only that Christopher was dead, had been dead for twenty years. And the death of her younger son, her special boy, to all intents and purposes had also killed her career.

On the Friday morning of *Murder in Triplicate*'s run in Norwich, Trevor Waterman was playing tennis with one of the other actors and, at match point in the third set apparently, fell and twisted his ankle. Alex, the company manager, called the cast together at lunchtime and explained the situation. They started to reblock in order to keep Trevor as static as possible, but it gradually became clear that there were scenes such as the fight, and the bit where he had to climb through the window, which it was going to be impossible to fake.

'Don't worry, m'dear,' Penny said, reaching up to put an arm around his shoulder. 'Let me give it a rub with some of my special cream. It worked for Alec Guinness at the Vaudeville in sixty-eight and it'll work for you.'

'It's not cream he needs, Pen, it's rest.' Gordon puffed on his pipe, the epitome of serenity as ever.

'Look, I'll be fine, really.' Trevor tried to demonstrate a jaunty step and promptly fell to the floor with a cry of pain.

'Hmm. Doesn't look good, does it, old boy?'

'Alec was just the same but he went on and did the show that night. He was marvellous.'

'Listen,' said Alex. 'I've spoken to Bryan on the phone and he agrees, we only have one option. The understudy goes on as Simon.'

'Understudy?' said Kate. 'Who's that?'

'Jack.' Seeing one or two slightly puzzled faces he added, 'Jack Fever, the ASM. He plays the policeman in the final scene. I'll go on as Sergeant Tanqueray; the costume'll have to be let out a bit.'

'But does Jack know the lines?'

'No, I'm sure he doesn't. But he's got . . .' he checked his watch. 'Six hours to learn them. Right, let's get rehearsing. Jack! We need you. Jack!'

'Well, it could be fun tonight!' Gordon beamed with delight at this turn of events.

Jack didn't know the lines for Simon, of course, as he'd been too busy doing props and sound and playing the policeman to learn them. But he'd heard them often enough in rehearsals and had a vague idea of how the scenes hung together. He looked a much better Simon than Trevor did, more compact and appealing to the eye than Trevor's baby giraffe look. Much of the afternoon was spent working out where they could stick bits of paper with his bigger speeches on them. The small table behind the settee could take two of them, a book from the shelf hid another, one piece of paper with the speech about love and duty was disguised as a label on a bottle of wine and the globe concealed another long bit of plot-laying carefully cut to fit the outline of North America.

'Apart from that, you're on your own,' Alex said.

He was anything but on his own. Anyone on stage with him knew where Trevor would normally be and so they were able to move Jack around the stage by the arm or with a flick of the eyes. He was a bit hesitant because of nerves, but his first show as Simon was deemed a huge success. There was much hugging and mutual congratulation in the bar and Bryan Harvey-Jones rang to arrange free drinks. Or rather one free drink each.

Kate even stayed for a while and pecked Jack briefly on the cheek.

'Well done, kid,' she said, coming on the leading lady. 'You did a great job.'

'Thanks, Miss Fitch. I hope it wasn't too ghastly for you. Oh, and I'm sorry about that bit in act one when I dried. I was so nervous. You were terrific, the way you covered.'

'Don't mention it. It keeps us all on our toes. I expect you'll be playing it most of next week too.'

'Yes, it looks like it.'

'Well, why don't you come to my dressing-room at the half on Monday and we'll have a chat about the part.'

'Yes, fine. I'd like that.' He looked doubtful. 'Was it really awful?'

'No. You were great. Really. Just some bits of business we didn't have time to explain today. Things Trevor and I had worked out, little things like . . . No, let's leave it until next week in . . . um . . .'

'Plymouth.'

'Yes,' she smiled. 'Tonight, just enjoy your new stardom. But don't drink too much, you've got a matinee tomorrow, remember. Goodnight.'

She brushed his cheek again with her lips. He really was quite sweet and so proud of himself, although he could only have been about Ben's age or even less.

Ben. There he was, haunting her again. Now, with all this business she hadn't got out to Northstrand as intended and tomorrow she'd agreed to do an interview on Radio

Hicksville or whatever the local station was called and then open some new supermarket, for Christ's sake. What the hell had Robin arranged that for anyway? Lousy money and so tacky. And when was she going to hear about the auctioneers and the disabled thing for telly?

She managed to keep smiling until she'd left the theatre, but once outside Kate let her despair sweep over her again. She was sure she was unwanted, unloved, unnecessary and she hugged her depression to herself, attempting to draw some comfort from that certainty at least.

Back at the hotel she got a large vodka and tonic at the bar and took it up to her room.

She stripped to her bra and pants, wiped all her make-up off and leaned close to the mirror in the bathroom, the harsh lights exposing every wrinkle and flaw in her skin. She felt a delicious self-indulgent thrill as she examined her face minutely, not allowing any part to be ignored.

The bones were good, that couldn't be denied. A strong, square jaw and good high cheekbones. And the hair wasn't too bad, although there was too much grey unless she kept it in check and she knew she really ought to stop back-combing it. It made her look like something out of a terrible American soap. Her almond-shaped eyes were now surrounded with a delicate filigree of lines and dark shadows of experience. The lids were heavier, lower than they had been, the eyebrows had a tendency to become wild like a garden that would return to its natural state unless constantly pruned. She stared deep into the reflection of her own eyes, green and . . . quite pleasant where once they'd been fiery and fascinating. The whites were off-white and red-flecked now after almost half a century of having the wool pulled over them by agents, husband and directors alike. They had once promised so much, hinting at secrets and pleasures withheld. Now they gazed at the world with a cynical matter-of-factness, a sense that she had no mysteries to keep from anyone, nor did the world hold any surprises for her any more.

She pursed her lips up like a dog's bottom to exaggerate the multitude of cracks there. They were thinner now and the colour was fading. Would it be worth having them filled out with injections? Or should she embrace the era of the character part, the dotty old aunts and spunky spinsters, and forget the glamorous roles entirely? Forty-eight was a difficult age for an actress. And fifty-two was worse. She'd stick to forty-eight for a couple more years.

She pinched the skin at her cheek and watched, fascinated, as it slowly recovered its former outline. Once upon a time it used to snap back like elastic. Not any more. The neck was turning scraggy too, the skin getting loose and wobbly. Where had all the years gone? Where was the excitement, or even contentment? Had she been on the other side of the street when the bus marked 'stardom' passed by?

She didn't need to torment herself by examining her sagging breasts, heavy hips and bulging stomach too closely. A cursory glance reaffirmed her state of depression.

She rang room service for another large vodka-tonic. Not such a brilliant idea, maybe, but she felt like getting drunk.

She thought about going back to the theatre to join the celebrations with Gordon and Penny and Alex and young Jack Fever. But she knew her arrival would take the edge off the affair, the decibels would drop, the conversation would be slightly cleaned up, nothing would be quite so relaxed. No, Kate Fitch could never quite be one of the boys.

The spotty youth who brought her drink looked at her with a lasciviousness remarkable in one so young, as if he could actually see through her dressing-gown. They must know more at seventeen than I did, she thought. Still, that wouldn't be difficult. His skin was very bad; red blotches and crusted pustules covered most of his face and she wondered how he managed to shave round them, like mowing a lawn dotted with flowerbeds.

'This'll do the trick,' he said.

'Thank you.' As he bent to put it down she noticed the flecks of dandruff on his maroon jacket. Why would anyone choose maroon?

'If not, just give me a buzz and we'll try something else, shall we? I'm sure I've got just the thing for you.' He gave her a lewd wink. 'If you know what I mean.' His greasy forehead shone at her and his smile revealed teeth of various shades of yellow and brown, like samples of paint colours on a card.

'Look, kid,' she said wearily. 'Don't mess with me, okay? I won't complain to the management about your behaviour if you just piss off. Otherwise you'll be out of this job and back in the gutter where you belong.' It was a line from a part she'd once played.

'Wow. Fantastic. You do anger really well. I saw your play on Tuesday. *Murder in Triplicate*. Great! You were dead sexy. For an older woman. I'd give anything to play Simon, especially in the snogging scene. Wow, a real tongue sandwich on stage. Yo!'

She had to sign his arm for him in felt pen before he'd go.

That's stopped me ordering from room service, she thought. Terrific.

She wondered what Ben was doing now, was he thinking of her? Did he want to talk? Did she?

She rang his number. No reply. He couldn't be out, he couldn't afford to do anything. He was probably there and refusing to pick up the phone just in case it was Kate. Oh God, she thought, I've been a terrible mother. I deserve all the pain he gives me.

She watched a pathetic game show on the television, shaved her legs, flossed her teeth, said her prayers to a God she didn't believe in and went to bed, clutching the dregs of her vodka.

9

In the tiny flint clifftop cottage Ben woke as usual with a coughing fit. It was light outside. A bright blue sky was visible through the small window, but he knew it would be another bitterly cold day.

Somewhere a dog barked, then a second one answered it. The throbbing engine of a heavy piece of farm machinery was just audible; now louder, now softer as it made its way up and down a nearby field. On the roof a bird's feet pattered. Underscoring the whole was the relentless crash-and-scrape, crash-and-scrape of waves on shingle.

His head hurt like hell and his bladder felt as if it was about to explode. The other half of the double bed was empty.

He let his coughing subside and then wrapped a blanket around his naked body and shuffled into the bathroom where he stood and watched in blurred amazement as his long, soft cock spewed dark yellow pee into the lavatory bowl with amazing force. It seemed to exist independently of him. While he waited for it to finish its task he ran a hand through his long hair, pushing it back from his face, and looked at himself in the mirror over the basin. Not a pretty sight.

He gave his cock a couple of shakes, threw some cold water into his face, licked a morsel of toothpaste from the tip of the tube, swooshed it around his stale mouth and spat it out. Tugging the blanket tighter around himself, he staggered down the narrow, squeaky stairs into the kitchen.

Sue was watching the black and white television on the table. The picture was breaking up as it always did.

'Hello, babe. How are you feeling?' she said in her nervous, breathless voice.

'Pretty bloody. That home-made beer of Terry's should have a government health warning. He could sell it at the garden centre as greenfly killer.' His breath condensed in the chill air when he spoke.

'Did you drink by yourself last night?'

'Just a few.'

'You must have been late. I didn't hear you come in.' She seemed to be avoiding his eyes. Ben looked at the lumpy form of men's sweaters hiding her scrawny body, at her lank hair and gaunt face. What had become of them both? They used to enjoy their fair share of health and contentment. Now he realized he didn't care about her at all. He wondered if she'd got up before him to avoid having any contact? Were things really that bad? Probably.

'Any tea?'

'There are a few bags in the tin, babe. I don't know if Terry's awake yet.'

Ben readjusted his blanket and went into the only other downstairs room. He kicked the side of the settee where, under another bundle of blankets, something was snoring.

'Kettle's on, d'you want a cup?'

There was a startled grunt and then a hairy head slowly emerged. Two bleary eyes stared at Ben, uncomprehending.

'Wha—?'

'D'you want tea?'

'Yeh. Wha'ser time?'

'Don't know. About eleven, I think.'

Ben made three mugs of weak tea from one bag and they sat down around a two-bar electric fire to their breakfast. Tea and some bread with margarine and jam. No one could be bothered to make toast.

'Oh, bugger off!' Terry said, throwing one of the three scrawny cats off the table. It was a perpetual task; they would return time after time to sniff and pick at any scraps of food that were left uncovered. Being dropped to the floor was a setback, not a deterrent.

Terry was rolling a thin cigarette with a few strands of tobacco. His Norfolk accent gave his voice a friendly tone. 'How was the play then? Was Mummy good?'

Ben's sigh was silent but visible, a long stream in the air between them. He wanted to be out of the whole world of his parents, television, the media, pretence and charade, people asking if his mum was really Kate Fitch, what his father was like in private. That's why he'd dropped out of university and come to this stone cottage on the cliffs near Cromer, to be himself. To see if he could find out who he really was. Not the son of George King and Kate Fitch. Ben King. He wanted to write the poems and stories that were inside his head, jumbling around and getting in the way. If he could only order them and put them down on paper perhaps he'd be able to clear all the crap out of his brain and get on with his real life.

He'd met Sue in the pub one night. He'd bought her a drink – that had been in the days when he still had some of his final grant cheque left – and they'd played a few games of darts. They were both alone, she'd left home and was drifting down the coast with vague plans of getting to Amsterdam to start some kind of new life there. Or maybe Denmark. She wasn't that fussy.

'Berlin's supposed to be a gas,' she'd said.

'Yes. I wouldn't use that expression in the post office, though.'

'Why not?'

'I don't think Mrs Lewenstein would approve.'

When she'd suggested in a desultory kind of way that they share the cost of renting a cottage he'd agreed that it made sense. They'd found this place for the summer and because it only had one bedroom they'd drifted into being a couple.

Sometimes they had sex. She seemed to get more out of it than Ben. She often told him how much she loved him. She liked his brooding, dark good looks, his hint of mystery and romance. And what she called her 'cockatoo',

94

nuzzling up to it at night as if it were a hot water bottle. Ben felt almost jealous of it. As if the rest of him could never live up to its promise. He still looked down on it and wondered why he'd been blessed – or cursed – with such a monster. Perhaps it was in compensation for being the last boy in the class to reach puberty. He was still squeaking while the others towered over him and spoke to each other in deep growls. They had hair under their arms, on their chests. He looked at their changing shapes in swimming lessons and marvelled, wondering all the time when his turn would come. When at last it did it was too late to impress anyone; he was already branded as the runt of the pack, singled out by his immaturity and his somehow having cheated by being the son of two famous people. He was apart from the crowd, not one of the lads. That feeling of not quite belonging, wherever he went, had never left him. He was still a loner.

Even in the so-called relationship with Sue. He knew he was not providing whatever it was she wanted from him. He couldn't help that. It wasn't in his nature to be lovey-dovey. He could sit for hours in the same room as someone else and never speak. It didn't strike him as unusual or anti-social, although he'd learnt that others thought it so. He had more than enough going on in his head to keep him occupied.

Just as he did now, thinking over what had and hadn't been said the night before.

'You did see the play, didn't you?' Sue was asking.

'Oh, yes, I saw it.'

'And how was it?'

'Well, it was everything you'd expect from something called *Murder in Triplicate*.'

'I wouldn't expect sod all, boy,' Terry laughed, proud of his ignorance.

'Then I stand corrected. It was everything *I* would expect from a play so entitled.'

'So what did you see?'

95

'I saw a sad and desperate woman trying to prove something, but I couldn't decipher quite what.'

Ben saw a look pass between the other two and wondered, not for the first time, what their relationship was. He wouldn't be surprised if they started sleeping together. Difficult though, with only one bed in the house.

Terry had befriended them on the beach one day and come to stay for 'a couple of nights', sleeping on the battered sofa. Three months later he was still there. Ben couldn't care less if he stayed or left. Presumably Sue liked to have him around. For one reason or another. Anyway, he was good at stealing food and always had a scheme to make them money.

Ben coughed and swilled some tea down.

'Did you have a good talk with your mum, babe?'

'We had a talk, yes.'

'How was she?'

He thought about this one. There didn't seem an appropriate answer so he let the question hang in the air, unattended like a piece of lost property whose owner had died.

'Look, man, what she means is did the old lady give you any dosh? Like, can we eat this week?'

'Terry . . .' Sue admonished him gently, then looked to Ben for the reply.

'I think I shall go for a walk along the beach. There are some things I need to sort out.'

'Yeh. Like how to pay the bleedin' bills.'

Ben went upstairs and pulled on as many clothes as he could. He knew they wouldn't stop the bitter wind from chilling his body. They said it came straight from Siberia. 'All the way from the Urals,' was the phrase, repeated sagely by the locals with a certain pride. Their wind was colder than anything namby-pamby Yorkshire or wimpish Northumberland had to endure.

As he left the house he heard Terry's voice whining, 'If his old man's so bloody rich and famous why doesn't he give Benny an allowance, then? Oh piss off!' This to one of the cats as it was deposited yet again on the floor.

The same inevitability was what fascinated Ben about the waves. As he stood on the clifftop, leaning into the wind and tasting the salt spray on his lips, he watched as each wave crashed down on the shingle, ran a few yards ahead and then was sucked back with a sinister wet rasp. The fact that the motion never stopped amazed and horrified Ben. It grew to the awesome power of the neap tides when the shingle mounds were remoulded overnight and flotsam was spewed up at the feet of the yellow, chalky cliffs. It shrank to the ripples that trickled up and down the sand with the delicacy of creeping spiders. But it never, ever ceased. It was the eternal energy of birth and life; the priapic thrust of sex that was, and he now understood why, inextricably intertwined with death.

Today the waves were not large, but their power could not be mistaken. He scrambled down the rough cliff path, grabbing at loose plants to steady himself, and relished the friendly clatter of his shoes on the grey stones as he walked as near to the sea as he could without being engulfed.

He saw from the wetness of the beach that the tide was on its way out. The undertow would be fierce, enough to pluck him from the safety of land and drag him down to the belly of the ocean.

It was like some giant creature to him. Roaring, pounding with its great hooves, threatening and always dangerously unpredictable. Even when calm and purring, able to kill with its smothering power. A shallow pool could still drown a child . . .

That was the fascination, of course. The thrill of the fear. The memories of the facts, the imagination of the alternative. If it had been him, Ben. If it was him next. Now . . .

He studied each wave as it dashed itself to destruction against the pebble floor and in his mind threw himself under it, giving his body willingly to its seductive tug, rehearsing the death he knew he deserved.

But he didn't fool himself it was anything but an empty gesture. He could never know how Christopher had felt. He could only find out by doing it. And even that wouldn't bring his brother back.

He took a notebook and pen from his pocket and quickly scribbled down the thoughts that were clogging his brain. They were variations of the usual, nothing new, nothing he didn't jot down every day. Thoughts on the sea, on death, on brothers and mothers and sex. His poem formed quickly and he spoke it aloud, matching the rhythm of his fatal friend the North Sea.

Then he tore the page from its spiral binding, screwed it up and threw it into the wind, watching it bob bravely on the foaming surface for a long time before disappearing.

For a few hours at least Ben was free to live his own life.

10

Just before eight o'clock on a frosty, foggy morning Becca Nichols parked her Volvo in the driveway next to the Rolls and let herself into the house. It was dark, quiet and cold. There was a lot to be done in time for the party the following night.

She put the coffee machine on and then set off around the main reception rooms with a notebook, jotting down ideas under different headings: preparation, design, catering. Then, in the room that she'd had converted into the office – whether hers or George's it was impossible to agree – she began telephoning. She rang the team of cleaners to confirm that they would be there later in the morning, the two painters and the interior decorator who were coming to finish off in the afternoon. Then she finalized the buffet menu with the caterers, co-ordinated the colour schemes with the florist, double-checking with the decorator again, and began to go through the guest list, marking those who would need a reminder tomorrow.

She revelled in her super-efficiency. George was fond of calling her his 'Girl Thursday, always ahead of the pack'. He thought this was very amusing. She smiled weakly each time she heard it. Some of his other favourite comments were not so pleasant, but she never argued with him. It was his prerogative, after all. Not that she was a doormat, far from it. But she dedicated herself to her work, proud that he could never catch her out or have cause for complaint. Complain he did, constantly, but never with justification. She knew that and she was sure he did too. He must know he was dependent on her for the smooth organization of ninety per cent of his life. If he could have got away with asking her to clean his teeth and wipe his bottom he would have.

She'd been eager to work for him when the chance arose. Four years earlier the agency had sent her to a television station to do some work for what had sounded like 'Mr Caine' and it had crossed her mind as she walked up to the impressive doors that it might be *the* Mr Caine. But when she'd seen who it really was her heart had almost stopped beating. George King! *The* George King! She knew him of course, well everyone knew George King. She felt destined to work for him.

She'd hardly dared to speak to him that first day, so terrified was she, so alarming the sensation of being in the same room as him. But once she'd revolutionized his filing system and suggested a score of improvements that could usefully be made in the running of his day-to-day affairs they had both realized she was indispensable to him and her empire began to grow, creeping into every part of his life like an insidious cancer.

Minding a Major Television Personality was a complex and highly skilled occupation, but Becca was more than equal to the task. She was devoted to it. Her devotion sprang not from any affection for George but from *amour propre* – being able to respect herself for the many unseen miracles she performed every day as she smoothed the path for The Product. That's all he was to Becca. A product to be promulgated, not a man with human fears and hopes but something manufactured which she now pushed in an eager market for a phenomenal financial return. There were a few design faults which needed disguising and the job demanded unsociable hours with total commitment but, if it hadn't been for one particular incident, it could have been satisfying, even enjoyable work.

Enjoyment was not a concept that meant a great deal to Becca. It pleased her to be able to pay her bills and afford occasional modest treats – a new Volvo, an outfit from Next or Laura Ashley, a weekend in Devon – but her only god was efficiency.

She'd been bright and friendly as a child, outgoing and a real giggler. The mature Becca was polite but aloof. She'd heard George describe her as 'a friend of Martina', believing her impassive features hid depths of raw passion. Little did he know quite what her quiet exterior concealed.

Neither George nor Kate had ever seen Becca laugh. She was unparalleled in looking over scripts and knowing what would amuse an audience but a sense of humour was not something she had ever been accused of possessing.

At nine-fifteen she heard the levee begin upstairs, and at nine-thirty George came into the study in sweatshirt and jeans. She knew without checking that his first 'on-the-record' appointment of the day was lunch at the Savoy with the publisher of his book. He sometimes took himself away on mysterious 'off-the-record' meetings that neither Becca nor Alec the chauffeur nor any of the less permanent staff were supposed to know anything about. They knew better than to ask for details. He went away, he came back.

Today was Friday, Show Day, so he would be in a particularly unpredictable mood.

'Good morning, Mr King,' she said pleasantly. It was always 'Mr King', never 'George'. Even after four years. She wouldn't have wanted to call him by his first name, it implied a familiarity she had no desire to claim.

'Ah. Yes.' Mid-yawn and crutch-scratch he noticed something odd. 'Has something happened?'

'I'm sorry, Mr King?'

'What's going on?'

'It's the party. Your official birthday party. On Saturday. Tomorrow. I'm organizing everything from here; it seemed easier to be on site.'

'Ah.'

'Would you like your breakfast in here?' He nodded his bald head. Becca buzzed through on the intercom. 'Marcella, would you bring Mr King's breakfast through

101

to the office, please? Now then, perhaps you could go through the list with me and let me know who you'd rather remind yourself and who you want me to contact.'

'Right. Um. There's a . . . I'm expecting a call . . .'

'Yes?' She expected him to say more, but he just turned and looked out of the window at the pale sunshine struggling to pierce the grey skies.

'I think I'll have a dump before we get down to business,' he said, leaving the room, bumping into the door frame on the way. A couple of minutes later the phone rang.

'Good morning, Mr King's house. Can I help you?'

There was a long silence.

'Hello? Is anyone there?' She was sure there was although there was no sound at the other end, not even breathing.

'Hello. Becca Nichols speaking. Can I help you?'

Then a strange voice – not British, maybe French – said, 'Is he there?'

'To whom did you wish to speak?'

'Hello, is he there?'

Becca's professional defences began to rise.

'What number did you want, caller?'

'What number is this?'

'This is Becca Nichols. Was it me you wanted?'

'Just put him on, please.'

'May I ask what it's about?'

Another pause, then: 'Oh, go lost!' and he rang off.

Odd, she thought. Still, nothing to detain her.

She busied herself at the computer, accessing the 'Showscript' file and printing out the list of that week's questions. Before she could fax them to the studio to be written out on the large white cardboard sheets he would have to okay them.

Marcella, the cook who'd been there almost three months without getting the sack or walking out, setting some kind of record, slunk in with a tray for George. As she left he returned, causing her to cower out of his way

102

against the wall before scuttling back to her own domain. She had very little English and just smiled shyly and nodded when George bawled at her.

'That's better. There's nothing like a nice soft shit, is there?'

Becca treated this as rhetorical.

'Who was that on the blower?' he asked as he scanned her lists.

'He didn't say. I think it was a wrong number.'

'Ah.' He wiggled a fat finger in his ear. 'Tiger lilies in the garden room, eh?'

'Yes. White, yellow and orange is going to be the colour scheme for the flowers.'

'Did he ask for me by name?'

'Sorry?'

'On the phone.'

'Oh. No,' said Becca, trying to remember. 'I don't think so. No, definitely not.'

'Right.' George looked up at her. 'Tiger lilies, they're the big orange buggers, aren't they?'

'Yes.'

'Great. Now, what did you want me to do with these lists?'

Don't tempt me, thought Becca.

The house was ablaze with lights as Kate pulled into the driveway the following evening just after midnight. Her way was blocked by another Mercedes, several bloated BMWs, two Rollers, neither of which was George's, a Maigret-type Citroën, a couple of Jaguar XJSs and a small clutch of Porsches – even the odd Japanese mock-Jeep. That was just their own driveway; Kate now realized that all the other parked cars she'd passed in Frognal Drive were here for the same function.

But what the hell was it? After two shows with the inexperienced Jack Fever and the drive back from Norwich she'd been looking forward to a large vodka in the bath and then going to bed and not setting the alarm.

As she climbed the stone steps and entered the house through the open front door someone took her photograph, then shot off several more in quick succession as she stared in amazement at the sight before her.

Becca had organized everything with her customary immaculate professionalism. The house had been transformed. Huge vases of flowers stood on every available surface, some exotic marble pedestals had been specially imported for the extravagant displays, white-coated waiters were circulating with champagne, two female cellists were playing a Schubertian arrangement of 'Bohemian Rhapsody' in the protective curve of the sweeping staircase and their music mingled uneasily with some raunchier funk further inside to which people were evidently dancing.

But the main impression Kate had was of people. Glamorous, noisy, laughing people, and a lot of them. In her house. White jackets, bow ties, fur wraps, halter necks and bare backs, the shimmer of black silk and the glitter of gold and diamonds all merged into one exotic image before Kate's eyes as she stood there gaping in disbelief.

The photographer was taking advantage of her immobility to shoot her from several unflattering angles.

'Oh go away, do,' she snapped back at him and moved forward into the room.

'Kate, darling. Wonderful party!'

'Ah, the hostess with the dope test.'

'Katie, lovey, congratulations . . .'

'Better late than even later, darling!'

Several people leaned forward to peck her on the cheek as she pushed through the crowd. The air was heady with expensive perfumes, all mixing into the noxious scent of money. Kate beamed a bemused but gracious smile and tried to fit names to all the faces which swam into her field of vision.

'Vanessa, darling . . . Judi, *so* glad you could make it . . . thank you, Karl, I want to hear all about the new baby later on . . . Klaus, how lovely of you to come, adored your shots of Clint . . . Simon, how are you now? In yourself, love . . . Good, good . . . Eddie! Poppet! And Jenny. Hi! Oh love, have you seen George, by the way?'

'Oh yes, he's very high profile tonight, my dear, but then when isn't he?' This was Charlie Wilson, a well-known television actor, famous for his portrayals of camp little men in situation comedies, whose guilty secret, well kept from the general public, was that he was one hundred per cent heterosexual and very happily married with three adorable children. Robin, who represented him, felt it would undermine his perceived persona if this ever got out, so Charlie continued to maintain an outrageously over-the-top image through game shows and risqué stories carefully placed in the gossip columns and hid his loyal and long-suffering family away from the prying lenses and microphones of the insatiably curious paparazzi. In complete contrast to so many others there.

'You could try the garden, my love. I saw him out there a while ago.'

'Thanks, Charlie.'

Suddenly, in a mirror that hadn't been there a week ago, Kate saw her reflection. She looked a wreck. Old, tired and unkempt. Her hair was hanging in loose straggles around her face which had been cleansed of all make-up after the show. Her simple white blouse was practical rather than pretty and her jeans were sticking to her as she sweated with the heat and her own embarrassment. She was even wearing flat shoes for driving and couldn't have felt less glamorous if she'd been playing the lead in *The Glenda Jackson Story*.

'What in God's name do you look like?' came an all too familiar growl close by her. 'Are you deliberately trying to make me look stupid? Go and get yourself tarted up for Christ's sake.'

'Hello, George darling,' Kate said brightly, aware of the many eyes and ears in close proximity. In pretence of kissing him she brushed his left cheek with her own and hissed in his ear, 'I want to talk to you. Now!'

As they reached the sanctuary of George's study they both began at once, 'What the hell do you think —?' and then became aware of someone sitting on the desk. It was a silver-haired man of about sixty in a white dinner jacket and red bow tie, but his naked legs dangled towards the floor, trousers and boxer shorts crumpled around the ankles just above his shiny patent leather shoes. The moustached face of the younger man kneeling between the hanging legs was vaguely familiar to Kate and she felt as if she ought to make a polite greeting, but thought that might seem a trifle inappropriate. Before she could say or do anything George spoke.

'Sorry, Freddie. This door doesn't lock, I'm afraid. Try a bedroom on the third floor. All yours. Carry on.' He grabbed Kate's arm and pushed her back into the hall. 'Come on!' and he pulled her inelegantly through the front door, down the steps and around to the side of the house. 'George, what the hell is going on? And what do you mean, "try the third floor"? What is this, a brothel?'

'Shut up.'

'What are they doing in our house, anyway?'

'It's fairly obvious what they're doing. It's called a blow-job, but you've probably forgotten what they are, haven't you?'

'Don't be any more disgusting than you can help, George.'

'Christ, I hate queers! They're everywhere now.'

'George! What is going on here?'

'Freddie Harris is important. He's a producer at BBTV. I may need him, even if he is a bum bandit.'

'Gay.'

'He's obviously important to that little cocksucker. He knows which side his bread's buggered.'

'George!'

'And stop pretending you didn't know about it,' he hissed.

106

'I did not. Do you honestly think I would turn up looking like this to my own party?'

'You're determined to humiliate me, aren't you? In front of some of the most important people in the business. Just because I'm a megastar and you're Little Miss Nobody.'

She noticed how mean his mouth was. The make-up girl always filled it out for him.

'Don't drag me down to your level of childishness, George. You've gone ahead and organized this for your own reasons and totally ignored me, as usual. I didn't know a thing about this.'

'We discussed it.'

'We did not.'

'Of course we did.'

'We did not!'

'Well how come all these other people knew about it, eh, clevercunt?'

'You tell me. And please don't use that expression.'

For a moment he looked nonplussed, then said defensively, 'Becca must have slipped up.'

'Oh, it's her fault, is it? The Girl in the Iron Mask. Computerbrain.'

'Jesus Christ, woman, this is a joint party.'

'What, me and you? What's to celebrate?'

'No, my fiftieth birthday and signing the new contract. You must know about that.'

'New contract?'

'Yes, we planted it in all the papers. Where the hell have you been all week?'

'You tell me. Where have I been? Come on, tell me.'

After only a moment's hesitation he said confidently, 'Nottingham.'

'Norwich! Knickers-off-ready-Norwich! I went to see our son this week. Is that how much he means to you? Oh . . . !'

'So that's why you're uptight.'

'No. If I'm uptight it's because of your infuriating

107

arrogance. Now, I'm going to go upstairs and get "tarted up" as you so delicately put it. And in half an hour I'm going to come down looking a million bloody dollars. And I want you to know, George, I would rather leave you to stew but I'm doing this for me, for my career, for Kate Fitch. So —' she smiled sweetly at him, as sweetly as if she was on camera, ' — fuck you!'

Upstairs she almost expected to have to compete with copulating couples for space in her own bedroom, but she was spared that. When she came out of the shower Becca was standing next to her bed. She looked small, neat and contrite.

'Mr King assured me you'd discussed it. He said he would remind you during the week. I assumed he knew best.'

'Wrong. You may organize his business life, but his marriage is totally dis-organized. But you knew that.'

Becca said nothing.

'Do you enjoy working for the old — for my husband?'

'There are considerable rewards, certainly.'

'Ah, your many skills include diplomacy.' Kate picked up a glass from the dressing-table and made a gesture as if toasting Becca. 'Congratulations.' She took a sip. 'Where did this come from?'

'I brought it when you were in the bathroom. It's vodka and tonic. Rather a strong one. I thought you might need it. If you'd rather have something else . . . ?'

'No. It's fine,' said Kate, beginning to relax. 'Thank you.' She took a large swig and sat down, looking at the image of Becca in the mirror. 'I used to think you and George were having an affair. Silly, eh?'

Becca looked genuinely shocked. Her pale face seemed to drain of all blood and her small mouth puckered slightly as if in moral outrage. Her eyes met Kate's in the mirror, proud and defiant, and then she turned away. Kate saw some clothes laid out on the bed.

'I thought . . . to save time . . . Perhaps the silver Versace with these blue shoes . . . ?'

'Hmm. Simple and elegant.'

'Yes.'

'How much is the new contract with Channel Four worth, Becca?'

'Well, there's been a lot of speculation in the press.'

'Oh come on, they print what you tell them.'

'I'm sorry, Miss Fitch, this must be terrible for you, coming back and finding all this going on in your house. If I'd known . . .'

'It's all right, Becca, I don't blame you. And after all the years of being married to George my skin has thickened. Nothing goes deep any more. What are the papers saying?'

'The figure of two million pounds over three years was quoted in the *Daily Mail*.'

'I wouldn't believe anything I read there. Still, two million? Even if it's exaggerated, that's a lot of fish suppers.'

'Of course, I'm only telling you what the paper said.'

'Don't worry, it's not a sackable offence. Not even if you work for my husband.' She took another slug of vodka and then a deep breath. 'Right! In that case, Becca, not the Versace. I think we'll go for the glittery emerald green Gaultier. With the six-inch stilettos, all the diamanté I can carry and — ha — pass me some ribbon from that box, will you? If my old man is celebrating conning someone out of a small fortune I think the least I can do is help him do it in style. I intend to enjoy this party.'

And twenty minutes later Kate descended the wide curve of the staircase, pausing half-way to pose for Klaus Zeschin to take a few informal shots and acknowledge her round of applause with a slight inclination of her head, then proceeded to give the performance of her life.

She outcamped and outvamped everyone else there, even Charlie Wilson, which very nearly involved her going over the top, which she'd have simply hated. But for nearly three hours she managed to maintain an elegance and charm while being flirtatious and outrageously suggestive to all the men and conspiratorial and witty with the

109

women. She seemed to know what everyone wanted and was able to provide it, from a comforting word to a useful introduction, from a rude rhyme for a limerick to the phone number of the best personal astrologer in town.

She even took a plate of canapés and a bottle of champagne up to Freddie Harris and his young friend who were by now involved in some very gymnastic enterprises in what was still known as Ben's room.

'Bottoms up, boys!' she called cheerfully as she entered the room. 'Oh, I see they already are. Now, now, don't speak with your mouth full, Freddie. When you come up for air you might enjoy some of these. You do eat meat, I suppose? Sorry, silly question.' She left them to it.

Everything seemed possible so long as she believed in the creation she was tonight, kept laughing and moving forward, never looking down to see if there was a safety net.

For ten minutes she even managed to slip her arm through George's and play at 'happy couples', but the last four of those ten minutes were quite an effort.

'Don't milk it,' he growled, a huge cigar clamped between his teeth.

'You asked for it, George. And it's all or nothing. Now excuse me, I'm going to try to find someone civilized to talk to.'

She wasn't even thrown by the sight of half a dozen ludicrously pink flamingoes around the pond and when she heard the strains of 'These Foolish Things' drifting in through the French windows she naturally stepped out into the vast mock-Victorian conservatory where among the palms and ferns she found a startlingly handsome young black man playing a white grand piano.

Well, of course there was a grand piano in the conservatory, she thought. And it *would* be white. And the pianist *had* to be black and stunningly attractive. It was fairy-tale time. Just stay on tonic water, she reminded herself; keep walking the wire and don't look down.

Kate leaned her body into the curve of the piano and smiled at him. She knew the face but . . .

'Well, hello again. I'm your guest this time. Great party.'

'Hal Brand, of course! So glad you could come. How's it all going on "Daytime . . ."?'

'"Lunchtime Live". Fine, fine. I stayed in kiddie's corner too long and it's not easy being accepted as one of the big boys. But then, you know telly.'

'Oh yes, telly,' she smiled airily, implying a weary over-acquaintance with the medium. He played some more and hummed along.

'It's a lovely song,' said Kate. 'But it needs a good pianist too.'

He laughed and looked away.

'What's funny?'

'Sorry. Family joke.'

'So?'

'Well, when I was young, asking lots of awkward questions, my father told me a pianist was the proper name for what little boys had between their legs. At least that's what I thought he said!'

Kate smiled and felt the tension that ran through her whole being untighten just a fraction.

'You've been to a lot of effort tonight. It's a great evening. Everyone's here.'

'Oh yes, Nunu and Nada and Nell.'

He looked puzzled. 'I don't think I know . . .'

'Forget it.' Explaining would date her. She looked around and noticed there was no one else in the conservatory.

'You know you look . . .' He played a few notes with his right hand.

'Go on, I dare you: "a million dollars"?'

'No. I never flatter. I was going to say you look elegant and rather fragile.'

'Oh, that makes me sound like Cinderella.'

'But you don't turn into a pumpkin at midnight.'

111

'I don't think that's quite right either. Did your father tell you that too?'

He smiled. Lovely teeth, she thought. I wonder if they're his. He's bound to be gay, the pretty ones always are.

'You've been very busy,' he was saying. 'The perfect hostess, rushing around, looking after everyone. But who looks after you, I wonder?'

Oh god, she thought, he's been in analysis. She tossed her teased mane of dark brown hair off her face. 'I can look after myself.'

He didn't reply, only raised one sceptical eyebrow.

Kate turned away and looked across the lawn to the stupid flamingoes, ridiculously incongruous in her Hampstead garden. She noticed for the first time a spotlit fountain in the pond that hadn't been there last weekend. Normally the pond was boarded over. Becca had forgotten nothing, damn her.

Despite the noise of the party inside the house there was a stillness in the conservatory, a calmness that stretched between Kate and this intriguing young man. She felt momentarily exposed and afraid. Where was the poise, the wit – her armour? She was looking down and there was no safety net.

'You're lucky,' he said.

'Oh?' She continued to survey the garden.

'If you really can look after yourself, you're very lucky.'

'Yes. I am.' She refused to let him see her aching vulnerability.

'George is a great chap. Tell me about him.'

'It's all in the biogs.'

'No, I mean the real George King. He can't be as perfect as he seems.'

'Can't he?' It would be unprofessional to shit on your own doorstep.

'Oh, come on. I bet he's really a wife-beater or into cabalistic goat sacrifice.'

'Darn it, who told you about the goats?'

'It's all over town. Is he a good husband?'

'I've nothing to compare him with. He's the only husband I've ever had.'

'Really?' His eyes danced with wicked humour.

'I mean, I've never been married to anyone else.'

'And how about . . . Ben, is it?'

'What is this, the questions you didn't get round to on the show?'

He thought for a moment before answering. 'I'm fishing for a good story, I thought I might find some dirt on George King.'

She looked at him. It was impossible to tell if this was bluff or double bluff.

'Katie, darling, there you are!' A raucous group of actors burst into the room from behind the largest of the palms. 'Come and play charades, darling. Charlie's got the perfect one for you!'

'I thought everything Charlie had was slightly imperfect,' she laughed. Waving a farewell to Hal she allowed herself to be pulled back into the library.

Just after four o'clock Kate said her long goodbyes to the last of the departing guests.

'Goodnight, goodnight. *So* glad you came. See you again *very* soon. Drive safely. Bye!'

She treated herself at last to the large vodka and tonic she had denied herself for too many hours and drank it as she walked around the ground floor, locking up and switching off everything she could find. The waiters and other hired help had long since departed. Presumably someone would come to reclaim the flamingoes in the morning. Still, wildlife was Becca's responsibility.

Upstairs George was already asleep and snoring. She could hear him as she climbed the stairs. He'd been persuaded to go to bed some time earlier 'for a short nap'. Kate suspected Becca of doctoring his champagne to knock him out; there seemed to be nothing that girl wasn't capable of. She would be a ruthless murderer, Kate thought.

She removed her jewellery and clothes, cleaned her face and got into bed. It was, appropriately, a king-sized double, like George's in his own room across the landing. They hadn't shared a bed for over eight years. Not for a whole night.

Kate suddenly felt exhausted. But also triumphant.

I did it, she said to herself. I bloody did it. I didn't just survive — I thrived. I blossomed. It was only for a few hours but I proved I could do it. On Monday the tacky tour continues, but tonight — tonight I was magnificent!

With a deep, satisfied sigh she snuggled into the friendly pillow. She thought about the attractive black man at the white piano. It was like something from a Walt Disney film. She was on the brink of slipping into oblivion when something struck her as wrong, out of place. There was too much light. And a noise, a muffled sound.

It was George, grunting something and staggering across the carpet towards her bed.

'Snoog brobben weggenorn . . .'

'What, George?'

'Snooger fobrits.'

She blinked herself back into full consciousness; George was half asleep and three-quarters pissed; he was wearing a pair of ill-fitting white jockey shorts and one black sock. Before she could take evasive action he had grabbed her duvet and thrown it aside with startling force. He teetered over her, swaying alarmingly.

'George!'

Too late. He fell across her, a dead weight and a dead loss.

Kate tried to squirm free of the mound of gross, ginger-fuzzed flesh and foul dog's breath but he sat up blearily and with surprising strength held her immobile, her arms above her head, and began to climb on top of her with obvious intent.

114

'George! What are you doing? *George!*' He was mauling at her breasts like a great bear. His eyes were barely open; he was too stupid to fake this, he didn't know what he was doing. 'George! Get off me!'

'Uh.' He opened his eyes and surveyed her with confusion. He seemed surprised to see her there, pinioned by the full weight of his bloated body. 'You were 'mazing tonight,' he slurred. 'You looked t'rrific. Real sexy. I wan' you.'

'Get off. How dare you! For goodness' sake, George, don't be ridiculous!'

For a few seconds he didn't move, then he muttered, 'Frigid cow,' and let his body collapse back on to the mattress. They both bounced gently, twice.

And this is worth two million pounds? she thought. He was already snoring again.

11

Kate sat in her dressing-room at the theatre in Plymouth on Monday night scowling at herself in the rust-spotted mirror. Christ, she thought, Robin had better have something good lined up next. Why hadn't she been called in to talk about *Cabbages and Kings*? There were a lot of good women's parts in that. And the wheelchair thing sounded great. But where were the interviews? Once they were in town, of course, he could really start earning his percentage, pulling all the stops out for the coveted part of Jackie O. What sort of agent was he anyway, to encourage her to do this crap? The only good part of the whole job was that it got her away from George for so many weeks.

She was examining the lines around her eyes, screwing her features up to make them worse and give herself a preview of what she'd look like in a few more years when there was a knock on the door. She readjusted her face and adopted her poised persona.

'Come in.'

A blond head appeared round the door. It was Jack Fever.

'Ah, good,' he said with a grin. 'I wasn't sure which dressing-room you were in.'

'Number one,' she said, a hint of reprimand in her voice. He should have known that.

Without being invited he turned a plastic chair around and almost threw it between his legs as he sat astride it, leaning on the back of it with his bare forearms. He was just to one side of Kate, slightly too close. She busied herself arranging her make-up and props, aware of his eyes watching her every move.

'Did you have a good weekend, Miss Fitch?'

'Fine. And you?'

'Lovely, thanks. I went to the Miró exhibition at the Royal Academy. Have you seen it yet? It's terrific.'

'No, I haven't. Not yet.'

'Do try to go, please; I think you'll enjoy it.'

He began to tell her about the exhibition. Listening to his animated explanations gave her the chance to look at him properly for the first time. He had an open, bright face, blue eyes, a slightly snub nose and lots of wavy straw-coloured hair cut in a very modern, rather rakish style. His teeth appeared to be perfect and his full mouth was a little bit lop-sided. She noticed he had very small ears and in one he wore a tiny gold stud. Another Bertie Woofter, no doubt.

He reminded her of a puppy with his energy and enthusiasm. Enjoy your youth while you have it, she thought. The doubts and regrets will come soon enough.

And the lines. She wondered if he was scrutinizing her face in the same way she was studying his. She turned self-consciously back to her regimented pencils and brushes.

'Did you go by yourself?' she asked.

'I went with a friend, Sam. Sam and I live together.'

Nicely ambiguous, she thought. Serves me right.

There was a moment's silence. Then the tannoy crackled into life. 'Good evening, ladies and gentlemen of the *Murder in Triplicate* company. This is Stevie, welcome to Plymouth. If any of you haven't got digs sorted out let me know during the show and I'll see what I can do. I'll be on the book tonight. The part of Simon will be played all this week by Mr Fever. Alex Farr will be playing the police sergeant. Laura will be doing props. Oh, and this is your half-hour call. Thirty minutes please. Thank you.'

'So,' said Jack Fever. 'You wanted to see me. About some bits of business. Some notes . . . ?'

'I . . . yes.' She was too slow to hide her confusion. He saw it and came to her rescue.

117

'Oh, I'm sorry, Miss Fitch. I must have misunderstood. Never mind. You've probably been far too busy over the weekend to think about that. Especially with the party and everything.'

She didn't react immediately. Then she said, 'Party?'

'I read about it in the paper this morning. There was a bit in one of the gossip columns.' He looked mischievous and rather sexy. 'It sounded quite a bash.'

Instinctively she blurted out, 'What did it say?' Damn, she thought at once. Why the hell was she sacrificing her superiority to this little jerk? And why did he seem such a threat?

'It just dropped a lot of names, said something about your husband being ubiquitous and described you as his finest and most glamorous asset. I've got it upstairs. Would you like me to pop up and get it for you?'

'No. No, don't bother, thank you.' He was getting far too intimate. 'Look. Jack. I did forget about giving you some notes. I'm sorry. Why don't you just play it as you did on Saturday? That was fine. I'll have a think during the show tonight and try to jot a few things down for you tomorrow.'

'Okay. Don't worry about forgetting, Miss Fitch, really.' His eyes crinkled up with his smile. 'And please don't be afraid to tell me exactly what you think of my perform-ance. I always prefer honesty to flattery as the basis for a relationship. Don't you?'

He got up to go and at the door stopped to pick up an eyebrow pencil from the floor. A rip in the back of his fashionably faded jeans yawned wide as he bent over and where Kate expected to see the fabric of underpants there was a gash of tanned skin. She felt excited and guilty at once.

'Better still,' he said, handing her the pencil, 'could we have a chat tonight after the show? How about back at your hotel so it wouldn't inconvenience you? Then I can sleep on it. We could talk over a drink. Or, tell you what, there's a smashing French restaurant just around the corner. Nothing too flash, just good food. Why don't I take you out for a meal? We could –'

'What? You take me out to dinner?' She laughed at him. His audacity amazed her. Most of the others in the company barely had the courage to speak to her at all, yet this boy, this child, who had been a mere understudy until last week was actually suggesting a date. And there was definitely a very dangerous look in those pretty blue eyes. Well, really!

'Okay,' he went on, undaunted by her mocking expression. 'Don't say anything now. Think about it. I'll ask you again after the show. I'm sure I've got the lines okay now; I won't let you down. Good lu– I mean, have a good one.'

And with a deft turn and a brisk step he was gone, leaving, like the Cheshire cat, a hint of his enigmatic smile in the suddenly warm room.

In fact she did have a good show. So did he. He was really very talented. He found a lot of new laughs, but they grew naturally out of the character, there was nothing cheap. He was also generous on stage and had a good rapport with the audience. There was something effortless and yet assured about his style. More relaxed Richardson than overdone Olivier. In her clinch scene with him he held her very tightly in his arms, pulling her whole body against him, and then when he kissed her it was urgent and impulsive. The audience's breath was held with hers until they parted; the biddies no doubt imagining the strength of Jack's young arms, the softness of his full lips. Kate didn't need to imagine; the kiss thrilled her in a way the moment didn't warrant.

As soon as the curtain was down – not bad applause on a two-for-the-price-of-one Monday night – she went to her dressing-room and wrote out a list of notes for him.

She began: 'You gave a very good performance but you know that. This is how I think you might improve it.' She

119

then proceeded to be highly critical of his voice, his timing, his gestures, his stagecraft and every other aspect of his performance. She finished: 'Remember that Simon is supposed to be a young fogey and rather dull. The audience doesn't need to know about your own personality. They have come to see Simon, not Jack Fever. Don't show off.'

She left the note in an envelope for him at the stage door. By the time he called at her dressing-room she was in a cab on her way back to the hotel. And by the time he got to the hotel she had hung the 'Do not disturb' sign on her door and taken the phone off the hook. Best to be on the safe side. Kids nowadays.

12

'So how d'you take your tea, young man?'

'Just lemon please. No sugar.'

'Splendid. I'm frightfully sorry I've only got Lapsang Souchong. Is that all right for you?'

'Oh, my favourite.'

'Jolly good. Jervis, get down! Honestly, these hounds think they own the place. Just push him off, he won't mind.'

'No, no, he's fine. Aren't you, boy?' He moved a hand towards the drooling beast as if to scratch his head but thought better of it and turned it into a reach for the proffered cup and saucer. The tea smelled of bonfires and tasted of nothing. He was dying for a mug of PG Tips with three sugars and the bag left in until it was 'properly drowned' as his father used to say.

'So, tell me again how I can help you, Mr . . . ?'

'Brand. Hal Brand. Well, I work in television, as a freelance presenter. And I'm a journalist. I don't know if you're familiar with any of my work . . . ?'

'No, 'fraid not. Don't get to see the box a great deal. So much utter drivel on it, isn't there? Still, it's here to stay, got to move with the times, eh?'

'Quite.'

'I know that Paxman fella. Big nose, politicians get up it. You're not on his programme, are you?'

'No. I tend to do . . . lighter things. I've been doing a stint on "Lunchtime Live" recently. Do you ever catch that?'

'When's that on then?'

'Well . . . it's on at lunchtime. It's called "Lunchtime Live".'

121

'Oh bugger me, sorry. Bloody stupid. Jervis, don't slobber on the poor man. Just push him off, Mr, er . . . Jervis, stop that!'

She waved a hand at the mutt, half wolfhound and half llama by the look of him. Jervis continued to growl, his curled lips seeming to guide the steady flow of thick saliva over Hal's tweed trousers. This settee was clearly Jervis's usual seat and he didn't take kindly to sharing it.

'Might have a biccie or two in here somewhere,' she was saying, ripping the lids off ancient faded tins and rustling the contents suspiciously. She sniffed inside one tin – covered in pictures of Princess Anne's marriage to Mark Phillips – and fished out something that looked rather like a semi-rotted dog turd.

'Dried banana? Smells disgusting but it's jolly yummy.'

'Thank you, no,' he smiled. 'I had a good lunch. Thanks though.'

'Hm. Bit past its prime but then aren't we all?' She threw it casually towards him and with a sudden lunge the monster in his lap caught it with a snap of his great jaws and chewed it noisily. Hal's tea was mostly in his saucer now; good, less for him to drink.

'If we find old Jerv the Perv dead in the morn we'll know the banana was the murder weapon, eh?' She slurped her own tea, picked a piece of black leaf from her tongue and flicked it to the floor.

Hal looked at her. Was she for real? The English aristocracy was renowned for eccentricity; was it in the blood or did they make a conscious effort to live up to the image?

He'd found her easily; she was in the phone book under 'C' for Combes-Howard. He'd assumed some butler or maid would answer, but her own booming voice had said yes he could call if he liked and ask her some questions as long as it wasn't for any article about her. She didn't mind if it was 'something to get the public into the Hall', but she didn't want it to be 'personal nonsense'.

A shame as there was a lot of great material. She looked·

122

slightly larger than life, heavy features gone rather to seed. A long nose and a firm Joan Sutherland chin that threatened to meet each other and block her wide, narrow mouth; wispy grey hair that floated and fell about her face like blades of grass that the mower had missed. Her complexion was raw and ruddy, it looked as if it hadn't seen blusher or lipstick for about three generations. Hal noticed she had fine, white hands, the fingers long and thin. He bet she'd grown up practising her piano scales in some freezing cold music-room. Her manner was otherworldly, distracted as if by a thousand things. She clearly didn't care what she looked like or what people thought of her. Good for her, thought Hal. So unlike the people he worked with. So unlike himself.

'And you work in the television? That's nice for you.'

'Yes. It's enjoyable.'

'I have a daughter. She works in the radio.' She enunciated it as if he might not know what that was.

'Really?'

'Yes. She's BBC. Makes programmes and things. Jolly interesting.' Her eyes almost disappeared as she smiled. 'I should think.'

'I'm sure.'

'And I can help you how?'

'Um . . . I'm interested in something I read about you in a magazine.'

'Lies, I expect. They never let you see it before they print it. Stick their little tape recorders on the table and then go away and make it all up. Scandalous. Don't like talking to journalists. Ask me, they're all parasites and wankers. Nothing personal.'

'No, well . . .'

'What d'you read about me?'

'You were at Cambridge in the sixties. Girton?'

'That's right. Daddy said I'd got a brain and it was a sin not to use it. Wish he'd had enough of one to keep the Hall up to snuff. 'Fraid not, though. Alcohol and betting took all the dough. Drink an' 'orses. Still, he enjoyed it, can't deny that.'

'They must have been heady times. The swinging sixties. A lot of people around you who went on to become household names, as you yourself did of course.'

'Yes, some interesting chaps.'

'Like George King, for example. Did you know him?'

She hesitated a fraction of a second and gave him a strange look, suspicious and angry perhaps. 'Knew lots of interesting chaps.'

Hal said nothing for a moment. Was there more or not? It became clear there was not.

'Was he as . . . popular at Cambridge as he is now?'

'Hardly knew him actually. Knew Boris van Bauer, liked him.'

'The film director?'

'And Caroline Trott. Tragic life she had. The Macclesfield Mae West they called her.'

'And George King wasn't really in your set?'

'Make me sound like a badger!' She pushed stray hair back into the various clips and combs that stuck out from her head like jumps in a paddock. 'What d'you say this article was about?'

'It's not exactly an article. More like background research.'

'Said on the telephone you were working on something that might help me get more people into the house in the summer months. That's why I invited you to call. If you're looking for a bit of twenty-year-old gossip you'd better leave, I think. Don't deal in tittle-tattle, young man. Ancient or modern. Journalists are bad enough, people who work in the television are the worst, I'm afraid.'

'Is that because of your early experience with George King?'

'Because of the number of times my words have been distorted and yours truly's looked jolly bloody silly.'

'Well, this could be your chance to put the record straight.'

'What could? Said you're not even writing an article. Background research. Direct quote.'

'Well, I'm sure the editor of "Lunchtime Live" would leap at it if I suggested a feature on you.'

'On the Hall?'

'Yes, but the viewers would want to get to know you. Flesh and blood beats bricks and mortar in the ratings.'

'You want to give the house some publicity you can film without me being here.'

'No, really, Lady Annabel, it's not like that in television. Believe me.'

'You get my daughter a job?'

'Your . . . ? Could I? Well, I don't know. Does she want one?'

'Sick of radio, she tells me. God knows why. Could be what I believe you call a "trade off" in this, after all.'

'Yes. Could be.'

Annabel smiled brightly at him for a moment; she was a strong, handsome and intriguing woman. Then the smile disappeared as if a venetian blind had been dropped over her features.

'More Lapsang?'

'No, thanks.'

'No, not a good cuppa, is it? Sorry about that. Things aren't very straight around here, what with the builders doing the brickwork on the west wing and the roof being half off.'

Hal nodded understandingly. Jervis put his head heavily across Hal's thigh and sighed. Hal gradually became aware that someone or something had farted; he hoped it was Jervis.

'True what they say about black men, is it?' she said, chewing the leaves in her last mouthful of tea.

'Er . . . I beg your . . . ?'

'Get this shaving rash 'cos the hairs are all curly. That right?'

'Well, yes, some people . . .'

125

'Hm. Ought to work on a product to sort that out.'

'There are one or two on the market. Look, can I clarify something?' he said tentatively, keen to steer her back on to safer ground but worried that the wrong tack would lose her completely. 'You did coincide with George King at university but you didn't know him well and you wouldn't be willing to discuss it?'

'Listen, young fella-me-lad, past is past and therefore no longer relevant. We were friends for a while. Short while. Kate Finkenberg came along. End of story.'

'But what sort of —?'

'End of story.' There was a half-smile on her lips but her huge jutting jaw and her narrowed eyes told him she was adamant.

Hal decided he'd leave it alone for a while. But he was sure there was more here for him to explore. It could be the big story he was after to effect the change in his career from lightweight ex-kids' telly presenter to someone taken seriously in the world of television journalism.

If any single story could do that for his career the low-down dirt on Mister Television was the one. And maybe this big pink hunk of upper-class English flesh would provide it. Maybe a softer approach was needed with Lady Annabel. He'd have to work on her another way. The other way.

13

Ben watched impassively from the doorway as the unappetizing white bodies humped away in virtual silence on the bed. His bed.

It occurred to him gradually that he ought to feel anger, jealousy, maybe a lust for revenge. He ought to be experiencing something . . . But there was an inevitability about the scene, a sense of *déjà vu* which gave him an air of even more detachment than he usually felt. There was almost relief that it had happened at last; now that it was a reality he needn't worry about its probability.

The last time he'd watched two people making love — although that was not really the term for it — he'd been a boy of four, nose pressed excitedly to the window, the scent of honeysuckle in his nostrils, eager to see the funny things his Daddy was doing, unaware at first of the girl's pain.

This time there was no excitement, no surprise. But his emotional memory was automatically providing the heady smell of honeysuckle.

It was Sue who noticed him first. She was deftly swivelling around as she sat astride the supine Terry, impaled in the way she always liked but which Ben wouldn't indulge her in for long. He preferred to lay her down and attack her, using his penis as a weapon to stab her into submission. The misogynistic symbolism wasn't wasted on either of them, he knew, although it was never discussed.

But here she was now in her favourite position, bouncing on Terry's pale, skinny body, her long hair falling across her face in straggles, sticking to her sweaty brow and catching in her mouth. She caught sight of Ben, continued with

127

her task and then did a comic double take, gaping in horror, unable to believe what she saw.

He was immobile and silent, an expression of calm acceptance on his face, almost a smile of amusement. Sue stopped her rhythmic bumping and shuddered to a halt, but beneath her Terry kept on thrusting, unaware of the change of circumstances.

'Oh, man, don't stop. This is so g-o-o-d.'

Unable to slip off him unobtrusively Sue pulled a sheet towards her and tried to shield them both, or at least the parts of them both which were interlocked. But, like a mother hen on a nest of restless chicks, parts of her kept moving by themselves. The smile on her embarrassed face rose and fell with Terry's shoving hips and her small breasts jiggled like jellies on a plate.

'Oh, Ben, hi!' she said, loud and cheerful, pretending all was well. 'Hi, BEN!'

'Yeh, that's right, babe,' came from the bearded figure below.

'Hello, *Ben!* Terry, Terry, *Ben's* here.'

'What?'

She stopped bobbing as his face emerged from the bed, peering round her naked body.

'Please, don't stop,' said Ben politely. 'I don't want to spoil your fun. In fact I was rather enjoying being a voyeur. You know, it's fascinating to see someone in a totally different light. No offence to either of you but sex really is a ridiculous carry-on, isn't it, when viewed objectively?'

'Um . . . I know this looks bad, but . . .' Sue extricated herself from Terry's no doubt rapidly shrivelling passion with a wet slurp and was searching for her knickers and a reasonable explanation, but her resources weren't up to either task.

'Hey, man, it's not what it looks like . . .'

'You mean you've just found a novel way to churn butter? Look, you have every right to do whatever you want.'

'Sue was cold, you know? We were just, like, tryin' to get warm, yeh?'

Ben laughed. 'Oh dear, nought out of ten for effort.'

'We thought you'd gone into Cromer. That's what you said.' She sounded annoyed with him.

'I did. I walked. Which is why you didn't hear the car. I'm sorry if I startled you.'

'Oh, man, this is really bad news. Like, shit, I feel terrible.'

Ben took in the objects on the upturned plastic milk-crate at the bedside. Two beakers of red wine, the remains of a joint, a packet of condoms, one used and lying limp and dead like the baby birds he used to find on the pavement as a child. This one had its neck tied.

'I suppose we shouldn't have, Ben, but, well, you know how it is . . .' Sue said with a shade of defiance in her little girl's voice.

'Have you been screwing for a long time?' Ben asked.

'Well, man, I mean . . .' Terry stroked his thick blond beard with embarrassment. 'Like, time kind of stands still when you're . . . you know.'

'I meant have you been sleeping together for weeks? Months?'

'Oh, right.'

'A couple of weeks. Sorry.'

'Good. I'm glad. I hope it works out for you.'

'Ben —'

'No, you carry on. I'm going for another walk. I don't want to interrupt.'

'Look, man . . .' Terry relaxed a bit, leaning on one shoulder, his body angled proprietorially towards Sue. He looked perfectly at home in Ben's bed. 'It's the way of the bleedin' world, isn't it? Nothing personal. I mean, you don't have to stop . . . you and Sue. Eh? Just because we've started. Right?'

'Ben, you okay?' Sue made as if to approach him, but something about the look in his eyes stopped her.

129

He pushed the cowlick of dark hair back off his face with both hands and left them there on top of his head. The two of them were watching him, waiting to see if he was about to explode with rage or break down in tears.

'Terry, do you have any of that dope left? I really think I'd like to get a little smashed.'

'Oh man, we finished it tonight, didn't we, babe? We'd have saved some if we'd known.'

'Not to worry.'

'Listen, man, we'll talk. We'll all talk, right? Tomorrow.'

'If you like. I'm going down to the beach. I'll sleep downstairs when I get back. Don't mind me. Please; I mean that.'

Kicking one of the scrawny cats aside he left the room and headed for the cliff path.

There was a moon but it was less than full and it cast a soft, subtle light on to the brown and orange cliffs and the grey shingle of the beach below. Ben scrambled down the path, slipping and grabbing for plants that he knew were there and could just make out as eerie shadows.

His favourite sounds welcomed him as he jumped down on to the pebbles, the scrape of his feet and the subdued crash of the waves. There was a distant throbbing of an engine from an invisible boat far out to sea and the intermittent screech of some airborne creature on a nocturnal hunt. He sat at the top of a steep bank of neat, oval stones and let the night sounds wrap around him. Here he felt safe; the noises spooked and thrilled him but he knew they were true, honest. A wave had the potential to suck you out to sea and drown you, but it didn't lie, cheat, deceive and resent you for being who you were. The night bird would pounce on the unwary mouse and devour it, but it wouldn't make its life a living hell for years with emotional blackmail and intolerance.

Ben felt the tears slide down his cold cheeks until he could taste them. But he wasn't crying for his relationship with Sue. That had finished long ago. He had left her emotionally and spiritually months before. She knew it, she'd told him so.

'You just can't commit to anything,' she'd shouted at him. 'You're stuck somewhere in your childhood and you can't grow up! You belong to Mummy and Daddy, but you can't marry them, Ben. You've got to cut the cord and go out into the world one day. I'll help you do it but you've got to commit to me. And you won't do it, will you?'

No. He hadn't committed himself to Sue or to anyone else. Whether her coffee-table psychology was right or wrong didn't interest him. All he was aware of was the gnawing sensation of inadequacy that permeated every corner of his life. It was the reason he had worked so hard at school to get to Cambridge, and yet, conversely, it was also the cause of his dropping out before completing his degree.

The weight of George and Kate's past dragged him down into the sludge at the bottom of the river. Everywhere he went their legends preceded him and prevented any chance he might have had of being accepted or rejected for himself. He was always 'George and Kate's boy' or 'the young Mr King'. If he wrote an article or went to an audition it was a story; if he didn't it was a bigger story. Would he go into journalism? Would he go on the stage? The world was waiting to hear about the son of Fitch and King.

But Ben knew what was missing. He was not 'the son of', he was 'a son of'. The surviving son of. Originally one of two sons of. He was the less talented, less beautiful, less loved son of his famous parents. The son who could have saved his brother from drowning but didn't. The son who could never be good enough, whose existence could never make up for the loss of baby bloody Christopher.

Anyone he had ever been close to had let him down one way or another, kicked him in the teeth, turned their back when he needed help or conveniently forgotten about him in times of crisis. That was why he preferred to reject them first, before they had a chance to do it to him. So

131

Sue had been old news before tonight. He'd reclaimed his emotions long ago, if ever he'd really invested them in her. Life was simpler without emotional involvement, other people only complicated things.

The simplest of all would be . . .

Ben watched the waves tumbling over and over in the hazy half-light and thought again about the sunny afternoon twenty years ago when his baby brother's life had ended so simply, his lungs filling with pond water just a few feet behind him as he watched his father's unforgivable actions with the babysitter. It was a scene he could replay from any point of view, but he couldn't change the ending. He could look from inside the room and see the tiny baby in danger at the water's edge and wanted to shout out to his younger self to turn, to do something, to save his brother's life. But his favourite pain was to put himself in the victim's part and know the terror of imminent drowning. It was a role he knew he didn't rule out playing himself some day.

He felt himself drawn by the lure of the waves, they seemed to be clawing at the shingle, pulling him to them inch by inch. He didn't resist, their cold embrace would answer so many questions for him.

As a child he'd held his breath and put his head under the water in the bath, just to see how Christopher had felt that day. He counted to see how long he could stay there, trying to be calm despite the throbbing heartbeat echoing through his head. For a long time ninety-six was his maximum; the figure of a hundred assumed a mythic significance for him and the first time he broke that barrier, bursting from the water and blowing like a whale, he felt he had altered his basic nature in some psychic way and searched for signs of it in his face. It was a step towards manhood, he was nearer to sharing his brother's fate.

One day, he was certain, he would finally achieve the ultimate sacrifice and accept the invitation of the beckoning waves. That was what they all wished had happened anyway. They'd have swapped one brother for the other if they had a choice. Ben agreed, his own life had been destroyed by the drowning as much as Christopher's. His own death would make up for Christopher's tragedy, perhaps even in some unspecified way restore him to life.

In the meantime Ben considered the mighty ocean and hugged himself for warmth, feeling the years of anxiety drain all energy from his chilled bones.

He was weary, so weary of this life.

14

Kate's attempt to keep Jack Fever's youthful exuberance at bay with her brusque criticism of his performance had completely the opposite effect. He seemed inspired by the honesty of her comments and assumed a new intimacy in their relationship.

'You're absolutely right, Miss Fitch,' he said to her conspiratorially in the green room the next night. 'I was showing off. Playing at the character instead of truly becoming Simon. Thank you so much. Your notes will make all the difference.'

It was true; his performance changed radically over the next few shows. He followed Kate's advice to the letter and it paid off. He simplified everything he did on stage and consequently the character became much clearer to himself and to the audience. It was believable and interesting. And a delight to play opposite. He really listened on stage, a rare quality in any actor let alone one so young, and he responded to little changes of mood or inflection that Kate introduced into the way she was playing Angela. They had a real rapport on stage, instinctive and imaginative, so much more rewarding than poor old Trevor Waterman.

In fact the only note Jack didn't seem able to put into practice was to make Simon dull. Whatever he did there was a quality about young Mr Fever that was very watchable. And very exciting. Kate knew she was attracted to that quality in him, on stage and off. Tonight, for the first time, she had felt his tongue seeking hers in the act two clinch and had desperately wanted to let him find it. But she'd pushed him away and continued with the scene:

'Simon, this is ridiculous. You'd better go and we'll pretend this never happened.'

But it had happened. And she had wanted him. And his breath in her mouth had tasted so sweet, his strong youthful body pressed into hers so enticing. And it would happen again tomorrow night. And every night this week. And twice on Saturday.

Kate felt about fifteen again, looking forward to a stolen kiss but at the same time dreading Jack's presence, afraid that somehow her own vulnerability would be embarrassingly obvious, that others would see her weakness and laugh at her.

After the Thursday night show he stood in her dressing-room. His extreme youth meant he needed only a few seconds to wipe off his eyeliner and the shading on his cheeks. He was already changed and ready to leave although she was still half-way between Angela and Kate.

He thanked her again for the notes and chatted about the production. He looked great in a loose yellow sweater, an old pair of Levis and battered cowboy boots. Kate was trying to put the finishing touches to her street make-up, but she discovered to her annoyance that her hand was shaking and it was impossible to apply her mascara.

'Did you get three the same?' he asked and leaned across her to look at the good luck cards stuck up around her mirror. His groin was only inches from her face, a faded part of the denim showing where the material had to stretch most. Kate looked away and put down the brush she'd been holding; it was a waste of time even trying.

'It's a joke,' she said. 'In triplicate.'

His innocent face showed he didn't understand.

'Like the play?'

'Oh yes, of course.' He giggled, not at the joke but at his own stupidity.

'They're from my agent.'

'You're with Robin Quick, aren't you? Is he good?'

His naïvety amused her. Robin Quick was the best agent in the country. Everyone knew that. 'Yes, he's good.'

'Has he seen this yet?'

'No.'

'Will he be coming, do you think?'

'If I ask him to, of course. Not otherwise.'

'But you do want him to see the play, don't you?'

Kate smiled indulgently, enjoying the look of horror on his face. 'Not particularly. I'm not doing anything he hasn't seen me do a hundred times before. And in scripts a thousand times better-written.'

'But surely . . . I mean, why would you do the play unless you believed in it?'

'Oh, Mr Fever, you have a lot to learn about the business.'

'Well, it may be my first job but I like to think I have a sense of ethics. I wouldn't want to accept work in plays I didn't respect.'

'So, you're the archetypal Ethics Man, are you?' No, he didn't get this either. 'Look, you have every right to your ideals; you should have them at your time of life. And — at my ripe old age — I have the right to be a little more pragmatic. You may say it's cynical, I prefer "practical".'

'Do you think it's a bad play, then?'

'No. But I don't think it's a good one. Look, why did you accept the role of Simon?'

'Why? Well, it was offered. And . . .'

'And you hope it'll lead to other, more interesting and challenging work?'

'Yes. Of course.'

'Exactly.' Their eyes met in a moment of silence, hers questioning, his uncertain.

'Well, yes, I see what you mean. I do have a lot to learn. I couldn't have a better mistress, though, could I?'

There was something about the way he said 'mistress' rather than 'teacher' that jolted her, like the shock of ice-cream on a filling.

136

'I do want to learn from you, you know,' he said, his features now set in an expression of fake sincerity. Or was it fake?

'I'm sure we can learn from each other,' said Kate quietly, unable to hold his gaze.

'We do have a great relationship, don't we? On stage, I mean. I find you totally inspiring.'

'Well, that's very . . . I don't know . . . Thank you.'

He was half-sitting, half-leaning on the make-up table, fingering one of her lucky charms, a little ivory elephant, in a way that seemed to Kate provocatively intimate, almost insolent, as was his physical proximity. In fact everything about him was over-familiar; Kate felt herself violated by his very presence but she couldn't resist him. His most telling weapon was a devastating innocence.

There was also the fear in the back of Kate's mind that his sexy charm was just youthful enthusiasm and if she was to accuse him of flirting with her he would be shocked. It wasn't a risk she was prepared to take. Meanwhile she had to put up with his dreadful up-front confidence. She wanted to scream, 'Give it to me or take it away. But don't tease me!' Instead she maintained an apparently cool and calm exterior.

'So . . .' She wanted to use his name but was afraid. Actually saying it out loud seemed too personal, too blatant, a statement of her interest and an invitation to further intimacy. Or was that what she wanted to convey?

'So, do you have an agent?'

'Not yet. Actually I'd appreciate some advice on that, Miss Fitch. Tell you what,' suddenly he was animated, excited. 'How do you fancy a bite to eat now? I'd love to pick your brain about the business. As you said, I've got a lot to learn and I can't think of anyone better qualified to teach me than someone with your . . . great wealth of experience.' His eyes crinkled up as he smiled at her.

He's managed not to mention my age, thought Kate. But only just. What's his game?

137

'Oh, I think you're an awful lot less ingenuous than you pretend.'

'I'm sorry?'

'Apology accepted,' she said quickly with her sweetest smile, deliberately choosing to misunderstand him. 'I have to go now . . . Jack.' She tried it for size, for taste and texture, slipping it into the sentence at the last moment, hoping to take herself by surprise as she did when sitting in a photo-booth. The one arrogant syllable thrilled and shocked her as it burst from her mouth. Its rough male brevity assaulted her tongue in a way that both appalled and appealed. It felt dangerous, as she knew it would, an admission of something in herself and an encouragement, a promise to him, perhaps, of future delights?

She stood up and held her hand out for the ivory elephant which he was absentmindedly turning in his pale fingers. She waited. He seemed reluctant to give it to her but she wasn't going to take it from him while he was resting his hands in his lap.

'Perhaps you'd put that back for me?' Kate turned away from his challenge − if challenge it was − and put on her coat. It was a fake silver fox with a high collar; very glamorous, very West End Star. She wrapped it around herself and felt protected now, back up on the pedestal he had threatened to shake.

'You haven't given me an answer about dinner,' he said.

'You haven't put my lucky charm back.' Their eyes met and the challenge was now unambiguous. For a long moment neither moved a muscle. Then a wry smile spread across his boyish face and he placed the trinket very carefully in the exact position he'd taken it from.

'There.'

'Thank you.'

'Now . . . ?'

'I'm sorry, dinner is out of the question.'

'But −'

'Excuse me. My cab is waiting to take me to the hotel.'

138

'It could take us to the restaurant.' His mouth was definitely lop-sided when he smiled. He looked absolutely gorgeous. She felt a terrible temptation to say yes.

'No.'

'Why not?'

God dammit, I don't owe you any explanations, thought Kate.

'Oh go on, don't run away from me like you did on Monday night,' he admonished.

That decided her. She'd hoped to avoid any reference to that and thought it had been conveniently ignored, but since he'd brought it up she would tell him exactly why she'd stood him up and why she would refuse to be won over by his charm. She simply had too much to lose. And she didn't trust him. This cocky little so-and-so needed taking down a peg or three and putting in his place.

'Look,' she began very firmly, with all the weight her status commanded. 'I don't know what you think you —'

But suddenly he came to her and put a hand on her arm. The unexpectedness of the seemingly gentle gesture made Kate flinch. Its implications were overwhelming and she tried not to let her troubled breathing show.

'I'm sorry,' he said quietly and through the coat she felt a soft squeeze of reassurance. 'I'm terribly sorry, Miss Fitch. I've gone too far. I do sometimes, I know. I don't mean to offend. It's just that I . . . that you make me . . . well . . . I do apologize. Please, forgive me?' And he waited for an answer, looking Kate directly in the eyes with an expression of such complete remorse that all her anger was diffused.

'Of course.' His eyes were grey, she saw now, not blue, and when he blinked she watched his contact lenses settle gently into place. She hadn't noticed that on stage.

'Thank you. I'd better go.'

'No, I . . . I . . . could give you a lift to your digs,' she said.

'No. Thanks very much but, well, I don't think you

139

should. It wouldn't look right, would it?' He walked to the door and then, in the best theatrical tradition, stopped with his hand on the handle and turned to speak.

'I hope you don't mind me saying, but you've only got mascara on one eye. It's very becoming but I have a suspicion that it's not deliberate. Just thought I'd mention it. 'Night.'

Only after he'd closed the door behind him did Kate realize she'd been smiling back at him. What am I doing? she thought, I'm old enough to be . . . to know better. And she noticed that her hands were still trembling. Oh Christ.

15

Kate's hands were trembling again on the following Sunday, but this time with anger.

'What do you bloody mean – you didn't watch the show?' George demanded.

'I mean I didn't watch it because I was busy working.'

'Pah!' he snorted and turned away.

'You know damn well I was.'

'Working? Poncing about in that fifth-rate tat? That's not working. Hosting a live talk show, now that's what I –'

'What right have you got to judge the play when you haven't even bothered to see it?' Kate snapped.

'You told me not to come until it goes into the West End. I'm doing as I'm told.'

'What I actually said was don't worry if you can't see it until then. I was trying to ease any sense of guilt you might feel at letting me down. Oh, how could I be so innocent after all these years of marriage to you?'

Kate flung herself on to one of the soft leather settees and gave a shake of her head to throw her hair back off her face. This was not the sort of day off she needed. She wished she'd stayed in Plymouth for a lazy Sunday beside the hotel pool or riding across the countryside before going on to Cardiff. Except that Jack Fever was in Plymouth and that was a potential problem she hadn't yet worked out how to handle.

'Oh, I see. That's the game you're playing, is it?' George persisted, adopting his lord-of-the-manor pose in front of the white Italian marble fireplace. Kate began to feel as she used to in the headmistress's study as a girl.

'Oh leave it, George, for God's sake just leave it. I'm sorry I didn't watch your wonderful show.' It wasn't worth drawing blood over. Why he needed her approval anyway she had no idea; it wasn't as if they meant anything to each other any more. Perhaps the vestiges of mutual respect remained somewhere deep down.

He ignored her token apology and a sing-song note of sarcasm crept into his voice as he went on: 'I won't watch my own husband's networked talk show — which, incidentally, was watched by more people than any other television programme last week so might just have something going for it — or even get anyone to record it for me because he hasn't been to Aberdeen or . . . or . . . Aberystwyth to see me give another classic performance in "Death by Cliché".'

Kate's lips were tight with barely-suppressed fury. 'No, George, that's not my game. Petty jealousy may be your own style but I don't operate on that level. Incidentally, Alistair Greene, the author of the play, has endless credits on something called television, which you have publicly said to your adoring millions — or at least one of your writers told you to say — is the eighth wonder of the world.'

'So what level do you operate on then, madam?'

'What?'

'Why didn't you come back last night? Why wait until today?'

'Oh George, did you sit up waiting for me? How thoughtful!' Kate mocked. 'You expect me to drive two hundred and fifty miles after doing two shows? To rush back to surprise parties and your childish sniping? What kind of masochist do you take me for?'

'Well, that's an interesting question.'

'Pardon?'

'Perhaps there's a different reason to stay away another night?'

'What?' What madness had gripped him now?

'Some romantic reason?'

'What are you talking about?' Her defences were up suddenly; what had he stumbled upon?

'I think you know.' There was a cold malice in his bloodshot eyes. Without cosmetics or corset he looked much older than his boyish television persona. And he wasn't wearing his hair. Kate had often thought in the last three or four years, since George had really hit the jackpot, that they were not the same person at all, the man she lived with and the person she saw on the screen. Brothers perhaps, but no more alike than Edgar and Edmund in *King Lear*. How cheated the doting housewives would feel if they could see their idol now, overweight, red-faced and bald, displaying all the style and wit of a delinquent cockroach.

'I refuse,' she said coldly, 'to be treated like a naughty schoolgirl.'

'Then you shouldn't behave like one, should you?' George smirked, his lips curling but the eyes cold and deadly. 'Have you been having a quick grope behind the bike sheds after an enlightening biology lesson, perhaps?'

'Don't be pathetic.' Kate began to pick at some black grapes in the fruit bowl. They must have been there since the party, but she needed to be distracted from George's searching gaze. She felt sure she was going to blush with unwarranted guilt at any moment.

'I know what I'm talking about,' George went on.

'Then perhaps you'd like to explain, since you're making absolutely no sense at all to me.'

He picked up a copy of one of the tabloids and threw it angrily into her lap. 'Read that. Page seven.'

Kate almost expected it to be her previous week's history essay, heavily marked in red.

'Since when have you cared what the gossips print?'

'Since the stories don't come from me or Becca. Read it!'

Kate prepared herself for the worst and lowered her eyes

143

to the text. It was Hal Brand's 'Mediaview' column. She read:

> Currently limping round the country is the new pot-boiler from Alistair 'Rich Pickings' Greene — 'Murder in Triplicate' — starring Kate (whatever happened to stardom?) Fitch, chiefly known for being the charming wife of the housewives' favourite 'Gorgeous' George King. Limping because one of the actors twisted an ankle on the squash court and had to be replaced by an understudy. And because of the box office returns. However, there's nothing limp about Miss Fitch's co-star, thrice-married ex-TV copper Gordon McCone of 'The Beat' fame. Father of five McCone, a sprightly fifty-three years young, plays Miss Fitch's husband, a man desperate for — no, I shan't reveal the play's flimsy plot. If it struggles into town go and see it. Miss Fitch's rumpled beauty is worth the price of a ticket. How about giving her a crack at La Jackie (Crackajackie!) in town? She does a nice line in grief. But how can bland bombshell George bear to let his lovely bird fly away from the nest to spend so many lonely weeks on tour with the virile Mr McCone? Can anyone be that nice? Or is there more to lightweight Mr King than meets the camera's eye? Come on and kiss me Kate!!

She let out a good strong peal of laughter in relief.

'What's it all about, then?' George's face was lumpy and ugly with suspicion.

' "Rumpled beauty". Bloody cheek. Still, they think I'm right for the part of Jackie. That's good. I wonder if Robin planted it.'

'What's going on between you and this McCone creep?'

'You said you knew what you were talking about. Surely you don't need my comments on this?' Kate felt strong now, knowing he was on the wrong track.

'What does it mean about you and McCone? It practically says you're having an affair.'

'Now that really is reading between the lines. Gordon is an absolute poppet,' she said and took a few grapes over to the French windows where she observed the newly smartened garden. She missed the flamingoes, but was pleased to notice the pond was boarded over again. 'A real sweetie.'

'Where did they get this?'

'Ask them, George.'

'I have.'

'Of course,' she said, keeping any trace of surprise or alarm out of her voice. 'And . . . ?'

'And I was told, Becca was told, Hal Jungle-Bunny couldn't reveal his sources.'

'Not even to George King? A commendably professional attitude.'

'I told them —'

'You mean Becca told them?'

'No. *I* fucking told them I'm going to sue for libel. Bland? Lightweight!'

'Fine, sue them.' He was obviously quite mad. 'The borders are still looking good. So having that bash wasn't a waste of time after all.'

'Stop pissing me around, woman!' Suddenly he was behind her, his hand on her shoulder. Before she could shrug him off he had spun her round to face him. 'I want to know now. Is this true or not?'

'What's that?' She was determined not to show him her fear.

'This fucking article! Is it true? Are you fucking fucking him or not?'

'My word, is that all on the autocue?'

'*Is it true?*' he screamed into her face, his own now purple with rage and distorted like an overripe aubergine.

Kate smiled very sweetly at him. 'No, George, of course it isn't. Trevor hurt his ankle playing tennis, not squash.'

But she had miscalculated the intensity of his fury. His big flat hand crashed across her cheek with a sharp crack before she even had time to wince. The slap nearly knocked her to the floor, but George grabbed her wrists and pulled her viciously to him, thrusting his face at hers.

'Don't fuck me about, bitch!'

'Let go. You bully! Let me go!' Kate screamed, struggling to escape. But he transferred both thin arms to one of his huge fists and grabbed her jaw tightly with the other. She couldn't even look away from his accusing eyes; now she was frightened and didn't try to hide it. She was used to his insecurity coming out as flashes of aggression but it was always verbal. This was different, he'd really flipped and she had no idea how far he would go. She felt stupid for having goaded him, but she wasn't to know. The phrase 'The Provok'd Husband' flashed through her mind as if on a hoarding glimpsed from the window of a high-speed train.

'Talk!' He shook her head with a sudden jolt hard enough to break her jaw. She wanted to cry out with the pain of his squeezing fingers but could manage only a strangled gargling sound which he ignored.

'Where did they get that story? Eh? Eh?' He shook her again. She tried to free her hands, but his grip tightened until she thought her wrists would snap. The pain was like a red-hot wire threading through her veins and there was no way to avoid or resist it. There was a string of saliva between his lips and he spat into her face as he bawled, 'Don't piss about, I want to know what's going on between you and this McCone creep.'

'Nothing,' she managed to squeeze out from her clenched teeth. 'Nothing. Nothing!'

He held her bruised and aching face inches from him own. There were beads of sweat on his top lip and his brow, flecks of white in the corners of his mouth and his eyes were narrowed as he scrutinized her for several long seconds. She could smell his smell, the one she hated, the one she once had loved. 'Christ I hate you,' she thought. 'You can't imagine how much. I want to crack your head open and watch you bleed.'

George licked his lips as he stared into Kate's eyes, then he spoke very quietly in measured tones.

'I hope you're telling me the truth. If I ever found out that you were fucking around behind my back . . . that would be it. If the press could prove anything they'd slaughter me. I'd be finished. And I'd make sure you didn't survive. Your so-called career, pathetic as it is, would be over, just like . . . *that!*' And he tightened his grip suddenly, making Kate gasp with shock as well as pain. 'And you know I'd do it!'

She did. Her determination to show defiance was forgotten now. She felt tears well up and prick her eyes and they wouldn't be blinked away. They rolled down her cheeks until they wet his fat fingers, still clenched across her jaw. He snatched his hand away sharply and wiped it on his jeans as if the wetness was an acid that would burn him.

'You bastard,' whispered Kate through her tears, still fighting for breath. 'Me sleeping around? What about you?'

'What about me?' He seemed poised to launch another attack.

'Well, it applies to you too. Doesn't it?' She knew he had someone tucked away. She'd seen that name and address scribbled down years ago and when she tackled him about it his bluster and bluff spoke volumes. The day would come when those details would be useful. But this was not it.

'Keep your nose clean. And out of my fucking business,' George said, wagging a stubby finger at her. 'No messing around, right? I'm Mister Fucking Nice Guy, remember? Any hint of scandal and the whole sodding bubble bursts. You jeopardize that and you're in big trouble. So no fucking around, geddit?'

When he was sure she'd got it he let her wrists fall from his grip, glared at her damp face for a long while and then

147

turned around and stomped out of the room, breathing heavily through his nose with exertion and fury.

'I'm not. I told you,' she sobbed, but she heard the front door slam and gratefully sank to the floor rubbing her sore face and weeping with pain and humiliation. And with a dangerous anger.

16

'I feel real bad about it, you know? Like, it's not a good trip to lay on a mucker, right?'

'As you so eloquently say, Terry. Still, these things happen.'

'Sue and me . . . me and Sue . . . we just kind of clicked. You know?'

'I hope it wasn't too painful,' said Ben.

'Now, come on, don't get all clever-clever. I know you're mad at me. That's okay. You probably want to hit me, right? I ought to let you, 'cept I gotta tell you I'd hit back. It's only fair to let you know, yeh?'

'Quite.'

'Look, it doesn't mean anything has to change in the house, does it?' Terry stuck his chin out and scratched his wild, hedge-like beard with his grubby fingers. His hands looked as if he'd been a labourer for years. Ben realized he knew nothing about the man beyond his skill for stealing food from the local shops. And stealing women.

'I don't know about that. Things are bound to change in subtle ways, wouldn't you say?'

'Well, we've got the bedroom, me and Sue, right? That makes sense, doesn't it? You're okay on the settee, aren't you? It's okay down there. But otherwise it's business as usual, yeh?'

'If you say so. I'm surprisingly indifferent to this whole episode. If anything it's something of a relief.'

'Right. So no bad karma about the new arrangements?'

Ben sighed and pushed his hair out of his eyes. 'Not at all. It seems to me that you and Sue, well, it's almost as if it had to happen.'

'Yeh, that's it, Benny-boy. It was kind of destined, wasn't it? We didn't do it, you know, deliberately, to hurt you. It was in the stars, yeh?'

'Very likely.'

Ben felt tired. Tired of the struggle. The struggle to survive, to prove himself worthy. Life was too hard and there was no end in sight.

They were making their pints last as long as they plausibly could in the Crown, Northstrand's only pub. They were both known there but not exactly warmly welcomed as they were neither local nor wealthy. Terry was from Norfolk, of course, but not that part of Norfolk and was therefore as much an outsider as Ben.

The place had recently been refurbished. This had involved tearing out the original timbers and opening up the dark, intimate corners of the lounge and the snug into one vast room. A brown and orange carpet had been fitted, the brewery's logo woven into the swirling design, and the mock-rustic tables had imitation oil lamps wired up and fitted to them. Even the bar stools had cushions that matched the carpet and had been permanently fixed to the floor at what somebody had decided was the correct distance from the bar. The old tinny piano had been replaced by a trio of video games that chattered to each other in weird electronic bleeps even when unattended.

It felt now like some kind of waiting-room, as if the pleasure of going out for a drink was being delayed just a little and this place would have to do meanwhile.

Terry's suggestion that they go there for a few pints had a heavy-handed ring to it, as if Sue had insisted they go to talk, man to man, about the new alignment of personnel in the house. Perhaps she liked the thought of being discussed, of two men arguing and even coming to blows over her. But that wasn't going to happen. Ben accepted completely her change of allegiance. It didn't touch him, bounced off rather, leaving no visible bruise.

He felt his whole existence was in a sort of trance. He

had no control and merely drifted where the winds blew him. To argue with Terry about Sue or about possession of the one bed in the house would have taken energy; something he didn't have.

'I don't know what we're going to do now about food,' Terry was saying, supping on his pint of Guinness and then pushing his bottom lip up over his moustache to suck the cream foam off.

'How d'you mean?'

'Didn't Sue tell you? I was spotted by the manager in Budgen's on Saturday stuffing a frozen turkey inside my coat. Christ, I was scared. He wanted to ring the filth but I went on about it being a mistake, I'd been under a lot of, like, strain with my granny dying and everything. I don't reckon he believed a word of it but he let me go anyway. Said I was banned from ever going in there again. He showed me to the checkout-chick and told her to call the police if she ever saw me in the shop again. I fuckin' ask you. Just over one turkey. They taste like shit anyway.'

'That bad, eh?'

'He wouldn't let me keep it, mean bastard.'

'So we have no money and no food. Or did you get anything else?'

'I'd only just started; the turkey was the first thing on my list. Don't know what we're going to do now, Benny. There's no other shop in Cromer I can get away with so much. Like, maybe a packet of biscuits here and there, but Budgen's was the best.' He looked wistful, nostalgic for the good old shoplifting days. 'Sue says she won't do it. She's too frightened.'

He gave Ben a questioning look.

'Lord, no. I blush with the embarrassment of lying if someone asks how I am and I say "Fine". Yet again you prove to be my superior. I would be a total failure. Would be? What am I saying?'

Terry swished the last mouthful of Guinness around in his glass and then threw it down his throat. 'What about your old man? Wouldn't he help us out? Help you out?'

'If I was on fire he wouldn't piss on me.'

'But he's a regular guy, right?'

'That's the image, not the reality. He's actually a . . . how can I put it? A selfish, petty, heartless, mercenary, mean-spirited cunt.'

'You don't like him, huh?'

'That's about the size of it.'

'As the choirboy said to the . . . hey!' He looked at Ben as if he'd finally worked out the answer to some great puzzle. Which he had.

'Yes? Was there something?'

'Well, of course!' Terry's whole face was alive, a mischievous smile lurking under the beard. 'There is a way, Benny.'

'A way where? A way in a manger?'

'A way we can make some money. A lot of money. Not just enough to eat this week, but enough to buy all the salmon and steak and ice cream you want. And fill up the tank of your car. And pay for dope and coke and new clothes. And endless fags. And some decent clothes too and —'

'Enterprising though your ambitions are, Sir Terence, I remain to be convinced of your methodology.'

'What?'

'How yer gonna do it, kid?'

Terry looked at him with a sly, secret expression. 'You may not like it, Benny, but there is a way.'

'And what way is that way?'

'We need money but we haven't got a bean, right? The answer is this: we have to sell something.'

'My God, that's brilliant! Lord Hanson could have learnt a thing or two from you. With business acumen like that the world is your lobster.'

'Oh shut up a minute and listen, will you?'

'Apologies.'

'You're thinking, we haven't got anything to sell. Well,

we have. Or rather you have, Benny, my boy.' Terry was smiling more broadly now. His teeth were stumps of black and brown and Ben wondered how Sue could bear to kiss him. She'd swapped him for that? And still he didn't greatly care. .

'You've got something a lot of people want, man. Or would like to have. Either for themselves or just to look at. No ideas? Look,' he lowered his voice to a conspiratorial whisper and with a flick of the eyes checked that the nearby tables were empty, ' 'scuse my, er, familiarity but this is purely a business deal, right? You've got something worth a lot of money and you've never even realized it.'

` Terry waited for him to catch up, studying Ben's puzzled features as he ran through his meagre possessions searching for something of any value. A ten-year-old 2CV? Abba's Greatest Hits? His two gold fillings?

'You'll have to spell this one out, I fear.'

'Okay, Benny-boy, it's right . . . there.' Terry's piggy eyes were dancing with glee. His grin widened and he lowered his gaze to stare down at Ben's body. Ben looked down too, expecting to see something unusual nestling in his lap, but all he saw were his denim jeans.

'What?'

'That's about the size of it.' He winked. 'You don't get many of those to the pound . . .'

'Sorry?'

'You're real lucky, man; that could be worth a lot of money to us.'

'What?'

'Your . . . *cockatoo*, huh?'

Ben thought about it. 'Really?'

'Sure. There you are, our problem's solved.'

'What the hell are you talking about? Prostitution? You want me to sell my body?'

'Ssh! Benny, Benny, please. Nothing so vulgar. Look,' with a small gesture he invited Ben to lean closer, 'a friend of a friend of mine's a photographer up London. He's

153

always on the look-out for new ... faces. People like yourself with something ... a bit special. And that's what you've got, isn't it? Sue was talking about you the other night.'

'Dear God.'

'Apparently I don't really *measure up* to what she's used to. You're something a bit out of the ordinary, eh? Someone up there's been kind to you. Well, my mate's mate pays by the yard. In a manner of speaking.'

'The mind boggles. The body too. Exactly what kind of photographs does this friend of a friend take?'

'He says he does licorice shots.'

'Lick what?'

'Licorice. All sorts. Girls, boys, girls-and-boys. Girls and girls, whatever. Stills, magazine stuff, mainly for the German market. It's bloody well paid. Not that I've done it myself. I would, like a shot, but I wouldn't interest him. I'm not well enough ... qualified. But I've put him in touch with one or two big boys like yourself. They were very grateful. They made a bob or two.'

'I'm sure they did. You know, I can't believe what you're suggesting. Take my clothes off for some total stranger so he can put photographs in a magazine of me bollock-naked? People staring at my meat-and-two-veg? Think again, Einstein.'

'Sue said you get off on being watched.'

'Jesus, you've been having some weird conversations. Talking about my dick and what we did in bed! Do you feel your relationship is progressing along the right lines? Because I fucking don't!'

In the sudden lull in background chat two shaggy heads at the bar turned in their direction with disapproving scowls.

'Hey, man, cool it. Don't get uptight. It was just an idea. If it doesn't turn you on forget it.'

'Too bloody right I will.'

They avoided each other's eyes; Terry looked out of the

window, Ben glared at the log-effect gas fire, glad of its heat to disguise the flush of embarrassment in his cheeks.

'Just thought you'd want to make a load of dosh, that's all.'

'Terry!'

'All right, all right, man. Bad idea. Forget it.'

'I already have.'

'Maybe I'll get some fencing work or gardening.'

'Right.' Ben drained his glass and then licked his finger to stick into the corner of the crisp packet for the last morsels.

'Mind you, wouldn't that be a turn-on, knowing people in Germany were tossing off over your picture?'

'Will you just leave it out!' Ben snapped.

'Yeh, sorry. Let's have another drink. Your round.'

Ben fished in his pockets and slapped the few coins on to the table. 'I haven't got enough,' he said. 'Forty-six p. Can't do anything with that.'

'Exactly.'

17

Kate was fairly sure that after his violent outburst George had gone off to his little friend. Suzi. In her Kensington mewsi. Kate had an image of the girl just from seeing the name and address written down that time. Blonde. A bit thick. But probably starstruck and therefore loyal. Poor creature. Was the other woman as badly treated as the wife? Kate wondered.

In case George did return to Hampstead, she sought refuge that night at her agent's flat in Holland Park.

'It's all right, my darling, you don't have to explain,' Robin had said when she rang. 'Just come on over. It's in my best interests to keep you in one piece too. I'll wash some flowers for the spare room.'

But she had explained. She needed to talk, to release the anger that George had stoked up inside her. So she let Robin have it, all the venom and resentment that surged just beneath the polite exterior of her marriage. He knew it was there, of course, but would never ask or interfere; he was too professional, too correct. And there was a limit as to how much he wanted to know about his clients' personal lives. Now he was a single and singular success he was out of all that messy business of emotions. Thank God for celibacy.

For an hour Kate stalked around Robin's immaculate sitting-room fuming and bitching about George, saying about her husband the things she would never dare say to his face.

Robin, as he had done years ago when he'd been a young and uninspiring actor, played a good feed. He let her ramble for a while, brought her back to the main theme with a gentle prompt, then asked simple but pertinent questions that forced Kate to be more objective about her situation.

Finally, when she was emotionally and mentally exhausted, Robin said briskly, 'Good girl, well done. Now then, I've been your shrink, I'd better be your mother too. This role may be slightly less convincing.'

He ran her a bath, supplying huge soft white towels, a vodka and tonic just how she liked it, candlelight and even music which actually Kate could have done without. The high drama of La Streisand's performance seemed to belittle her own problems. Otherwise she wallowed in complete comfort in the hot, steamy atmosphere. When she emerged from the bathroom the table was set for two and the wine was breathing.

'How do you like your steak done?' Robin called from the kitchen.

'Like a laugh in Ibsen,' said Kate, testing him.

A slight pause, then he called, 'That rare? You got it!'

After the meal, as she gulped decaffeinated coffee and he sipped blackcurrant tea, Kate said with a smile, 'Why don't I just divorce the bastard and then we can get married?'

'Because, my darling, marriage and I are as compatible as haddock and custard. For me, unlike the redoubtable Jacqueline Susann, once was quite enough, thank you. And because you seem to believe you need someone who will not only shrink you and steak-and-salad you once in a blue bruise but will cherish you each and every night. And that someone is not me.' He looked at her seriously and said firmly, 'Nor is it George King.'

'No,' she said sadly. 'It isn't.' There was no point in arguing, they both knew he was right. Nor was it Jack Fever. At least not yet. He might take a little moulding to bring him up to scratch, but he was mature for his years and could certainly give her a lot of the things she needed: affection, tenderness, passion, fun. Does he cherish me? she wondered. Damn it, there's only one way to find out . . .

'More decaf?'

'Thank you. So, Robin, who do you have all day and all night?'

'All day I have my lovely clients and their lovely problems.' He looked at his watch. 'And sometimes into the night too. You really should get a good night's sleep with that long *schlepp* to Cardiff tomorrow.'

'Don't avoid the question. Who do you have to cherish and be cherished by?'

Kate had drunk enough to make her persistent but not enough to make her rude. She'd always been curious about Robin. He seemed so cool and self-contained. He'd been married before but now was witty and waspish in a camp Jack Tinker, Kenneth Williams sort of way that meant people assumed he was gay. But he never spoke of his own desires and disappointments, preferring to involve himself in contracts, percentages and scripts, so nobody knew for certain about his sexuality.

'I cherish nobody but myself. Nor do I covet my neighbour's ox and certainly not his ass. And that's the way, uh-huh uh-huh, I like it.'

'But –'

'Now I don't know about you, m'dear, but I have to be up and in the office by nine-thirty to talk to your dear producer.'

'Oh, has the West End been sorted out?' Kate was easily deflected from the subject of Robin's love life. 'Which theatre will it be? Not the bloody Fortune. Isn't the Haymarket dark at the moment? Mind you, we'd never fill the Haymarket with this vehicle, would we?'

'It's not as simple as that, lovey. There's a lot of talking to be done yet. Which is why, Little Miss Chatterbox, it's time to go up the wooden hill.'

'Oh God, I want to work in town again! I've had enough of the bloody provinces. They're so . . . provincial. I want people to see me. They must think I'm dead.'

'No, my love, if you were dead George would milk his

158

grief for every last ounce of public sympathy. Take Mother's word for it, you are alive and kicking. Sheets and blankets or a duvet?'

The spare room was in the turret which ran up one corner of the building. It was a small, circular room and Robin had had it decorated in the same black and white as the rest of his apartment. Even the Hockney over the bed was a simple sketch in black ink of a strong female face. In a tall black vase stood a dozen white plastic tulips, newly washed. Everything was antiseptically immaculate.

Kate slept deeply and dreamt of Jack Fever. They were naked in each other's arms, floating in mid-air. He was strong and urgent but patient too, attuned to her physical and emotional whims. His tongue traced a path over her pliant body and she tingled with a joy she had never known before. When he entered her it was a shaft of fire, burning with a cold, bright flame. And the moment of pulsating orgasm — simultaneous, naturally — was accompanied by the sweet sounds of applause and ringing cheers.

She woke horny as hell.

'Robin,' she said over breakfast — coffee and croissants for her, vitamin pills with fresh mango and rosehip tea for him — 'would you come and see the show sometime?'

'Of course, my love. I thought you didn't want me to until you come into town.'

'Well, for my perf yes, but by that time Trevor will be back. It's his understudy you might be interested in. Jack . . . um . . . Fever, I think it is. He's rather good. Only young, of course, and no track record to speak of but . . . well, there's something there. A certain quality. With the right management I think he could make it.'

She managed to keep busy with her knife and plate and didn't make eye contact with Robin while she spoke; she knew she'd blush crimson under his cynical gaze. He had a weird, indefinable quality, something extra-terrestrial, Kate had always said. As if he listened not to the words your mouth spoke but the thoughts in your head. Perhaps he came from a planet where they didn't need love or sex. How much simpler that must be. Everyone living life in monochrome and existing on vitamin pills and herbal tea.

'I'm honestly not looking for new clients, love. Especially juves. It's hard enough keeping my family of thesps happy as it is without adding to my worries. Anyway, what's your interest in promoting new talent all of a sudden?'

'I'd just like to restore a little natural justice to this lousy business. He's good, he deserves a break. It's as simple as that.' Again she was inordinately engrossed in her croissant.

'Is it?' He sounded arch.

'Robin, he's barely out of his teens. I told him I'd mention him to you. There, now I've done my duty. Any more coffee in that pot?'

'Plenty. Here, let me be Mother. Are you sure you won't have some kelp tablets? You really should, you know. George has drained you of all your . . . well, spunk.'

'Mr Quick, please!' Kate feigned shock and fanned herself with her napkin. She was happy to be able to perform again; pretending to be natural was too much like hard work.

'Ah, you're all right, still floating despite the great George King. Kate Fitch is one of life's unsinkables.'

She laughed. 'Am I? That sounds vaguely unsavoury. Like something that won't flush away.'

'Really! Not at breakfast.'

'Sorry. No news about the disabled thing yet?'

'No. But leave it with me. Now, you're happy about this morning's appointment with Klaus, aren't you? You won't be too tired for the show tonight?'

'No. Better to press on and get it done as soon as poss, don't you think?' He nodded. 'And you've arranged for an art director to be there?'

'Michi B.'

'Oh, he's wonderful!'

'He's got it all in hand. The wig, the slap, the cozzie. All you have to do is turn up and think Jackie.'

'No problem.'

'That's my girl. Keep taking the positive pills. Now, chop-chop, Klaus is expecting you at nine. I've told him you have to be through by one at the latest. Is there anything else I can do?'

'Yes. Come and see Jack Fever next week.' If she could tell Jack she'd persuaded Robin to come and watch his performance he'd be so grateful she'd have him in the palm of her hand. Literally.

'He certainly must have something. What exactly is going on?' Robin was tuning into her brain again.

'Nothing,' Kate smiled. 'Not yet.'

But he's going to put back into me what George has drained out, she thought. Maybe even tonight.

18

The razor blade chattered against the mirror's surface, dicing the tiny white crystals ever finer. The ritual was part of the pleasure; the anticipation added to the excitement.

But the snicker-snack of the metal on glass brought an echo of Ben's childhood and he shuddered to remember the flash of his mother's sharpest kitchen knife as she chopped leaves of mint to make a sauce. He could picture the leggy green plants growing around the foot of the sundial, just past the dry concrete bowl that had once been the pond.

The sound of the busily chattering blade heralded another frosty mealtime of tight lips and verbal sniping. How jealous he'd been of children at school whose parents were divorced. Even now he hated to sit down at a table to eat, the stifled emotions it evoked were too uncomfortable. Tonight he had eaten alone from a tray on his knees and the remains of the meal were before him on the floor.

Terry and Sue had gone out together, just like a proper couple. They'd taken Ben's car and gone to see friends of Terry's over towards Stiffkey. A carpenter and a designer who were married with two children. A proper family. Ben wondered how long it would be before he had to borrow the car keys back from Terry, before they began to make noises about wanting the house to themselves. Eventually no doubt she'd be swaying backwards, hand on back, bulging with babies. And he would feel as rejected by them and their new coupledom as he always had by his parents.

I shall never be free of their influence, he thought. I will always be their son, never an individual, valid in my own right.

The old dilemma and frustration threatened to bring the usual depression and Ben chopped away furiously, trying not to let the stuttering blade remind him of his impotence and despair.

He divided the fine snow into eight parallel lines, wiped the razor clean and rubbed the dust on his finger around his gums. Escape into unreality could begin. A rolled up final reminder from British Telecom was all Ben could manage to snort the coke through.

Four lines now, four later, to give the desired supplementary buzz. He welcomed the clean, bright sensation of the initial hit; his nasal passages tingled with a slight irritation and sent the first excited messages to the brain that something wonderful was beginning.

'Business as usual,' Terry had said. Oh yes, of course. Which is why he and Sue were suddenly going away for the weekend in his car. Since when did any of them have weekends away? That was never part of the schemes they had as a household. Mostly they talked about how to get enough to eat, drink and smoke. Other luxuries were denied them. Once sex with Sue had seemed to alleviate the daily drudge, but that soon became mechanical and pointless. Then they brought each other to orgasm. Then they just masturbated, the last one putting out the light. Hardly a meaningful relationship.

Still, a good wank was the only way to get it just how you liked it, after all. That and the other obvious possibility that was open to Ben.

Terry had suggested parading about naked for money. Oh come on, how could you just stand there with a camera pointed at you? It would be so . . . well, what would it be like? Embarrassing, presumably. What did you do with your hands?

Imperceptibly Charlie was taking control. Ben surrendered all responsibility to it, letting its energy ignite him.

He swilled the last of a bottle of cheap sherry down his throat and relished the fire that began to burn inside. A fire of power and strength. His feelings of inadequacy evaporated and he knew now that he had drive and potential. He took two more lines of his precious fuel and seemed to rise on a crest of confidence.

The real fire was blazing too and Ben felt stifled by the intensity of its heat. His body needed freedom and space. He took off his grubby sweater and shirt and saw his lightly-furred chest glistening in the golden glow of the flames. Impatiently he tore off the rest of his clothes — ancient trainers, jeans, boxer shorts — lay back on the soft rug and breathed deeply, relishing the serene release. He propped himself up on one elbow and gazed down at his crutch where his thick dick hung arrogantly over one thigh.

What if there was a camera pointing at him now? How would he feel?

He'd feel great!

His cock began to come to life. It lifted its head ponderously like some lazy jungle animal scenting distant prey, then as it gradually gorged itself with blood, began to fill out and rise with little bobbing movements, swaying heavily and still extending as if by magic. Ben loved to watch it grow all by itself; it was his toy, his baby, his secret. The one thing in his life he was proud of. He knew it was a rare specimen; it delighted and fascinated those privileged to make its acquaintance. It was magnificent and massively beautiful with a mysterious power.

The blood continued to flow and it grew longer still, the head emerging from its protective cowl and its wrinkly neck smoothing. Then with a final effort the great beast reared up and flopped helplessly back, exposing its vulnerable, blue-veined underside like a salmon lying exhausted on the river bank.

It lay there, stiff and throbbing, stretching beyond Ben's navel, its single slant-eye weeping slightly. It seemed to be teasing Ben, daring him to ignore it.

Of course he couldn't. He could deny it nothing. He scooped some soft butter into his hand from the dish on the tray and began to massage it indulgently into the delicate flesh.

The idea of being watched, admired and desired by anonymous thousands; what a kick that would be, an exhilaration like nothing else he knew. The thought of performing to a camera's unblinking gaze inspired him; he wanted to put on a real display.

Imagining a photographer clicking away appreciatively all the while, he lay back, swung his legs right over his head until his feet touched the floor behind him and then, as if swallowing a particularly delicious spear of buttery asparagus, began to give himself exactly the blow-job he wanted.

19

The sleek red Merc ate up the M4 tarmac with ease. Kate drove at a steady ninety. So what if she got done for speeding? It would be good publicity. 'Speed cops trap Fitch in fast lane' had a nice ring to it. Unlike George she had no super-clean image to uphold; for her any mention in the papers – even 'Whatever happened to . . . ?' columns – was better than nothing.

But soon, she was sure, she'd see her face plastered over the tabloids, the posters, the colour supps. 'Katie F. IS Jackie O.' Not yet, she ain't baby, but soon, very soon.

The session with Klaus had been a dream. He and Michi B. the art director and their two female assistants had fussed and fidgeted over her until every hair of the wig was in place and the shade of make-up precisely accurate. The clothes were genuine sixties items and they referred constantly to their stills for the absolutely correct nuance of lighting and expression. Klaus even played the original Broadway cast recording of the show while they worked. She'd posed in the large, cool, ground-floor studio in different outfits and a variety of moods, each time to fulsome praise from all present about the uncanny resemblance she bore to the late former First Lady.

Yes, this was what she craved; a little star treatment. She could get used to it all over again. Her comeback was long overdue.

'Eyes to me now, good, and thinking of your dead husband . . . oh, *ja*, so perfect . . .'

God, she loved this business. The way a handful of talented people could come together and create a make-believe world. It was a kind of magic, something that amazed her every time she was a part of it.

Strictly professional to the last, they had finished her final shot on the stroke of one o'clock and now she was tearing down the motorway with a thrill of anticipation about her chances of landing the part of the year.

The fast lane. It seemed an appropriate place to be to prepare herself for her more immediate project: The Seduction of a Toy Boy.

Kate was now determined it would take place that night. She would 'go at it' as her Swiss ski instructor used to say. The Gershwin tape was ignored as she sped west planning her clothes, her behaviour, her words for the big night. She even dared to speculate about their relationship after the tour. Once the play was in the West End it would be quite simple to meet Jack at the theatre during the day or at a nearby restaurant for a meal. She presumed they wouldn't be able to use Jack's flat because of the mysterious 'Sam', but Kate didn't mind the expense of hotel rooms for the time being. Later . . . well, they would see how it progressed. She knew what George's attitude would be if anything leaked out. She'd had ample warning from his outrageous behaviour over that silly piece by Hal Brand. What was he up to, anyway? No, the affair must be conducted with discretion and very definitely on her terms. She was going to control everything from the beginning, and that beginning would be in . . . she checked the clock . . . about seven hours' time.

In Cardiff she went first to her hotel. It was just round the corner from the theatre; Robin had booked it for her, or rather one of his angels had.

Her room was large and rather grand with a four-poster bed and heavy swagged curtains in tones of pale green. Yes, she thought, perfect for tonight's business.

'The seduction suite, madam? Certainly. With a spare toothbrush and a selection of condoms? Of course.'

Only flowers were missing, so she rang room service to

167

order several large displays; she intended to impress young Mr Fever with her style and there were to be no half-measures.

She just caught the shops before they closed; she needed some bits and pieces and she did buy a toothbrush to put in the bathroom as a spare; it was too early in the relationship for him to use hers. There was intimacy and intimacy, after all. She'd bought the condoms from a garage earlier. She was sure the moronic salesman didn't recognize her; but then, why should he? She hoped her own supply wouldn't be necessary; Jack seemed the type to be properly prepared.

Then she went to the theatre, checked the billing and photographs front-of-house, gave the set a quick once-over and organized her dressing-room for the week. There was a battered old chaise-longue against one wall; Kate pulled it around so that it faced the door — much better for receiving one's prey. She tried it for comfort, it was over-stuffed (some chaises-longues have all the luck, she thought), but the carpet was threadbare and none too clean so the chaise would have to suffice for any action that took place there. In the interval, maybe, later in the week? Perhaps with her fur draped over it? Yes, now that was very camp . . . But not tonight, the first time would be very romantic in the pale green bedroom . . .

She ate at the hotel, taking care to order a garlic-free meal, and then lay down for half an hour before walking back to the theatre.

As usual on a Monday night there seemed to be a lot of backstage activity as people got used to the layout of a new theatre. This week it was the New Theatre; ironic in view of the fact that it was a grubby and crumbling Victorian pile.

Beate had everything in hand. Her frocks were clean and pressed and hanging on the rail in the order she preferred so she could work her way through them in the course of the evening from left to right. Anything else she would have taken as an ill omen not just for that show, that week or the tour but as a positive blight on her career. So Beate got the dresses right.

Alex, the company manager, had put a bunch of carnations in the dressing-room for her and he called round just before the half more out of a sense of etiquette than from any need to pass on information. They chatted politely about their weekends; he told her it was 'not a bad house for a Monday' and she didn't embarrass him by pressing him for exact figures. It was important for him to feel that his presence was reassuring and she had no desire to disabuse him of this illusion. He asked tentatively which interviews she would be willing to do and she happily agreed to them all as long as none of them was before lunchtime; she imagined long erotic lie-ins at the hotel, lovely tender 'horizontal chats' of discovery and confession with her pretty Jack-the-Lad.

At the quarter-hour call Kate sent a message via Beate to 'Mr Fever'.

'Could you ask him to pop in at "beginners" please? Just for two seconds. Thanks.' All very calm and businesslike, although Kate was secretly tingling like a teenager with anticipation at the rest of her scheme.

She was ready at the five and already listening for the knock on her door. She studied herself in the full-length mirror and was more than satisfied with the effect. Despite everything that George had inflicted on her over the years, despite the fact that she would never see forty-seven again and despite the tawdry setting and her nervously pounding heart she appeared serene, and radiant. Even − yes − beautiful. Her eyes shone with faith and pride. She hoped Jack Fever would appreciate the rare treasure he was about to be awarded: a woman in her prime.

The sharp knock startled her for a second and a sudden pang of doubt made her shudder, but in a moment her technique had regained supremacy over her nerves and she was again in charge of her emotions. She draped herself along the fur-covered but still uncomfortable Victorian chaise in an attitude that she hoped was sensual but not too obvious and called, brightly, 'Come in.'

He looked stunning. He didn't appear until page eighteen of act one so he was clearly only half-way through his routine. He'd obviously just finished shaving and was dabbing at his face with the end of a white towel that was draped around his neck. The other end hung tantalizingly over his bare chest. There was hair, but not too much and he had worked at his body. He was strong and sexy like a man and yet with his bare feet, those worn denim jeans and the tousled hair he still gave off the erotic aura of a naughty, vulnerable boy.

But what really made Kate fight to control her breathing even more than the bare tanned flesh was the wicked expression in his eyes. She knew at once that he had calculated the details of his appearance as carefully as she had hers, even down to the speck of shaving foam by his ear.

If we're both playing the same game, she thought, let's get on with it. Come to me now, I want to smooth your ruffled hair and unbuckle those restricting jeans, let me taste those sweet, smirking lips. Take me here on the fur, I'm yours. Oh God, I want you . . .

'You wanted me, Miss Fitch?' He stopped dabbing with the towel and thrust his thumbs into his pockets with wonderful arrogance. This couldn't be accidental.

'I certainly did,' said Kate, matching the subtle tone of his innuendo. 'I certainly do. Did you have a good weekend, by the way?'

'Tolerable, thank you, Miss Fitch. Although there's not a great deal of excitement in Cardiff on a wet Sunday in November.'

'Ah, well, let's hope it gets a little more interesting for you during the week.' Kate could hardly believe it was her own voice she heard, but she didn't regret it. It was thrilling to be playing this game again after so many years, flirting dangerously and yet certain – surely – of success.

170

They kept eye contact in a highly charged silence for what seemed to Kate an outrageously long time. But their script was good; it could take a slow pace.

The tannoy crackled. 'Ladies and gentlemen of the *Murder in Triplicate* company, this is your act one beginners call. Your calls please, Miss Fitch, Miss Stiles and Mr McCone. Miss Fitch, Miss Stiles and Mr McCone, your calls please. Thank you.'

Kate stood up and made a show of checking her already immaculate costume and hair in the mirror, confident that Jack's eyes were on her the whole time.

'I just wanted to say that I think you're absolutely on the right lines with your performance.'

'Thank you. You're very kind.'

'There's a little way to go yet before you master all the subtleties but stick with it, your approach will reap rich rewards.'

She picked up her act one props – the handkerchief and the compact – and then, exactly as she'd rehearsed earlier, pretended to have just remembered why she had summoned him.

'Oh, I almost forgot. I've got some good news for you, Jack. I mentioned you to Robin at the weekend. Robin Quick. He'd like to come and see the show but I wasn't sure if you'd really like to be seen in something so . . . well, so downmarket. Perhaps you should wait until you're playing a part that tests you more. What do you think?'

'Robin Quick? You spoke to him about me?'

'Yes.'

'Wow! Well, thanks. What did you say?'

'Ah, now that's confidential, Jack. But I did say I thought you were worth . . . looking at.' Her eyes roamed over his towel-covered chest as she said it. 'You did say you didn't have an agent?'

'Yes. Hey, that's fantastic! You asked him to come to see me? Shit! I mean, thank you.' His cool poise had vanished; he was like an eight-year-old with a new train

171

set. 'Fantastic! Robin Quick, he's the best, I mean, he represents . . . well, really good people . . .'

'He'd like to see you. I said you were worth the trip.' Kate smiled; she had him at her mercy now.

His jaw dropped. 'You said that? Wow!'

'Well, I think you are. When you've really got the part under your belt I'll let him know and he'll come to the show. But not until I give you the nod. You won't let me down, will you?'

'No way. What can I say? Well, great! That's really great, Miss Fitch. How can I thank you?'

Oh, we'll find a way, she thought.

'You can buy me a drink after the show tonight,' Kate said straightaway. Really, it was as if he'd learnt her script too. 'Why don't you come to my hotel? Shall we say eleven o'clock? I'll meet you in the bar. Our little secret. And . . .'

She was ready to leave now, Beate would be here any second; she approached him and stood very close. His eager face was beaming with delight, and yet he was trying to recapture his sophisticated image; his confusion pleased her enormously, everything was going precisely according to plan.

'. . . And . . .'

Slowly, provocatively she took the edge of the towel, fighting her almost uncontrollable desire to grab him and hug him to her there and then, and gently lifted it to wipe away the stray fleck of soap from the side of his face, just below his ear. It really was tiny, like a succulent sea creature freshly prised from its shell. A squeeze of lemon juice and it would slip down a treat. Before she let the towel fall back into place she allowed her eyes to wander over the exposed torso for just a few seconds, knowing he was watching her, and was gratified to see hard rippled flesh above his belt pulsing faster than was normal. The left nipple was very dark and looked as if it would be hard to the touch. She longed to stroke him and to feel his young, clean skin against her own. How could she wait another three hours? But she met his eyes and was in no doubt that he wanted the same thing.

He was about to speak but Kate feared it might be something explicit and unmagical, taking the delicious ambiguity out of the scene so she quickly cut in.

'. . . And I think you can call me Kate. When it's just the two of us. It's more . . . appropriate. Until tonight, Jack.' And, resting a hand for a second on his shoulder, she leant forward, breathing in his odour of sweet soap and raw sex, and placed the most delicate of kisses on his cheek, to confirm her unspoken promise of what was to come.

In a silence more dramatic than anything in the play, broken suddenly by a shudder in the heating pipes that seemed unable to take the tension, they held another look, then she smiled her professional, leading lady smile at him and said simply, 'Have a good show.'

As she opened the door, there was Beate approaching to escort her to the stage. Perfect timing. She hadn't lost her touch.

The Cardiff audience didn't seem to appreciate it, but the show had an extra energy that night. Even Beate thought it was lighter and fresher. 'Like one of those lovely omelettes the French make,' she whispered in the wings during one of Kate's quick changes. 'The sort where you whip up the egg whites separately and then fold in the yolks. If you pop it under a hot grill to brown it and then serve —'

'Beate, please, the shoes!' She was a sweet girl but batty as hell.

'Oh, yes, Miss F. Sorry.' She placed the black shoes for Kate to step into and then checked her hair and make-up as well as she could while Kate held her face close to the little blue bulb in the makeshift black tent tucked into the wings. Beate powdered her down and then said, 'Perfect. They are good, you know, those omelettes. That's how my mum makes them. They're delicious, just like your performance tonight.' Kate assumed the management had told Beate to keep the star happy. This was her attempt?

But she was right. It was delicious. Kate floated through the most turgid dialogue, buoyant with anticipation, savouring every scene with Jack and discovering new opportunities to add intimate looks or smiles which he responded to in a way that was so natural it could have been rehearsed. Kate felt the audience must surely know what was going on, it seemed they were being so blatant, but apart from Beate's culinary comparisons no other comments were made. At least not to her face.

In the act two clinch their tongues wrestled eagerly together and Jack pulled her tight against him, holding her there in a highly-charged kiss for a dangerously long time. Kate finally had to fight to release herself from his passionate grasp.

'Simon, this is ridiculous,' she gasped, struggling to regain her composure. 'You'd better go and we'll pretend this never happened.' But there was a lifetime of regret in her voice. Don't listen to the script, she wanted to reassure him. It's only words. Listen to what my body's telling you. But she knew. She was sure of him now.

As soon as the curtain was down Kate changed and left the theatre. There was only a handful of autograph hunters at the stage door and she was well practised in the skill of being charming but brief. From George she'd learnt to sign and smile and chat and walk at once without giving offence. She showered at the hotel and changed again, this time into a simple John Richmond dress in yellow and grey. By the time she went down to the bar, at eleven-fifteen, Jack was just ordering his second drink. Beer, she noticed with a little disappointment.

'May I buy you a drink, Miss Fitch?' he asked politely, on his best non-seductive behaviour for the benefit of any inquisitive eyes and ears. She asked for a vodka and tonic. Soon he'd know and be able to get her 'usual' without asking.

'You look very nice,' he said as he joined her on the low-slung sofa. It was bottle-green and she was sure she clashed horribly with it.

'So do you,' she said, and added quietly, 'Very sexy.'

His hair was still damp from the shower. Good boy, nice and clean. He had baggy grey cotton trousers on and a loose black leather jacket over a big white tee-shirt. There was some slogan on the shirt but she could only see certain letters. Was it a Katharine Hamnett? Something political about nuclear families or nuclear weapons? Well, he was young. The jacket wasn't Armani but it was a very good imitation. Kate wondered what Acting-ASMs got paid. It was eight pounds a week when she'd started out. Clearly they got more these days. Much more, if they played their cards right.

'Cheers, Jack. To new adventures.'

'Oh, absolutely.'

They drank without breaking eye contact.

'It really was very kind of you to ask your agent to see me, Miss Fitch – er . . .' he caught her questioning expression and corrected himself: 'Kate.'

They smiled. 'Not at all, you're very good as Simon. I'm sure Robin won't have a wasted journey when he comes.'

'When d'you think that'll be?'

'Oh, we'll give it a week or so yet, shall we? Give you time to make the part your own.'

'Right. I hope I won't be a disappointment to him. Or you.'

'Silly boy. I'm sure you won't.'

'Well, I do appreciate it. Really.'

Kate was bored with his gratitude and tried to move the conversation on to more stimulating areas. She fished for information about his background and present situation but it was all very conventional. Parents both teachers, happily married; contented childhood, good grammar school in Shropshire, English degree at Southampton, then drama school in Bristol for two years. And now his first job. And that was it. No rough edges, no real life yet. Everything still came in the major key, the subtleties of the minor had not entered his emotional consciousness. No wonder he looks so smooth and clean, she thought. He hasn't even begun to live, he doesn't know anything. Dear God, he's just a boy. What am I doing here? And even as she envied him his simplicity and undentable self-assurance she felt contemptuous of his immaturity. We're worlds apart, she realized, watching his bright face as he enthused in his young man's vocabulary about the merits of some football team called the Saints.

'You get a real buzz on a Saturday afternoon at a home game; it's a cauldron of white-hot emotions.'

'Is it really?'

'You bet it is!' And he proudly opened his jacket to show her the slogan on his tee-shirt: 'Oh when the Saints! Go marching in!'

This precise moment would have been the one for Kate to withdraw the unspoken offer, if she was so minded. She could have thanked him for the drink, stood up and gone to the lift. He wouldn't have made a scene; he would assume he'd misinterpreted all the way down the line and be grateful things hadn't progressed to a further stage where he could really have put his foot in it. But the moment slipped by unmarked and five minutes later Jack finished his beer with a final gulp and said in what he probably thought was a seductive voice, 'Do you think we'd be more comfortable upstairs?'

Before Kate had even nodded her assent he was on his feet; but nod she did. There was no going back now. She had handed him the reins and he'd seized them eagerly and was quite happy to drive hard and fast for as long as it took. What she had deliberately begun could not now be halted. The inevitability of it gave her a frisson of apprehension.

Kate had never enjoyed the rides at fairgrounds as a child; they terrified her and made her sick. She hated the raucous music, the insistent throb of generators and the stench of fried food and diesel fumes. She screamed not out of a thrilling sense of erotic danger but from simple fear. Why had it been so hard to explain that to the smiling adults who had put her into the dreadful metal seats that felt horribly unsafe? Even at the age of eight she had known, somehow, that she was having to undergo this terrible ordeal because she was a child and therefore easily manipulated and because it was something the adults were too afraid to do themselves. She was being used to cover their own fear.

But the very worst part of all the rides was the moment at the top of the steepest, tallest, fastest drop on the Big Dipper. A moment that seemed to last for ever, when it was too late to change anything but too soon to abandon hope. You just had to survive by hanging on tight and holding your breath.

Was it just the motion of the lift that reminded her of the Big Dipper or was it also the same fear that crept into her stomach like slimy pondlife under a stone? And why, if she had engineered this whole thing herself, was a voice somewhere inside her skull whispering, 'It's too late now – you've really done it this time . . .'?

The teenage groping began the moment they were in the room. There was nothing tender or romantic about him. He was urgent and rough with her, pulling at her expensive clothes as he bit her neck and kneaded her breasts crudely with his cupped hands.

As suddenly as he had attacked her he stopped his frenetic scrabbling about her body, walked around to the far side of the bed and began to undress, slowly, teasing out the moment when she would see him naked. He knew his body was terrific and relished the feeling of her eyes feasting on his hard, bulging muscles. His striptease was a performance in itself; he dropped his clothes to the floor with studied insouciance. His boxer shorts had a picture of a giraffe on the front and some slogan which she didn't try to read. He stepped out of them and stood before her, hands on slender hips, cock up and eager, tensing his stomach muscles.

'What d'you think? Not bad, eh? Look at that washboard. Hit me. Go on, hit me; I won't feel it.'

She said nothing, hoping not to show her acute embarrassment.

But Jack didn't need a response. He threw back the covers on the bed and fell in, stretching out on his back, hands behind his head, legs crossed at the ankles.

'Here you go, then; tonight it's all yours,' he smirked. The grin that before had seemed cheeky and erotic was now simply dirty and smug. It seemed to challenge Kate to some sort of test. She felt waves of doubt engulf her. This wasn't right. Not at all how it was meant to be. She hadn't planned the details of disrobing and actual lovemaking, but she'd assumed that Jack would take the lead in creating something magical. Not talk about football and say, 'It's all yours . . .' What did he expect her to do? Strip for action while he watched and then dive on top?

She couldn't have been that wrong, could she? Surely her instincts couldn't lie; he was a sexy, intelligent and potentially romantic stud worthy of her time and attention. She had to believe that the fantasy was still a possibility. This far in there was no turning back; that would be an admission of defeat and defeat was something she'd already tasted too frequently in her life. It was time to start winning for a change. Jack Fever represented the chance to claim a prize for herself. She had to go through with this.

Oh, go for it, girl, she told herself. It'll come right in the end.

She couldn't bear his arrogant eyes roving over her cellulite so she gave him a small smile and went to undress in the bathroom. She returned wrapped from breasts to knees in a hard white towel with the name of the hotel emblazoned across it like a name tag: 'Diana'.

'Very coy,' said Jack and as soon as she was near enough leapt up to tug it off and pull her down on to the bed. He quickly reached for the light switch and plunged the room into darkness. Kate tried to mould herself into him, thinking they would stroke and tenderly kiss as they talked, gradually accustoming themselves to the dark and the curves of each other's bodies, but tenderness didn't seem to be within Jack's repertoire.

He began a bizarre exhibition of sexual techniques, using Kate's bewildered body as a gymnast would a piece of apparatus to demonstrate his skills. His display was vigorous and energetic but quite devoid of any emotion. He put himself through every exertion imaginable and many Kate would never have believed possible. As the minutes went by the tricks became more uncomfortable and even less enjoyable. The sheer novelty value of seeing a part of his body or her own from a new angle didn't outweigh the 'so what?' factor.

This was not in her script; not what she had been dreaming about.

She had no say in his performance; it was a one-man show. He grunted and moaned to himself – or maybe it was for her benefit? – as he turned her round, stood her up or bent her over. First backwards, then forwards. And he weaved himself between her legs, around her head, over her back and across her belly. His fingers and tongue were forced up inside her with a vigour that felt more like a gynaecologist with a grudge than a lover. When he touched her breasts they might just as well have been lumps of recalcitrant clay on the wheel of a bad-tempered potter. Occasionally she heard him mutter something meaningless – 'Oh, isn't this great?' or 'You're the best, this is the real thing' – at what Kate guessed must have been particularly erotic moments for him, but mostly he manoeuvred his handsome, inexpressive, sweaty body around in silence, probing into her with his fingers, tongue, cock and even toes; she wasn't always sure which.

179

But he didn't stroke her. Or cuddle her. Or kiss her eyelids. Or lie quietly with her, gently rocking her head to and fro. He didn't even call her by her name.

Nor for a long time did he notice that she was crying. Finally, after he'd performed his final trick and loudly enjoyed his own orgasm, he saw her in tears, flashed her his smug, lop-sided grin and said, 'That great, huh? Wow, what a raunchy session!' Then he collapsed on the bed some feet from her and let out the deep, contented sigh of a job well done.

Kate lay there for several minutes completely immobile, crying silent tears of regret. After a few minutes she felt the bed bounce as Jack got up.

'Well, I'd better get back,' he said brightly, switching on a small light by the bed. He checked his image in the mirror, posing briefly with obvious approval, then beginning to dress. Kate turned away from him and pushed her wet face into the pillow.

'Thanks for having me, glad you could come,' he goofed in a stupid voice.

'Go,' she thought. 'Just go.'

But now — too late — he seemed to think that conversation was required.

'You know, that's the first time I've been with — well, I was going to say an older woman, but that wouldn't be very kind, would it?' And he laughed with a dismissive snort. 'I thought it might be a bit . . . kinky, you know. But it wasn't. It was great, wasn't it? Listen, we'll do it again real soon, okay? Are you awake? Kate? Miss Fitch?'

She closed her eyes and didn't move a muscle as he approached the bed. He didn't even pull a sheet over her used, bruised body, just patted her on the leg as if she was a horse he'd taken for a canter and clicked his tongue.

'See ya, babe,' he said and left the scene of the crime.

20

Terry insisted on going into Northstrand to make the call from the smelly, old-fashioned red callbox.

'You can't be too careful, boy,' he said, covering the mouthpiece with his hand. 'Oh, hi. Dave? Hi! It's Terry . . . Yeh. Look, haven't got too much dosh to put in the slot. I've got someone your friend might be interested in . . . Yes, that's right. He's got all the qualities your mate's looking for . . . Yeh. Well, hang on, he's with me now.'

Terry passed the phone over to Ben.

'Don't say anything to arouse the suspicions of the operator,' he whispered dramatically. 'Here.'

Ben took the receiver as if it might bite him and placed it tentatively to his ear.

'Hello?'

'You Terry's mate?'

'Yes.'

'How old are you?'

'Twenty-four. Is that all right?'

'No physical deformities, birthmarks, other peculiarities?'

'Well, no.'

'You done this before?'

'No, I'm afraid not. Is that a problem?'

'Look, I can't make any promises, like, but I'll have a look at you and if you're any good I'll pass you on to my mate who'll do the shots. Okay? Can you be at Leytonstone tube station tomorrow evening? Six-thirty?'

'Leytonstone? I don't . . .'

'Central line.'

'Oh. Yes, I suppose so.'

'See you there. I'll pull up in a blue Fiesta with a roof

rack. Ask me the way to Wanstead Flats. Okay? Oh, I'm Dave.'

'Okay. Do I need to bring – ?' But Dave had rung off.

'He's a good mucker,' said Terry. 'He won't mess you about.'

'No. Good.'

'Don't look so worried. Just do it, Benny boy!'

So the next day he did it. He took the train to London, dodging and bluffing his way past the ticket inspectors, and got to Leytonstone tube station ten minutes early. It was dark and there was a pre-Christmas buzz about the commuters who swarmed around him on their way home, a warm, friendly atmosphere that Ben hated. It made him jealous of their cosy lives and happy homes. Each car that swung round and approached he watched until the glare of headlights had passed and he could identify the vehicle clearly. He suddenly wondered if he had been set up by Terry, or whether he would be alone. Perhaps when the Fiesta pulled up another half-dozen young men would appear from the dark shadows of the station and pile into the car, each one of them to be vetted by Dave to see if they were 'any good'.

When it did arrive at last Ben walked quickly to the car and leant down to the driver's window.

'Um . . . excuse me. Do you know the way to Wanstead Flats?'

'Yeh. Hop in.'

The driver was a swarthy type in his forties with a few days of stubble, an unruly cloud of grey curly hair and deep-set eyes which he screwed up as he peered out into the drizzly winter gloom. He could have come off a building site. Except that he wouldn't have been much use there as his left hand appeared to have been mangled by some machinery or beast, leaving a swollen, twisted stump with one finger and one thumb sticking out at odd angles as if they'd been stuck on as an afterthought. He poked and grabbed at the gear lever with this claw. How did he come to be vetting boys for dirty pictures? Ben didn't ask and Dave volunteered only a succession of post-nasal snorts.

They drove to a car park about a mile away where Dave parked by a skip overflowing with spare bits of people's lives, tugged the handbrake on and got out with a nod of his head to Ben saying, 'Come on,' as he would to a pet. He led the way into the ground floor of a sixties tower block, all echoing corridors, misspelt graffiti and broken light bulbs.

Ben began to feel apprehensive. Was he being incredibly stupid to follow or overly suspicious to hang back? They stepped into a deep, silvery lift that had the same pungent odour as the call box in Northstrand. Other people piled in, squeezing Ben and Dave to the back. A man with a dog, a woman with a basket on wheels, three boys with a football and two girls with the same giggle. Nobody greeted anyone else.

At the sixteenth floor Dave led Ben out and down a narrow, empty landing to a door marked 1622. Ben tried to fix it in his mind in case of later necessity.

'I remember particularly, officer, because I thought "Great Fire of London".' No, that wasn't right. 'In sixteen hundred and twenty-two Columbus sailed . . .' No.

'Come in. You want a tea?'

Ben saw the state of the place and shook his head. 'No, thanks.'

Dave sifted a handful of brown envelopes with windows and dropped them back on the carpet. He clicked his tongue at a scrawny-looking black bird in a cage. It gave a whistle and said 'Howay the lads!' in a perfect Geordie accent.

'In here,' said Dave and disappeared into another room. Ben followed slowly, wondering what would be the best excuse to give for a sudden departure.

In the bedroom Dave was gathering clothes off the floor and throwing them on to the double mattress which took up most of the room. Then he arranged two Anglepoise lamps, twisting the heads into a corner until their combined light made a stark little stage, ready for Ben's big moment.

'You wanna take yer shirt off and stand in there for me?'

Without comment or questioning Ben did as invited. He was cold despite the heat from the lights and he noticed his nipples were hard like boils. Dave took a camera from among the pile of clothes on the bed and with difficulty adjusted it, balancing it on his mangled claw while he took a photograph. The camera vomited a small square of paper from the front. Dave took another, then said, 'Push yer trousers and stuff down now.'

Ben undid his belt and his flies and shoved his jeans and boxers down to his ankles. He was reminded of his one visit to the clap clinic where he hadn't understood the nurse's broad Ulster brogue. What? Do what? She'd had to repeat it three times. 'Pull-back-your-foreskin!' Oh, right. As he stood up the camera flashed at him. Then again. He crossed his arms, not sure what else to do with them and Dave took another shot.

'Yeh. That's okay. Now get it hard.'

'Pardon?'

'Get it stiff, can you? You stand a better chance of getting work if my mate can see it big.'

'Oh, sure.' Ben pulled at it half-heartedly while Dave waited with camera poised, sensitive as a traffic warden with a pad of tickets.

'Terry said it was a whopper.' There was a note of doubt in his voice.

'Sometimes it is.' Ben tugged at his flexible friend which was playing dead and seemed if anything to be shrinking with shame. He and Dave both stared at it as it lay in Ben's clammy palm like a small, furry pet about to breathe its last.

'Look, I don't think this is going to work. It doesn't want to come out and play.'

'I'll give the others to my mate and see what he says.

184

Give me a number I can ring you on. Oh, and what name d'you wanna be known by?'

'Ben?' said Ben.

'Yeh. That's good. Sounds plausible, doesn't it? And we haven't got a Ben. Can you find your own way to the tube? I've got someone else coming round in a minute. Turn left out of the lift and straight down past the mosque.'

'Sure. Well, thanks. That's it, is it?'

'Yeh. He'll ring you if he's interested.'

Ben was out of the flat less than five minutes after entering it. It was only in the train on the way back to Norwich that it occurred to him the whole thing was a gigantic rip-off. Dave was getting pictures of naked young men without paying for them. Could photographs of that standard be sold for profit? If so, why take only three? He felt very queasy about the whole thing.

A week later the sorry episode was forgotten, written off as experience – 'the name everyone gives to their mistakes': who the hell said that, thought Ben – when the phone rang. In itself that was a surprise, so rarely did it happen. But hearing the soft foreign accent was an even bigger shock.

'Ben? I'm the friend of Dave. I think we might be able to do some business together.' He pronounced it 'togezzer'. 'You want to come and meet?'

'Actually I'm not sure. I've been thinking about it and really . . .'

'Don't worry. It is something very friendly and relaxed. Just you and me and the camera, only what you want. Nothing more.'

'Would I need to bring anything with me?'

'Would you like to bring anything?'

'Such as?'

'Any special clothes or something that you find sexy.'

'You mean like a copy of *Ulysses*?'

'Please?'

'You know, James Joyce.'

'If he is sexy, bring him too.'

'Now that's kinky.'

'Just your body is all we need. The rest will happen all by itself, I promise you. Lunchtimes are best for me. Say, tomorrow, one o'clock?'

'Tomorrow, one o'clock.'

Ben found the house easily enough. It was a large, three-storey semi with a decent garden in Turnham Green. From his years in London Ben could tell just by looking at the building that it was not divided into flats. Only one bell, no bicycles, an air of being cared for, a certain uniformity of external decor. There must be good money in this business for some, he thought. Good, that was what he was after. Money and the power it brought.

As he stood there in another grey shower literally on the threshold of what he hoped would prove to be a whole new phase of his life, checking his watch to see that he was not early and likely to interrupt some previous session, Ben was surprised to discover he was terrified as he hadn't been for years. Was this how his mother felt before going on stage? Or his father before a live transmission?

Forget them, forget them. This was for him, for Ben. This was his adventure. He pressed the bell and heard it ring inside.

What if the whole thing was a con? An excuse to mug and rob him? Not that he had anything worth stealing; he'd arrived as instructed with just his body. Probably no one would answer the door. Or someone who knew nothing about a photographer. Or, more probably, a couple of burly policemen would be there demanding his name and address.

Even if the whole set-up did turn out to be genuine what would be expected of him? A dog was barking inside the house; was it going to be involved in the photographs? He'd heard of such things — and if they drugged him anything could be done to him without his knowledge. And

186

what about those 'snuff' movies? Where people were filmed actually being murdered . . .

Perhaps he should just go away and think about it again . . .

'Hello, you are Ben, yes? I am Klaus. Come in, please.' A small, elfin man with a round, smiling face stood at the now open door. He was completely bald although a huge walrus moustache drooped over his mouth, hiding his lips completely.

'Thank you.'

'You are wet, no umbrella?'

They shook hands and Klaus led him through a large, panelled hallway into a light, richly furnished sitting-room.

'Now then, Ben, what would you like?'

'Like?' What did he mean?

'Tea? Coffee? Maybe a whisky or something?' It sounded like 'visky or zumzing'.

'Ah, well, a coffee would be fine.'

'Good. You have had some lunch?'

'I was going to eat on the way but somehow I lost my appetite. Nerves, you know.'

'No, no. No need for that. I will make you one of my best sandwiches, okay? So, sit down; relax. Back in two minutes.'

Ben looked around at the room. It was decorated almost entirely in shades of cream: the carpets, walls, curtains, and a pair of leather sofas with small piles of books and groups of quaint little *objets d'art* dotted about on several lacquered tables. A large anonymous stone bust, the features worn away by time and the elements, stood in the white marble fireplace.

Ben felt as if he had stepped into the pages of a design magazine. This wasn't at all what he had expected.

Klaus brought a cup of rich, real coffee and a BLT for Ben and sipped a tinkling glass of iced orange juice while they talked.

'So. You are a friend of Dave?'

'Well, not really a friend. We have someone in common. Somebody I shared a house with. Is Dave . . . ? Do you and he work together?'

'Yes. He puts out the feelers for me. Finds me people who might be suitable for my . . . contacts in Germany. I am German, you see.'

'Really?'

'How is your sandwich, Ben?'

'Fine. The sandwich is fine.'

He began to wonder if accepting the coffee and sandwich constituted some sort of contract or could he still get up and walk out? 'I haven't actually done this before, you know.'

'No, no, of course not,' Klaus said with a little smile. 'First, you know, Ben, I should say that you are no use to me. Not like you are. How you are looking now I cannot use.'

'What? Now hang on —'

'I have been told something of your supposed qualities so I am sure we will take some fine shots. But this and this . . .' he gestured towards Ben's hair and his stubbly chin. 'Looking good for the camera is not the question of centimetres. It is about being . . . appetizing, you say? You must look clean and nice. Not so, like you now. You have a terrible feeling about yourself, I think. The outside and the inside too. Do you feel bad? You look bad.'

'I didn't come here to be analysed and insulted. If you want a model for a beauty parade, fine. Get someone else. I thought this was going to be a few dirty pictures.'

'There is nothing dirty about what I do!'

'Oh come on. Smutty pictures for porn mags? Let's not get too grand. It clearly pays the bills. Money talks in any language. *Sprechen Sie Deutschmark?*'

'Ben, I would like you to know I do this for pleasure. I have another job at which I am very good and so make a happy income. I am rather well known, in fact. These "dirty pictures" too I am good at making but they are not

188

bringing such much money. These I enjoy. I think enjoy is a word you do not use in your life, *ja*?'

Ben stood up and walked over to the mantelpiece.

'Look, I shouldn't have come. I'm wasting your time.'

He helped himself to a cigarette from a silver box and lit it with a lighter embedded in pale green onyx. Inhaling its sweet bitterness helped.

'Jesus Christ, this is so embarrassing. What am I doing here?' He gave a short, humourless laugh. 'You must think I'm so stupid. God, I can't get anything right. I never have before so I suppose I never will. I'd better go.'

'Wait. The anger is good. Very good. You have strong eyes, Ben. Such an interesting face once you let your feelings show.'

'Don't patronize me.'

'No, no. No sulking again, that is very, very dull for the expression.' He clicked his fingers. 'Okay. Here is the deal.'

'What deal?'

'You need money. I will give you forty pounds now and you go. Right?'

'Forty?'

'And the lunch is free.'

'But —'

'But if you want another sixty, then you let me take photos and you let me . . . arrange you better.'

'Arrange me? What the hell are you talking about? I'm not a bleeding bunch of flowers.'

'Tch, tch. You said it. You are a prickly cactus plant. No, don't argue with me. Listen. I want to clean you. Prepare you. You need to bath. You will wash and I will cut your disgusting hair. Your fingernails make me want to be sick. If you stand up straight and put back the shoulders you have perhaps a chest. Maybe you look not too bad. But like you look now, no way we do pictures. Forty or one hundred. You choose, Ben. You choose now.'

'Now wait a minute —'

'No. This is professional business and I have other fish

to be fried. You make up your mind. Go now or stay and play my way. Come. Decision.'

'Jesus fucking Christ . . .'

'And you stop all this "fucking, fucking". You look nice and you talk nice when you work with Klaus. Why you feel so sorry for yourself I don't know; this is your problem and I think you need to think about it. But for me and my camera you must have some respect. Come, which is it? Quick!'

Ben sucked on the cigarette again, buying time. He didn't like what this odd little man had said. He needed the money. No, he wouldn't be pushed around by anyone else. His father, his mother, his best friend. Now a total stranger. On the other hand . . .

'I'll do it.'

Klaus's round face broke into a beam of delight.

'Good! I am so pleased.' He stood up and grabbed Ben's hand. His own was small and damp. He took the cigarette from between Ben's fingers and threw it into the grate. 'Shake. To a good piece of work. Tch, those nails. So, let's go. The bathroom!'

Upstairs Klaus ran a bath for Ben, made him shave the stubble from his face and then left him to scrub and polish the body about which he now felt extremely self-conscious. It was true, his nails were filthy.

Klaus bustled in suddenly and placed a wooden stool in front of the basin and handed Ben a can of beer.

'When you are clean, sit here please and we will try to do something with your hair. The hippie look is no good. No hippie was ever sexy.'

Trying to hide among the bubbles Ben finished washing and then clambered awkwardly into a big towel that Klaus held up for him. If he felt this embarrassed being seen naked how the hell was he going to do the pictures?

Klaus was very businesslike. He sat Ben on the stool, pushed his head back into the warm water and began to rub shampoo into his scalp. It was a good feeling and neither of them spoke while the process took place. When Klaus was ready to start cutting he turned Ben round and stood behind him, looking at his image in the mirror.

'So. Short, *ja*?'

'I really don't know. What do you think?'

'You ask my opinion. That's good. I think short. A strong shape, show off your bones. You have a good face, you know.'

He started to comb and snip, comb and snip the curtain of wet hair. Ben couldn't remember the last time he'd had it cut, apart from by Sue. He was beginning to enjoy being spoilt.

'You know, Ben, if the pictures are good and you want to we can do you in some duos maybe later on. Coming to London is not so difficult for you?'

'No problem, no. There's nothing to keep me at home.'

'Good. Well, with a nice blond girl would be nice since you have the olive tones, yes?'

'Fine. But today . . . ?'

'By yourself.'

'Right. And what'll happen to the pictures?'

'Don't worry. I sell them, if they are okay, to a German magazine which one can buy only in Germany and sometimes in Holland. So neither you will see yourself here in England neither your friends will.'

'Good. What if they're . . . you know . . . no good, the pictures?'

'Then I give you the negs. You can burn them if you want or take them to Boots the Chemist, but I think they will not print them. But they will be good. Photographs by Klaus are always good.'

When the cut was complete he blew the hair dry with a tiny, tinny drier and then set about the manicure – cleaning, filing and shaping the nails to best effect. Then came the pedicure. Ben squirmed like a child while Klaus held his feet against his own trousered thigh to smarten up what was surely not going to be exactly the main focus of

191

the pictures. He felt embarrassed and yet oddly flattered to have so much attention paid to the minutiae of his appearance. It made him feel as if he were someone, after all.

'So, now a little slap to help the complexion.' Klaus dampened a small sponge which he then dipped into a soft brownish cake of something and dabbed on Ben's face. 'Just to cover the shave marks and so on. *Ja*, this is much better. You were very handsome all the time, you see, under the hair and the . . . attitude. So!'

He stood back to admire his work and, after a couple more strategic dabs, clearly approved.

'When you are ready, please to come into the room opposite. We use the upstairs studio. Okay?'

'Okay.'

Ben wasn't sure what more he could do to make himself ready. Left alone he considered his new image in the round mirror that extended from the wall on an adjustable arm. Klaus was right, he looked a hundred times better than an hour ago. Cleaner, smarter, younger, nicer. Sexier? Well, more appetizing. What the hell did he mean 'attitude'?

'Hi,' said Klaus pulling a blind down over the window as Ben went into the studio. Quickly, expertly his eyes ran over the reworked body.

'Yes. Looks good. You want to sit on the bed while I finish off these lights? Two minutes, then I will be ready.'

Ben sat cross-legged on the double bed, primly checking that the towel sagged between his knees, hiding his crutch from view. He knew it was silly but even so . . .

'Michael Jackson. Off the wall?'

'Yes, I think so. Totally.'

'Some music. The album?'

'Oh, yes. Fine.'

Klaus put the cassette in the machine and turned it on. In a few seconds the familiar rhythms began to pound.

Klaus adjusted the silver umbrellas with an efficient, professional touch. He held a light-meter up to Ben's face, then against the white sheet, moved the lights a little, then measured again.

He was so intent on his work Ben had the chance to look at him properly for the first time.

Klaus was in his late fifties or even sixties, Ben thought. On the short side with a compact body, but fit and healthy-looking. He had no hair on his head at all, as if it had dropped out after a shock or an accident. His face, though, was dominated by the wide and bushy moustache that looked faintly ridiculous on the round, bland, babylike face. His skin had an unnaturally even tan and apart from three moles grouped together so closely on one cheek that a twenty pence piece would have covered them, his features were curiously unmarked by character or experience.

He was dressed in a yellow sweatshirt with the word 'Zipper' emblazoned across it in black, denim jeans just an inch too tight around the waist, an inch too short in the leg and with an immaculate crease ironed down them. White socks and trainers that had seen no surface rougher than a thick pile carpet. He wore a heavy gold chain round his left wrist which he would shake out of his way every so often with a gesture that gave him an odd one-sided palsy.

Ben began to relax a little and take in his surroundings. They were in an attic room with one mirrored wall, a double bed and a couple of nasty Conran chairs. The black roller blind was down now over the window and the light came from four lamps on tripods. They were all focused on Ben, sitting demurely on the bed.

'So. We are ready, I think. It looks good, you are nice there on the bed. Whatever you like, you can do. But first some simple shots just as you are.'

He began to click away, moving around the floor. Ben wasn't sure what was expected of him, he gazed levelly at the camera, waiting to be told. As he looked up at the phalanx of eyes staring down at him – lights, cameras and photographer – he felt something stir. He could hear the tick and whirr as Klaus stole frozen moments. Something about the attention on him induced a response. The towel no longer sagged, it was lifted up, then became stretched like a tent over a pole. Ben was about to tear it off, but Klaus's voice stopped him.

'No, no, not yet. Wait, I will put film in the camera. Normally I spend ten minutes or so without film until the boys are relaxed. But you are natural. One moment. There, now I can shoot you. Yes, just like this is very good. Very sexy. The haircut is just right. Yes . . . lean back some more . . . the chin down . . . very well . . . and give me your eyes . . . Yes! Think about something sexy . . . oh yes . . .'

The music continued, Ben felt the rhythms pulse through his body. He felt safe here, he felt good.

Klaus snapped away for a while and then said quietly, 'Now perhaps we lose the towel, okay?'

Ben pulled it off with a little flourish and met the stare of the camera with his own arrogantly cool gaze.

Klaus stood up from behind the lens to look at his naked model with his naked eye. For a few seconds he just stared, as if it was a clever trick, then a broad grin spread across his babyface, making the moustache quiver.

'But this is wonderful,' he chuckled, delighted with his find. 'Look at you. Fantastic! Pretty face, good body and — well! You are Ben Nevis with a Loch Ness monster.'

Ben laughed. 'I think you mean —'

'Let's go!'

Klaus quickly focused the apparatus slung around his neck on the apparatus slung between Ben's thighs and started to duck and weave about as Ben posed and writhed on the white sheet. Klaus fired off shot after shot in quick succession and muttered his own running commentary. 'Oh yes, this is nice . . . very nice . . . good . . . and hold it . . . hold it . . . now hold it with both hands . . . yes, pull it back and look down at it . . . the other hand to the nipple . . . fine . . . give me the eyes, Ben, and lick the lips . . . bend this knee some more and . . . lovely . . . so . . . hold

194

the balls in your hand, that's it . . . but open the fingers so we can see . . . Yes, oh yes! . . .'

Eventually Klaus had to pause to reload the cameras with more film.

'You are very good, did you know?'

'Thank you.'

'But I think we can make still one more improvement.'

Klaus went to the shelves and from a box took a small pair of scissors. He must have registered Ben's alarm but he couldn't have seen the frisson in Ben's scrotum as a sudden panic seized him.

'I think we can find even one more inch covered up by all this.' Klaus had stretched out his arm and was brushing the thick, dark curls of Ben's pubic fuzz with his fingertips. Ben didn't have time to be affronted, Klaus was pulling a few hairs out to their full extent with an experienced eye, as if examining the quality of a coat or carpet for sale.

'You see how they hide you? When did you last cut them? Ah, your face tells me never. Naughty boy. Come.'

So while Ben lay back, propped up on his elbows, Klaus began to snip away quickly but carefully at the black curls, handling Ben's soft cock deftly to shield it from the snapping blades.

Ben looked down at the activity with curiosity. It should have shocked him to feel this strange man's fingers touching him, cupping his balls together as he would himself, holding them first to one side then to the other as he clipped away, but he simply lay back and accepted it.

'This is the first time I've done anything like this,' Ben said. 'I think I told you.'

'I think I believe you now. The boys always say it is the first time even when they must know I recognize them from magazines or the films.'

'You make films too?'

'No, I do not make them but often I choose the boys and girls. I know the best models and I have the contacts in Germany too. The producers and so on. I am what is

195

called, Ben, a useful man to know! Open the legs, please. I just trim down here as well.'

Klaus carried on with his work, blowing gently to clear the cut hair away. It was rather pleasant.

'There.' One final puff of warm breath made Ben flinch.

'Is that nice? A blow-job! Now, that looks much better, you think?' Klaus was pleased with his topiary.

Ben looked. Yes, it was much better. Neater and cleaner somehow, like a trimmed lawn or a shorn sheep. More streamlined. And definitely flattering.

They cleared the hair away and then shook the sheet like lovers making the bed.

'Now,' said Klaus, 'I think – *Ach, Scheiße!*'

His bell was ringing.

'So sorry, Ben. This is simple, I take only two minutes. Please to relax until I return.'

'Okay. I need a pee anyway.'

Klaus checked his appearance in the mirrored wardrobe doors, put on his public face and went downstairs. As he crossed the landing to the bathroom Ben heard Klaus's voice drifting up from below.

'Ah, my lovely Jackie! Come inside, I have the contact sheets for you and you will be delighted, I know. But I must tell you I am middle in a session upstairs in my other studio – no, not another Jackie, a young man for his *Spotlight* shot. Very, very boring but it must be done. So, come through . . .'

He heard no more before a door closed. Muffled voices seemed to be discussing something and then there were some female noises of delight and much mingled laughter. More nude shots being admired?

He had his pee and took the opportunity to touch up his face with the sponge and . . . what did they call it? . . . pancake. 'Quite the old pro,' he thought. 'Mother would be proud of me. What would she think if she knew what I was up to? This is not quite her idea of acting. Not exactly legit . . .'

196

The thought delighted him. He wondered where she was and what she was doing while he was here with Klaus. He couldn't imagine.

As he crossed the landing again back to the attic room he heard the two voices saying their farewells. He looked down the stairwell and caught a glimpse of a blue skirt swishing as Klaus kissed a woman on both cheeks and seemed almost to hustle her towards the door.

'So now we are agreed about the ones to be blown up. I will do them this afternoon after the upstairs session. I know they will pull the strings for you. I will send them to Chelsea Harbour tomorrow, *ja*?'

Ben looked from the window and saw the blue dress and a pair of legs striding out under a huge golf umbrella towards a waiting taxi at the kerb. It takes all sorts, he thought.

'So sorry. One of my official customers. A very important little job.'

'Pictures like the ones we're doing?'

Klaus laughed. 'Oh my God, no! The opposite. Not a young man who likes undressing but an older woman who likes dressing up as other people!'

'That's weird.'

'No. Nothing is weird, just different. Now,' he considered Ben seriously for a second. 'Perhaps you like to dress up? Anything you like here?'

He threw open the wardrobe doors and Ben was amazed to see a whole fancy dress department. There were dresses trimmed with feathers, multi-zippered boiler suits, padded jockstraps hanging neatly next to football shirts, a wet-suit with two bright orange flippers; a khaki regimental uniform complete with medals, torn tee-shirts, leather shorts and a real suit of armour. On a top shelf he saw a variety of headgear from black leather caps with chains to sailors' hats, boaters, a construction-worker's hard-hat, a black balaclava with a zipped slash for the mouth and huge creations fashioned in silk, ribbons and lace that could have graced the Royal Enclosure at Ascot.

It was amazing. An outfit for every possible fantasy. Ben gazed in wonder and tried to imagine whose sexual day-dreams could possibly involve West Ham soccer players or scuba divers.

'So, nothing there to excite you?' Klaus smiled. Ben looked down; he was flaccid again.

'Up and down like a Cabinet Minister's undershorts!'

'Sorry.'

'Something from the kitchen, perhaps? I have cream or chocolate sauce. Some yoghurt? What is it that you find most sexy?'

'The camera,' said Ben simply.

'Ah-ha. Like Marilyn Monroe, are you? So, we shall see. Stay just there; the lighting is good.'

Klaus lifted the camera to his face. Once more the scrutiny of the lens exercised its extraordinary power; in ten seconds he was rock hard, jutting up massively towards the glaring lights and staring eyes of the Pentax and of Klaus.

'Oh this is so great . . . superb . . .'

Ben posed in a ripped tee-shirt and then with a top hat and cane but he wasn't interested in play-acting. He was into the idea of himself as sex-object. Soon he was back on the bed, curling and writhing in a display of erotic excitement that was only slightly exaggerated for the camera.

'Brilliant . . . *ja* . . . now hold the head back – no, Ben, *your* head . . . aah, lovely . . .'

Klaus's enthusiasm mounted with the rate he was taking photographs and Ben was in such a heightened state of arousal that he could almost believe the camera's eye and the faceless voice were making love to his willing body.

'Oh that is very beautiful . . . my god, yes . . . let me see it all . . . give it to me, Ben . . . *yes* . . . *oh* . . .'

Klaus urged him on eagerly in whispered, breathy tones. Otherwise only the click-and-hum of the camera broke the silence. The music had finished; no other distractions disturbed the private and strangely intimate ritual.

Ben's body shone with sweat induced by the heat of the lamps and his exertion as he squirmed among the rumpled sheets.

Klaus handed him a tiny bottle. 'You want poppers? Like this . . .' He showed him how.

Ben inhaled the sweet odour and immediately felt an intense surge of hot energy rush through his entire body making his heart pump overtime as if it would burst. He was almost sure he could feel fingers that were not his own caressing his sensitized flesh. He didn't care. He sniffed again, filling his lungs with the drug. A second wave of heat followed the first and he clung on, trying to live with it.

'You like that, yes?'

In reply Ben moaned aloud, no longer completely certain what was real and what was imagined, but not too bothered. His jaw dropped as all his muscles were overcome with exhaustion. As his mouth hung open he suddenly knew what he wanted in there and with an enormous effort he eased his legs back over his head and began to perform his party trick.

'Oh, Ben, look at you! You are the best ever . . . *so schön* . . .'

Ben could hold back no longer. As he came he heard Klaus's ecstatic commentary reach its own climax and the shutter clicked more furiously than ever, capturing every moment, every drop.

As Ben subsided and began to shrink again Klaus's lens was still there, intent on capturing a few final close-ups of his splashed, contented features. Finally he sat on the bed and rested a hand on Ben's gently panting stomach.

'Oh, Big Ben, what a find. We can do great things, you know. You could be really big.'

'What d'you mean, could be? Bloody cheek.'

They shared a smile.

199

21

'Miss Fitch, are you all right?' Jack Fever whispered to her in the wings on the Friday night. 'You've been avoiding me, haven't you?'

Kate stared ahead at Gordon and Penny's scene about the secret panel in the library, refusing to meet Jack's eyes.

'Miss Fitch. Kate. What's wrong?'

'I'm sorry, I have an entrance in a few lines. I need to concentrate. Excuse me.'

'Please, can we talk? I think we should.'

'I really don't think there's anything to discuss.'

'But –'

She raised a hand to finish the discussion and he backed off into the darkness again. Kate breathed a deep sigh. She thought she was going to get through the whole week without being confronted by him. Now he was trying to spoil everything. Even more than he already had.

The morning after their disastrous gymnastic session it had rained in Cardiff. Which suited Kate just fine.

After a long soak in the bath and some tears of regret she'd had a late breakfast sent up to her room but found that she had no appetite and pushed some eggs and mushrooms around her plate.

She spent an hour dressing – finally choosing her least flattering outfit, a baggy old sweater and tracksuit bottoms with flat shoes – and then, paradoxically, made up her face with great care and skill. She wanted to look good even though she didn't want to be seen to have made an effort.

She wandered the quiet, uninspiring streets of Cardiff in a daze, replaying the embarrassment of the previous night again and again in her head. How could she have made such a total fool of herself?

Kate dreaded the thought of having to face Jack Fever at the theatre that night. Would there be loud recriminations? Or boasting to the others, maybe, that he'd 'had Kate Fitch'? Would he tell them? Of course he would. But would they believe him? Perhaps he'd only done it for a bet.

She wouldn't go on that night. She'd phone and say she was ill. But she knew her understudy had had no rehearsal; they'd have to cancel the show. Perhaps she could have Jack Fever removed, she was the leading lady after all, the box office draw. But on what grounds? Besides, he was already the Understudy Who Had Saved the Show and was therefore flavour of the month.

What could she do? Phone Robin and — and what? Tell him she'd slept with a boy in the company half her own age mainly out of lust but partly out of a crazy notion that it would help regain her son's affection. For that's what she now suspected she'd been up to. Robin wouldn't understand. Not even about the lust, let alone about the other thing. And certainly not her present despair.

The plan she'd pinned her hopes on, the plan she'd confidently expected to lead to a bright, new future had plunged her deeper than ever into misery.

She trudged around the shiny streets in the fine, soft rain, welcoming the anonymity it brought. Nobody recognized her or approached with shy congratulations or a request for her autograph. Irritating as it could be to be pestered, to be ignored would normally have annoyed her much more, but today she welcomed the fact that the citizens of Cardiff bustled past her without even a glance.

Usually on a Tuesday on tour Kate would be keen to see the critic's opinion in the local paper as soon as possible, to discover just how much of a celebrity she was going to be for the rest of the week. But today she didn't care. Things were so bad now it was more a question of survival. Somehow she had to face that arrogant, emotionally disabled boy at the theatre. Tonight. And every night for the next month. Apart from the Sundays which she would spend with her arrogant and emotionally disabled husband.

She did ring Robin, more because she needed to hear his uninvolved professional voice than to pour her heart out. That particular part of her body she was convinced would never be allowed out of its protective casing again.

'I'm glad you called, lovey. I was just about to ring you. We have a commercial casting for you next week. If it's mid-morning in town you'll be okay, won't you?'

'Oh, yes. Fine. Where is it?'

He gave her the address of a studio in Soho.

'It's Allan Findlater. He's asked for you especially, says it could be right up your boulevard.'

'I don't know why I go up for commercials; I never get them.'

'Now, that's not the attitude. Anyway, what about the Cheezichips campaign?'

'Robin, that was when I was in the "Young Mums" category. Back in the days of black and white telly, pounds shillings and pence and the National Health Service.'

'Good lordie, was it that long ago?'

'I'm practically "Character" now.'

'Ah. Funny you should say that . . .'

'What's the product?'

'Well, it's something along the granny lines. I don't know if you've heard of Auntie Annabel's Country Kitchen?'

Kate let a short laugh snort from her nose. 'Annabel Combes-Howard. I know her. Knew. Years ago, at university.'

'Oh, it's a real person, is it? I thought it was just an image for the cookbooks. Like Edwardian Lady or that fake farmer with the turkeys. Well, they're . . . she's pushing a new line of jams and chutneys and so on. It's going to be a big campaign. Whoever they choose could make megabucks if the ads work.'

202

'It's not money I need. It's respect.'

'Lovey, are you all right? I sense a tightness in your *chakras*. Would that be true?'

'I . . . something's . . . someone has . . . disappointed me. I can't say any more. But I'm okay. Really. Any news about Jackie?'

'Robin will do his best, believe me. You should take some rosehip tea.'

'Yes, yes, I will. Listen, there's something else. Forget what I said about the juve lead. I was wrong.'

'Your young Mr Fever?'

'Yes. Don't waste your time coming to see him. He has no talent.'

'Well, you've changed your *chanson*.'

'Please.'

'If you say so, m'dear.'

Kate went earlier than usual to the theatre that night. She gave the stage-door keeper a weak smile and scurried quickly down the corridor, unseen by anyone, to her dressing-room. Once inside she locked the door and tried to figure out how to handle the inevitable meeting on stage with . . . him.

She heard the pre-show bustle as the crew and the company began to turn up. Nobody disturbed her. Then, just after the half-hour call she heard footsteps stop by her door. There was a knock. She waited for the caller to speak but no voice came. She stayed still and silent and then the footsteps went away. She pictured the torn jeans, the hair flopping, the self-satisfied half-smile disappearing down the narrow corridor. Something inside her wanted to fling the door open and run after him and hug him, to forgive him and teach him how to love.

The moment passed, but the confrontation couldn't be postponed for ever.

Beate came and chatted brightly as she prepared the costumes for the show. Kate managed to keep the conversation going with minimal input.

Finally it was act one beginners and Kate took her short walk to the stage. Standing in the comforting darkness, surrounded by the whispers in the wings and the untempered chatter of the audience, Kate did some deep breathing exercises. Anyone tempted to speak to her didn't, they could see she was otherwise engaged.

'Okay, Houston, we've got front of house clearance, here we go,' Stevie whispered into his microphone at the poky little blue-lit desk just off the stage. 'Stand-by sound and LX cues one . . . and sound cue one . . . go. LXQ one . . . go. Stand by on tabs.'

The music started, the house lights faded to black and Kate moved round to wait by the upstage left entrance, trying to concentrate on the play.

Never mind Jack Fever, leave it alone, think about Angela, think about the way she walks and speaks. Have I got my props? What are my first words . . . ? 'God, what a miserable day for June. Donald will get soaked, poor thing.' God, what a miserable day . . . Concentrate!

Her stand-by light glowed red, she pressed the button to acknowledge it.

'God, what a miserable day for June . . .'

The music began to fade. The chatter had silenced now. There were one or two coughs as people settled. The green light came on and she opened the door and swept on to the set. She busied herself with a bit of hair-straightening-in-the-mirror acting to give them time to appreciate who she was and give their polite spattering of applause.

'God,' she said to no one in particular, trying to sound as if she wasn't really laying important plot, 'what a miserable day for June. Donald will get soaked, poor thing.'

Her performance was cold and correct. Page eighteen approached apace with the inevitability of a dental checkup. It could be delayed but not avoided.

And then he arrived with his jaunty air and clever little stammer on his first line as he put the suitcase down by the desk and held out his hand.

'G-good morning. Your husband let me in as he was leaving. He t-told me to come through. I'm Simon, by the way. Hello.'

As they shook hands Kate adjusted her brooch so she didn't have to make eye contact with him. Incredibly he gave a 'last week's' performance. She could scarcely believe it but he was still giving her little looks and smiles, obviously expecting a response. Did he seriously imagine that last night had been a success? Could anyone be that insensitive?

When it came to the act two clinch Jack had barely put his hand on Kate's shoulder and his lips were still several inches from hers when she pushed him away and said brusquely, with the tone of an exasperated schoolteacher to a naughty child, 'Simon, this is ridiculous. You'd better go and we'll pretend this never happened.' Which, of course, it hadn't. Only then did she see a look of genuine surprise on his stupid, pretty face.

Beate, who had no desire to be on the stage but said she loved 'watching you all doing your acting', thought it was wonderful. 'The way you change bits every night to stop it being boring.' There's no fear of that, thought Kate.

While Beate buttoned her into her dress for the confrontation scene Kate thought about the dialogue she had just spoken.

'. . . pretend this never happened . . .'

She had the answer to coping with the whole messy situation.

She would simply pretend nothing had taken place between them at all. No sexual contortions, no drinks, not even a flirtatious glance. That way there was literally nothing to be ashamed of.

So that night she avoided Jack after the show and she continued not to be where he was for the rest of the week. He seemed at least confused enough by her attitude to leave her alone.

But now here he was during the Friday night show, pestering her with the persistence of a terrier pup.

'Please,' he hissed into her ear. 'We can't go on pretending nothing's happened. People are talking.'

She turned to him. 'Who? What are they saying?' It was a shock to see him so close, for his lips to be so near to her own.

'We can't talk here. Let's go for a coffee or something later. We have to talk.'

She felt the warmth of his sweet breath on her cheek and could smell that lemony scent of his after-shave. He took her hand and gently squeezed it, rubbing his thumb across the back of her fingers. She enjoyed the sensation for no more than a second or two before she removed her hand.

'Come to my dressing-room in the interval,' she said, turning away.

The audience was restless, unable to concentrate. So was Kate. She couldn't be bothered with the show and sketched in an approximation of her performance. Enough to impress the punters but without any real passion behind it.

The interval was only fifteen minutes but neither Kate nor Jack was needed in the first scene of act two. Most people gathered in the green room for a quick coffee. Gordon, of course, would have brought a carton of apple juice and sandwiches which he would eat with his library book on his lap.

'You really know how to live, don't you?' Kate said as she passed him, settling down to his little treat.

'Mmm. Corned beef and tomato. What a lucky chap I am, eh?'

In her dressing-room Kate waited for the knock and tried to prepare her mind for the meeting. But nothing seemed clear and she resolved only to maintain her dignity.

When Jack arrived he had taken off his act one suit but not yet changed into his jacket and trousers for act two. He had a cotton kimono on as a dressing-gown. A dressing-gown! Who did he think he was – Noël bloody Coward?

'I brought us some coffee,' he said, putting down a tray with cups, a milk jug and even a sugar bowl and teaspoons.

'Very civilized. Thank you.'

She helped herself and sipped while he poured his. Then he sat in a plastic chair a respectful distance from her. Neither of them spoke. The tannoy over Kate's head buzzed with the chatter of the punters.

'Jack,' she said at last but he interrupted her.

'Miss Fitch, I'm sorry. I'm terribly sorry.'

'Sorry?'

'Yes. This week has been horrible. You've been avoiding me, even on stage you won't look at me. The play doesn't work properly and I don't know what I've done.'

'You said people have been talking?'

'Yes. One or two comments, you know.'

'About . . . us?'

'Oh no, about you. Being a bit odd this week.'

'Odd?'

'Well, aloof. Depressed perhaps.'

'I see.' Kate looked away from him; she couldn't bear the yearning in his eyes.

'Is that right? Are you depressed? Or angry with me because of . . . because of Monday?' He saw her flinch slightly but pressed on. 'I'm sorry but I need to know. We can't pretend it didn't happen, can we? Can we, Miss Fitch?'

She looked at him again and knew she couldn't resist his appeal to her common sense.

'No, Jack, we can't. You're right.'

'I've been thinking about it. About everything. You might think it was all a big mistake. If so, that was my fault. I was silly, immature.'

He leaned forward to put his coffee on the floor and stayed there, elbows on thighs and head hung down, a hand raking through his floppy blond fringe. The dressing-gown was loose and Kate was annoyed to discover she wanted to thrust a hand down into his dark chest hair.

'I was a real jerk, I know. I was just showing off. I treated you like you were a . . . a blow-up doll or something. I was so stupid. I knew as soon as I'd gone. I nearly came back to apologize and then the next day you were cutting me dead. I didn't do anything I should have; I didn't share any of it with you. It was all my fault that it was a disaster. I should have . . . cherished you. Kissed you and hugged you. I was like a silly teenager. I'm really embarrassed but I just want to say . . . I'm sorry. If you don't want to . . . see me again I don't blame you.'

He looked up at her through those long lashes, his expression contrite, pleading for her mercy. 'But if you'll give me another chance I know we could really . . . make love.'

'Oh, Jack . . .'

'I understand if you hate me. You've every right.'

'No. No, I don't hate you. I couldn't do that.'

'Thank you.' His head came up an inch. He smiled at her and she knew in that moment she was lost. 'Can I stay?' he asked. 'We could just talk.'

'We could. And there's a lot we need to say.' Kate got up and stood at his side. She gently stroked his hair back and watched it fall over his eyes again. She rubbed the back of his warm neck and felt the tension beneath the skin. His fantastic body was covered only by the thin cotton. She knew she couldn't let him go, not after that pretty speech. He'd said more than she could have hoped for.

'You're right, it wasn't the greatest night I've spent. And we do need to talk. But we can talk at the same time as doing other things, can't we?'

'Yes. Yes. Miss Fitch, Kate, will you teach me?'

She went to the door. The key turned silently in the lock. 'Oh you silly boy, of course I'll teach you. Come here and we'll start right at the beginning with a proper kiss. And let's take that dressing-gown off . . .'

208

22

At exactly the same moment that Jack was going down on Kate in Cardiff, Becca was going down the usual pre-show check list with George in the studios of Kingvision in Camden.

The toupee had been styled and carefully positioned, powder had been subtly applied to disguise the dark shadows under his eyes and to combat the natural loosening of ageing skin. The contact lenses were in and eyedrops added for extra sparkle.

Becca had chosen his clothes some days previously and brought them to the studios. She knew which companies paid him to wear their designs, although not how much, and whose turn it was for some close-ups on nation-wide TV.

There was an art to making logos visible and George knew every trick. And then some. He would rehearse positions and gestures with Becca until it all seemed natural but had the desired effect of showing off a particular product. Becca would phone one of the team of pet writers for 'a spontaneous anecdote that needs a close-up of feet' if George had just signed a deal with a shoe manufacturer. Later in the day a story about treading in dog shit ('doggie doo-doos' on the air) or getting stuck to a piece of chewing gum would be faxed through to her. She'd go through it with George, refining its artlessness until they'd got it to conform to the George King style.

George checked the image in the full-length mirror on the back of the dressing-room door, tilted his head to scrut-inize the line of the hairpiece and then switched on his famous dimpled smile. Yes, it was working. As quickly as it came on it went off again. No need to waste it.

Becca handed the make-up girl an envelope containing an over-generous tip and ushered her out. She picked up a heavy glass ashtray and held it in front of him. George obediently took one long last drag and stubbed out his cigar. He extended his hands, palms down, and they both quickly checked that his nails were clean. She noticed the small tremor in his fingers. Situation normal.

'Cimetidine. Ranitidine.' She shook the prescribed number of each of his ulcer pills into his cupped hand. He gulped them down.

'Cue cards double checked and set?'

'Yes, Mr King.'

'And the order is actor, author, minister.'

'That's right, Mr King.'

'Good. Get the crap out of the way first before the grownups start talking. Which set is it tonight?'

'Set B, that's the lemon and grey. The sweater will tone nicely with –'

'Just give me the facts, fuckwit. I don't want your opinions,' he snapped.

'No, Mr King.' Becca remained uncannily calm at all times. 'Here's the badge.' She pinned a charity motif on his sweater just above the designer's logo on the left breast. The tight shots would work very well, and Becca would send stills to the States to show them they were getting their dollars' worth.

'Well,' she said, stepping back for a final appraisal. 'I think we're ready, don't you?'

'Don't patronize me, clevercunt!'

'No, Mr King.'

'Bland bombshell, eh?' He cleared some mucus from his nasal passages and swallowed it. 'Lightweight, am I? Okay, you bastards, stand by for George "Mister Television" King! Tonight you get the works. This ain't gonna be bland. Ready or not, here I come!'

*   *   *

After her fourth large whisky Gina Howard was pumped up and ready for action.

Unfortunately she had nothing lined up.

She wondered who she could call for a night's entertainment that wouldn't end up between the sheets. She wasn't into that. She couldn't be bothered to put out unless there was something to be gained.

She stubbed out her cheroot and flipped open her personal organizer, browsing among the address files, seeking inspiration. There was Rodney the ex-public school company director who liked being pissed on, Anton the psychiatrist who had more hang-ups than all of his patients together – if they had been together. There was Duane the Aussie bodybuilder who was overdeveloped in every place bar one but, like a boomerang, kept coming back for more. Or Tommy the tennis pro whose penchant was for nappies and a dummy.

No, they were all too simple. Men – what a breed. All that testosterone sloshing about their systems, giving them a totally fucked-up idea of who they were and how they were supposed to behave. Only women truly understood the way of the world.

She decided that as soon as her hair was dry she'd take a cab up to Park Lane and cruise the cocktail bars of the hotels; the men staying there had everything that turned her on – money, position . . . and power, the ultimate aphrodisiac. Yes, an oil magnate or visiting US senator would do nicely.

Just as she was about to turn the television off to begin the preparations for her night's adventure Gina hesitated. There was something odd about the programme on Channel Four. There were the familiar features of George King; the open, friendly face, the perfect coiffure, the smiling mouth, the top lip shiny with perspiration. But he was alone, without guests, and talking to camera. And there was something about the eyes . . .

She turned the sound up.

'– and that is precisely why Great Britain has been going to the dogs. What d'you say to that? It may not be popular to go about old-fashioned, Victorian, basic values, but there are things that need to be said about certain trends in this country and I'm not afraid to speak out. Take the education system, for example. Now when I was a boy . . .'

Gina quickly grabbed the remote control and set the video to record. She knew something bizarre was happening but couldn't figure out quite what. George King was in the middle of a right-wing harangue on the state of the nation. It seemed to be a sort of Queen's speech from the King of Broadcasting and the studio audience was finding it very uncomfortable to listen to. This wasn't for laughs. Nor was it the usual highly successful recipe for the George King Show: slick, bland, carefully packaged and pre-digested. This was rough and dangerous. It was real, opinionated, even offensive. And to Gina infinitely more exciting.

She studied George's eyes closely and was sure he wasn't reading from an autocue. He was improvising, talking off the top of his head. She wondered what the show's producer was doing now. His nut probably.

'– so don't tell me about hard work and just deserts. It's not a fair world and there's no point pretending otherwise. It's the survival of the fittest and the weakest go to the wall. That's not a pretty thought, is it? But it's reality and we'll get nowhere by burying our heads in the sand. Some harsh things need to be said, and for all our benefits I'm prepared to say them.'

He held a long, unblinking gaze straight to camera for fully five seconds. There was a total hush in the studio. Eventually he crinkled his eyes in that old avuncular way. 'Right, that's all for the Week in Focus. After the break back to the safety of the script.' His eyes darted sideways presumably to acknowledge the floor manager and there was a nervous shuffling in the audience.

'We'll have more lovely guests plugging their fabby old

products. First up will be gorgeous dumb blonde Dillie Davies. Stay tuned to find out if she's any of those things: gorgeous, dumb or even a natural blonde. Join me, George King, in a couple of minutes!'

Cue applause, sig tune and run VT. Cut to shot of audience clapping while staring at themselves in the overhead monitors and fade to black.

What was he up to? Gina lit another cheroot and waited impatiently for the commercials to finish. He was the undisputed lightweight champion of the small screen, he surely didn't need a change of image to boost his popularity. The ratings for his show could hardly be better. There was no serious competition since Aspel's retirement and the boy Schofield's recent return to Oz. Not since the late Sir Terry Wogan in the eighties had there been a chat show host so dominant in the ratings. It had even been suggested by some that his murder had been staged by irate BBC television executives who claimed that his fees were bankrupting the corporation. Gina couldn't think what George King's motives were. Was he trying to move up to be a heavyweight in the mould of Lord Dimbleby?

She could imagine the frantic scenes in the studio now as the make-up girls powdered George's top lip and checked the idiot boards for part two. The floor manager would be diluting angry messages from the gallery and relaying them to George in a diplomatic way, the audience would be shuffling and giggling and rustling sweet wrappers, the cameramen lining up their shots of the empty guest chair. And in the centre of it all that smug bastard George King. Whatever he was up to it was quite deliberate, Gina was sure of that. Calculated and cynical.

That's my kind of guy, she thought.

And she desperately wanted to be there, to be a part of it. Like a first aider hearing an ambulance's wail she knew she ought to be involved in the thrilling danger of it all.

She didn't understand it but there was definitely something attractive about him. Not physically; he was past his

213

best. But that didn't bother her. It was his power and the way he used it. She didn't agree with what he'd been saying; it was the fact that he was saying it that turned her on. She felt a tug of desire, an elemental urge to get involved.

Oh yes, she thought. This is my inspiration, my new challenge. My opportunity. Fuck the Arabs and senators. Or rather, don't. I want a part of you, George King. And Gina Howard gets what Gina Howard wants.

George was back to his usual bland, slick self as he did his closing spiel. But he departed from the agreed text, throwing the autocue operator into temporary confusion, to invite letters or calls from the viewers on the night's show.

'Critical or even, heavens to Murgatroyd, complimentary – your old Uncle George would be ever so grateful to know what you reckon. How're we doin' up here? Let us know, would you?' He'd arranged with Becca to have a cue card next to camera two with the switchboard number on so he could read it out a couple of times.

He gave his famous silly smile, allowing him the briefest pause to hear the PA's count in his ear as the melodramatic theme music began to build under his voice. '. . . twelve . . . eleven . . . ten . . . nine . . .'

'Until the next time, then, be kind to yourselves and – if you can find it in your hearts – to each other as well. Have a good one. From me, George Mister Television King, ta-ta!'

'. . . two . . . one . . . and off air. Thank you, gallery, thank you, studio.'

Up in the gallery, unheard by George, Derek the director snarled, 'What the blazes is he up to? Not only does he put our whole future at risk by charging off on his own little reactionary tirade, now he's begging for hate mail. He really is a jolly arrogant so-and-so and this time he's darned well gone too far!'

But George didn't need to hear. He knew what Derek's reaction would be and he didn't give a flying fuck. He thanked the studio audience for coming, called ostentatiously loudly, 'Thanks on the floor, thanks, gallery,' and then before his radio mike was removed by the floor assistant he said into it quietly, 'Sorry, Derek, can't manage a drink tonight. Urgent business. We'll talk on Monday. G'night.'

And, pausing only to cast a handful of jellybeans from the bowl on the set to the still avid audience, he walked into the darkness, collected a towel from Becca and stalked down to his dressing-room.

'Fucking great, eh?' he said, slamming the door behind him and loosening his shirt collar. 'Fucking great! That Week in Focus – brilliant! They didn't know what the fuck was going on. Ha! I'll show 'em. George King has plenty more surprises for them yet!'

He dropped heavily into his favourite armchair as Becca entered. He held out his hand and she obediently placed a cigar in it and waited with the lighter. George began the ritual rolling and sniffing, biting and spitting before the flame of life could be brought to his treasured Havana. Becca stood patiently; in a moment he would start firing orders at her, instructions about fans, restaurant tables, gifts for the guests or whatever else concerned him.

But tonight he was obsessed with his own achievement.

'Fucking brilliant!' he crowed, then glared at her for agreement. 'Hey, what's up with you, Little Miss Frigid? Disapprove of something?'

'As you frequently tell me, Mr King, I'm not paid to have opinions.'

'Right! So there's no need to look down your nose like that. It was a fucking good show, wasn't it?'

'I'm sure it will generate a great deal of feedback,' Becca said quietly with a small smile.

'Ha! Too fucking right it will!' George cried. 'And it's only the fucking beginning.'

His voice rang in the confined space and he was beginning to go an interesting shade of red which even the make-up couldn't disguise.

There was a knock on the door.

'Send them away!' He shrugged his jacket off and it dropped to the floor.

'I'm sorry, Mr King can't see anyone just now . . . Very well, I'll see he gets them. Thank you.'

As Becca was doing her diplomatic bit at the door the phone rang.

'Yeh?' George barked. 'What? . . . What? . . . Terrific! . . . Right!' He slammed down the receiver and let out a whoop of delight.

'The feedback has started,' Becca said calmly, turning from the door with a sheaf of papers in her hand. 'Messages taken by the duty officer.'

George snatched them from her. He was really sweating now. 'That was the switchboard. They've been jammed since the first five minutes of the show. Said they'd never known anything like it. Not even for that Yid spoon-bender.'

He began to skim through the papers. '"Outrageous, shouldn't be allowed" . . . "who does he think he is?" . . . "speaking for us all, high time it was said" . . . "opinion-ated and obnoxious". Oh, yes!' he boomed. 'George King makes headlines. Oh, this feels so friggin' great!' One hand clutched the slips of paper and a stinking cigar, the other he thrust deep into a trouser pocket and clutched himself with glee.

Becca said nothing as she picked up his jacket from the carpet.

'It's a whole new chapter is this. Oh, bloody hell, I need to – to have a meeting about this. Is the Roller outside?'

'Yes, Mr King. You were driven here in it.'

'Don't get clever, it doesn't suit you. You can drop me off in Kensington; I need to celebrate. Be an hour early on Monday. There'll be more mail to answer after that.'

'Yes, Mr King.'

'Ha! "Who does he think he is?" George fucking King, that's who!'

Back in Cardiff, Jack Fever had proved to be a fast learner. Kate had only had time in the interval to teach him the rudiments of the delights a slowly applied tongue could bring, but he'd made remarkable progress. After the show they'd returned by separate routes to the scene of their Monday night débâcle, the large bed in room 104 of the Hotel Diana, for the fuller course on lovemaking.

This time Kate insisted on dictating the pace of operations, talking to him with sweet words of encouragement, taking everything slowly, sharing each moment and relishing the subtlest change of emphasis.

'There, now, isn't that better?' she whispered, nibbling on his pretty little earlobe as they lay side by side on rumpled sheets after an hour of advanced instruction.

'Mmm. You bet.'

'You see, it doesn't have to be a performance worthy of a SWET award. Something more understated can be just as effective. Oooh, do that again, that's lovely . . .'

He brushed the back of his hand lightly over her breast as it hung over his body, his hairs tickling her nipple and making her gasp.

'But it's never completely spontaneous, is it?' he said. 'I mean, some of it's for show, it must be.'

'Well, perhaps. It's hard to divorce one's technique from one's instincts.'

'Ever the star thespian.'

'Not here, Jack. Here we're partners. Although I suppose you could say you're up and coming . . .'

He grinned, pointing his perfect teeth at her like weapons.

Kate sighed. 'You really are very, very sexy, young Mr Fever.' She leaned on one elbow and looked down at his beautiful face. 'But you know that.'

217

His grey eyes were wicked and alive. She closed them with a stroke of her finger and kissed them – one, two. When he opened them again they were serious, questioning.

'I'm really sorry about the other night,' he said. 'I was only –'

'Sssh. It's gone, forgotten. Now you're learning a better way.' And she kissed him, exploring around his mouth with her muscular tongue, practically eating him as she would a ripe fig. Against her leg she could feel him getting hard again. Never letting their lips part, she adjusted herself until she felt him slip comfortably inside her. Just the sensation of having him there made her want to cry out. This was everything she wanted, now that he was submitting to her tuition.

She sat up and studied his features. He looked softer now, less self-consciously handsome with his hair ruffled and stuck to his sweaty face, his lips smudged and swollen.

'The Older Woman and the Toy Boy. Quite a plot. Let's see, you were born in . . . oh God, the dreary seventies. Platform heels and loon pants.'

'What pants?'

'You're such a baby, aren't you? I'm going to have to explain all about florins and the Beatles and hula hoops, aren't I? It's no use asking you where you were when JFK was shot.'

'That was shot in ninety-two, wasn't it? Oliver Stone.'

Kate laughed and bent to kiss the patch of hairs in the centre of his chest. 'Yes, my darling.'

He stretched up his hands to weigh and press her breasts as if they were something on a market stall he was considering purchasing. Kate tried to arch her back unobtrusively.

'You don't have to do that,' he said. 'I like the way they hang.'

'You're funny. Why should you like that? I'm . . . twice your age. There, I've said it. Forty-eight. Nobody else in the company knows that, by the way. That's off the record.'

'But why hide it? You're great for your age, you should celebrate it.'

'"Gee, I really dig your cellulite"? You won't say that when you're my age. My God, I'll be . . .'

'Seventy-two!' He laughed, horrified.

'Yes, all right, all right! What a depressing thought.'

'Come here.' He pulled her to him and rolled over so he was on top of her. 'You'll be giving a brilliant Juliet's Nurse at the National. Acclaimed by all the critics. And I'll be Mercutio.'

'At forty-eight? A bit long in the tooth for that. Capulet?'

'Macbeth, that's the one I want a crack at.'

'I'm sure you'll get it. I think you get the things you want in life, don't you?'

'Yes. I tend to.'

There was a blatant matter-of-factness in his eyes. His hands were on her shoulders, the ones he'd marvelled at because he'd never seen freckles there on anyone before.

'What about Robin Quick?'

'What about him?'

'He is going to come and see the play, isn't he?'

'I don't know.'

'His secretary said he had no plans to.'

'You rang him?'

'Yes. I thought you were going to fix it.'

'Fix it?'

'Invite him. To see me.'

'He's . . . a very busy man, Jack.'

'Not too busy to come if you tell him to. You said you thought I was worth it.'

'Did I?'

'Yes. I am worth it, aren't I?' He was rubbing his thumb along her collar bone, near to the vein that was throbbing in her neck. Somewhere in her head, faintly as if a long way off, an alarm bell began to ring.

23

When the phone rang Kate jumped. She felt like a burglar, padding around her own house and hoping George or Becca wouldn't appear. She wasn't going to answer the ringing but then it occurred to her it could be Ben. Or even Jack.

'Hello?'

'Katey, it's I.'

'Oh, hello, Robin.'

'It's good news, lovey. I've just spoken to Barney Jungsheimer's office in New York and the latest is that British Equity are going to agree to an American John F. K. but they're insisting that Jackie is played by a British actrine.'

'Oh Robin, that's wonderful! So I will get a chance to audition!'

'It's possible, although I should stress the Equity deal's not final yet. Jungsheimer's secretary said they have certain ideas about casting, but they're open to suggestions. They're quite happy to consider an unknown. Sorry, love, but to them you are. I'm putting together a promo package about you to send to the States. I'll get the angels to come up with something really special. Biog, video, stills, all presented magnificently.'

'Yes, he'll have to see me then.'

'Oh, he will, especially now we have Klaus's piccies. They are, of course, totally wonderful. You look more like Jackie than she did some days.'

'We had a lot in common.'

'I know; I'm stressing that — some of that — when I speak to Barney's office. Oh, by the way, Klaus apologizes for

220

hustling you out the other day instead of offering you lunch. He had a client upstairs in his other studio.'

'Yes, he explained. So long as it wasn't another Jackie lookalike.'

'No, I don't think it was. From his shifty tones I'd say it was one of his Tadzio sessions.'

'Tadzio? What's that?'

'It's a kind of . . . enlarging process.'

'Did you agree with the list of mine to be blown up to ten by eights?'

'Totally. I may not send all of them straightaway; I want to keep some of my powder dry so I can blast him with more later.'

'God, this is so exciting!' she squealed. 'This and – well . . .'

'There's a long, long way to go yet, you know.'

'But I just feel right about this part. It's got my name on it.'

'Well, in the words of Dame Doris, "Que sera sera".'

'Kerry, this could be the start of a whole new Kate Fitch.'

'I was always very fond of the old one. I mean the previous one.'

'Thank you, sweetie. I do appreciate what you're doing. Everything's going to work out fine, I just know it is.'

'You had a good week in Cardiff after all, then?'

'Oh, so-so. Nothing special.'

'No?'

'It was okay.' She tried to keep the excitement out of her voice, although she wanted so much to tell someone all about her newfound lover. How tender and romantic he was, how hard his muscles and soft his skin. And how flattered she felt by his attention.

'And this young man – Mr Fever.'

He was listening to her thoughts again.

'Fever . . . ?' she feigned confusion. 'Oh, Jack Fever. The young understudy.'

'Do you want me to see him? Or not? Which way is the wind blowing now?'

'Well, if you come and see the show this week or next you'll see his performance anyway. But don't make a special trip.'

'So I'm not banned from the theatre? He hasn't earned your disapproval in any way?'

'Good lord, no! Why?'

'Just an impression I got last time we spoke.'

Kate laughed, just like in the scene from act one where Donald asked about her relationship with Simon.

'Ridiculous. What an idea.' She even used the same line.

'Well, maybe I'll come to Brighton this week. Is George there or can you speak?'

'He's out at the office.'

'Are you going to stay there again? Is it . . . safe?'

'Yes, for a while. But I'm going to look for a house to rent. I don't want to keep imposing on you every time he gets . . . every time we have a row.'

'Darling, I'm here when you need me.'

'Thank you. That's very kind.'

'Now you get some rest before your next perf. We'll speak soon. Good luck with the Findlater casting.'

'Thanks, Robin. Bye.'

'Adios!'

Robin put the receiver down and took the call that was waiting on line three.

'Robin Quick, yes? . . . Ah, good morning! *Parlant du diable*! . . . No, never mind. Now, young understudy, what can you do for me?'

The traffic in Greek Street had to stop and wait while Kate stepped from her cab and paid the driver. Without waiting for change she turned and walked through the revolving door of Aspertions Casting.

'Hello. Kate Fitch to see Allan Findlater.'

Allan was from Sri Lanka, a shock to people who had

only heard his cut-glass Etonian accent on the phone. The deep chocolatey brown complexion disguised his age. He was probably in his early sixties but he looked about forty, as he had since he was in his teens.

'Kate Fitch! Come in, come in,' he fussed around her. 'Look at you. Why don't I ask for you more often? You're perfect for this part. Let's hope the client sees sense for once and gets it right. Now then, let me just brief you on what they're after.'

It was a series of short television commercials for the various jams and chutneys from Auntie Annabel's Country Kitchen. They wanted someone Kate's sort of age, open face, warm personality but not mumsy. More businesslike. 'Nothing too Tiggywinkle,' as Allan said.

'Is she in there?' Kate nodded to the other room. 'Annabel Combes-Howard?'

'Oh no. She's terribly reclusive apparently. People don't believe she exists, hence the ads to promote a real person. Or rather an actress pretending to be a real person. Well, one real person portraying another. Oh, you know what I mean. She won't do it herself, you see. The director's going to choose the actress, with her approval of course.'

'Of course,' said Kate. 'I might as well leave now, then.'

'No, you're perfect.'

'Not quite. She can't stand me. I'm glad she's not here.'

'You might see her though. She's coming in to meet Boris, the director, at lunchtime. And you're the last one before they break.'

The director was pleasant enough. He got her to do the usual routine, name and agent to camera, then they recorded a tight close-up, a full-length shot and both profiles on to video. She then had to improvise selling jams on a busy market stall in a room with all the ambiance of a morgue. The director and his assistant watched the monitor rather than her and were very complimentary, but she didn't believe a word of it. Commercial castings were all the same. 'Somebody has to get it, love,' Robin always said. But it was never Kate. Yet again she vowed to tell him she wouldn't go up for any more.

As she left the studio a figure in a huge orange poncho swept in. Kate had a quick impression of grey, wispy hair floating around a pair of big sunglasses and a strong jaw. The mouth was set firm, devoid of lipstick.

Lady Annabel Combes-Howard. My God, she's aged, thought Kate. But then, haven't we all? But she looked . . . old. Not the way Kate thought of herself. The great entrepreneurial aristocrat, ducking into the building like a movie star. While she, the real star, stood unnoticed on the pavement trying unsuccessfully to be noticed by a passing cab.

'Good morning, Miss Fitch.'

Kate hadn't noticed him at first. He'd been walking two paces behind Annabel Combes-Howard. She didn't associate him with her, or vice versa.

'Well hello. Mr Brand, isn't it?'

'Yes.'

'Are you . . . ?' She indicated with her head the swirl of orange blanket. 'With Lady Annabel?'

'I'm accompanying her today, yes. She finds this sort of occasion very difficult.'

'Does she indeed? You, however, breeze through anything like this, as you breeze through life. Even other people's.'

'Pardon?'

'Is that the way to get a good story? And I use the word story in the sense of "fiction".'

'I'm sorry?'

'Your snide piece last week about me and the play. Implying there was something other than professional between myself and Gordon McCone.'

'No such implication was meant, I assure you.'

'Oh no! I'm sure it was all checked with the lawyers first. Nothing libellous. You just throw enough mud and see what sticks.'

224

'Please, Miss Fitch. I thought after your charming party I could give you some good publicity for the tour. I promise you, I had no intention of causing you embarrassment. Quite the opposite.'

He looked genuinely contrite. But then he was a journo first, a kids' telly presenter second and a human being only third, if at all.

'Would you like to see the bruises that story caused?' Kate asked dramatically, making as if to unbutton her blouse.

'Bruises? Are you serious?'

'Oh don't get excited, there's no story there for your cheap column.' Although even as she said it she realized there could be . . .

'Hal? Are you coming?'

Kate was aware that the pale face atop the splash of orange in the shadows of the open door had been watching them. She looked at the solid blackness of the glasses behind which she felt sure two cold eyes were scrutinizing her. Neither spoke. Kate wanted to say something, to make contact, to explain to Annabel that she hadn't known at the time how big a mistake she was making by luring George away.

But it was too late. Decades too late. The imposing figure withdrew into the darkness, her stern features giving away nothing of her feelings.

'Look, Miss Fitch. Kate. May I call you? To explain. To apologize properly?'

'No,' Kate said quickly, still looking at the space where Annabel's face had been. 'But give me your number. I might need you to do something.'

'Of course.' He took a business card from his jacket pocket and held it out to her between the tips of two fingers.

'I'd better go with her. We're choosing someone to be her in a series of ads.'

'Really? How fascinating. I hope you find someone with

the right qualities. I'll call you. Or not. But no more lies or my lawyer gets this number.'

'Of course. Look I —'

'Hal!' A sepulchral echo rang in the empty hall.

'I'd better go. Goodbye. Please ring me.'

'We'll see.'

24

'Hey, it's for you!' Terry called down the stairs.

'Is it my mother?'

'No, man, it's some foreign guy.'

'Oh, right.'

Ben had been drying himself in front of the fire after a bath, admiring his two new haircuts, head and groin. He wrapped the towel around himself and climbed upstairs to the bedroom, where the phone was.

It had been 'the bedroom' first of all, then 'Sue and Ben's room' until the other week. Now it was 'Sue and Terry's room'. It was different already, the furniture rearranged, Terry's clothes mingling with Sue's on the bed and the floor. The cats were welcome now where Ben used to throw them out. And it smelled different too, more spicy and lived in. It smelled as if their relationship was working. Ben stood awkwardly, unable to relax.

'Ben, is this private?' said Sue with a concerned look.

'Yeh, like you want us to get under the blankets so we can't hear?'

'No, that won't be necessary, I'm sure. Hello?'

'Hello. Ben? This is Klaus. You remember?'

'Oh yes.'

'I thought you were not in perhaps.'

'Sorry, I was in the bath.'

'Ah-ha. Alone?'

'Unfortunately.'

'So you are now standing naked and wet, yes?'

'Well, sort of,' said Ben, aware of two pairs of ears pretending not to listen.

'I wish I was with you with my cameras; we could make

227

some good pictures. What do you think? You standing at the bath with soap all over your big cock. Lots of close-ups, yes?'

'Possibly.'

'No regrets about doing the photographs with me, Ben?'

'No, not at all.'

'So, that's good. And you think you would like to do some more work?'

'Yes. I would.'

'Very good. Well, I think we have something for you. I have developed your shots and they are fantastic. Really top class. I have shown them to my friends in Germany and just now I have a telephone call to ask me if you will be available to make a film with us. What do you think — exciting, *ja*? . . . Ben? Hello? Are you there?'

'Er . . . yes, I'm here.'

'Ben? You okay? You don't sound so good.'

'No, I'm fine.'

'I thought you'd be pleased, Herr Dover.'

'What?'

'Mister Dover. Ben Dover. Ha! Funny, no?'

'Yes, very amusing.'

'You know, it's true what we say about the British, you have no sense of humour.'

'Right.'

'Well, you want to do it, Ben?'

'Oh yes, definitely. If I can. I mean, if you think I can.'

'You want four hundred pounds?'

'Of course.'

'Then you can do it.'

'But what if — well . . .'

'You like to fuck girlies?'

'Well, yes.'

'And to taste their pussycats?'

'Their — ? Yes.'

'And you like it if people, if girlies go down to you?'

'Oh yes, of course.'

'So, that's it. No problems.'

'But what if I . . . can't . . . you know . . .'

'What? If you get nervous? Were you nervous with me? A total stranger?'

'Well . . .'

'Your shots were tip-top. *Prima!* First class! Your stiff cock in your stiff upper lip. You are a natural, you know. You will be my special discovery. My protégé, okay? Happy?'

'Well, yes, I suppose so.'

'Then I am happy. Look, I must go. I will ring you with the details but I tell Boris you are the boy for him. Mister Dover! Ha-ha! *Wiedersehen!*'

'Man, that's great,' said Terry the moment the receiver was down. 'Four hundred quid for a blue movie! And those pictures you did sound amazing! Phwaw!'

'Did you hear that?'

'You bet. A star is born, eh, Sue? It runs in the family. He's a bloody star! Just like his mum and dad!'

Ben glared at him.

'Shut up. Don't ever say that again.'

25

Becca collected the usual pile of mail from the box let into the electronic gate before driving her Volvo up to the back door and letting herself into the house.

It was quiet. Kate was probably away, George was certainly still in bed.

Good. She liked to get herself established without interruption and she didn't need him around to tell her what to do. He'd done it once and that was enough. She was now perfectly capable of running her own life as well as his.

The day's post contained the usual assortment: a couple of letters for Kate and about fifty for George, mostly forwarded from Charlotte Street. Becca put Kate's letters on the hall table and began to sort out the rest into various piles. One for George with the envelopes marked 'personal'. There were usually about a dozen of these; they would be love letters from lonely women — some pathetically old, some surprisingly young — suggesting anything from dinner or marriage to a torrid night of intimacy with full anatomical descriptions of the delights they offered, frequently accompanied by a Polaroid photograph of themselves in a bikini or worse. After reading these George passed them all on to Becca anyway, although he always kept the photographs, and she wrote carefully-worded replies which she then signed with his name, along with all the other fan mail and photographs. Only the business letters needed his genuine signature — the inquiries about availability or his willingness to endorse certain products, the wheeling and dealing of life at the top of his particular shit-heap.

Becca was sorting out this pile into an order of importance when one letter caught her eye. It was four neatly-
typed pages stapled together with numbered paragraphs.
She'd assumed it was a business letter but glancing at it
again it looked like fan mail.

It began: 'I've just been watching your show and I wanted
to write to say how much I admired your performance . . .'
But near the bottom of the page Becca read, '. . . and I feel
that you could go much further with the political piece you
open with. Be specific. A flick knife, not a blunt instrument.
And hone your anger with the abrasion of wit. I wasn't sure
about that tie tonight. A bit provincial . . . ?'

Becca skipped to the end. It was signed G. Howard (Ms).
The name rang a distant bell . . .

She read the letter through. It was a well-thought-out
and carefully-argued critique of the commodity known as
George King. In general it was complimentary, but there
were several more points of criticism of the style, or rather
lack of it, of George's presentation and suggestions for
improvements. Dress, haircut and speech all came in for
adverse comment and Ms Howard even hinted that he
should consider minor plastic surgery 'to ensure your continued appeal to what used to be called the yuppie market.
Nobody loves a "wrinklie" . . .' She proposed a meeting
to discuss 'these and other salient points' in the next few
weeks.

Becca felt odd. She poured herself a coffee and read the
letter again.

This woman was clearly not a crank. The advice she gave
was actually very good. George might well be impressed.
Insulted at first, no doubt, as he always was at any implication of his own fallibility. But if he thought about it he'd
see the wisdom of what Ms Howard had to say.

Becca sifted through her mental software trying to
remember why she recognized the name of Howard. She
went to the computer and called it up on the 'people' file,
but there was nothing there.

She tried to analyse her own feelings. Why did she feel strange, uncomfortable? What was it?

She felt threatened, that was it. Someone was muscling in on her domain. George King was her own property, an image she packaged and controlled virtually single-handed – barring a business manager, a part-time publicity consultant, a team of researchers and writers, an accountant, a chauffeur and domestic staff – and here was someone from outside daring to try to influence him herself.

'I won't have it,' she thought. 'George King may be a bastard, but I want the bastard all to myself. I need that control of his life, need him on a tight rein. I don't need you, Ms Howard, getting in my way. So just leave well alone.'

The smell of a freshly-lit cigar and the sound of a phlegm-shifting cough preceded George's appearance by several seconds. By the time he waddled through the door Becca was already standing at the shredder, watching the thin strips of paper drop into the bin.

He grunted a kind of all-purpose greeting without looking at her and went to the coffee pot on the desk. He poured a cup for himself and sloshed some down his throat.

Every morning Becca saw him it was like the first time; she was appalled anew each day, the sight and sound of him assaulted her senses in a shockingly intimate fashion. But he was oblivious to her finer feelings; he hadn't got where he was by being sensitive to other people's emotions.

'Jesus I feel rough. My guts are totally fucked.' He inhaled hard on his fat cigar and belched out a mouthful of smoke. 'Mail?'

'All carefully filed for you, Mr King. The ones you need to see are on your desk.'

George flicked through the envelopes and opened one or two. He snorted at the pictures of flabby thighs and pendulous breasts that met his gaze.

'God, these women know nothing about turning men on. Nothing. I could really show them some decent porn. Classy stuff, the sort of thing they — well, never mind. Speaking of which . . .'

He unlocked a drawer in the huge desk and took out his little black book of phone numbers. He still refused to put this information on to the computer despite Becca's best efforts to persuade him to move into the nineties.

'You just do the job you're paid for,' he always said. Since that had never been defined it was difficult. But it was a job that she was stealthily expanding as the months went by. She would eventually have total control of his life, and he wouldn't even realize it. Until it was too late.

George dialled a long number on one of the phones.

'This coffee tastes like shit. And it's cold. Deal with it, will you?'

'Of course.'

Becca left the study and spoke to the kitchen staff. When she returned something made her pause for a moment outside the door. George was speaking fast and low.

'Yes, everything looked great . . . No, I'm at home. Don't ring me here, right? Listen, I need a favour. Your latest legit project . . . Yes, that's the one . . . Because I keep an ear to the ground. Well, don't let the Finkenberg bitch get it, all right? . . . Because I say so, that's why! . . . All right. Now back to work, make us rich. Okay, richer!'

He rang off.

Becca left a beat and went in.

'Coffee's on its way.'

'Never mind that. Let's make a start. What arseholes am I interviewing this week?'

26

'So, are you gay?'

'What?'

'Are you gay?' Jack Fever repeated, continuing to eat his snails with dexterity, apparently unconcerned by Robin's confusion. They were sitting, appropriately, in L'Escargot. Downstairs.

A lot of people assumed he was, Robin knew that. But he didn't think of himself as homosexual. Nor hetero any more. Since his marriage split up a good fifteen years ago he'd been practically celibate, and happily so. He preferred work to relationships. He got a real kick from negotiating a big deal and his own soul was not at stake. At the end of each day's business he could go back to his own apartment and be his own person.

And work was good at the moment. He was riding high and acknowledged to be the best agent in town. Apart from Kate Fitch and her obsession with *O Jackie* almost all his clients were fixed up with something. This week he'd placed one older actor at the National on a ridiculous salary for theatre, finalized a deal for a well-known character actress to play Judi Dench's mother in a good British movie set in the fifties, got a new girl a job as presenter of a popular teenage programme, stitched up a package deal for two of his clients to star in a TV movie by Alan Bennett and started the negotiations for a telly-face to take over in one of Cooney's West End farces. All that and a definite 'heavy pencil' for one of his girls to do a commercial for a new washing-up liquid. It was what they called a 'T-C-K' – two cunts in a kitchen – but the repeats would be terrific and fifteen per cent of terrific was still very nice, thank you.

Those were the deals he got a buzz from. Not the negotiation that was part of being involved with another person in a relationship, an intimate alliance of body, mind and spirit. That was just asking for trouble. All that coaxing and wheedling just to live your life, to enter the interminable round of row, guilt, concession, make up, resentment, row . . . And for what? Companionship and sex. How pathetic.

At least that's what Robin had thought until now.

Suddenly, though, things looked different. They smelled different, tasted and felt different. It was all too alarming. This he hadn't expected and had no contingency plans for.

Here he was confronted by an extraordinary beauty. Those grey eyes, the square jaw, small nose, full ripe lips, artfully tousled hair. Above all the strength, conviction and health that oozed from every pore. But especially those clear, smiling grey eyes which belonged to the curiously beguiling and undoubtedly sexy Jack Fever . . .

Sexy? What in Cliff's name was he doing, thinking of someone as sexy? And this creature was asking him if he was gay.

'Or bisexual, perhaps?'

'I . . . well, no, I'm not. That is, I —'

'Oh, I am sorry. I'm terribly sorry. You should tell me to mind my own business. I'm always barging in, saying things that cause offence and I don't realize I'm doing it until it's too late. Forgive me.'

Robin tried not to look flustered and busied himself with his salade niçoise.

'Forgive me?' Jack persisted with an angelic smile.

'Of course. Yes. No offence taken.'

'Good.' The smile became even more intimate and the sparkle in his eyes was devastating. Robin wished the blush would drain from his own flushed cheeks. He dabbed at the corners of his mouth with his napkin to hide his embarrassment.

For a while they ate in silence but the subject seemed to hang in the air like a cloud waiting to burst.

'It's just that I was wondering,' Jack eventually went on, tugging at a reluctant mollusc, 'why such an eligible chap wasn't married.'

'I was.'

'Oh. Widower?'

'Divorcé.'

'Ah. But not a gay divorcé.' Jack turned on his smile again and once more Robin hid behind his napkin.

'But then we didn't meet to discuss your sex-life, did we?' Jack said and pushed his plate to one side. 'This is a business lunch, right?'

Robin nodded. 'Correct.'

'Right. To business. Cards on the table. I need an agent. A good agent. And I'm led to believe you're one of the best. You've seen my work. All right, the vehicle was a tacky thriller, but the part wasn't too bad and I gave a good performance. I know that. Now, you don't have anybody like me on your books so I know I wouldn't clash. I'd like you, Robin, to represent me. There, what do you say?'

Jack filled both their glasses with Muscadet and stared calmly at Robin, waiting for an answer. Robin couldn't get over his eyes, those deep grey pools, so large and bright and clear.

'How do you know you wouldn't clash?' he said.

'I've done a little research. It seemed . . . prudent.'

'Then you will also know that I represent only a few clients and they all have a considerable amount of experience in the business.'

'Yes, sure, my inexperience counts against me but doesn't talent outweigh that argument?' Jack gazed straight at Robin, his pretty eyes wide and unblinking, challenging him to deny the existence of that talent. 'Presumably,' he went on, 'you also want to cover the more youthful end of the market? That's just good business sense.'

236

'I already have a number of younger actors on my books. As, of course, you must know from your . . . "research".'

'I don't mean mid-thirties, Robin! I'm talking about young actors, early twenties. That's a whole different casting group, isn't it? C'mon, be honest.'

Never, thought Robin, not if I can help it. Not with an actor and certainly not one as dangerous as you.

'Well . . .' he sipped his wine, buying time. He was able to snatch another secret glance over the rim of his glass. He certainly was very castable. So handsome. But intelligent-looking too. Not just a male model type. A younger version of Jason Connery perhaps? Something of the early Maxwell Caulfield look. And yet very much his own man. He really could go far with the necessary luck. And if he was well handled . . .

'Well . . . yes, you have a point. It can be.' He felt himself soften, and rather liked the feeling of being charmed by this extraordinary young man. He wasn't used to having the initiative taken from him. For Robin Quick control was everything. But now, with this Jack Fever, something odd was happening.

The waiter cleared their plates and topped up their glasses again, unnecessarily.

'It's warm in here, isn't it?' Jack was saying, and he undid a button on his shirt. 'What I suggest,' he went on, 'is that we give it a trial period – three months, say, or maybe six – to see how it works out. Give us time to get to know each other, professionally speaking. Socially too. It's all part of the Biz, isn't it? Then we can re-appraise and see if we both want to put the arrangement on a more permanent footing. So, Robin,' he picked up his wine glass, ready to toast their liaison, 'what do you reckon?'

For a few moments Robin said nothing. He'd been watching Jack as he spoke. So positive, arrogant even. No doubts, no thoughts of failure or frailty crossed his mind. His handsome features were bright, alive and eager with the quest for success. How attractive such assurance was.

Robin interlocked his fingers and rested them precisely in front of him on the crisp white tablecloth. He licked his dry lips, gave Jack a polite half-smile and, ready at last, spoke.

'I'm afraid it's not as simple as that.' His delivery was slow and deliberate; he was determined not to let Jack have everything his own way. 'I really can't tell very much from your performance in *Murder in Triplicate*, you know. I would need to see further examples of your work before I could even discuss the possibility of representing you. Something rather more . . . ah . . . demanding, shall we say? Do you have anything on video you'd like me to look at?'

He knew the boy didn't. That was why he'd asked. Jack's brightness dulled visibly as he said, 'No. Nothing as yet.'

Jack wore the sleeves of his black leather jacket pushed up to the elbow and one bare arm lay across the table where he'd returned his glass to its place. Robin felt a powerful impulse to touch it, to reassure Jack that it would be all right in the end. He would represent him, Robin knew that already, but he couldn't compromise his reputation and this relationship by appearing too eager. There was a whole game of take and take to be played yet.

Just a pat on the arm, surely that would be acceptable? No, of course it wouldn't! What the hell was he thinking of?

'Look, Jack, if I'm to represent a client's best interests I need to know more about his, or her, work. So that if we did decide to form a . . . an association I could promote you more effectively. As you say, it's just good business sense.'

'All right, you don't know me one hundred per cent yet; you may not do me full justice until you do. But that's a chance I'm prepared to take.'

'But I'm not. I don't gamble with my reputation. My good name is based on many years' experience. I can't risk losing it with one mistake.'

Jack's brightness faded a little more on being called a mistake. Robin felt a pang of guilt on causing the downturn of those pretty lips, which he noticed now were endearingly asymmetrical.

'Don't misunderstand me, you were good in the play. Very good. And Kate Fitch spoke very highly of you. That's why I agreed to come and see you last night in Brighton. But I'm sure you wouldn't want that performance to be representative of your talent, would you?' Good, appeal to his vanity. Clever. No actor could resist that.

'No, of course not.' He brightened again. 'So she did tell you about me? Miss Fitch?'

'Yes, she told me something. I suspect there's a lot more she didn't tell me, but she said you might be . . . "worth looking at" were her precise words, as I recall.'

'Good for her; she said she would.'

Robin smiled encouragingly at him.

'What I suggest is that you go away and meet the other agents on your list. You have got others to see, I take it?'

'Oh yes.' Taken unawares he was not a good liar.

'And then have a think and contact me again when you're in a good play in town. Or at least not too far out of London.'

'Right.'

'Maybe we can do business then.'

'I hope so.'

'Yes, Jack, I hope so too.' Keep him dangling, he'd appreciate his good fortune all the more when it came. 'Now, that's the business out of the way. Look, here comes the main course. Let's enjoy our lunch and have a bit of a chat. Tell me all about yourself. Are you a family man . . . ?'

27

Ben stood on deck filling his lungs with the cold air, feeling the salt spray on his face and anticipating his voyage.

The boat was only just nosing out of the dock into the choppy seas but even so Ben felt an acute sense of danger. Being so close to the fatal power of the sea thrilled and terrified him. Had the passengers on the *Herald of Free Enterprise* had a sense of foreboding when they set off from Zeebrugge that day? Did Christopher know what was happening to him just before he drowned? Had he called out Ben's name, held a tiny arm up for help and believed he was being ignored? Did his baby brother, wherever he was now, in the place that dead babies went, blame him for that wasted life? Or had he, unlike their parents, forgiven Ben?

The water's threat could not be ignored.

Perhaps he shouldn't have had that joint in the train loo.

And yet, and yet . . . Despite the fear that swirled in Ben's guts, there was also something wickedly intoxicating about the forthcoming project. He was looking forward to making the film, sure he could do the job well. Soon he'd be appreciated for his prowess. Soon they'd be fawning over him for qualities which he alone possessed; he'd be wanted in his own right. They only knew him as 'Ben', and they assumed that name was assumed. His parentage was of no interest to them.

He'd been given a ticket for the cross-Channel ferry, some cash to cover his expenses and the name of a contact who would meet him in Ostend. Hans. The rest, he assumed, would be − ha! − plain sailing. Klaus had told him there would be another 'actor' on the boat, a girl called Jo. He called Ben an 'actor' too. Ben wasn't sure he liked that; it made him sound as if he'd entered his mother's profession and that was no part of his plan.

'She is a good girl, Ben,' Klaus had said. 'She has a few problems but don't we all, then? Jo is a good girl, really.'

Good in what sense? And what sort of problems? Still, he was being paid to travel to Germany to make a blue movie; what did he care? He was in demand and he felt good.

So good he felt a familiar stirring below decks. It didn't take much to get that old bilge pump working.

The boat ducked and rolled alarmingly as it ventured out into the Channel; the black waves seeming to toy with the vessel contemptuously as if waiting for the right moment to capsize it and pull it below. Ben stayed on deck, refusing to turn his back on his enemy the sea, clinging to the rail and willing the voyage over.

Suddenly a large hairy animal lurched into him, hung itself over the rail and promptly threw up with a full soundtrack of guttural evacuation.

Ben wondered whether to offer his assistance but decided that none was really necessary and sympathy would be equally useless. He was about to stagger away to another part of the deck when the figure unsteadily uncurled, grabbing at him for support.

It turned out to be a woman, very tall and made to appear even bigger by the tattered fur coat and high heels. Her hair was darkish but mostly grey and very long but so unkempt as so have no recognizable style. A grubby red beret compounded the down-and-out look and flecks of sick were dotted over the pale, washed-out face.

'Ow, shit,' she said with an Antipodean twang. 'I didn't chunder over you, did I?'

'No, you didn't,' said Ben primly. 'Not quite.' He didn't want this ill-bred colonial denting his feelgood factor. All the same he was in generous mood so he asked icily, as if

241

even by enquiring he was doing her an enormous favour, 'Are you all right?'

'That's a fuckin' stupid question. Of course I'm fuckin' not,' she declared as if it were his fault. 'I'm fuckin' – oh shit.' Her attack was cut short by the need to throw up again. She scraped her hair to the nape of her neck with both hands and thrust her head over the rail again.

This time Ben left her to suffer alone. He was vulnerable, being downwind, and rather than the smell of vomit or even sea spray, there was something much more stimulating he wanted to get up his nostrils. It would be difficult in the ship's tiny lavatory with the crazy pitching and rolling; difficult, but for the experienced and determined coke-snorter not impossible.

It was a rough crossing and he was forced to spend most of it lying down contemplating not so much the mystical powers of the sea as its power to induce nausea.

Once the boat had docked at Ostend, Ben hung about as instructed and was soon approached by his contact. Hans had a sallow, pock-marked face, suspicious slits for eyes and, despite the driving rain, gave off a stench of stale tobacco. He couldn't have been much more than twenty but looked as if he'd packed a lot of sleaze into his two decades.

'You Ben, huh?' As he spoke he referred to a photograph, one of Klaus's, checking that he'd found the right person. Ben felt decidedly odd, rather offended, seeing his own naked image so casually treated in this youth's hands. He thought Hans might ask him to strip off there in the damp car park to prove his identity in every respect. Ah well, he'd have to get used to that, he supposed.

'Yes, I'm Ben. You must be Hans. How nice to make your acquaintance.'

Hans ignored the proffered hand and said something terse in German with a nod towards a sleek white 7 Series BMW parked a little way off. To Ben's puzzled expression he added, 'You wait. *Zwei Minuten*. Is not locked.' He took

242

a second photograph from the pocket of his brown flying jacket and, his snake-eyes darting from left to right, searching for the corresponding girl, moved off into the crowd.

Ben got into the back seat of the car and waited. He had no idea how this weekend would turn out but for once in his life he felt no apprehension. Come who may, it was his very own adventure.

Twenty minutes he waited, peering out into the black, rain-torn evening from his cocoon of silence but seeing nothing. All was blurred and vague.

Suddenly, in a flurry of noise and movement, the door next to him was flung open and with a cry of 'Shift over, I'm half drowned,' a large wet woman collapsed on to the seat he'd just been occupying. Hans climbed in behind the wheel, started the powerful engine and began to ease the BMW forward through the rows of parked cars, heading for the open road.

Ben recognized the coat first, then the voice. It was the girl who'd almost puked over him on the boat. God, this surely couldn't be her?

'Hi. I'm Ben.'

'Right.'

'Are you Jo?'

'Sure am.' She carried on shaking the water out of her hair and wiping her face on the sleeve of her coat.

'We met on the boat, sort of. You were being sick at the time!' Ben laughed. Jolly her along, he thought, get to know her.

'Yeh, I spent the whole friggin' trip heavin'. Some fuckin' company. Why they can't fly us over, fuck knows.'

'You're involved in the . . . filming, then?'

'Yeh.'

'Have you done it before?'

'Ha! Is a rabbi Jewish?' Ben was about to answer what he took to be a very silly question when she said something in German to Hans who grunted a reply. Then she studied his face for a moment and said, 'This your first time then?'

243

'Is it that obvious?' He thought he was hiding his inexperience rather well.

'If you'd done a fuck-film before you'd know me.'

'Oh.' Was she famous? Within the underworld of blue movies at least? But she looked such a mess. 'What happens, then?' he asked, no longer bothering to conceal his innocence. 'What's it like?'

'You'll soon find out, mate.' She wrapped her tatty coat around her and settled down to sleep.

In the beams of street lamps and passing cars Ben studied her more closely. She was thirtyish, looked every day of it and more. She had no make-up on and her skin was pale and unhealthy, dull like an old coin. Her eyes were deep set in dark hollows, underlined by large grey semi-circles like twin bruises. Her thin lips were pursed even in sleep, set against some real or imagined adversary, her cheeks sunken and her hair a greasy mop. Even her nails were bitten or broken.

His mind did a quick flashback to an image of someone; it was someone he had been once, before Klaus had smartened him up.

Ben couldn't tell what her body was like under the mounds of fur but her whole aura was one of exhaustion and defeat.

How could this be the glamorous star of what she called 'fuck-films'? She looked ill, unsavoury. Who the hell would be turned on by looking at her on a screen? There must be more to it than pointing a camera up between her legs, surely? There had to be some eroticism. But this woman blatantly had none. How was he supposed to get a hard-on for this old hag? He just hoped the Fräulein was something to get hot about . . .

Hans drove the long, phallic car fast, changing the radio station every couple of miles. Once or twice Ben tried to make conversation but the German's brusqueness and the language barrier defeated him and so he settled back into the soft leather and closed his eyes, grateful for this little

244

taste of luxury after the harshness of the Norfolk winter. The BMW sped down the autobahn into the night.

Sometime later Hans woke the two of them, now snuggled up like babes in the wood, as they pulled up at a restaurant garishly lit in neon. They stumbled inside, blinking at this untimely invasion of deep sleep. Jo coughed and muttered incomprehensibly like an old bag-woman. They pointed at the food and drinks they wanted – frankfurters, sauerkraut, chocolate cake and coffee – and Hans paid from a thick wad of notes pulled from his back pocket. He took a bottle of beer for himself and two packets of chewing gum. At a plastic table they ate in silence, Hans absorbed in a hi-fi magazine. Around them one or two other subdued figures shovelled vast quantities of strange-looking food into their mouths. Oompah music, seventies decor and fluorescent lighting completed the impression of being in the pit stop from Hell.

'How much further is it?' Ben asked Jo. 'Do you know?'

She shrugged, asked Hans without bothering to look at him and translated his equally uninterested reply: 'We'll be there in another couple of hours.'

Ben looked at his watch. He hadn't put it forward – or should it be back? He had no idea what the local time was, but it didn't seem to matter. Hans would take care of everything. And when they got wherever they were going, then what? Then he'd meet Boris, the director, and he'd take care of everything else.

Back in the car Jo produced three joints she'd rolled in the ladies' and handed them round without comment as if dealing cards. They smoked in silence without even a word exchanged, producing a good heady fug that continued to give them a buzz for many miles after the dog-ends had been jettisoned on to the passing tarmac.

Without ceremony Jo lay down on the back seat, rested her dishevelled head on Ben's thigh, hid herself completely under her sour-smelling fur and was soon snoring gently. Ben accepted this without complaining and also nodded off again, his ear banging against the tinted window.

The next time Hans woke them it was with a prod and a long string of words none of which Ben understood. He took their bags from the boot and led them through the cold darkness over some loose gravelly surface and into the warmth of what seemed to be a large and elegant house. Up a wide wooden staircase they climbed, still more asleep than awake, past framed portraits and stuffed animal heads on panelled walls. They were shown to a room each, Hans said something which could well have been 'Sleep well' and something else that sounded very much like 'Good night' and Ben fell gratefully into a wide bed, wondering if it would be possible to smoke a stronger joint and survive. If he never saw another day he'd die happy.

28

It really had been the perfect day and Kate was feeling plump with pride. She was licking this young man into shape. Jack may have been rough around the edges a couple of weeks ago but now, both offstage and on, he was coming on apace.

They'd spent the afternoon together wandering around Brighton. They strolled arm in arm along the narrow strip of sand exposed at low tide, huddled close for warmth with heads bowed into the wind. They took tea in a tacky little shop on the front, giggling like teenagers about 'crumpets' and what the crusty old waitress called 'capu-China' coffee.

In an antique shop no bigger than a generous broom cupboard they browsed through trays of brooches, cufflinks, tiepins and earrings. Kate sought Jack's opinion on various pretty things, finding out about his taste and preferences. She wasn't entirely surprised to find that he liked the showy items more than anything subtle. Well, he was young. For Kate it was all part of the fascination, getting to know the kind of person he was. And judging the kind of potential he had under her guidance.

On the pretence of having forgotten to pick up her gloves from the counter in the shop she left him on the front, saying, 'You stay just here looking out to sea and I'll come and goose you in a couple of minutes. If anyone else squeezes your hunky buns before I do, you're a dead man!'

Back in the shop she bought the badge he'd liked most and took it to him. She walked quietly up behind him and discreetly fondled his backside. He pushed himself into her open palm and muttered, 'Ooh, don't tell Miss Fitch about this . . .'

She walloped him hard and they hugged. She didn't care who saw; this was honest and good and true. There was nothing underhand or sleazy about it. Nothing to be ashamed of. What was growing between them was full of tender affection and bright laughter. It was a kind of love.

'Jack. You are so good for me, do you know that?' she whispered into his ear, letting her tongue trace around its narrow corners and then jiggling his gold earring.

'You're too kind.'

'Oh, God, I do love you.' She held his face in her hands and stared into his eyes, seeing her own reflection in his lenses as he blinked and they floated back down into place. 'I know I shouldn't but I love you so much.'

'I love being with you too.' He couldn't hold her gaze, his own shifted to focus on the waves that were gently rearranging the wet pebbles. Kate thought of their footprints in the sand, not obliterated but somehow preserved by the encroaching tide.

'I'm sorry, I don't mean to put pressure on you. I should have said I'm very fond of you. That I love to spend time with you like this. Just us two together doing silly things. I really enjoy your company. You seem so much more mature than your years and you make me feel ten — oh, what the hell — twenty years younger! I feel like a teenager.'

'But where can we get one at this time of day?'

She giggled. It didn't matter what the joke was, just feeling the sensation of laughter creaking through her tired bones like fresh air in a musty house brought a joy to her deep-frozen heart.

'Look, darling, I've got something for you.' She took the tissue-wrapped gift from her pocket and watched his face as he undid the paper. He was a good actor but he couldn't disguise his discomfort as he saw the silver aeroplane badge.

'Oh. It's the one we were just looking at.'

'Yes. What's the matter? You said you thought it was beautiful.'

'I do. It's wonderful. But I can't take this. It's real silver and it's deco. It must have cost –'

'It doesn't matter what it cost. I can afford it, and you're worth it to me. If you like it.'

'But what if we . . . ? I mean, if I lose it or something?'

'Darling, it's a gift. A token of my love for you. No strings attached. If you lose it I'll just chop your balls off. Here, give me a kiss and say thank you.'

'Oh, thank you. You're too kind to me, you know. I don't deserve it.'

'That's your opinion. Do I get that kiss?'

'Of course.'

Later, as they passed a sweet shop Jack bought her a stick of Brighton rock and presented it to her on his knees right there on the pavement.

'It's not deco; it's rocko. It's all I can afford.'

'If it's from you I shall treasure it for ever.'

'Think of me when you eat it.'

'You dirty boy!'

They hugged again.

'Whoa, let me breathe. That's some grip you've got, Miss Fitch. Kate.'

'Sorry. I just want to hold you as tight as I can. I'm afraid you might get away.' She couldn't see his eyes so she brushed his hair back off his face, but he was looking down at her hands which he was holding in his own.

'You all right, Jack?'

'I'm okay. A bit mellow. You really are fond of me, aren't you?'

'Silly boy. I love you. I know I shouldn't but I do. Don't you worry; it's my heart and I'm in control of it. You just go on being your wonderful self. Okay?'

'Yeh, sure.'

He looked out to sea, biting his lip. Sometimes his vulnerability made her feel more a mother than a lover to him but whatever mood or profile he presented to her, the unmistakable aroma of lust couldn't be disguised. Her appetite for him was insatiable, every new trick she taught him came back with his own improvised cadences, his signature lovingly applied.

'Kate. We've had such a good time. Thank you.'

'Yes, it's been a lovely day.'

'Let's go and make love. Would you like that?'

'Would I? My God, every time I see you on stage I get wet with anticipation. Come on, let's go to my hotel.'

'No, let's do it in your dressing-room.'

'What? Why?'

'Oh go on, indulge me. It's extra sexy when it's in a forbidden place. Like in the school chapel.'

'You didn't!'

'That's where I lost my virginity. I used to be hymn book monitor. I was allowed into the chapel in the lunch-hour. One day I found this girl from the sixth form praying.'

'And in you came, the answer to her prayers, and you said to her, "While you're down there . . ."'

'Well, yes, something like that.'

'So that's what they mean by a comprehensive education. Come on, I can't bear to hear the end of this, let's get inside and get warm.'

Kate told the stage doorman not to tell anyone she was in the building because she needed a quiet lie down before the show. Her dressing-room was set away from all the others just off the stage itself. Exclusive as ever. Jack came through the pass door from front of house and locked the door behind him. Nobody could surprise them now. They stood face to face in her seedy, chilly room, listening to the moaning wind and the creak of timbers somewhere up in the flies.

'Well,' he said softly, his expression so solemn it could have been taken for one of melancholy. 'This is it.'

'What, my darling?'

'Everything you've wanted.'

250

And he was right. It was more than she thought he could ever give her.

He slowly undressed her, despite her initial self-consciousness about the privacy of her unadorned body. But there was something reverential, almost holy in the way he revealed parts of her, kissing them gently as they appeared and laying her clothes carefully over a chair. He undressed himself quickly, as if his own body was nothing special, not parading or preening as he used to. He led her into the shower and washed her all over, slowly and with care as if she were an invalid, rubbing soap over her legs and her breasts and then rinsing them until the water ran clear. Nothing sexual happened although Kate was on the point of screaming for him to take her while the water poured over them both.

She looked at him; he wasn't even erect. Was he really so into this role of serving her, worshipping her? Or was he just not turned on by her now, seeing all the flaws in her mundane, middle-aged body?

He was stunningly sexy. More so than ever with his hair and body wet from the shower. He dried her with a soft towel, first dabbing and pressing to mop up the moisture and then rubbing hard to warm her. She didn't have a dash of make-up on and from the glimpse she saw of herself in the mirror this was a Kate he had never seen before. But he was not put off. He laid her down on the narrow bed, turned off all but one small light and then snuggled up to her soft, damp flesh and kissed her on the shoulders and the breasts.

'Oh, Kate, thank you for everything you've done for me.'

'Jack, my lovely Jack. I do so love you.'

'You're something special, you know. I really do appreciate you.'

'What do you –?'

'Ssh, now.' He touched his finger to her lips. 'Just relax and enjoy.'

251

But unlike the first time this was no display of technique. He had learnt from her words and actions and blended them thoughtfully into his own creation. Where before he'd been bluff and bluster now he was seductive and slow. Everything he did was soft and tender; his lips sought out the backs of her knees, the inside of her elbows, the soles of her feet and when he sucked her toes she could have come with the delicious tingle it gave her. Wherever his fingers caressed her his tongue was playing somewhere else like a counterpoint to the main theme. She sighed and squirmed and let it all happen; she was the instrument and he the maestro, his touch confident but sensitive to nuance.

He stroked her arms, barely touching the skin but making her giggle as the goosepimples appeared. He grazed upon her body, finding areas that she thought of as commonplace which gave him special pleasure. And he shared his body with her, letting corners of it come within reach of her hands or her lips and taking his pleasure from whatever she chose to do.

He talked to her too, nuzzling his nose around her hair and under her chin. He whispered little noises, her name, a sound of pleasure and breathed his sweet breath across her face.

'Yes? Yes? Is that good? Do you like that? Oh, Kate, let me do it all for you . . . oh, yes . . .'

'Jack . . . Jack . . .' was all she could manage. She needed to concentrate on the messages of pleasure various parts of her body were sending to her brain.

He dabbled his fingers between her legs, parting her lips and dipping into her far enough and for long enough to make her groan with delight, and then tantalizingly leaving her alone while she anticipated what was to come.

At exactly the right moment, when he knew she couldn't bear to be empty of him another second, he unrolled a condom on to himself and slipped quickly into her. She moaned aloud with the rightness of it all.

'God, Jack, I love you. I love you. I do love you. This is everything I want. Do it, this is perfect. You are perfection. Oh . . .'

'Sssh . . . just enjoy . . . enjoy and treasure this for ever . . .'

He moved so slowly inside her, even when she wanted him to hammer like an engine. He kissed her hard on the lips, his mouth wet and soft like a doting dog, while she repeated his name again and again and stared at his so handsome face.

She was lucky, too lucky. She kissed him as if he was about to go to war, and they might never meet again. She began to feel a grim urgency about their situation. She wrapped her legs around his back and pulled him into her, digging her nails into his broad back, grimacing with the effort and the intensity of what they shared. Nothing could ever be like this again, so powerful, so right. So full of love.

When she was ready to come he did everything right. Slowly he brought her to the point and then, judging her mood to perfection, fucked her like crazy as she seemed to feel herself thrown into the air like a rag doll and dashed to pieces on the ground.

He came at exactly the right beat of her heart too, joining her but not stealing the moment.

They clung to each other, silently feeling the energy die, unwilling to let the moment go. Kate almost wept with the intensity of it, the joy and unbearable sadness commingled in one unique experience.

Minutes passed and she felt the cold air encroach again on parts of her skin. When she moved her arms to hold him, if possible, even closer to her he kissed her on the neck, then the lips and around her eyes.

'You're very beautiful, Kate,' he said.

'You're sweet, but that's not true. You are the beautiful one.' She ran a finger along his nose, across his lips and down his chin. 'Very, very beautiful. And a very special lover. I don't think this room has ever seen anything quite like that.'

'Good. I wanted it to be special.'

'It certainly was.' She sighed. 'You're amazing. Who'd have thought we could be so . . . well-suited.'

'Yes.'

'Did I say perfection? You're better than that!'

He propped himself up on one elbow and smiled down at her. 'Better than in Cardiff?'

'Only about a million times.'

'Good.' He sat up.

'Wait, come back and hold me.'

'We haven't got long until the show. The stage crew will be arriving soon. I can't keep appearing from your dressing-room every night.'

'Why not? If we're having an affair, it's the most logical thing. People will just have to accept it.'

'Well, *if* we're having an affair . . .'

Kate waited but he didn't finish the sentence. He stood up and began to dress.

'Jack? What is it? Is there something wrong?'

He pulled up his jeans, stepped into his trainers and then slung his sweatshirt around his neck and grabbed the ends. No wonder it was his favourite pose. It suited him.

'Jack. Don't ignore me, please. Tell me what's the matter.'

He turned to look at her and his expression shot a sudden shiver of fear into her like a bullet that passed right through her body, causing fatal internal damage but leaving only the tiniest external mark.

'Look, Miss Fitch . . .'

'"Miss Fitch"? Oh dear, this is serious.' She felt stupid, lying there naked while he looked down at her, his eyes half-smiling, half-apologetic.

'I don't know how to say this. It's not easy.'

'The condom burst?'

254

'No, no. Nothing like that.' He laughed. So, she thought, it can't be that bad.

'Oh come on. You can tell me. We can talk about anything.'

'Okay. Look, I did want that to be something really special. Something you'd remember. Remember always. Because it's not going to happen again.'

She was listening but she didn't hear. She was distracted by thoughts of how attractive his shoulders looked in that profile. Even now he chose his most flattering angle.

'What, Jack?' She smiled up at him. She was getting cold without him lying on top of her; she'd have to encourage him back in a minute when they'd got this business out of the way.

'That was the last time, Kate.'

'What last time? What do you mean?'

'The last time we make love. That's why it had to be right. So you remember me the way I want you to. The best.'

He must have realized she was gazing at him, uncomprehending. He spoke again, as if to a child.

'Kate, listen. It's over. You and me. Finished. It was great. Well, it was good. But it wasn't really right, was it? So, thanks. No hard feeling, I hope? I'll always remember you with affection. Really.'

Only now did she get it. Every muscle in her body froze; her power of speech temporarily died. No, this didn't compute. She had misheard. Or he was joking. Some joke. Don't panic. Get it clear.

She pulled the thin blanket around her and stood up, trying not to catch sight of her reflection. She stood away from him, giving him space.

'What do you mean, over?' she said quietly, trying to maintain at least some of her dignity.

'I just think that our relationship has come to a natural conclusion. Hell, it was only a fling, after all.'

Jack's face was calm and pleasant, half-smiling and

friendly, as if the words coming from his cruel, pretty lips were the most reasonable thing in the world.

But they weren't. They were tearing Kate apart.

'I'm sorry. I don't understand.' She searched his features for some hint of the reason behind his savage message. 'Have I done something? Said something?'

'No, it's nothing like that, Miss Fitch.'

'Don't call me that, please. Has someone else said something? Have they been teasing you about going out with me?'

'Listen, I just think it's . . . not right anymore.'

'But we're just beginning. It'll get better, even better than it is now. Please, Jack, don't do this to me. I don't think I can take it.'

Kate grabbed his arm, desperate to make contact with him somehow, to persuade him he was wrong. He tried to pull away but she wouldn't let him go. She kissed the back of his hand, the brown hairy skin, and then the dry palm; she held it to her cheek, feeling its coolness against her hot face.

'Look, Miss Fitch, please don't make a scene. It'll only be embarrassing for us both. It was good, really it was and I'm grateful.'

'Grateful? What do you mean, *grateful?* I haven't been having an affair with you to do you a favour. I did it for me, Jack. I wanted you and I thought it was just a silly fantasy, that you'd never look at me. But you felt it too. Don't pretend you didn't. It was meant. I can't just stop what I feel inside, it's too strong for that. It's growing, it's blossoming. I feel so much for you.' She kissed his fingers one by one as she spoke, smelling the lovely sweetness she was already so familiar with. 'I'm so fond of you, I care for you, oh God I –'

'No, don't say it.'

'Jack, I love you.'

'No.'

'I do. *I am in love with you!*' Tears welled in her eyes,

blurring her vision. He stepped back from her but it was a small room and there was only a wall behind him. Kate threw her arms around his bare shoulders and hugged him tight. With the blanket around her it was like a moth capturing its prey. She nuzzled her face into his neck below his ear and bit at his shoulder, surprised to taste her own tears as they wet his tanned skin.

'I can't help it, Jack, I do love you. You made it happen. You knew what you were doing. Oh, you're so special. Please, please, don't do this to me. I need you. You mean so much, I can't just let you go.'

'Listen, you have to.' There was an unpleasant edge in his voice now. 'I don't want to go on with this.'

'But why? Tell me why.' She grabbed his face roughly and held it in her two hands, staring through her tears into his angry grey eyes, searching there for answers. 'Is it that woman, Sam? Is she involved?'

'No, I've told you. She's a flatmate, not my girlfriend. It just doesn't . . . suit me any more.'

'Suit you? This is a love affair. It's not something you start and stop like having milk delivered.'

'I can't help that. It's over. It's my fault, I shouldn't have let it happen in the first place. Look, it was never right, was it? That first time in Cardiff was terrible. We should have left it as a quick fuck and quit there and then.'

'No! It was not a quick fuck! You came back to me and asked me to teach you how to make love, to be tender and kind. And now we have something beautiful; we have love.'

Jack extricated himself from Kate's grip and moved away. The shocking beauty of his bare back made her want to cry out loud. She had to force herself not to go to him, wrap her arms around his body and reach them up to his strong chest. She knew he would shrug her off. Desperate now, she changed her tactics.

'Listen, Jack,' she said quietly. 'We can't talk now. Let's go out for dinner after the show and discuss it properly.

257

Whatever's troubling you about the relationship, I'm sure —'

'Christ, woman!' he snapped, spinning round. 'It's over! Do you hear what I'm saying? Over! I didn't ask you to fall in love with me. You're old enough to know better. I mean, you're the one who said it was ridiculous, you were twice my age, could have been my mother.'

'I didn't say that. Not that!' She was shaking, quivering with the shock.

'But it's true! Isn't it? It's true!' His mouth was tight, ugly. His eyes narrow, his fists gripping the sleeves of his sweatshirt as they hung down his chest. He looked as if he was about to go into a fight.

'You have to get this into your head. Don't pretend to be so stupid. You can't really believe I was in love with you; that's ridiculous. It was convenient, for both of us. But now I don't need it. And I don't care whether you need it or not.'

There was a moment of horrified stillness as they stared at each other, a few feet apart but a deep chasm between them. He was the first to look away.

Something settled into place in Kate's head, a child's toy brick falling through the right-shaped hole, simple and obvious.

'You don't need this? It was convenient. What the hell is that supposed to mean?'

Kate wiped the tears from her cheeks with the back of her hand.

'So you did need me to start with, eh? Why did you need me? What for?'

He looked away from her, pushed his hand through his fringe and said nothing. Kate could only think as she watched him that she would never touch that hair again, never kiss those full lips, feel his warm, soft skin against her own. It was too much, she felt she would crumple to the floor and wail unless she stayed hard with anger.

'Come on, tell me. What's this all about? Why did you need me?'

'Why do you think?' He glared at her with fury in his eyes, as if she was the one tearing his world apart.

No, she didn't get it.

'Are you seriously telling me you felt nothing for me all the time? Even when we were making love? Even tonight? I thought . . .'

'Oh, it had its moments. It was an interesting exercise.'

'And today, on the beach . . . the silver aeroplane . . . everything was a sham. You knew what you were going to do tonight. That whole business on the bed just now – it was just a performance, was it? Like playing Simon. A part to learn. Gestures and words and reactions. And then see if it's well received. Christ!'

'Come on, Kate. Life's just a part.'

'You cheap little shit.'

'You used me too. Of course you did. You wanted me for my body, for my youth; I know how flattering it was for you to taste young flesh again.'

'How could you do that to me?'

'Listen, lady, it's a tough business. I intend to be one of the few who make it big. I don't want to be touring the provinces in rubbish like this when I'm –'

'When you're what? My age? Well, thanks. Don't worry, the way you're going you never will be my age. Someone else whose face you trample on won't be as resilient as I am.'

'Look, I'm sorry if –'

'Forget it!' She took a step back as he came towards her, wrapping the blanket tighter around her body, as if it could protect her from his vicious words. 'I don't want your apology. I'm not going to let you off the hook. You're a nasty human being.'

'I'm genuinely sorry you feel like that. I thought we had some pleasant times. Especially on stage. You've been very useful in the development of my career and I thank you for that. Sincerely. And, Miss Fitch – Kate – can I also just say how much I've learned from you.' He gave a cute little laugh. 'Not in bed, of course, I prefer it my way to yours but then that's a question of generations, I expect. But you've been a joy to work with. And I do mean that. Thank you.'

He kissed his fingertips and blew the kiss to her as the tannoy crackled.

'Ladies and gentlemen of the *Murder in Triplicate* company, this is your half-hour call. Half an hour, please. Thank you.'

'I'd better start getting ready. So had you. Now, don't get broody about this. It's been a ball. See you on the green.'

He walked calmly out of the room.

Beate marvelled at the subtle differences in the show that night.

'You're still finding new ways of doin' the lines. Amazin' innit?'

'Yes.'

'There was a real nasty vibe between Angela and Simon tonight, a proper sort of buzz. So clever how you do that, even though you're friends.'

'Quite.'

Kate was drained by having to keep up the pretence on stage of infatuation with Jack's character, Simon. She alternated between trying to woo him with the lines and keeping coolly detached from her real emotions. He played it dead straight, as if they were strangers off stage. As if he was showing her that, yes, he could do everything on sheer emotionless technique. Was he bluffing or did he really feel nothing? No, she'd felt his passion, nobody could be that cynical.

At the risk of attracting gossip Kate went to his dressing-room after the show; perhaps he was already regretting what he'd said earlier. With a quiet talk they could probably sort out whatever it was that was bugging him. He was young, confused. She'd be able to sort him out. He'd apologize and be hers again.

But Jack had left the theatre, the bare room was almost empty save a faint scent of his freshness. There was nothing of him left; it was as if he'd never been there at all. Never even been in her life.

29

Kate spent Saturday's two shows in a bewildered daze, unsure whether to try to speak to Jack backstage or not, hoping for the best but fearing the worst. In the event they had no contact and she drove back to town tranquillized by the misery of rejection.

On Sunday she slobbed about the house, sharing it with George but neither of them really acknowledging the existence of the other. He pottered around in and out of his office, papers in hand, glasses down his nose, a cigar clamped in his teeth. She flicked through the worst of the Sunday supplements, gazed at the garden, bathed and half-heartedly watched an old film with Peter Sellers and Terry-Thomas on TV.

And thought about Jack.

'What's up with you? You look bloody awful.'

'Thank you for your concern, George. I'm a bit under the weather, that's all.'

'Can't take the pressure, eh?'

'I think I may be getting this flu that's going round.'

'Don't come near me, then. I can't afford to be ill, too many deals up in the air.'

'Of course. Look, if you could find it in whatever you have instead of a heart not to be too foul-mouthed and unpleasant to me just for today I really would appreciate it. I'm feeling a little . . . tender. I'll be out of your way tomorrow morning. We're playing Birmingham this week.'

'It's a glamorous old life, isn't it?'

'And if you so much as raise a finger to me, George, I'll call the police.'

'Don't threaten me, you silly old cunt. You need proof

before you make stupid allegations. Nobody in this country would believe you otherwise. And I just don't leave myself open to charges like that.'

Nothing had been said about his violence towards her. What could she say? She'd seen his fits of rage many times before and had always come back to him after a night or two away. She knew he needed her for his public image.

Why she needed him she couldn't quite define. In the past the thought of living without him was just too huge a subject to contemplate. She'd considered it so many times. The first was after Christopher died. She'd blamed him totally for that. Slowly she'd reached some kind of acceptance, if not forgiveness. In a way the more she had exonerated George the more culpable Ben had come to seem. But to leave them both and start afresh had always struck her as even more terrifying than staying together as a family unit.

'Oh George,' she sighed. 'I feel so weary of all this pathetic fighting. Why do we hate each other so much?'

'Hate? No such thing in my book. No time for bollocks like that.'

'There you go again. You can't even agree with me about that; would it compromise you too much? It's so ridiculous. Individually we're both sane, successful people to a greater or lesser degree – no, George, don't bother to make a cheap dig about my career, please. Why do we go on sniping at each other? After all these years? If nothing else it's such a waste of energy.'

'My dear, you're getting very philosophical. Is this wise?'

'We loved each other once. It's hard to remember now but we did. At Cambridge and then in the early days. Before . . . when we were still a proper family,' she said quietly. Losing Christopher was something they never spoke about, something they couldn't bear to admit had ever happened. 'Those early successes were so good, weren't they?'

'Good? For you maybe. I've never been so miserable in my life.'

'Oh George, you never told me about that. I knew you weren't happy about your career, of course.'

'God, I was so jealous of you, taking off before I did. Everybody wanted to interview you, photograph you, cast you in plays. I couldn't get a look in.'

'But you've made up for that since. It never occurred to me that you were jealous. Of me! Imagine that. For my few brief years in the bright lights? But you've had decades of life at the top, that far eclipses any fame I once had.'

'Of course it does. Nobody remembers when you were a box office attraction. But I'm not going to take the risk of your ever being in a position to rise up again from the dead. I'm never going to be second fiddle to you again, Kate Finkenberg. I make sure of that. Daily.'

'What do you mean?'

'Are you disappointed you didn't get the commercial?' He had a smug look in his puffy eyes, like a child who's put the tortoise in the microwave.

'What commercial?'

'The TV ad for Auntie Annabel's Country Kitchen.'

'Did I tell you about that?'

'No, you didn't.'

'Then . . . I don't know if I got it or not.'

'Oh, you didn't. Believe me.'

'How do you know?'

'I happen to know the director rather well. We've done some business in the past, some filming for various projects. We spoke the other day and he mentioned that you'd tested for Annabel's campaign. He said you were just what he was looking for.'

'Really? Did he?'

'Yes.' George puffed on the fat cigar a few times, making sure it didn't go out. 'Said you'd been pencilled in for it.'

'Yes, Robin told me that. A heavy pencil.'

'Well, don't get too excited. I managed to persuade him that you weren't quite right.'

'You did what?'

'Yes. He didn't need much nudging. You see, whatever I say he goes along with. It's that kind of business arrangement. He needs me. So many people do, don't they?'

His smile was pure evil.

'You miserable . . .'

'More wasted energy? Don't bother. You'll never even scratch my paintwork, let alone dent the image. I'm a smooth operator, isn't that what they say?'

'You got me removed from a lousy commercial? But why? That's just pathetic.'

'I told you. I'm not going to run the risk of your career taking off and outshining me again. Still, fat chance of that now, eh? You're well and truly down the pan.'

'My God, you're serious, aren't you? Have you done this before?'

'Does skunks' sweat stink? How about the telly adaptation of that "Provincial Lady" thing, wasn't that going to be your big break last year?'

'You were involved in that?'

'Let's say I took an interest. As I did more recently with a series for Central about a family of market gardeners. Terrible crap, perhaps I should have let you do it. And then there was a cracking part in a wheelchair for some telly-film. You wouldn't have enjoyed it.' He was relishing the demonstration of his power and her horrified expression. 'You came pretty close on that one. Unfortunately the director thought better of casting you when he heard about your little problem.'

'My . . . what problem?'

George mimed a shaky hand holding a glass near his mouth.

'I don't have a drink problem! I'm about the only actor who doesn't these days. You told him that?'

'No, no. Not me. Nothing that could be traced back to

me. But if he got that impression well . . .' He smiled as if he was on camera. 'No biz like showbiz, eh?'

'You despicable, pathetic animal. How can you live with yourself?' She was shaking with rage, she wanted to flail at his smug features with her nails but she knew his strength was superior to hers. She needed to think of some other way to damage him.

'When it comes to television, my dear, you don't stand a chance.' He gave a hearty laugh, the most natural thing she'd heard from his lips for months. 'I've been controlling the jobs you get and don't get for years! I'm surprised you hadn't worked it out for yourself before now. But then you're just a washed-up minor celeb, aren't you?'

Suddenly he became very serious. 'Has anyone told you you look just like Jackie Onassis?' he said, studying her face closely. 'Because it's not true, you're nothing like her. Far too old, for one thing!' And he roared with laughter, throwing his head back in delight at her confusion.

'George King, you're an evil bastard and you won't get away with this!'

'Oh, oh, please don't threaten me; I'm really frightened!'

On the verge of tears Kate walked from the room, reeling from the blow he had dealt her so soon after being dumped by Jack.

As she grabbed her keys and a coat she heard him call after her, 'Oh, what was that about feeling a bit tender today?'

She pressed the remote control to open the electronic gates, revving the Merc's engine hard with impatience. Once on the road she pushed her car aggressively through the traffic, forcing gaps to open so she could put as much distance between herself and George as quickly as possible. As she drove her plan for revenge began to firm in her mind.

Once on the Heath she pulled off the road into an illegal parking space and took her three calming deep breaths.

She dialled the number on the card and waited while it

266

rang. There couldn't be any way George could monitor calls from her car, could there?

'Hello?'

'Hello, is that Hal Brand?'

'Speaking.'

'This is Kate Fitch.'

'Well, hello. How nice to hear from you. How are you?'

'Can you talk?'

'Certainly. What can I do for you?'

'It's more a case of what I can do for you, Mr Brand.'

'Hal, please. We are friends, aren't we? I'd like us to be, you know.'

'You're so full of shit, aren't you?'

'Am I?'

'You'll go far. Listen, cut the crap. I'm feeling generous. I have something that may interest you.'

'Oh yes?'

'It concerns an address in South Kensington.'

It did interest him, of course. It also intrigued him why Kate should be dishing the dirt on her husband to him, but that she wasn't revealing.

The moment she finished the conversation the phone buzzed.

'Katie, darling, it's I. If you're on the move pull over.'

'Why? I'm stationary, what is it?'

'No, no, remove that note of hysterical dread from your voice, my dear. It's good. I've just been speaking to Barney Jungsheimer's office and . . . you are parked, aren't you?'

'Yes! Tell me!'

'They want to see you for the part of Jackie. They loved the photos. Isn't that terrific? Hello . . . ? Katie . . . ? Are you there . . . ?'

'Oh God. Robin.'

'Isn't this fantastic news?'

'Robin, there's no point. I won't get it anyway.'

'Come along, that's not the attitude. He said he's happy to see all kinds of people; he's not looking for a big star but someone who can look right and act right. And you, my darling, fit that bill.'

'It's useless, Robin. Believe me. George'll make sure I don't get it. He can stop me doing anything. Oh, just when I thought I was doing something right . . .' She began to sob as she spoke and the words tumbled out. 'That's not all. That arrogant little jerk. He used me to get to you. It was just a performance to him all the time. Oh, Robin . . .'

Tears trickled down her face and she made no effort to stop them. Choking for breath she spoke slowly into the phone.

'Tell them . . . tell them I don't want to be seen for the part of Jackie.'

30

In the morning at breakfast Ben met the others involved in the film. The two German actors were both blond, *natürlich*, and in their twenties. Jürgen was big and very butch, with a little moustache; Anna was small and slim with bright, bird-like eyes. They looked up as he came into the room.

Ben smiled at them but his schoolboy German wasn't up to conversation. He helped himself to coffee while they talked together.

Boris, the director, burst in with a stream of abuse thrown over his shoulder to some minion. He was in his late fifties, with silvery grey hair, and he had the air of a provincial librarian or a distinguished Oxbridge academic rather than a director of porn movies.

Before Jo emerged there was some talk in German about her. Snake-Eyes' opinion was sought. From the tone of his thin, cracked voice and the expressions on the listening faces Ben guessed that the beans were being spilled about her having been a wreck the night before.

In a mixture of German and pretty good English, Boris explained the film's plot. Its subtleties would not have taxed a *Hello* reader. It was to begin with a man and his wife at home in their big country house. They get horny and start to fuck. Cut to second man and woman driving through the countryside. Their car breaks down. Nearby is – well, well – a big country house. They knock at the door, interrupting the first couple at a crucial point. The car owner is dirty from trying to mend the car so he takes a shower. The lady of the house brings some towels in and can't resist joining him in the shower where she gives him

269

a blow-job. Meanwhile the owner of the house and the woman from the car have got it together downstairs. All four meet in the bedroom and do the business in various combinations. General rapture all round. Much of it in slow-motion.

At this point the garage mechanic arrives, repairs the car, and as the visitors drive off they see him being led inside by the owners of the house so he can have a shower with all the trimmings. The end.

They all applauded Boris' bilingual plot summary, then he said in careful English, 'Ben, you will be the owner of the house, please. Your wife is to be Anna. Jürgen will be driving the car with Jo if she is well. Today we shoot only the, ah, innocent shots for you. At the house, meeting the two driving people *und so weiter*. Only tomorrow will we take off your clothes!'

'I'm not exactly sure what –'

'Yes, yes. Klaus tells me that for you it is a first film. So I will not be . . . er . . . unkind. Tonight we film Anna and Jürgen, after the car has break down, okay? You will see them working, they are the best.'

He spoke in German to the other pair who shrugged and whispered to each other.

Boris seemed to reprimand them with his next comments. Then to Ben he said, 'Today you watch, tomorrow you hump. Okay?'

'Fine by me.'

The rest of the morning was taken up with technical details, deciding what each should wear – ironic really, thought Ben – writing dialogue, deciding which rooms to use and shifting furniture accordingly.

At exactly midday, as a clock somewhere in the building was striking the hour, there was a sound of footsteps treading slowly down the main stairs and across the bare boards of the hall. In the midst of a discussion about locations with the actors and crew in one of the main reception rooms, Ben turned to see a tall, dark and stunningly

270

glamorous woman standing in the doorway, one arm above her head against the frame, the other on her hip. She stood frozen in this pose, inviting scrutiny and praise from the group in the room all of whom for a few moments did nothing but gaze in silence. Finally they started to applaud and Boris went to her, arms outstretched.

'Jo, you look terrific. Really good. Still you know how to be the star, eh?' He kissed her on both cheeks and the others went over to her, greeting her fondly.

Ben could hardly believe it was the same woman he'd seen yesterday on the boat. She'd transformed herself with clothes, make-up and willpower. Her hair was dark now and shiny; it had been crimped into pre-Raphaelite waves. Her face was bright, her eyes clear and she moved in her simple blouse and skirt with a relaxed, easy confidence that was both ingenuous and erotic. Only the voice identified her as the same bedraggled gypsy he'd shared a car with the previous evening.

'Oh struth, I'm sorry about last night, Ben. I was right out of it, wasn't I? Was I really foul? Bloody hell, I'm so horrible sometimes I hate meself.'

Soon after Jo's arrival the action began. Jürgen and Jo in the car, driving, breaking down, arriving at the house, phoning a garage, drinking with Ben and Anna, Jürgen being shown upstairs to the bathroom. Boris called out instructions as they were being filmed. Snake-Eyes seemed to fulfil the role of general gofer, moving vases, checking light meters and showing the actors their 'marks' which they were supposed to 'hit' during a 'take'.

Three other boys set up the lights and worked the camera and sound recording equipment, although Boris told Ben that they would be dubbing other voices on later. One of the boys, a spotty kid who looked like an inveterate wanker, would also play the mechanic.

Ben was amazed how banal the whole process was. Mostly he hung around, waiting with the other actors in a spare room. Anna and Jürgen sat in a corner playing backgammon and every so often giggling over some private joke. Jo sat with Ben chain-smoking German cigarettes.

'Bugger me if I know why Boris always uses them. Old Tweedledum and Tweedledee. Guess they must be cheap.'

'You've worked with them before?' Ben asked, primly sipping an apple juice.

'Hell, about ninety-three times. Can't stand them. So into each other.'

'Are they lovers, really?'

'Yeh.'

'That's nice.'

'Nice! It's fucking crazy. They're brother and sister.'

'Oh. But surely they don't . . . with each other?'

'Oh yes they do. She does it with dogs too. That's how nice she is. It's her spesh. I expect they'll work that in somewhere. Ha, look at your face! There's fuck all nice about this business, kid. Just get out of your head enough to do the tricks they want. It's take the money and come. Look out, here we go.'

She checked her face in a mirror and went to do her shot of arriving at the front door.

Ben started to wonder what the hell he was doing here. What if he couldn't deliver the goods tomorrow? There was nothing erotic about the set-up or any of the other actors. How would he get an erection? Perhaps he could talk to Boris, explain his misgivings.

Most of his 'innocent' shots were with Jo. However rough she started to look during the day, whenever required to appear before the camera she was able to recreate her new, sexy image just long enough for a take.

'Listen,' Ben said during yet another lull for technical readjustments, 'I don't know if I can do this. I feel silly. I don't think I'll be any good tomorrow. What if I can't . . . you know.'

'Get it up? You've got to. Whatever it takes. We don't have a choice, kid. None of us. Just stand and deliver.'

'It's easier for you, isn't it? You can fake it. How the hell am I supposed to fake an erection?'

'You got me there. Steel rods down your dingo?'

'What? They don't. Do they?'

'It's worth a try. I know they can spray you with something if you're going to come too soon but the other way round, now that's a problem. And they don't like problems.'

'Oh shit.' Ben lit a joint that was lying in the ashtray by his side and took a lungful of the sweet weed. 'Have you been in this . . . line of work long?'

'Too fucking long. I'm gonna quit in another year. That's all I'm doing, one more year. As long as I can stay based in the UK. What I'd really like to do is get married to someone so I can stay. I haven't been well you see, Ben, and I just need to make some fast dollars to put me back on my feet. Then I can get out of this lousy business. It really fucks you up. Everyone thinks they're going to be different. But they get fucked up too.'

'But you're not fucked up.'

'Oh no? Look a bit deeper, kid. If the truth were known — no, it's better it isn't . . .' She trailed off, a sad, wistful look in her green eyes.

'What will I have to do?' he asked. 'Tomorrow, I mean.'

Jo shrugged. 'There's not much to it for the boys. Fuck. Suck. Don't come. Come. Come again. And again. Stay hard for hours. The toughest thing is to look as if you're having the time of your life. And think of things to say. Do as you're told. Don't say no to anything they want you to do, however disgusting. Otherwise you won't get paid. Basically, bare it and grin.'

'Do you watch them, the films you've made?'

'Jeez no! I do them for the money, fuck all else!'

'What about the — well, the glamour.'

'The glamour?' Jo laughed. 'You're unreal! But cute with it. Come on, Mr de Mille wants us for a close-up.'

31

'Take a seat please, Miss Fitch. They're running a little behind.'

Surprise, surprise. She'd never been to an audition where they weren't. Come to think of it, she hadn't been to an audition for . . . five, six years. Normally the jobs came through as straight offers. If they came through at all.

Kate couldn't decide if she was excited at being considered for the part of Jackie O., insulted at having to audition, despondent at knowing that George would ensure she didn't get the part or just plain terrified at having to strut her stuff.

Robin had persuaded her to come and 'give it her best shot', even though she was convinced it was a waste of time.

Thinking about it logically she had no reason to be nervous. Everything was prepared; more photographs had been biked round before with her video showreel and a cassette of her singing, she'd rehearsed the songs with Brad Good, her usual pianist, now here she was at the stage door of the Albery Theatre dressed like Jackie and made up by Michi B. to look like Jackie. She'd meditated that morning, done her breathing exercises and centred herself.

Or she'd tried to. Somehow everything seemed to have unravelled itself in her head. She wanted this part so much. She understood what people meant when they said they'd kill for something. If that would convince Barney Jungsheimer to cast her she'd happily pull a trigger or wield an axe. It might come to that yet, she thought, if George's influence was really universal.

Or had those terrible threats been his stupid idea of a joke?

Oh God, how much longer were they going to be? She'd been all geared up for eleven o'clock and now it was twenty past. For months she'd been dreaming of nothing but this moment, the chance to prove herself again, to climb back to the very top of the thespian tree, to show George, Ben, the world that Kate Fitch was a star once more.

Now she was going off the boil.

Her thick pancake make-up felt sticky and blotched, her hair was lacquered like a helmet, her sixties outfit was too small and now she wanted to pee.

'Kate Filch?'

The girl was trying to decipher the name on her clipboard. She was dressed in a black poloneck sweater, black skirt, black tights and shoes. She wore big black plastic earrings. Even her hair and glasses were black. She could have been on her way to a very hip funeral.

'Fitch. Kate Fitch.'

'Yah, right. Can't read my own writing. Come through.'

Trying not to think about her bladder Kate followed the petite figure down the stairs, past the two main dressing-rooms — where Larry and Johnnie and Ralph and Edith and Peggy and all the dear, dear luvvies had once held court — through the heavy iron sliding door into the wings and suddenly, too suddenly, on to the bright stage.

'Gentlemen, this is Kate . . . er . . . Felch.'

'Fitch.'

She blinked out into the dark auditorium. A tiny pin-point of light shone down on to a desk half-way back in the stalls. A small group of heads seemed to be clustered around the light, deep in conversation.

Kate waited. And waited. Her smile didn't feel quite so natural now. Her bladder reminded her of its existence. Perhaps they were so stunned by her resemblance to Jackie O. that they were drinking in the slowly-dawning implication that their long search was over.

275

'Bella!' bellowed a male American voice. 'Are you up there? Is she up there in the wings? Can you look for me? Yes, you.'

'I'm sorry; are you talking to me?' Kate smiled into the void.

'Yeh. The girl showed you in. Black dress. She there? Take a look, would you?'

Was this some kind of power game? Improvisation? They were big on 'improv', weren't they? She'd better go along with it. She walked into the wings and found the girl with her personal stereo on. She tapped her shoulder.

'Excuse me, I think they'd like a word with you.'

'Uh-huh.' She stuck her head around the tall flat. 'Yah?'

'Bella, honey. Tell the restaurant we'll be a half-hour later for lunch. And bring some coffees, would you. Four . . . J-P? Five, then. Cappuccinos, yeh?'

'You got 'em.'

'Now then, who's this? Pauline Adams, right? Hi, Pauline.'

'No, I'm Kate Fitch.'

'Who?'

'Kate . . . Fitch. F – I – T –'

'Oh, right. Here we are. Eleven o'clock. What in Christ's name happened to Pauline Adams, then? Oh, what the hell. Now then, honey, I'm Dwight. I'm going to be recreating the piece here in your West End of London. Alongside me are Jean-Pierre, Lars and Miguel. Oh and Mr Jungsheimer, our Executive Producer, of course.'

'My, how cosmopolitan,' Kate quipped, still peering vaguely at the half-lit figures. There was an ominous silence. She smiled nevertheless, wondering if the next move was up to her.

'How so: "cosmopolitan"?' came the voice of this 'Dwight' again, echoing in the empty space. 'Mr Jungsheimer would like to know.'

'Well, I just meant, the names, you know. Lars and

276

Miguel and . . . very international. That's nice. That's good.' She was dying. Oh God, she was dying.

There was some hushed discussion around the spot of light.

'You didn't mean the magazine, then?' came the voice. '*Cosmopolitan* the magazine?'

'No,' she laughed. 'Certainly not.'

'Good. That's good. Mr Jungsheimer is pleased about that. Would you walk around a little, please?'

'Walk around?'

'Yes. You have any objections to walking around for Mr Jungsheimer?'

'No, I suppose not,' said Kate uncertainly. 'I just thought perhaps . . . oh well. Where would you like me to walk?'

'Where? There, on the stage. Just up and down a little. We'd like to see you move. Our choreographer, Lars, is here and he'd like to watch you walk.'

'Fine.' She surveyed the empty space around her. 'Um . . . How would you like me to walk?'

'How?' There was an edge to the Voice Called Dwight. It seemed to have a sort of drawl to it, lazy and slow, but not relaxed.

'In what way? What kind of walking do you want to see?'

'Listen, lady, how many ways of walking you know? Let's see the walk you do every day of your life, okay? Begin now, please.'

Kate thought better of commenting further and crossed down stage left, turned and strode across the width of the stage to the opposite prompt corner. From there she moved upstage centre and held it briefly before slowly approaching the staring faces again. She did it with a challenge in her eyes, daring them to mess her about any more. If they asked to see her walk again she'd show them how she could walk right out of the theatre.

She stood down centre, square on to the rows of seats and her body language saying 'angry', not caring about the Jackie look any more. It obviously hadn't grabbed them or they would have said something. She just wanted to get through this with the minimum of further embarrassment.

'Yeh, good walking. So, Katherine, tell us about yourself.'

'It's Kate and what do you want to know? Or do you just want to hear me talk now?'

Another muffled conflab ensued in the shadows.

'Mr Jungsheimer would like to hear about your most recent piece of stage work.'

'You've received my full cv with photographs and videos of various pieces of work from my agent, Robin Quick.' Another discussion seemed to be about to start so she pressed on. 'However, I'm currently appearing, well, starring in a play called *Murder in Triplicate* which is, guess what, a murder mystery. It's produced by Bryan Harvey-Jones and we're in the middle of a six-week pre-West End tour. We hope to be in town in a few weeks or maybe just after Christmas. I play Angela Browne who is a rather uptight middle-class English woman — hardly typecasting at all, eh? — whose marriage is going through a very sticky patch and who thinks about taking as a lover a young researcher who's recently started to work for her husband. They flirt and we're led to believe they're having an affair but in the final analysis they don't actually go to bed together because . . . well, because it's not that sort of play. How much did you want to know?'

'That's fine. Have you prepared a song from the show?'

'I have.'

'Good. Hold on there, please.'

After a moment she became aware of some movement and then a figure emerged from the stalls, climbing up a flight of wooden steps over the orchestra pit.

He was slight, only about twentyish, dressed in a huge loose suit and he had lank blond hair that he wore in a scrawny ponytail down his back. He smiled at Kate through little round glasses. She held out her hand but he walked straight past her into the wings and then re-emerged pushing an upright piano onstage.

'You're going to do '"Marry me", aren't you?' he said quietly while he adjusted a chair under him.

'Yes, is that okay?'

'Sure, honey, they all do. You look great, by the way, although they'd never bother to tell you. I'm Miguel da Santos, music and lyrics, hi.'

'Hi. What was all that stuff about *Cosmopolitan*?'

'Mr Jungsheimer sued them once for libel over an article. He lost.'

'Oh great. Well done, Kate. Listen, can you take it down a tad?'

'Uh-oh. What's your top note?'

'In the bath or on stage?'

He took her up and down a few scales to warm up 'la vochay' as he called it. Then he said, 'Just remember, she wants him. Give it pizazz, okay? Mister Jungsheimer is a big fan of pizazz.'

He went into the familiar limping intro to the only song Kate felt confident enough to attempt. She stepped away from the piano – 'Don't lean on it, dear, you look lopsided and sing lopsided', her teacher used to say – planted her feet and belted her guts out with all the passion that she could muster.

> Hello J.F.K. I'm a Bouvier, won't you choose the day
>   we'll wed?
> Make my surname the same as your brother Ted.
> They call me Jackie, I'm never tacky
> I'll be your rave, your slave, your lackey;
> I want to be with you
> On your journey to the top,
> But while you press the flesh
> I'll dump the kids at the creche
> And shop!
> For Balmain and Gucci, Chanel, Fiorucci

279

I'm not that choosy, but I'm no floosie
I got 'je ne sais quoi' – I know how to talk and dance,
It's a savoir faire as they say over there in France.
And since you hanker
For the casa blanca
(That's White House to you if don't speak the lingua
*   franca)*
Show me off and win the casting vote,
I've the qualities that'll float your boat.
Oh Johnnie K. don't turn away, why won't you make
*   me your wifey?*
Oh Mr Jack, don't turn your back, just propose and
*   change my lifey.*
I got taste and, you gotta admit, a cute ass –
What a team, you got the brains and I got the class!

She hit the last high note right smack bang in the middle,
like a crisp winning volley on match point. She held it the
full eight beats and came off cleanly, her head high with
defiance. It was bloody good. She knew it but did they?

There was silence in the auditorium.

She glanced at the pianist, expecting him to give a little
private nod of approval. But he was looking oddly at her.
She'd remembered the words, hit the right notes and given
it pizazz, for Christ's sake; what more could they ask?

'You gave it a different slant,' he said to her. 'Kinda
ironic.'

'Thank you.'

'No, no, it's totally wrong.'

'Oh. I thought it was interesting that she sings "Call me
Jackie" when in fact she liked to be known by her full
name. "Jacqueline – it rhymes with queen" she's supposed
to have said.'

'Is that right?'

'According to my research.'

'Great.' He closed the sheet music and stared at her.

There was still a colossal silence in the stalls. She waited for some comment. Something. Anything. Even, 'thank you for coming'.

'Thank you for coming, Miss Felch. That was okay. We'll be in touch. Would you tell Bella to show the next Jackie in, please?'

Kate stood immobile, wondering how much to say and how much to leave unsaid. She heard the voices muttering to each other in the darkness. She had been dismissed.

No, she wasn't going to put up with this. Not again. She'd had more than her share of rejection lately. It was time to register a formal complaint.

'Before I go,' she said and noted with satisfaction the fact that the voices quietened at once. 'I can't say it's been nice to meet you because you haven't actually bothered to get off your backsides and come to the stage to shake my hand. Having kept me waiting nearly half an hour I think the least you could have done would be to apologize. And you have also repeatedly called me by the wrong name. It's Fitch. Not Filch or Felch. *Fitch*.'

She paused to see if anyone wanted to get a word of apology in. Apparently not. Fine, she was warming to her task now.

'I've been in this business for nearly thirty years and I have never been so insulted as to be asked if I can walk! I came here wanting this part more than anything I've wanted for . . . well, for damn near thirty years. I saw *O Jackie* on Broadway last year and it knocked me out. I thought it was fantastic. A brilliant portrayal of the woman and the times. For the audience a proper gut-wrencher. And for the actress — Dyane Schotts on Broadway and, I dared to hope, perhaps me in the West End — a real ball-squeezer of a part. Something to remind me why I'm in this profession. But, gentlemen, if your attitude this morning is indicative of the style of the London production, then I pity you. I pity you. That's all.'

The pianist was hunched over, head buried in hands, fair hair spilling through artistic fingers. Kate stared out into the near-black silence, ready to accept an apology.

But none came. She wondered how long she'd have to wait. Then a throat was cleared and an American voice she hadn't heard before, deep and resonant and powerful, surely the mysterious Mr Jungsheimer, rumbled out across the empty seats.

'Miss Fitch. Thank you for coming. Would you ask Bella to show the next Jackie in, please? Goodbye. Oh, and have a good career.'

The sound of her shoes on the bare stage rang out with terrible finality as Kate stalked into the wings.

32

A high-pitched scream echoed around the vast empty rooms of the west wing of Combes Hall.

'No! No! Please don't!' came the cut-glass tones of Lady Annabel Combes-Howard. 'Don't, please!'

'Don't you like it?'

'I love it. But it tickles, damn you.'

'Tough titties.'

She lay back in the elegant four-poster – rumoured to have been slept in once by George the Second – holding her knees in the crooks of her elbows and tingling to the thrust of her new lover's tongue.

He was pouring champagne into her navel and slurping it out noisily, following the stray dribbles with his tongue over her rounded mounds of pink flesh. He took another mouthful from the bottle, buried his face between her thighs and let the wine mix with her own juices.

'Oh God, you naughty, naughty man.'

Suddenly his bright face appeared between her ample thighs and with a giggle he spluttered champagne over her belly.

'I'm sorry? Something amusing going on down there?'

'I was just thinking, what would the customers say if they could see Aunty Annabel now, eh? Spreadeagled on her ''Cornflower'' sheets, being serviced by her young stud.'

'Stud? Hardly! Anyway, they're ''Poppyland''.'

Suddenly she sat up and stared at him, a look of shock on her aristocratic features.

'Good Lord,' she said. 'Blackcurrant meringue pie!'

'What?'

'Look at us. The colours, the textures. That's what we're

like. And it's because you're black. I know you are but I hadn't realized. If you see what I mean.'

'What are you talking about?'

'I've never been to bed with a black man before. Can't think why not. No prejudice intended. Just an oversight, I suppose. Now, here I am, practically geriatric, and new experiences are still falling into my lap. In a manner of speaking. Don't you think that's bloody wonderful?'

'Well . . .'

She wrapped her hefty legs around him as if he was her mount for the hunt and squeezed hard.

'Please, don't,' said Hal, squirming his way out from between her great thighs. 'I'm only little.'

'Yes,' she said haughtily, 'that's another thing. I thought all black men were supposed to be hung like elephants. What happened to your equipment?'

She flicked a finger at it. When it was soft like this it reminded her of the leather knob on the gear stick in the old Austin Healey Sprite she'd driven around Cambridge the year she and George had been together. Before everything changed.

Immediately she touched him the wrinkles began to smooth out as he became aroused again.

'Ha! You think that's going to impress me? I've seen bigger thingummies on garden gnomes! You're a bloody fraud, sir!' She brought her open palm down with a loud crack on his bare backside.

'Ow!' he yelled. 'I'll show you what damage this thingummy can do when it gets angry!'

Hal sprang up and pushed Annabel back on to the sheets with a display of mock machismo.

'Please,' she whimpered unconvincingly. 'Please don't hurt me . . .'

Hal sat astride her and gently pinned her arms to the bed.

'Whether it hurts or not, old lady, is entirely up to you. You're gonna get it, the only question: wet or dry?'

284

Annabel laughed at the sight of Hal, wielding what looked to her like a piece of black pudding against the pale crème caramels of her chest.

'Ooh, which do you recommend?' she asked coyly.

'Well, wet hurts.'

'And dry?'

'Dry hurts like hell.'

'Do you have any medium dry?'

In reply he thwacked her breast with his stocky cock. They let out simultaneous yelps of pain.

'All right, I'll have it wet.'

'Right answer, Auntie. Now, get wetting!'

She did as she was told.

The trill of the phone at the bedside surprised them both.

'Ow; that hurt!'

'Sorry, darling. Ignore it.'

'How can I? It's throbbing.'

'I mean the phone. Let's ignore it; they'll give up in a minute.'

They waited, marking time, unwilling to stop, unable to carry on. The phone continued to ring.

'It might be important,' Hal offered at last. 'Go on, you may as well answer it and then we can get down to business.' He rolled off her and began to examine himself for teeth marks.

'Good morning,' Annabel said brightly into the handset. Then, 'Oh, hello, Gina,' making no attempt to conceal her disappointment on hearing her daughter's voice.

'How are you, Mother?'

'I'm fine, dear. You?'

'Yeh, okay.'

'Good. Look, dear, what do you want?'

'Want? Well, I just phoned for a chat. To see how you were and so on . . .'

'No, dear. What else? What do you really want?'

'Oh, you in the middle of something?'

'Yes, I do have . . .' She reached out and fitted her action to her words. 'Something in hand right now.'

'Oh,' said Gina. 'I didn't realize. I thought –'

'Don't worry. It's not a meeting. Hal and I were just indulging in a little rumpy-pumpy.'

'Jesus. Again?'

'We didn't get it quite right before so we thought we'd have another bash at it.'

'Mother, you're fifty. And it's lunchtime, for Christ's sake!'

'I wasn't aware there was an age limit on sex. Or a curfew for that matter.'

'Dear God.'

'So how are things? You any nearer to being happy?'

'I'm getting there, Mother. Good jobs are thin on the ground, you know.'

'I said happy, not successful.'

'They're the same thing.'

'Oh dear.'

'Don't you want me to be a success?'

'Did you phone to have a row, dear, or was there some other reason?'

She heard Gina inhale deeply on one of her silly little cigars.

'Success will make me happy, Mother. I want you to help me.'

'Of course, dear, if I can.'

'I want an introduction to George King.'

Silence.

'Hello? Mother? Can you hear me? Oh, bloody British Telecom. Hello . . . ?'

'It's all right, I can hear you. Don't shout.' Annabel's voice was low and measured. She gently pulled away from Hal and sat up, hugging her knees to her chest and drawing a 'Poppyland' sheet around her as if in protection from something. 'Why? Why this fascination with him? Someone else came to me recently wanting me to bad-mouth him. He got distracted. Why do you want an introduction to him?'

'Why? It's obvious. He's at the pinnacle of the profession. Mister Television. I want to work for him. With him. I'm aiming straight at the top.'

'He's the dregs as a human being.'

'Maybe. But in the public eye he's a god. I want a part of that action. And you know him, don't you?'

'I knew him. At university. That was a long time ago. But he was a shit even then.'

'Are you still in contact with him? Do you have his private number?'

'Six, six, six.'

'What? Is that his phone number?'

'Never mind. If I did have his number I wouldn't give it to you.'

'But he's mega-famous. That's what counts.'

'Not in my book.'

'So, Mother, you won't help me?'

'No.'

'God, you're determined to thwart me at every move, aren't you?' Gina exploded. 'You want to see me suffer! You can't stand the thought of me being Someone, can you? You want all the attention yourself. Christ! What sort of fucking mother are you?'

'I don't know.' Annabel was quiet, considering it. 'I don't know. I do what I think is right, that's all. I always have. In hindsight . . .'

'Well, thanks for nothing!'

'I don't think you should be involved with someone who has the morals of –'

'I'm a big girl now; you can't vet my playmates any more.'

'I don't mean –'

'I'm sorry to have interrupted your meeting,' Gina's voice was ugly with sarcasm. 'You can get back to your nigger-fucking now!'

'Gina!'

But the line was dead.

Hal said nothing. He watched her and waited. She looked tired and confused. All of her fifty-something years. She replaced the phone slowly, frowned and shook her head slightly. Then she pinched the bridge of her nose with finger and thumb, trying to keep her self-induced sinusitis at bay.

Hal slipped a hand under the sheet and between her cold thighs. She seemed not to notice.

'Jig-a-jig?' he asked quietly.

'Hm?' She looked through him, almost uncertain who he was. 'Oh. No, Hal. Just hold me. Hold me tight.'

33

At breakfast on the second day Boris stood up, clapped his hands and said brightly, 'So — let's fuck!'

The whole troupe went upstairs to the bathroom for the first scene of the day.

While the German boys set up lights on spindly stands and fussed over the cameras — one on a wheeled tripod, the other a smaller, hand-held job — Boris came over to talk to Ben.

'When we come to your scenes remember, never please to look at the camera. Otherwise it's so simple. Klaus says you will be a natural.'

'Well, I hope so.'

In the first scene Jürgen, grease marks across his face from his 'breakdown', was to take a shower and be surprised by Anna, the lady of the house, who would climb in with him.

Boris said a few words to Jürgen and Anna and then patted them on the shoulders like a football coach with his players before a big match.

Ben stood in a steamy corner behind one of the cameras to watch the action. It was a large bathroom but even so it was crowded with bodies, equipment and cables. He had to peer between other heads to glimpse the action. He felt the tingle of nerves even though it wasn't his scene and wished his own baptism wasn't so far off.

When Jürgen got the nod from Boris and the camera began to whir he slowly took off his tee-shirt and jeans and stepped into the shower. He soaped himself, apparently alone and unaware of the staring people and lenses.

'Ja. Sehr gut, Jürgchen. Und jetzt kommt Anna . . .'

Anna now stepped up to the shower. She had far too much eyeshadow on, Ben thought. He hoped it was waterproof. Jürgen turned his back as instructed and responded to her hands softly rubbing the soap across his broad shoulders, down his back and over his buttocks. Then she reached in between his thighs and as she grasped him he flinched visibly, then turned to her and smiled.

The cameras closed in, greedily absorbing every nuance of touch and taste as the two bodies began to entwine and enfold. Jürgen demonstrated his professional versatility by licking Anna's breasts for the benefit of one camera while probing his fingers between her spread legs for the other.

Ben lost sight of some of the subtler nuances of their performances as the crew moved around and blocked his line of sight. He didn't feel at too much of a loss. It was stuffy and airless in the bathroom and his head was beginning to ache.

For a second his mind was filled with panic. A brother and sister making love in a shower with six people filming? She did it with dogs and later he was going to be doing it with her himself. Who were these people? What was he doing with them? What had happened to his life to bring him to this?

Anna had a confident, professional touch. She kissed Jürgen on the lips, turning him slightly to make sure the camera could see their tongues slithering together like a pair of writhing pink slugs. Then she knelt before him and cupped his flesh in her hands, nuzzling her face into his groin as she would into a convenient roller towel. Jürgen made little whimpering sounds like an anxious puppy. Then she licked his balls with the kind of relish she might be expected to show if they were two scoops of her favourite ice-cream and held his dick in her immaculately manicured fingers, gazing at it with fascination as if it were the first one she'd seen, all the while working it up and down with incongruously elegant movements. She rolled it over her face and neck as if it had magic powers, overacting wildly and groaning with mock — or maybe genuine — delight.

This went on for some time and Ben had the curious sensation of wanting to fast-forward reality. On a quiet word from Boris, Anna's jaw dropped and she engulfed him into the bright red gash of her mouth, her steadying hand carefully preventing him from going too far. Her other hand wandered down the contours of her body to her own crotch, taking with it the staring eye of the smaller camera. Whatever she did there her dexterity brought mutterings of praise from Boris.

He was still giving instructions to them, every so often leaning into the shot to pluck a stray hair from her lips or touch up her blusher. At a sudden cry from Jürgen, Boris grabbed a plastic bottle from one of the assistants and quickly sprayed something all over his lead actor's groin.

'It's novocaine,' said Jo at Ben's side. 'It deadens the feeling in his dingo and stops him coming. He's only got to see his little sis naked and he practically creams his jockey shorts. Odd. Does she do anything for you?'

'No, but . . .'

'They'll use it on you if you get overheated. Don't worry, there's no lasting effect. You can still be a father one day.'

'What a terrible thought.'

The siblings returned to their task and Ben didn't strain to watch too much more between the others' shoulders. His mind wandered to the first time he'd observed two people doing something like this and he could almost taste the sticky scent of summer honeysuckle. He breathed the steamy air deep into his lungs and fought to control his rising panic.

'*Oh, ja! Jetzt! Ich komme!*'

Jürgen did his duty with groans and grimaces that implied he was gushing like a thermal geyser. Once he'd shuddered himself dry there were general rumblings of satisfaction. He coyly wrapped the offered towel around his waist and nonchalantly left the room.

291

Anna, still on her knees in the shower tray, let herself be filmed in extreme close-up, first in gynaecological detail by one of the German boys lying on his back and then from above while Boris dipped a turkey-baster into a tub of creamy gloop and squirted it over her cheeks and across her open mouth. Gob after gob he splashed into her hair and her eyes and she smiled through it all as if kneeling too near an explosion in a glue factory was her idea of heaven.

By the afternoon Ben's headache was in danger of becoming a fully-fledged migraine. He went for a walk around the impressive formal gardens and wondered how far he'd get down the road before Snake-Eyes caught up with him in the BMW and brought him back.

Inside the house again he sought out the only friendly face.

'Come on in. It'll be nice to speak English to someone.'

Jo was naked as a lie. She had one leg up on the edge of the basin and a tube of something in her hand.

'Oh, sorry, is this private?'

'Honey, there's nothing private about my privates. The only bit of my body the camera hasn't seen inside is my head. And that is not a pretty sight.'

Ben voiced his fears to her, primly averting his eyes.

'I mean, watching them in the shower didn't turn me on. I just felt . . . embarrassment. Anna's about as erotic as . . . Chelsea Clinton.'

'Aw, don't give a toss about old Hansel and Gretel,' said Jo. 'They're just into each other. Literally. Ignore them.'

'How can I ignore them if I'm supposed to be having sex with her?'

'Just think of Michelle Pfeiffer or Virginia Bottomley or whatever your fantasy is. Do it all in your head. I do.'

'I don't have a fantasy. It's the camera that turns me on.'

'The camera? Hey, that's kinky.'

'What's yours? Tom Cruise? Michael Portillo?'

'D'you really think I'd stand a chance there? No, my fantasy is getting out of fuck-films,' she said. 'Shit, this is so cold.' She was applying handfuls of the greasy stuff to herself. 'Pass me that, will you, kid?'

She was pointing at a glass bowl that contained a small bottle, some packets of something wrapped in silver foil, matches, a length of rubber tube and a syringe.

'Oh.'

'Come on, don't get squeamish. You're out in the big wide world now.'

'But . . .'

'It's just to get me through this crap. I'm not hooked. I can kick it any time I like.'

'Yeh, right.'

She picked up the syringe, licked her fingers and wiped them down the needle.

'Don't look at me like that, okay? It's all right, I'll wash it first.' She turned the cold tap on.

Downstairs in the dining-room where the big orgy scene was to be shot there was much activity by the time Ben and Jo were called. A large alsatian dog was loping about.

'He'll be doing his shots with the Aryans later on,' said Jo.

Ben laughed, then realized she hadn't been joking.

'You mean she really . . . ?'

'Yeh. Not just any dog, though. It has to be Adolf – that's his name.'

'You're winding me up.'

'I swear to you. Anyway, that's nothing. I once saw her shove this eel right up her black hole of Calcutta! Yeh, a live eel! While it's in there she warms up some butter in a pan. Weird, I thought. Then she whips it out, chops it into pieces, fries it up and eats the thing there and then. And she did the whole business *in one take*. Jeez, what a pro.'

'No!'

'I tell you, if your Walkman goes missing this weekend you know where to look!'

Boris came over to talk to Ben. He explained that they'd be shooting the cum-scenes first while he and Jürgen were 'up to it', then starting right at the beginning with the 'soft dickie' stuff and going on into the humping, so they could stay hard for a long time with less danger of coming. But there was always the novocaine. When they were able to come again Boris would take more cum-shots to be edited in somewhere.

'But, you know, it's not the boys who are the attraction, *ja*? The wankers at home want to see up the girlies' pussy-cats. You just come for me, then get hard again for lots of pumpy-shots, okay?'

'I'll see what I can do. But, you know, Anna's not exactly easy to relate to, Boris.'

'Relate to? Who the hell do you think you are? Dustin Hoffman? Just be up and coming, boy, that's what you're getting paid for!'

Ben went upstairs and stripped off, feeling distinctly unsexy. He wrapped a towel around his goosepimply body and joined the others. With a little flourish he discarded the towel and awaited instructions, arms folded protectively across his chest. His head was throbbing now. Nothing else was.

Boris and Snake-Eyes put the four of them into position; Anna on her back on the smelly carpet, Ben astride her, Jo over Anna's face and Jürgen standing ready to get his second blow of the day, this time from Jo. Holding their pose like a Victorian family they waited while one of the crew took a Polaroid for the sake of continuity.

'So, remember, this is what we are calling the cum-positions, Ben. Okay? You remember?'

'I'm hardly likely to forget.'

'We come back to this later. Okay, if we are all set, turnover, sound and . . . action.'

The other three who knew the ropes immediately went

into their pre-orgasm rituals, moaning and writhing with straight abandon. Ben tentatively pressed his face between Jo's small breasts, feeling rather impolite, wondering if he should ask her permission. But she was busy with Jürgen and didn't seem to need him at all. Below him Anna was lapping at Jo like a thirsty dog at a bowl. Where Ben expected to see a fuzz of dark hair there was none; she'd shaved completely. Waves of shame engulfed him and he wanted nothing more than to disappear.

Boris and the cameras were concentrating on the activity above his head. He whispered comments in German and English, encouraging and instructing his willing puppets. Then, with much shrieking and fake spasms Jo pretended to come, clutching at her own breasts and squeezing Ben's face between them until he thought he might never breathe again. Then Jürgen did his glue factory impersonation again and Boris applied his turkey-baster to Jo's features.

After a quick dab with Kleenex they readopted more or less their previous positions and Boris and his boys prepared to focus on Ben's fabled equipment rogering Anna.

Or so they thought.

'What the hell is wrong?' Boris demanded. 'Where is your cock?'

'I'm sorry. Give me a minute.' It was short and soft and evidently not intending to stand up for itself. Ben grabbed it and tried to bring it to life with a few jerks of his fist but it lay dormant in his palm, mocking him with its torpor. The more violent he was with it the lower it hung its sulking head.

'For Christ's sake, Ben. Anna is most insulted. What do you need to get yourself big?'

'I don't know. The camera did it before.'

'Okay, here is the camera, here are two cameras. Where is your dickie?'

'Hang on, Boris, he'll be okay; I'll fluff him. Come here, kid.' Jo dropped to her knees and matter-of-factly scooped his reluctant cock into her mouth. Half a dozen strangers watched to see if she could do the trick. Ben didn't know where to look so he closed his eyes but visions of Michael Portillo and Virginia Bottomley made him open them again.

After a couple of minutes Jo checked on the state of play, leaning back as other bodies leaned forward optimistically to see if she'd had any joy. Or rather given any.

She hadn't.

'*Ach!*'

'What's up, kid? Stage fright?' Jo held his mopy dick as if it were a raw chipolata she was about to throw on the barbie.

Jürgen helped his sister up, muttered something presumably Anglophobic and they went off into the safe area behind the cameras.

'You want drugs?' asked Boris. 'Dope? Coke? Smack? Eh? We got it.'

'No, that's not it.'

Boris leaned closer to him and spoke confidentially. 'Is it Jürgen you want? Just say so and he's yours, any which way.'

'No.'

'Adolf?'

'No!'

'Look, Boris,' said Jo. 'Why don't we get on with all the pumpy-shots and soon he'll be up like a stallion. Just like the photos. Yeh? Okay, Ben?'

'No. I don't want him in the frame flopping that thing about like a wet sock. This is not a comedy. What about my reputation? You three will fuck and the boy can watch. Perhaps it's his bent. He can join when he has a stiff Sir Dickie. Not unless!'

Boris gave Ben a look of total disdain. Without warning he grabbed Ben's 'dickie' and squeezed it as if testing an inner tube for punctures.

'Tch! So soft still. So, we shoot the three professionals. Come!'

And so while Ben sat to one side like a naughty school-boy, checking himself for any stirrings, the others duly showed him how it should be done.

They fucked and sucked and groped and probed each other, all the while in a state of apparently imminent climax. Boris instructed them and gave orders to the cameras about which body part to film and in what detail. He took them back over good moments, lining up limbs with precision to ensure each frame was an erotic master-piece. He was clearly the Busby Berkeley of fuck-films.

And his cast never let him down.

Supine on the carpet Jürgen massaged himself for a while, then Jo strode in and stood over him, straddling his slim hips. She wore shiny high heels, suspenders and cheap fishnet stockings and looked stunning. Cheap and tacky, but stunning.

Ben checked: nothing doing down below.

As Jo lowered herself down the cluster of shadowy figures behind the cameras moved around and Ben heard her moan and gurgle with convincing rapture.

When they broke to reload the camera with film Jo came over to him.

'Well, anything stirring in the close tonight?'

He checked. His cock had curled up to sleep against his thigh, its hood pulled up over its head to keep the light out of its eye. It had shrunk to almost normal proportions. 'Nothing stirring. I don't think it ever will again.'

Boris called for quiet, the cameras began to purr and Jo was pressed into action again, this time with both Jürgen and Anna.

Now there were few instructions from Boris. The three pros knew what they had to do and they got on with it. Another day at the orifice.

Tongues and fingers strayed over soft white and hard brown skin. Mouths and breasts and one Sir Dickie all met in hungry conjunction and three writhing bodies, bathed in a glow of sweat, humped and pumped in candid abandon on the flawless floor. They all moaned and sighed and cried out loud as the pitch of erotic pleasure was squeezed to new heights of make-believe.

Boris breathed heavily. '*Ja*,' he said quietly. '*Prima*.'

Ben turned aside, found a damp towel to cover his nakedness and slunk quietly away from the sticky knot of human flesh.

'You're not Boris' favourite person,' Jo said to him later that evening as they shared a joint in the kitchen. Anna and Jürgen were busy elsewhere. The plot was out of the window by now.

'I'm not surprised. He must be furious.'

'Hey, we all got nervous first time.'

'It wasn't just nerves. I was watching, thinking . . . well, it's so . . . sordid, isn't it? What a waste of a life. Lying there in the water while he was at it . . .'

'What water? You're rambling. You've smoked too much.'

'I mean, lying there on the carpet.'

'Couldn't switch your brain off, eh? Maybe you're lucky.'

'What did Boris say?'

'Oh, a lot of crap about "bloody English public school wankers". But don't take it personally.'

'Klaus'll be furious. I've let him down as well.'

'Tough. It happens.' She passed him the joint. 'I saw the pics he did of you. Terrific stuff.'

'You think so?'

'Yeh. Good face; lovely eyes.'

'Funny, I didn't think those were what would catch your attention.'

'Oh, big dick, sure. But that's nothing to do with character, is it?'

'I don't know. I was starting to think that's all I had.'

'Bullshit. Ben – is that your real name?'

'Yes.'

'I thought it probably was. Look, don't undervalue yourself, Ben. Just because everyone else does. I don't think of myself as "just a fuck-queen". I'm Jo. And one day . . . oh, sod it.'

'I've fouled up again, haven't I?' Ben said. 'I shouldn't be here. I've wasted everyone's time and messed up your filming.'

'Bollocks. Boris will get another sour Kraut out here in an hour or so. He'll boldly come where every other man has come before and another masterpiece'll be in the can. It's only a bit of hanky wanky. Here, don't waste that.'

He passed her the soggy joint.

'You know, kid, I'm glad we didn't do it for the cameras. It wouldn't have been right. You're too good for this shit-heap. I feel somehow . . .' She looked very serious for a moment and then sucked on the stub of the joint and said, 'Oh, don't let me get sentimental and go all soft. I've got to stay hard to finish my last scene.'

'*You've* got to stay hard?'

'Listen, mate, would you mind if I . . . ? No, never mind.'

'What?'

She leaned over and kissed him on the cheek like a six-year-old with her first sweetheart.

'There. Good luck, kid.'

'You didn't have to ask permission for that.'

'No, it was something else. Doesn't matter.'

'May I . . . ?' He kissed her. Gently, shyly, not sure if this was allowed. When their tongues met he pulled away, embarrassed.

'What's the matter?'

'Boris would be proud of me,' he said, looking down at the tell-tale bump in his jeans. 'I suppose it's too late now?'

'Too late for Boris, maybe . . .'

34

'Fuckingbastardcuntingshittinghell!'

Gina Howard was not happy.

As she muttered to herself she paced her cramped flat, the image of a caged lion with her thick hair loose around her pinched face. From time to time she raked through her red mane the hand that wasn't holding the burning cheroot.

'Oh buggerit!'

Why her mother was being so intransigent she didn't know. Her own frustration at the stagnancy of her career was heightened by the news that a college contemporary had become co-presenter of an afternoon chat show on Channel Four. It was a pretty naff show that tried with the desperation of an ageing whore to appeal to all of the people all of the time, on one glorious occasion following an item on bereavement with a vicar juggling exotic fruit, but to present even a bad show was still to win brownie points in the eternal struggle for 'Success'. The world, or at least a small part of it, would soon know who Felicity Hosken was. Who the hell was aware of Gina Howard's existence?

'Soddit.'

But what was afternoon exposure on 'Pull up a Chair' compared with controlling the George King Show? For that's where Gina had set her sights. There was nobody and nothing bigger than George King in the media, he was everywhere on the small screen, in voice-overs, commercials, guesting on other people's talk shows, endorsing products, profiled in the papers and magazines, on roadside hoardings, he was discussed in gossip columns, pubs and houses throughout the country. He was at the very top — and Gina intended to be up there with him.

Her letters had been ignored. Three now. And her mother, too busy making millions and indulging her new-found taste for dark meat, was now refusing to help her make contact with this demigod.

She'd get there somehow. By foul means or worse. She wasn't sure where yet but there was a way in, she was certain of that. She'd have to get at this one through his manager, his agent, his PA or maybe even his wife . . .

Ah. Now something was beginning to happen. A scheme began to bubble to the surface of the slimy murk of her mind. She stood still, feet set apart as if braced for a blow, one hand on bony hip, one at her mouth, feeding another rush of nicotine to the brain. Her eyes were shut tight in concentration on both the drug and the plan, tasting the moment.

For a long minute the only movement was the curl of grey smoke spiralling up from the tip of her cheroot to the already stained ceiling. Then she exhaled noisily. Yes, she had it. The cathedral tapes. That was it. You never knew when a good bit of juicy gossip would come in useful.

'Hello, Jasper?' she breathed down the phone. 'It's Gina. Gina Howard. Yah . . . Hi. Yes, fine. You? . . . Good, great. Look, babe, I thought you might like to know that a few very choice turds are about to hit the fan and I'm afraid you're in danger of catching it full face. Well, not everyone can boast of a threesome in the organ loft with a boxer and a bishop's wife. And during Evensong too. Really! No, Jasp, don't interrupt. Just listen. You see, the thing is I know the person who was holding a camcorder . . . Quite . . . Hm? . . . No, I'm afraid it's not as simple as that. I have a little proposition to make . . .'

Really, Jasper couldn't have been more co-operative. His ecclesiastical connection was obviously too much of a social cachet to risk losing.

Gina was actually smiling as she dialled the next number.

'Hello?'

'Hello. May I speak to George King, please?'

'I'm afraid Mr King is not available at the moment,' said a tight-arsed female voice. 'Who's calling?'

'It's Gina Howard. Of the BBC.'

'Gina Howard?'

'Yes.'

'Can I help, Miss Howard?'

'You are . . . ?'

'I'm Mr King's personal assistant.'

'Oh yes, of course, we met at that party in Kensington the other month. I'm so sorry, I didn't recognize your voice,' Gina bluffed.

'Er, well . . .'

'Carol, isn't it?'

'Becca.'

'Becca, of course!' It never failed. 'How are you, Becca?'

'Fine. I'm sorry, Miss Howard I –'

'Is George there, Becca, sweetie? I just need a quick word.'

'I'm afraid not. He's gone to –' She stopped, professionalism intact. 'He's not here at the moment. May I be of assistance, Miss Howard?'

'Gina, please. Well, I do really need to speak to George but . . .' Get her on your side, it could pay dividends later. 'You see, Becca, we're planning a series on the top media figures. The face behind the mask, you know the sort of thing. Nothing intrusive; home life, wife, kids, hobbies and so on. Very *Hello*. What they're like away from the camera, ordinary people with ordinary problems. We're thinking about Frost, Dimbleby – either one, it doesn't make any difference – Bragg and so on. But we really want to launch the series with the biggest fish of all. George. If he's agreeable. So I'd really like to discuss it with him. Is it the sort of thing that would interest him? What do you think,

Becca? You know him even better than any of us, after all.'

'I think it might interest him,' Becca said. 'But obviously I can't answer for Mr King. You should really write to his agent, you know.'

'Yes, I've done that. I've also written to George himself but I've had no reply.'

There was a silence from the other end of the line, which Gina sensed was a guilty one, confirming her suspicion that this prissie Missie was responsible for intercepting George King's mail. 'Mind you, perhaps they were lost in the post,' she said, offering a way out. She needed Becca's trust after all.

'Yes. Perhaps.'

'Look, Becca, this may seem an awful imposition but I do want to give this baby the best chance of success — I was wondering if I could buy you lunch one day next week and ask your advice about how to present my case to George?'

There was no reply. A good sign; no outright rejection. Gina pressed home her advantage.

'It's just that with your knowledge of the great man you could point me in the right direction so that I wouldn't be wasting my time when it comes to interesting George in the project. I wouldn't take up too much of your time, Becca, I promise.'

'I'm not sure that I'm that much of an authority on Mr King but yes, all right. It would have to be Tuesday, though. That's the only day I'm free for lunch.'

'Tuesday's fine,' said Gina, mentally deleting two other appointments. 'Now, where shall we meet?'

When Becca put the phone down she checked with the computer again. No, still no entry for 'Gina Howard'. Strange. She wondered what this 'Gina Howard of the BBC' was up to. Whatever it was Becca wasn't afraid to find out.

*   *   *

'Large gin and tonic, no ice, no lemon. And . . . ?'

'Perrier, please, with a slice of lemon. But I only want ice if it's cubes of Perrier. Not tap water.'

'No ice then.'

When the pretty but vacant waiter brought their drinks he took their order for food. Gina chose the quail's egg salad with garlic bread followed by fish pie and the *légumes du jour*. When asked what they were the waiter explained, 'They're the vegetables of the day.' Becca asked for the board of French and English cheeses with wholewheat crackers.

'I don't usually eat lunch,' she explained. 'That will be quite sufficient.'

Gina tried to mask the supercilious curl of her lip with a polite smile, but her eyes were cold and critical as she observed Becca's style and tried to work her out.

They were eating at Brasserie Zeppo, the brand-newest and super-trendiest of Soho's recent plethora of locations for the smart set to be seen. Around them men in funny suits and silly glasses and women in tiny hats and dramatic lipstick talked too loudly of deals, dates and diets.

Gina's instincts prompted her to catch eyes and phrases as she could – anything might prove useful one day – but with an effort of will she concentrated on her current project: Ms Becca Nichols.

They discussed the mythical series on media people at great length. Gina hoped she was giving the impression of being enthusiastic, candid and even – she'd do it if it killed her – charming.

'The working title is "At Home with the Stars", but that could change.'

'Yes, I see.' Becca nibbled at her food antiseptically and gazed levelly back. Gina knew she was being measured up by those large, calm, cow-like eyes.

'What aspects of Mr King's life would you be interested in, in particular?'

'Well . . . Becca . . . that's what I really need you for.

Since you know his typical working day better than anyone else I'd like to pick your brains. What do you think the public would be most interested and entertained to learn about their idol?'

Gina pushed her oversized specs up into the exotic mass of hair piled and pinned on her head. She waited as Becca dabbed deliberately at the corners of her mouth with the thick linen napkin before replying. 'Frankly I think that Mr King is of the opinion that he reveals to the general public already just as much as he wishes to reveal.'

'Yes. Except that it seems odd, to his fans, to see him so often on the small screen and yet know so little about him. As a man. As a husband and a father. As a boss, too. What's he like to work for? Work with? That's what we'd want to cover. Fly on the wall for a few days; you know the routine. See him chatting with friends over dinner, washing the car, walking the dog.'

'I can't believe you'd want your name attached to such a dull hagiography. Whether as researcher or producer.'

'Well, no, not dull. But there is a fascination with the ordinary details of extraordinary people's lives. Maybe we'd catch a family row over something trivial. You know, let the world see him as he really is.'

Becca smiled and delivered her well-practised dismissal.

'If you have a written proposal you'd like Mr King to consider I'd be happy to put it to him on your behalf. Formally, through the correct channels, of course.'

'Of course.'

Yes, you do everything formally, don't you? thought Gina. All your channels are correct. Don't you ever sweat, belch, fart? Or come? No, I don't think you do.

She looked at Becca with new eyes, suddenly reading the neat, mean body language in quite a different way.

My God, she thought, you poor frightened little thing. I know what your trouble is. Do you guiltily finger yourself under the duvet and feel remorse even before any pleasure has begun? You need help, my girl, you need a helping

305

hand. Maybe a tongue. *And I think I'm just the person to provide them . . .*

They carried on talking, ostensibly about the theoretical series, but gradually, and as subtly as anything she did ever could be, Gina turned the conversation around more and more to focus on Becca herself until finally Becca placed her short, clean, unvarnished nails together as if about to pray and said, 'Miss Howard, I thought it was my employer you wished to discuss. You seem to be more interested in my life than his . . . ?'

Gina said nothing but raised her eyebrows in a way that said, 'Yes, so?' and held Becca's reproving gaze for a long, challenging moment. She was delighted to notice twin spots of colour high on Becca's cheeks as she broke eye contact first. Good! Embarrassment was always useful. She was making progress here.

'Look, Becca,' Gina leaned forward on the table and toyed with a salt cellar to avoid coming on too strong. 'It's a long shot but I find you very interesting. I feel we have a certain . . . rapport. I have these two tickets for a show next week and I've been let down. I don't suppose you'd be interested . . . ?'

'How kind. What's the show?'

'It's the new Lloyd Webber.'

'Oh, sorry, I'm busy.'

'I haven't said which night yet.'

'You don't need to.'

Gina smiled. 'How about a movie then?'

'Very well. After all, I can cut my toenails some other time.'

Becca smiled back, acknowledging the game they were both playing.

'Cheers,' said Becca, holding up her Perrier. 'Here's to a pleasant evening.'

Gina held up her G & T.

'Cheers,' she said. 'Here's to a *useful* evening.'

35

Hal pressed the entryphone and waited.

'Hello?' came a tinny voice.

'Hi, I'm a friend of George's,' he said.

Silence.

'He suggested I should call and see you.'

'George who?'

'Well, I don't like to say, out here in the street. But, he's not a queen . . .' No response. 'He's *your* George.'

There was a beat. Then: 'What do you want?'

'Look, it would be much easier if we could talk inside. Less public.'

He waited while she considered this.

'Hang on.'

The box went dead and in a few seconds he heard locks and chains being released on the other side of the pale lemon mock Georgian door. Through frosted glass he could see a vague shape moving.

The door opened a crack and above a restraining chain one eye looked up at him.

'Who are you, then?'

'Do you recognize me?'

She thought about it. 'No. Should I? Have we met?'

'No. My name's Harold.' He held out a hand which she looked down at briefly.

'Harold what?'

'Oh. Um . . . Harold Steptoe.'

'Oh yeh. I think I've heard of you, haven't I?'

'Possibly. I work in . . . the media. It was George . . .' he lowered his voice dramatically, 'Mr K. who suggested I should call. You see, I'm involved in the advertising campaign for Auntie Annabel's Country Kitchen and we're scouting for interior locations at the moment. He happened to mention to me that your home might be just what we're looking for. I don't know if you'd be interested? There'd be a considerable sum involved, of course.'

'Adverts?'

'Yes. Posters and television. The client is happy to spend a lot of money on this and we've got to get exactly the right look. We'd naturally take care of the cost of any redecoration necessary. If I could just have a quick gander, it wouldn't take more than five minutes, I promise.'

'I don't know. I'm not supposed to talk to people who come to the door.'

'Yes, he told me that. But I think Mr King, George, was hoping you'd be interested.'

The door opened a couple of inches so they could each see more of each other. She had tight denim jeans on and an even tighter red sweater; the two items failed to meet by about three bulging inches.

'Well . . . all right. You can come in. But only for a few minutes.'

The door closed and the chain came off. As she let him into the small hall Hal noticed that she cast a suspicious eye into the empty mews.

She showed him through into the sitting-room.

'Oh yes, yes,' Hal enthused, noticing that he was getting camper by the minute. 'Divine. I think this could be just what we're after. George was right, bless him. But he so often is, isn't he? I've always said if you want a decision taken ask George. Have you known him long?'

'Oh, Georgie and I go back a long way,' she said with a proud little smile, then looked guilty and added quickly, 'But he wouldn't like me to tell you about things like that.'

'No, no, I understand,' said Hal. 'You can trust me, Miss . . . Oh, I'm such a muddlehead, I've forgotten your name. I had it written down in my papers in the car.'

'Sparks. Suzi Sparks,' she said obediently. This was going to be a doddle.

'Of course, how could I forget? Suzi with an "i"? Yes, I had a feeling it might be. Much classier, somehow, Suzi.' Hal took a notebook from his pocket and jotted in it. 'This room is exactly the sort of thing the client is after. I wonder, could I just take some measurements?' His steel rule was at the ready.

'Well, I don't see that can do any harm.'

'Oh thank you. Some people get so fussy about everything, when in fact if their property is used they get a complete do-over all at our expense so it's in their interest to be as co-operative as poss. Could you hold this a mo? Up against the wall, if you would.' He gave a little giggle.

She held the end of the tape while Hal fussed about and pretended to note down dimensions.

Suzi Sparks. Red sweater. Dyed blonde. Blue eyes. Early 30s??? Empty chocbox. Candlesticks. Love nest. G and I go back a long way. Thank God he'd learnt shorthand.

'Nice curtains. Austrian swags always flatter, don't you find?'

'They were here when I moved in.'

'Mm-hm. And what is it exactly that you do now, professionally speaking, as your line of work?'

'I don't work now. I used to be a model.'

'A model? No! I was saying to myself that's what you were, 'cos you've got the looks for it and the bearing too. I said, Harold, she's a model or I'm Dorothy Squires. It's the way you hold yourself, isn't it? And how did you and George meet, then?'

'Well, we . . . he . . . our work brought us together.'

'Oh yes? Eight feet and ten inches . . . How was that?'

'Oh you know . . .' He waited but nothing more came.

'Would it be okey-dokey to have a look-see in the *boudoir*?'

'Sorry?'

'The master bedroom? Or should I say "mistress" . . . ?'

309

They giggled together, neither quite sure which way to take this.

'Well, I suppose so. Just a look would be all right. It's through here.' She waddled ahead of him.

'Oh, it's the bee's balls,' he enthused, gazing at the circular bed with scarlet leather headboard and white fluffy pillows. He could already feel the buzz of scandal as the story hit the streets. Something about 'King's Lady in Waiting' perhaps.

'And look at that, you've got the same Snoopy poster I've got in my bedroom. Isn't that amazing? We're soulmates you and me, Suzi. I'll bet you're a . . . wait, don't tell me . . . Libra?'

'Libra-Virgo cusp, yes.'

'I knew it. Oh, this is so perfect and I'll never be able to do it justice when I try to describe it to the boss back at base. I wonder . . . Do you think . . . ? I hardly like to ask, but since we have this special understanding I'm going to be bold. I just couldn't live with myself if I didn't put it to you. Now, here I go. Do you think I could just snap a quickie or two so I'm not misrepresenting you and your *scrummy* bedroom ambience at our locations meeting?'

'Ah, no, I don't think –'

'I understand, it's a bit of an imposition. Tell you what, my darling, after I've shown the girls at the office I'll send you back the photies and that way we're all happy, yes?'

'Well, I still don't –'

'The negs, I mean. And you can destroy them if you want. Oh, this is *such* perfection. George will be so pleased we've found the location.' He took the camera from his briefcase and lined up some shots. 'Oh, yes. It could have been built for the Auntie Annabel campaign. So classy, so chic . . .'

'Classy? Is it, really?'

'It *reeks* of sophistication! Like something out of "Dynasty". I'll just take one or two.'

He clicked away quickly, moving around and trying to

catch her in each one but she stayed behind him all the time.

'Hm. It's just the sense of scale I'm missing.'

'I thought that's why you were measuring.'

'Well, yes, you're right. For literal scale, but for a sense of visual proportion I need something the eye can relate to. Let's see, what about . . . ?'

'My Garfield pyjama case?'

'Love it to death, natch, but it does nothing to define the space. It's something more *human* I need. Let's see . . .' He looked about, waiting for her to get there.

'Human? Um . . . well . . . oh, what about me?' She got there.

'You?'

'Yes, me. Something human. If I sit on the bed you'll get a sense of visual scale from me, won't you?'

'Lordy me, you're right.'

She sat on the edge of the bed, legs crossed, leaning back on straight arms, one shoulder slightly dipped and her chin lowered so she could look up through her blue-tinted lashes at the camera.

'Gosh. You're naturally creative. Typical Libra-Virgo cusp. You've done this before, haven't you?'

'Well, sort of.'

'Hmm. Nice, but I'm not sure sweater and jeans quite show the room off to its best advantage. A tad — forgive me Suzi — suburban? What do you think we should do?'

'Well I could put something different on.'

'You're a one hundred per cent trezh, you know that? I don't want to be a nuisance but I do think that might just make the diff. If you were in something more . . . well, more in keeping with the *tout ensemble*, with the slightly *fin de siècle* character of the *chambre*, do you think? Then we'd really get a sense of how the commercials would work. This is the location, I just know it!'

'Fan de . . . ?'

'Naughty Nineties. Something saucy?'

'Ooh, I've got some lovely saucy outfits. Give me a couple of ticks and you'll get your pics, I promise.'

She laughed, into the whole thing now.

Candy from a retarded baby, thought Hal with just a tinge of remorse.

36

'They want to see you again, lovey.'

Kate was confused. 'Who? What about?'

'You've got a recall for the show.'

'Sorry, Robin. What show?' She'd wiped it from her mind.

'What show? Only the show you've been obsessed with for the past three months. The J.F. bloody K. show. They want to see you again. To work with the choreographer and the MD.'

'But I was so rude to them.'

'Yes, they said something about your being . . . "feisty", I think the word was. I told them you were always like that when you were pissed off.'

'Oh Robin, you didn't.'

'Yes, I explained that an actress of your calibre is not used to being treated to the cattle market audition. They ought to handle you in a more civilized manner next time. As befits your status.'

He was right. The next meeting with the *O Jackie* team was in a very nice room of a very large suite in their very expensive Park Lane hotel. The mysterious Mr Jungsheimer was absent this time; Kate met Miguel again with the choreographer Lars, Dwight-the-Director and the willowy Jean-Pierre whose role was never clearly defined but who seemed to know everything about everything. He might have been Dwight-the-Director's assistant or maybe Mr J.'s right-hand man. He made a lot of notes and even pointed a video camera at her while she was going through some simple steps with Lars. After asking her permission, of course.

The longer she was there dancing, talking, reading scenes, singing and discussing the project, the more definitely she knew she really did want this part. She tried to explain to Miguel, the most approachable of the boys — and they were boys, not much more than Jack Fever's age — how determined she was to play Jackie, but she guessed every actress they were seeing presented an equally vehement case.

For three hours she sweated, desperate to convince them that she could sing, act, dance, take direction and be a good guy to have in the company. Even when they took breaks for tea and sandwiches she was on trial. How she sat, reacted with them, the way she spoke, her political and cultural attitudes all had a bearing on the report they would make to Mr Jungsheimer.

And all the time she felt the part slipping away. She could tell by their struggling questions and encouragement that she just wasn't up to scratch.

'Well, let's try it one more time,' Dwight-the-Director would say. 'Maybe we'll get closer to the heart this time.'

'Don't worry,' from Lars. 'It'll come, just relax.'

Miguel played the white Bechstein grand for her, urging her to ever greater theatricality in his clever-clever songs, then ignored her interpretation and sang it himself for his own enjoyment and said, 'Let's take a break, shall we? J-P, you wanna order some beers?'

He stopped his note-taking just long enough to ring room service then picked up his pen again and returned to his task.

Kate was heartbroken. She knew she was failing the unspoken test and yet there was nothing she could do. Would she have to accept the cruellest rejection of all? 'You just weren't right for the part.'

'Well, thanks for coming, it's been great,' Jean-Pierre said to her with an air of finality and apology. 'I'll be in touch with your agent when we know a little more. We have a lot of people to see and then a great deal to do.

And listen, Kate, you were right to bawl us out last week. We were a bit . . . American, weren't we? You Britishers do things more politely. Keep it that way. We love your quaint customs. Have a good day, now. Ta-ta!'

In the cab on the way home she replayed every moment, every comment in her mind, looking for positive interpretations but finding none. She'd lost it, the part of the season, the part of her life.

Lost it to whom? One of the regulars? Maggie, Judi, Vanessa or Emma. Seagrove, Suzman or Rigg. She was known neither by her Christian nor surname. Even as Kate Fitch in full she was less of a household name than Domestos or Andrex.

'I could have been Judi Dench!' she muttered to the beautiful, empty house as she went in the front door. 'Dame sodding Judi. Hibernating like Mrs Tiggywinkle in my country cottage with my comfortable marriage, making forays into sitcoms and the odd limited run in another classic on the South Bank! That's what I was supposed to do!'

Except that she'd got pregnant because of George's incompetence and he'd convinced her a child would be wonderful publicity and in those days she'd believed everything he said. By the time she discovered it was only good publicity for him and disfiguring hard work for her it was too late. His star rose as hers sank. First she couldn't work, then when she was available again nobody wanted to know. They had other, more marketable products whose momentum had not been interrupted by a 'mistake'. She'd been slowly working her way back into the public eye when . . .

'I could have been Vanessa!' she shouted. 'But let's face it who'd want to be?' Then the waves of bitter disappointment hit her, tumbling over her like the crashing breakers on the north Devon coast that had so frightened her as a little girl.

She checked her watch. Yes, she still had time to shower,

change and relax before driving up to bloody Birmingham for that night's show.

The show with Jack. They were both giving terrible performances, neither making proper contact with the other in any of their scenes. Even Beate had noticed.

As if the Jackie disappointment and the Jack Fever disaster and the George feud weren't enough, there was the Ben situation. That needed to be resolved somehow, but Kate couldn't see how. One day maybe they would be able to sit and talk to each other as adults without all the shared pain preventing them from making emotional contact. No, she doubted it. Their moment was past.

Anyway, this wasn't the time to get her brain around that one; she had to get going and head north.

'Hello, Mother.'

Ben's face was there before her, peering round the high side of a chair by the fire, as if conjured up by her thought-power.

'My God, Ben! I mean, hello.'

'Hello.'

They stared at each other, not sure whether to touch, uncertain quite what relationship they had. If any.

'I thought I might drop in. If that's all right. I was on my way home.'

'Of course it's all right. This is your home.'

'Not any more. I thought we should . . . look, if you're busy I'll go.' He stood up.

'No, no. Stay. I have to drive up to Birmingham but not just yet. Let's have some tea. Would you like that? I'll ring for Marcella. Or coffee? Have you had lunch? Or a drink?'

'I don't want anything.'

'All right.'

They both sat, opposite each other in huge leather chairs and neither spoke for a long time.

'So, Ben, how are you?'

'I'm okay.'

'That's nice. You've been away then?'

'Yes, I've just been to Germany. I went to . . . to see some friends.'

'Oh. Friends from university?'

'No, friends . . . just friends.'

'Uh-huh. That's nice.' God, she thought, why is this so difficult? It's my fault, I've alienated him, he has no trust or respect for me. It's like — what was that Hopkins play she'd been up for all those years ago with Maurice Denham? — *Talking to a Stranger.* Judi got that too.

'You weren't in Stuttgart, were you? I played the theatre there once as Lady —'

'Yes, yes,' he said quickly. 'You told me. I wasn't in Stuttgart.'

'Ah. You've had your hair cut.'

'I know.'

What now? Surely it wasn't always like this. Hadn't they been friends once? When he had reached for her hand before crossing the road and run to her side and snuggled into the folds of her skirt when danger threatened. When she had kissed his grazed knees better, played games with him on boxes that became monsters and spaceships and sung 'Puff the Magic Dragon' to him at bedtime. How could that special intimacy just die and leave no trace in him of affection, let alone love?

'Ben, about the future, about work . . .'

'Mother.'

'You have to think about it. You can't just drop out and —'

'I am thinking about it. And when I've come to some conclusion I'll let you know.'

'But you're a talented young man. You could do all sorts of things. If you asked him I'm sure your father could help you.'

'I wouldn't ask him for the time of day.'

'Ben. Give him a chance. He is your father.'

'Unfortunately.'

'Once you're back on the rails again —'

'You know, Mother, I sometimes feel like lying across them and waiting for the train to come.'

'Oh, Ben. Let me talk to George. You could work as a researcher.'

'No.'

'Just for a few weeks, to earn some pocket money, I'm sure he –'

'*No, Mother!* I want nothing to do with him.'

They backed off, leaving each other a breathing space. Kate looked at him and saw a little boy who needed a hug and a 'there, there'. But she didn't move.

'How are you?' he asked at last and Kate's heart leapt with gratitude. 'All right?'

'Me? Oh, I'm . . .' A mess, clinging on to reality, on the verge of a breakdown, drinking too much, distraught, depressed, desperate . . . 'I'm fine.'

'I thought you looked a little, well . . .'

'Ben, I'm sorry.'

'Look, Mother –'

'I'm sorry for what happened when you came to the play. We both said . . . I said some things I had no right to say.'

'Please, you don't have to –'

'It's not a good time at the moment, you see. That's no excuse for being insensitive, but I wanted you to know.'

'I didn't come here for –'

'Ben, let me try to – I want to apologize for all the – You see, I'm under a certain amount of pressure. I mean, your father's being – he's very . . . well, you know your father. And what with one thing and another . . . Sorry, I'm not being very – I'm sorry. I suppose I just don't want you to think badly of me because of what was said. I can't blame you if you do, of course, but I am your mother, after all, and that's very special, isn't it?'

'You don't have to go on with this,' Ben said. 'At least not for my benefit. What you said isn't in reality all that important.'

318

'There you are, you see. You dismiss everything so easily. I don't believe this brittle façade is you at all. You push everything so deep to stop it hurting you and it'll only work its way out in some other way. It's not healthy, Ben.'

He got up and pretended to browse along the bookshelf. 'This coffee-table analysis is fascinating but very wide of the mark, I fear. Or are you rehearsing for something? "Who's a-Freud of Virginia Woolf"?'

He turned to her with a smart expression but she didn't smile.

'Ben, don't. You don't need to show off now. Why can't you just talk to me?'

'Why? I'd have thought you could work that one out.' He walked over to the window. For once it wasn't raining. 'Your garden's looking rather the worse for wear. Aren't you keeping the domestics up to scratch?'

'Why did you come? Just to score points? I have to go to work. If there's nothing –?'

'I'm sorry if my presence is not convenient for you. Mind you, it never has been. I'm a bit of an embarrassment all round, really, aren't I?'

'Ben . . .'

'Have been for twenty years. Getting in the way, saying the wrong things, doing the wrong things, like breathing, like living! Well, pardon my existence. Not that I expect you to. Not at this stage of events. I'll just crawl off to my hole and leave you alone. I shan't bother you again. If you see my father –'

'Ben, stop it!' Kate stood up and confronted him. She searched his eyes for the truth behind his bitterness but all she saw was ingrained, seething anger. 'Please, don't do this. I don't understand why you're punishing me. If you hate me so much, tell me what I've done wrong. I'd like to put it right if I can.'

She reached out to brush his hair back from his face but he jerked his head sharply away, never taking his eyes off her.

'You can't. Not now. So many years you could have tried to make it better but it's no longer ... You can't undo what you've done. You've got to live with it, just as you forced me to do. I've been trying to get my head sorted out with my writing. I thought the winds in Norfolk would blow the cobwebs out of my head. But they're cold winds and all they do is chill my blood. I'm alone in this. It's up to me to get things straight. Your role is over. You're not a part of my life. Not any more. You have to understand that.'

Kate felt a tightness in her chest that increased with his every word.

'No, no, darling. I'll always be a part of you because you were a part of me. That can never be undone. Don't reject me when I need you. Please!'

He gave a short laugh. 'Oh, I see; you're getting a taste of rejection now. It's not much fun, is it?'

'But I didn't reject you. Is that what you're saying? You were special to me. You are special. I gave you everything.'

'Yes, everything your husband's money could buy.'

'No,' she whispered. 'Time, affection. Love. Things only a mother can give.'

Wearily he looked away from her, down to the floor.

'I feel as if I don't have any parents. I think of myself as an orphan.'

Kate crumpled into a chair and was surprised by the delicate splash of a tear bursting into a neat dark stain on the pale silk of her dress. She sniffed and wiped her hand across her eyes, thinking that she'd been making a fool of herself too many times in recent days. With Barney Jungsheimer, with George, with Jack. Now here she was again.

'I may have made mistakes — what parent doesn't? — but I do love you and I want to hear you say you still love me.'

She was sniffling quietly, trying not to cry but knowing there was no hope now of retaining her dignity. She

320

needed Ben to salvage her self-respect with his forgiveness.

He was staring at her, appalled.

'I love you, Ben. Do you hear me? I love you.'

Still he was silent.

'Ben. Say it. Please,' she begged him urgently. 'I need to hear you say it. Say you love me.'

For a long moment she thought he wasn't going to respond at all. She was about to run to him and clutch him to her, hoping she could squeeze the words from him.

'I'll say it if that's what you want. I l—'

'No! I want you to mean it. You do, don't you?' She was desperate now, a love-junkie clamouring for a fix. 'I'm your mother. You're my baby. You do love me. Say it.'

Ben was quiet and undramatic. 'I don't know if I do. I'm not saying I don't. The fact of the matter is, Mother, I'm not sure.'

'Ben!' Her cry was full of anguish, her route to salvation blocked. 'Please don't do this! *Help me!*'

'I'm afraid I simply don't have the space in my head to worry about your problems. I've been screwing up my life. I learned it all from you. I just carried on what you started.'

His eyes were unfeeling and unkind. Cold and capable of witnessing any torture, of watching any amount of pain.

'Ben, don't do this to me. Not today. I've been . . . I can't take any more, I can't . . .'

But he had no pity; his voice took on a new hardness and he seemed to change up a gear to drive his point home.

'What about taking responsibility for your own actions? Wouldn't that be the mature thing to do? Oh no, you always blame others, don't you? Do you ever wonder why I've never felt good enough for you? Why my whole life I've had a gnawing sense of inadequacy? Of not measuring up, not at school, not with my writing, not with my friends. Nothing could ever have been good enough, could it? I was always a failure to you, always. Because of who I was. And more to the point who I wasn't and never could be!'

She turned her face to him, her dark eyes blazing with

a passion that was hers alone, not manufactured for an audience. She took a deep breath. But she knew something that really mattered was happening here. It was a row they needed to have. Not *the* row — maybe they would never be strong enough to have that one — but it was a step towards dealing with the big problem.

'Have I been such a terrible mother?'

'Yes,' he said calmly. 'You've really fucked my life up.'

'My own is messed up too, you know.'

'That doesn't make mine any better. What happened, happened. We've never accepted it. It's eaten you away too. Which is why you're touring in shit plays pretending to be a star.'

'Don't, Ben.'

'And why I'm throwing my life away.'

'Please, I'm sorry if —'

'And you still think it was all my fault, don't you? I mean all of it. Everything. The thing this is really all about.'

'No, don't let's bring that up. It's gone.'

She reached out, wanting to touch him, hide the ugliness of his cruel face against her breast and make them both feel all right. It used to work, twenty years ago.

'It's not gone! It's not gone! It can't go away, because it's in us both. *It's killing us both.*'

'Ben, no!'

'It might just as well have been me who went under that day! I've been dead ever since! There! Does that make you feel better? Does that make you happy?'

'Don't say things like that.'

'I know why you hated me so much. I can't bring him back, Mother. Neither can you. He's dead and he's taken us both with him. We don't function properly any more. We're finished. Face it! We might just as well have died with him that day. We're dead people! *We're just as dead as Christopher!*'

The calculated venom of his words shocked and terrified her. For a second she wasn't sure if the figure glaring at her was George and was about to hit her or Jack who might make love to her. It was both of them and neither of them.

Ben held her gaze with his own, challenging her to call him a liar. She couldn't. For a few dreadful seconds there was a silence like the sound after a gunshot when it seems to echo in the mind. Then, very quietly, a lifetime of regret in his tired voice, he said, 'I shouldn't have come. I had no right to expect anything from you.'

Dragging his heavy limbs he walked past her just out of reach, denying her contact with him.

'Wait —'

'Look. I understand why you feel guilty about ruining my life,' he said. 'I don't forgive you, but I understand. Now I have to get on with it by myself. Somehow. All I've been doing so far is making it worse. Maybe there's no hope. I'll find out. But I see now that I have to do it without you.' He was about to go but there was one last barb. 'And incidentally, the answer is no. I don't think I do love you.'

He walked from the room and she heard the heavy front door slam. She was still and silent. And cold. Nothing, nothing else could hurt her now.

37

After ten minutes of shocked immobility Kate began to feel again. She felt pain and anger and grief.

And she felt desperate for the sanctuary that her one safe and true friend could provide. She craved Robin's calm influence, needed to unload her misery over Ben before facing the torment of Jack. After her recent flight there she had the keys to his flat 'for emergencies'. This certainly counted.

As she packed her Birmingham bag she did a quick calculation in her head. Yes, she had time to go via Holland Park.

Kate ran from the house leaving the front door swinging open. Twenty minutes later she was at Robin's. She left the Merc with three wheels on the pavement and the front bumper jammed up against a post box. If only a passing policeman had spotted her erratic parking and detained her she might have been spared the final insult, but fate — and the Metropolitan Police — turned a blind eye in order that her humiliation should be complete.

As she stumbled up the steps to Robin's front door, Kate was groping to see through the mist of her tears. She let herself in and, hearing Robin's voice from the bedroom, made her way towards it, over thick carpets and through open doors.

Even if she hadn't been in such a state of panic she certainly wouldn't have stopped to consider that he might be doing something private; Robin didn't. She had space in her tormented head only for the thought of salvation which Robin now represented. His objective ear would receive her garbled and hysterical moans, his practical eye would see the best course of action for her redemption.

She stopped in the open doorway and stared in bewilderment at the scene before her.

At first her brain simply couldn't compute the message it was being sent by her eyes. Surely it was jumbling up different parts of her life, or her imagination, or someone else's imagination perhaps, like a re-recorded video tape when the old picture still breaks through.

What she was seeing couldn't be true. It was a mistake.

She shook her head to erase the image, but nothing changed.

Two naked bodies lay across the bed, a pair of pale interlocking shapes splashed diagonally on the black silk, a pair of feet at opposite corners. For several painfully slow seconds Kate watched in a blur of incomprehension until they eventually became aware of her presence and ceased their rhythmic bobbing and looked up at her, two faces so familiar in other contexts.

Robin's narrow back was towards her; he had to twist around to stare over his shoulder at the cause of the intrusion. His features were a mask of astonishment and guilt as he stuttered stupidly, trying to find words to explain.

Just beyond Robin's white flesh was another body, one Kate knew well. The fuller, darker, softer shape of Jack Fever.

His face, a mixture of amusement and triumph, was propped up on his muscular arm and he gazed levelly at Kate over the top of Robin's scrawny thigh. He seemed happy to have an audience, amused by the comic possibilities of the scenario. A half-smile flickered around his loose lips that were glinting wet with saliva.

Kate could scarcely breathe. There was silence in her head and the moment was frozen. For a second or two nothing happened. There was no movement or sound. Just the tableau of three bodies petrified in unresolved triangular ambiguity. She had an odd sense of peace.

Finally Jack spoke.

'Come and join us, Miss Fitch. I'm sure we can fit you in somewhere. But it'll only be a supporting role . . .'

She didn't decide to scream, hadn't chosen to do it. It simply started somewhere inside her and blasted its way effortlessly out of her body through her throat, a continuous stream of air in a high screech like a kettle that wouldn't turn off. It had its own existence, was entirely independent of her control.

Robin instantly leapt into action. He grabbed a piece of clothing from the floor and pulled it around his waist, trying to tuck it and arrange it to cover his bare white flesh and at the same time get to her to quieten her down. But he'd picked up a tee-shirt and it wasn't equal to the task. As he fumbled with it and then searched at the side of the bed for something more substantial he was talking, too. Kate knew he was speaking because she could see his thin lips making tiny urgent movements and his tongue darting between his teeth. She heard words but they made no sense, it was merely a flow of sound, the dreary noise of self-justification and excuses.

'. . . I can explain . . . don't get upset . . . try to stay calm . . . not what it looks like . . . we'll talk about it . . . it's too complicated . . .'

She ignored his efforts at reassurance; she had no intention of being calmed or silenced. And his nakedness was a matter of complete indifference to her. She shrugged his pawing hands aside, clearing the visual and physical path to the target of her wrath.

Jack was lying back now, hands behind his neck, his long legs crossed at the ankles as they'd been that first night in her hotel room in Cardiff. This smug display of flesh was compounded by the arrogant laughter which now shook that body, the body she'd given herself to, the body she'd had over and under and around and inside her.

The body that she'd loved so much, had believed for a while was hers for the asking but now despised. The body that was so beautiful, so strong.

And so vulnerable.

Kate retook control of her voice, shut down the shattering scream and spat down at him, her voice satisfyingly clear and loud. 'You shit. You little bastard-shit! All the time you were with me you were thinking about this, how to get to my agent. That was the sum total of your feelings for me. How useful I could be! So you dump me when it suits you, when you've used me as a stepping stone to get what you want. That's the only way you know how to behave, isn't it? You pathetic little creep. You've really ballsed up this time!'

'Kate, please, let me try to —'

Robin, by now wrapped in a white bathrobe, tried to intervene but she ordered him to 'Shut up!' with such command that he obeyed at once.

Jack was still laughing and trying to speak at the same time.

'You're ridiculous,' he said, looking up at Kate with no awareness of the danger he was in. 'You really can't expect to dictate my sex life for me. So we got it together in the sack —'

'It was more than that. I was in love with you.'

'Yeh, I know. You were really in deep. Pardon the expression.'

'You little worm!'

'Honestly, if you could see yourself.'

'Stop it! Stop laughing at me!'

But he carried on. He couldn't have known what a mistake he was making.

'Now why don't you just relax? Come on, lie down and for old times' sake let me give you a nice massage.'

'I don't need a massage,' she said calmly, turning away and looking around the room.

The huge glass vases on the tables by the bed were

327

Robin's most treasured possessions. He'd spent thousands of pounds on them in Venice years ago because, he said, he couldn't bear to be parted from their exquisite beauty. They were translucent with intertwining patterns of blue and gold dramatically swirling through the glass. They were the only splashes of colour in his starkly mono-chrome bedroom. He often said they were the sexiest thing in his life.

Kate reached for one now. Not because of its beauty but because it was two feet high and weighed twenty pounds. Perfect.

She was surprised how easily she was able to lift it above her head. Her fury had given her a strength she'd never known before.

'No, Katie, not the Murano!'

Jack Fever was a man and therefore considered his groin his most prized and precious feature. His hands reached down to protect it from the anticipated blow by the great glass vase which Kate now held behind her head with both hands like a basketball player about to launch the ball through the ring. Jack's nakedness clearly alarmed him; his delicate soft tissue could be so easily damaged.

But he got it wrong. It was not his overactive penis Kate wanted to spoil but his face; his stupid, grinning, pretty face. That was conveniently unprotected, turned up to watch her arms as they heaved the huge vase downwards on its avenging arc.

Robin's cry and extended arm were ineffectual. Jack saw his mistake too late and winced pathetically as one pre-cious object fell dramatically towards another. For a milli-second Kate enjoyed the inevitability of what was to come, the power she now wielded over him.

Then it happened. There was a satisfying splintering crunch as the glass crashed into flesh and bone. Sharp splintered shards of gold and blue shot across the room, catching the light and twinkling like exotic insects in a foreign land.

From the damaged face on the bed came a terrible high scream, an inhuman cry like a fox in a snare, and then as the pieces settled on the floor and the bed and on the brown, quivering flesh, Kate became aware of a weird stillness, the only sound now Jack's gasping breath, a mixture of shock and pain.

The vase had disintegrated, only a small piece of the rim was left in her hand. She let it fall on to his bare stomach where it rocked with the rhythm of his terrified panting. He still had his eyes screwed up tight as if fearing another attack, a second stab of sharp glass.

But Robin had found a modicum of strength and was pushing Kate back, trying to stop her from doing any more damage.

But she had no desire to. That would have been common. She had made her point, hurt his body and his pride. She didn't want to go too far.

She heard voices as they shouted at her, one trying to calm her and the other pleading for succour. She wouldn't dignify such cheap behaviour by sinking to their raucous level. She said nothing, but stood her ground, watching as one thin pink line above Jack's lip opened into a broad crimson gash, the blood welling up thick and dark and trickling into his open mouth. And from it, at the same time, came a low, guttural moan.

It had worked. He wasn't laughing any more. He was quiet now – subdued. Put firmly in his place. He looked terrible; his face a real mess of blood. Red-blotched and wet. But at least it wasn't laughing at her.

That would teach him. That would teach Ben. That would teach George. That would teach that Barney Jungsheimer. They'd all have to take notice of her now. Respect her as she deserved.

She felt a pulsing in her hand and saw her fingers gashed and leaking blood. Again, she thought.

'Oh, Robin. Your white carpet. I'm so sorry. Let me get a cloth.'

But he wasn't bothered about the carpet. He was staring at her as if she was from another planet. He looked terrified.

'Katie.' He was shaking, his voice querulous with terror. 'Oh, Katie, my love. *What have we done?*'

38

'I suppose the thing is . . . what I'm trying to say is that I'm not very good at . . . well, you know, communicating,' ventured Becca hesitantly. 'I mean, when it comes to organizing or arranging anything I know what I'm doing. I'm good at that. But if you want to chit-chat about weather and politics and so on then I just don't do that very well because I'm . . .' She petered out and sipped her Evian water. 'Sorry,' she added.

'Don't be silly,' Gina encouraged, leaning forward with a warm smile and lightly touching the white skin of Becca's thin arm. Sincerity was the thing she wasn't too hot at, but she hoped she was faking it convincingly. This was bloody hard work, but after several expensive and faltering meals together the ice was beginning to show the first signs of melting. By flattering and wooing her, Gina reckoned that Becca would eventually soften up and let her into the private world of which she so much wanted to be part.

Tonight's bout of professional seduction was taking place at Langan's.

'You're just a naturally private person,' she reassured Becca. 'There's nothing wrong with that. In fact I'd have thought it was essential in your position.'

'Well, professionally yes. But I do sometimes wonder what it would be like to have more . . . to be more . . . more like you,' she smiled shyly.

'Oh God.' Gina pulled a face and reached for another cheroot. 'What does that mean, irresponsible?'

'Actually, yes, I suppose it does, in a way. Able to let yourself go, not live life on too tight a rein. It must be

331

rather . . .' she searched meticulously for *le mot juste*, '. . . refreshing.'

There was a questioning note in her voice, something sad and yearning for guidance. Right, thought Gina, this I can work on. She wants to be corrupted. No problem, honey, you've come to the right gal!

'Oh yes, Becca, you're so right. My life is nothing if not refreshing. The trick is knowing how much to do and how much to leave undone. But when in doubt hang it out, that's what I say.'

'Really?'

'Oh yes, oh yes.' Her impersonation of John Major was wasted on Becca.

'Not that I'm unhappy, you understand,' Becca said a little too swiftly.

'Of course not.'

'But happiness is a concept in which I find it very hard to believe.' Her glass was empty and she gazed into it apparently hoping to find contentment there. How many poor fools had done likewise and not just with Evian water?

'But that's tragic! A talented, intelligent and beautiful woman like you? You should be alive with constant excitement and thrills.'

Becca laughed. 'I'm not beautiful, don't be silly.'

'You are very, very attractive and if you only believed that you would bloom like an exotic plant.' Careful, Howard, don't lay it on too thick or the poor dumbo will clam up again. 'I'll tell you what, I want to take responsibility for giving you some of the buzz that's missing from your life. How about that?'

'Oh no, I wouldn't want to be any trouble. I don't think . . .'

'Balls! No trouble, I'll enjoy it. You need to loosen up for a start. Let's toast the beginning of your new life. Come on.' She took the bottle of Dom Perignon that only she had been enjoying from the ice bucket at her elbow and made to pour despite Becca's covering hand into the empty glass.

'No, no, really, I don't drink. I need a clear head.' But she snatched her hand away all the same.

'One glass of fizzy wine isn't going to turn you into a lush. Trust me.'

'Well . . .'

'Trust me, Becca. You do, don't you?' Come on, girl, you can do it. Eyebrows raised, demanding a response, head tilted slightly and then hold her gaze in silence. She'll crack. Hold it, hold it . . .

'Yes, Gina, I do trust you.'

Bingo!

'Here's to your renaissance. To the new, raunchy Becca Nichols!'

'Cheers.' They clinked glasses and drank. 'Gosh, it's rather nice, isn't it?'

'You see what you've been missing all this time. And there's more.' Believe me, honey, there's much more to tickle your tonsils. But give me time . . .

That had been three weeks ago. Becca's AmEx card bore testament to the evenings shared since then. Like a good therapist Gina was encouraging her patient to talk about herself in this apparent relationship of trust to the point of dependency. Little did poor Miss Tightarse know that the kind and sympathetic Ms Gina Howard would drop her the moment it suited her darker ends. But until then she carried on treading innocently on the strands of the web Gina spun.

The list of loosening exercises for Becca's tight knotball of a life included a long session at the women-only health club The Haven, being massaged, pummelled and pampered by hard, probing fingers. They had also had a trip to Madam Jo-Jo's – 'No, honey, it's nothing like Madame Tussaud's' – to watch the wonderfully tacky androgynes' floor show.

Becca's reaction had been refreshingly predictable. 'You mean they're really men? That's amazing. Where do they put . . . well, you know, their things?'

'In the cloakroom, like everyone else, I suppose,' Gina had deadpanned. 'Actually I know a couple of the boys; if you'd like to meet them out of their frocks we could.'

This had been another revelation to Becca, seeing the gorgeous 'Betty' and 'Sherilee' revert to plain Darryl from Chigwell and Tony from Billericay.

A trip round a few of the capital's gay bars had helped to remove some of the fog before Becca's eyes, as had a night playing blackjack at a casino in Knightsbridge where several Arabs had approached them and discreetly offered vast sums of money for 'a little company tonight'. Whereas Gina might have been tempted Becca was merely intrigued. Gina also took her to see the greyhound racing in Walthamstow, a circus in Clapham and a very dreary play in a room over a pub in Hackney in which an over-weight Canadian actress performed a one-woman show about the politicization of lesbianism. 'Or was it the other way round?' as Gina said in the cab home.

They had even smoked a few joints together and Becca had daringly snorted a minute quantity of cocaine. She said she 'appreciated' it but didn't like being out of control.

'That,' said Gina, a rolled fifty-pound note to her nostril, 'is your whole problem.'

Nevertheless, as her education continued Becca's shoulders lowered little by little and the corners of her mouth began to rise. She started to talk about herself too; only the odd snippet here and there but giant leaps forward for someone who had, after all, spent much of her childhood wanting to grow up to be a tractor. She began to develop the beginnings of a sense of enjoyment in life. Gina persuaded her to go to Smile and get her hair cut in a new geometric shape which she could wear loose instead of her usual fashion, scraped back against her skull like a punishment for being born.

'Mr King won't like this,' she said with a naughty child's mixture of fear and glee as she checked the new image in the one small mirror she possessed.

They were spending the evening together in her immaculate but soulless house in Muswell Hill. Gina was allowed into the inner sanctum now, witness to Becca's personal space. They had even got into something of a habit of opening a bottle of Krug on their evenings together, although Becca always protested beforehand and had to be gently persuaded.

Gina watched from the uncomfortable leather Chesterfield as Becca swung her head around to watch how the new cut fell neatly back into place. She had to admit it was practical so it met her criteria for change.

'Even so, it's jolly . . . dramatic. He's bound to make some sarcastic comment tomorrow.'

'Tough shit! What the hell business is it of his if you get your hair cut? What kind of hold has he got over you for Christ's sakes? You're his PA, his minder, his right-hand person and a bloody good one. Full stop.'

'Yes. You're right, Gina. Tough shit,' she said tentatively, trying the wicked words out and rather liking them. 'Tough bloody shit. I'm his PA and the bloody best.'

'The fucking best!' encouraged Gina.

Becca giggled. 'Yes! I'm the . . . the *fucking* best! Ha!'

They clinked their glasses of champagne and laughed out loud together like schoolgirls sharing a smutty joke in the dorm after lights out.

Gina secretly congratulated herself. In all the weeks of trying she'd finally got that pale, freckly face to split into a genuine full-blooded laugh. Whatever next? She knew what should come next but wasn't sure if the time was right.

'Sod him,' Becca said suddenly, shocked by these strange new words that fitted thrillingly in her mouth. 'He's only jealous that he can't get his hair cut because he hasn't got any!'

'What?'

'It's a wig, didn't you know?'

'No!' She topped up Becca's glass.

'Oh yes, he's a total fraud. Sod him! I'm not his slave. He thinks that just because he once . . . well, because I work for him he owns me. And he can't do that. I won't let him!'

'Right.' She didn't need Gina's encouragement now, she was freewheeling solo.

'You wouldn't let anyone do that to you, would you? Because you're too strong and brave and free.'

'You make me sound like something from the wild west!'

'You *are* wild, Gina. That's what I like about you.'

'Tell me about George. He must be a fascinating person to be around.'

'Oh, the things I could tell you about him . . . But not now, that's not important. I want to talk about you, Gina. I do respect you, you know. You're the sort of person I'd like to be. You seem to challenge life instead of accepting things. You re-invent the rules as you go along; you make things happen on your terms. I think that's so . . . admirable.' She was speaking quietly now, intensely, keen to express exactly what she meant.

'The other man's arse is always cleaner,' said Gina flippantly and with a shrug. 'I mean, that's your impression, but believe me it doesn't feel like that from the inside.'

'But your whole attitude is so iconoclastic. I've always been afraid of life, well, not always but ever since . . . I've been fearful of what people would say, trying to do the right thing. And do you know what? I don't think there is a right or wrong thing at all.'

'Becca, honey, don't undersell yourself.'

'You've been so good to me. So kind.'

'I've only done what I wanted to do. Because I care.'

'You're a real friend. My only friend.'

Their eyes were locked on the same beam. Gina was aware where this could be leading, but she wasn't sure if

336

Becca did too. Their gaze continued beyond the point where British politeness would have dictated a break. None came and Gina knew now she had a green light to proceed.

She reached out a hand slowly and deliberately, still offering a last chance for her protégée to look away and talk about the weather. But Becca let the hand cup her chin and tilt her face upwards to meet the advancing lips. Her neck muscles were tight and when Gina pressed her own lips to Becca's they were hard and dry. Gina tried to open them and enter with her tongue but she met resistance and pulled away.

'Sorry, honey, I couldn't help myself. Was that wrong?'

'No. Not wrong, but I don't ... I can't ... respond. I don't know how. It's not part of me, you see. I can't explain.'

'I understand. You're not turned on by women. That's okay. I'm just lucky, I guess. I like skin; male, female or anywhere in between.'

She threw an arm around Becca's shoulder and gently rubbed the bare skin at the top of her arm. Damn, she'd miscalculated. And yet all the vibes had felt right.

'It's not that I don't want you to ... it's just that I don't think I can do anything in return. Not because I don't feel it. I do. I'm very fond of you. And not just spiritually.' She looked down and a slight flush rose to a pink blotch on her cheeks. 'I'd like to ... try things with you. But I don't think my body will let me. It's not you, it's me, it's something that I ... oh God, I don't know how to ...'

She got up and walked away. Gina thought she was going to cry. What about? One lezzie kiss? Sister, this was one repressed female.

'Listen, honey,' Gina stood behind her, close but not too close. 'If this is my fault I apologize. I went too far. But don't worry, it doesn't mean you have to start taking tennis lessons.'

Becca was quiet for a second, then she got it and laughed. She turned around, looked deep into Gina's eyes

337

behind the big glasses. Her own were sad although her mouth was smiling.

'I want to but . . . there's sort of somebody else.'

'That's all right. I don't want to marry you. Besides, I ought to break the bad news to you: I'm not a virgin.'

Becca's smile disappeared. Seriously and very deliberately she leaned forward and gently pushed her puckered lips to Gina's. She pressed them tighter, they relaxed and then Gina felt a tongue searching for her own. Both women had their eyes open, watching each other's reaction.

Arms turned the kiss into a hug and soon the kiss was wet and their bodies pressed together, still tentative but moving positively forward.

Christ, I'm such a cow, thought Gina even as she held Becca's new hairstyle in her two hands, burying her tongue in Becca's face as if extracting the juice from a piece of succulent melon. All this to get close to George King. I wonder how far I'll have to go. Ah well, whatever it takes. There are less pleasant ways of passing a few hours.

In silence they kissed, not gently but with a fierce passion and firm determination. Becca seemed to be forcing herself to do it, overriding her doubts and scruples.

Gina moved things on, exploring Becca's neck and ears with her lips, all the while monitoring the resistance or compliance of the response. She sensed Becca's willingness but also a fear, as if this was a hurdle she wanted to clear but wasn't sure of her own ability.

Gina was struck by the perfection of the skin and the lack of any kind of smell, natural or synthetic. It was a long time since she'd tasted the flavour of a woman; she preferred the harsh surface of stubble and the potent scent of male hormones. But this was work, not pleasure, and she didn't mind putting in a bit of overtime. Her fingers had soon traced down the slim throat to the neckline on the sensible white silk Laura Ashley blouse and as she undid the buttons there was a frisson from the body within.

'All right?' Gina whispered.

'Yes. Yes. But slowly, please. I'm not . . .'

'Not what, honey?'

'I'm not experienced. It's been a long time and then . . .'

'Did someone break your heart?'

'Mm. Sort of.'

Jesus Christ, she's like a teenager on a first date. This is going to be one helluva drag unless she loosens up.

'We don't have to do this, you know. Not if you'd —'

'No. We must.' She was adamant. 'I need to. I want you to make love to me. Properly. But be . . . considerate, please.'

'Honey, I'll give you the five star treatment. Relax and enjoy.'

So, it's going to be hard fucking work. Hard work fucking. And I get sod all in return. At least not tonight.

She took her glasses off, led her unprotected protégée to the sofa, sat her down and bent to her task. The blouse came off and then the bra. Gina dutifully began to lick the small white breasts, delicately lined with pale blue veins like Blue Cheshire cheeses.

She heard Becca gasp at this sensation and then whimper as if a well of grief were being tapped after years of upper-lip stiffness.

After four and a half minutes of fondling and sucking — the producer in her could still 'feel' the second hand ticking round and knew when it was time to move on — Gina checked that her fingernails were bitten short and smooth and then ran her hand up a thin white thigh, above and beyond a point of decency, and she sensed the whole body flinch and clench beneath her. After the initial resistance came a slight relaxation and a deep sigh of something like regret.

All right, my girl, here I go. Her fingers strayed where she doubted even Becca's own hand had been. She wouldn't have been surprised to find a filigree of cobwebs there.

Becca seemed to have stopped breathing, to be bracing herself for some dreadful ordeal. But she didn't make any move to halt Gina's advance.

'Yes,' she whispered. 'Go on. Do it. *Go on.*' There was no pleasure or anticipation in her voice, her throat was as tight as her thighs.

'Look, hon, this ain't compulsory. We could just play backgammon . . .'

'No, we have to. I want you to, really,' Becca said, but her eyes were closed in grim resolve. 'I mean, if you don't mind.'

'Mind? I want to. You're allowed to enjoy it too, you know. If you don't there's not much point.'

Becca opened her eyes.

'I'm sorry, Gina, I'm not being very fair. One day I'll explain. For now, will you just . . . do it?'

'Okay, let's go for it. We'll write a note for the milkman and see what he leaves on the step.'

Slowly, watching Becca's face for signs of pleasure that never materialized, she began to deliver the goods. This time, in response to her digital dexterity she felt the slim white legs open very slightly to give her easier access. Delicately, expecting all the time a cry of horror and the gates to slam shut, she parted the petal-like folds of flesh and found the hard pea she was seeking, gently rubbing and pressing it, hoping this would have the usual magic effect.

'Oh no, no . . .' Becca muttered, frowning at some private mental anguish, although her body was less negative.

Gina worked away for a while, checking her watch surreptitiously and then upping her work-rate. Whatever this silly Tightbutt's problem was she didn't want it to stop her getting some sleep later.

Gradually Gina felt the resistance lessen, everything seemed to warm and soften and her hand became moist with Becca's juices. Still watching the unhappy face before her she pushed a finger right up inside Becca, exploring and stimulating, then two, then three, the way she liked

340

it herself. As she always said, only a woman knows how to turn a woman on. Men were at most a useful second best. She was gratified to feel her hand gripped and squeezed. A response at last.

She looked at Becca's rather unattractive face, eyes and mouth shut tight against this whole experience although her legs were now spread shamelessly wide.

'No . . . please . . . don't . . .' she was still moaning but clearly talking to some ghost in her past, not to Gina.

It was time to move on again.

Okay, you want the full muff dive? You got it.

Still fearing a shocked refusal Gina removed her hand and quickly buried her face where it had been, pushing out with the tip of her tongue. A gasped intake of breath was followed by another sigh, longer and louder this time, seeming to express all the years of neglect and repression. The whimper sounded as if it was a real cry, not of pain but sadness. How come?

'No . . . this isn't right . . . *please* . . .'

But Gina felt the narrow hips push forward to meet her tongue, seeming to welcome and relish the hard softness twisting and burrowing away. Like a brat at a birthday trifle she chewed at Becca, her tongue sliding in and out of the wet cunt-crevices, seeking every possible avenue that would give pleasure.

Becca's hands reached out blindly for Gina and she let them find her breasts. Half-heartedly Becca fondled her, more out of duty than desire, Gina thought. With her nose pressed into the curiously odourless black bush she worked her jaw muscles, chewing away on the now tenderized meat in the hope of bringing it to shivering orgasm. Preferably before too long.

The minutes passed in a silence broken only by the slurping and moaning and the occasional hissing sound outside of a car passing by on the wet tarmac. Like the good Girl Guide she'd never been Gina stuck to her task, wiggling and jiggling her tongue until it ached.

When the moment finally came it began as a breathy, panting, guilty affair. Gina had forgotten how surprising an orgasm could be. Becca gave little gasps and seemed unsure how to deal with it as the waves of energy pulsed through her. It was as if apprehension or uncertainty didn't quite allow her to give way to sheer pleasure. Even now she wouldn't relinquish control; spontaneity was too much to ask. Gina said nothing, unwilling to impose anything that Becca didn't want. This was her own special treat to enjoy however she wanted.

She was groaning, almost keening for something lost. Without warning her slight body arched up with amazing power, juddered for a few seconds and then heaved violently and she huffed and puffed, her head rolling from side to side, as if she was in labour, trying to hang on to a huge, overdue baby and not let it be born.

'Oh! Is this it?'

'Yes, come on, honey, do it, let's do it,' Gina whispered encouragement. 'Enjoy – this is for you. Let it go.'

'No,' Becca moaned. '*No* . . . please don't . . . *let me go* . . .'

'It's all right, honey. Go for it. It's okay, just ride the wave.'

Time after time she shared the shudder of another shock as it washed through Becca's frail, defenceless form. She saw with no surprise that Becca was crying and wondered what private hell was being confronted, what horrors relived with such anguish.

Eventually Becca collapsed back on to the Chesterfield, a dead weight, come and gone. Gina marvelled at her own handiwork with some pride and not a little envy. That delicious moment of corruption could never be repeated.

'So that's an orgasm,' said Becca ten minutes later as they sat side by side on the floor in front of the log-effect gas fire, cupping mugs of chocolate in their hands.

Gina laughed and lit a cheroot.

342

'Wait, you're kidding me. You've never...? Seriously?'

'Seriously.'

'Spooky. But why?'

'I've never been ... brave enough.'

'Brave? Why do you have to be brave?'

'To trust someone enough to let them.'

'You don't have to've been awarded a medal for gallantry to have a wank, honey.'

'You have to be relaxed.'

'Which is not your forte, right. But never to have wondered what it was like and had a go.'

'Oh, I've wondered. But that's as far as it went. I thought it was, well, dirty. Not quite the sort of thing one did. Like picking your nose.'

'But a lot more fun.'

'Yes...' she said doubtfully.

'Wasn't it? Or was I wasting my time?'

'No, no. It was ... jolly pleasant. Thank you.'

'Don't mention it.'

'I'm sorry I couldn't ... share more. You see, I'm not used to people being kind to me. And so when you are – and you are very kind to me, Gina – I don't quite know how to react. Sorry.'

'Oh, God. I thought we were making love, and then you politely say thank you as if I'm a maiden aunt who's sent you a book token for Christmas.'

'I'm a disappointment, aren't I?'

'Come here, give me a hug. Christ, now I feel like your mother.'

They clung together, Gina unsure if this was progress or not.

'Don't worry,' she said as their hug broke apart. 'It doesn't mean we have to get married or have babies or anything. It doesn't even mean you're a dyke. I'm not.'

'Does it mean anything then?'

'You tell me.'

'I . . . I'm not sure. It's not something I thought would ever happen.'

'That's good then. Being taken by surprise, being unpredictable. That's what you want, isn't it, in your new life?'

'In a way. But sex without love. It feels so depraved.'

'Exactly. It's wicked!'

Becca wasn't smiling. She sat hugging her own knees and staring into the flames in deep contemplation.

'You know, Bec, you think too much. You've got to start leaping in with both feet, legs akimbo.'

'I just did, didn't I?'

'Well, you swam out of your depth a little. But now you feel guilty,' said Gina, a little petulantly. Had all her efforts been wasted, and only driven Miss Perfect further away? Along, of course, with Mister Television.

'Guilty? Don't start projecting your own feelings on to me, thank you. It's not a question of guilt. Not even confusion. Just certain barriers I need to overcome, in time.'

'That's healthy,' Gina ventured.

'Anyway, I think it's too early to say what it means. Obviously I wanted it to happen otherwise I would have stopped it. But do I want it to happen again?'

'Do you?'

Becca turned to her. The look in her eyes was enigmatic. At least, it was to Gina. Her glasses were on the other side of the room so everything was slightly soft-focus.

'I don't understand what the hell is going on. But I think something very important has happened to me today. And, on the whole, I have to say I don't think I'd object if it were to happen again.'

'You're saying I'm a good lay?'

'I suppose I am.'

'You randy old sleazebucket! Now don't look so wounded; from me that's a compliment.'

'Really? I have got a lot to learn, haven't I?'

'Well, I'm happy to teach you. Shall we fix a date?'

'Yes, although I'm not very available. You-Know-Who

344

practically has to have someone to hold his you-know-what when he goes to the you-know-where. But I should be able to find some time to come out and play.'

'Play anyway, I don't think there's any need to come out yet.'

'I mean, if you want to?' There was a note of panic in Becca's voice.

'Of course,' Gina reassured her. 'We must see a lot of each other.' She stroked Becca's hair. 'Yes, we'll have fun.' She held Becca tight and kissed her on the ear. 'Why were you crying, honey? Is it something to do with this man, the one who broke your heart?'

'I . . . he . . . look, I really don't want to talk about it. Sorry.'

'Okay. My fault for asking. So, change of subject. Something uncomplicated. Er . . . tell me about your boss. What's he really like?'

'Mr King? Oh, you don't want to hear about him.'

'Yes, I do. Go on, honey, tell me about him. Tell me *all* about George King.'

345

39

Fear of flying. It wasn't something Kate ever experienced.
She always found the actual journey dreadfully dull apart
from the take-off and landing. At least they brought the
frisson of danger, the terrible possibility that something
might go wrong. This time she doubted anything in her
life could be more horribly wrong than it already was.

'Another drink, madam?'

She looked at the steward through her Wayfarers. It was
the lack of sexual energy in his look she noticed. Another
airy-fairy. A trolley dolly. Funny how they conformed to
the stereotype every time.

'Yes, vodka-tonic. Make it a double.' This new taste for
alcohol in quantity helped to dull the pain of living. She
didn't have a drink problem. She could stop any time she
wanted to; she just didn't want to.

As the second and then the third drink went down Kate
began to relax a little and allow herself space to reflect.

That afternoon at Robin's flat she'd resisted all his pleas
to stay for camomile tea and homemade herbal Rescue
Remedy. She remembered brushing off his restraining
arms and, head held high with the pride of a job well
done, sweeping down the wide stairs and out into the
refreshingly cold night air.

She drove too fast, oblivious of red lights, and tore
several times up and down Park Lane, the Merc's engine
racing as she deliberately didn't change up to top gear,
preferring instead to hear the urgent whine begging for
relief which she took pleasure in denying it. As she threw
the car round corners and bounced it off kerbstones, Kate
allowed herself the privilege of losing her cool alone inside

her little cocoon. She screamed aloud in bitter fury at Jack Fever for the humiliation he had inflicted on her. And she screamed at herself for being stupid enough to allow him direct access to her feelings. He had hurt her even more than she'd realized he was able.

'You arrogant, selfish, insensitive bastard!' she shouted until it hurt her throat. 'Just because you're young and . . .' she was reluctant to admit it, '. . . attractive you think no one else matters. You treat people like shit because you are a shit! And you'll never be anything else! *I hope you die!* No, I hope you live and your face is a mass of scars! I hope you're disfigured for life!'

She'd stopped the car in the street and walked through glass doors to a reception desk and found herself checking in to the Four Seasons Inn on the Park. For three days she stayed in her suite, having food and drink sent up and living in the hotel's dressing-gowns and bathrobes. She slept, watched television – apart from George's show – and spent long hours in the bath, wondering how long it would take the police to track her down and come calling.

And she thought about death. She didn't actually contemplate suicide, but she wondered what it would be like to slip out of life now, alone and unnoticed. After all, no one knew she was there, it would be easy enough to disappear. To take too many of her sleeping pills with a bottle of vodka or to fall conveniently and gracefully to her death one chilly night from her sixth floor balcony, making a loud and messy impact on the pavement below.

A bigger impact than she'd made in life.

But just as she no longer had the lust to live, nor could she summon the energy to die. It would all be too much effort. So she slept and bathed and sank lower into depression. The heady days of optimism seemed so far off now. The days a few weeks ago when she thought a fling with Jack Fever would sort out her mid-life crisis. She couldn't have been more wrong.

She'd wasted it all, half a century of existence, thrown

347

it away on worthless people, worthless men, and become worthless herself. She cried until no more tears would come and still she heaved dry, empty sobs.

Eventually the realities of life reimposed themselves. She needed clothes for one thing. And her mascara and diary and books and all the things in her life she could rely on.

She'd missed the show for three nights. That was so unprofessional. Unforgivable. She thought about dialling Robin's number to ask him as usual to contact the producer on her behalf, but now he was soiled with the Jack Fever connection it was unthinkable. A row with him now would only add to her troubles. Instead she rang Bryan Harvey-Jones herself. His exasperation at her disappearance was countered by his relief at hearing from her at last.

'So you're all right, then? We've all been so worried. Even Robin didn't know where you were. We were going to contact the police. We had to put your understudy on.'

'Zoe? How was she?'

There was the briefest pause. 'Marvellous. Marvellous. She was very frightened, of course, at such short notice, but she worked so hard and she's really grown into the part, really started to make it her own.'

Kate knew what his game was, of course, and briefly wondered whether to call his bluff. But her thespian feathers were ruffled. In her most off-hand manner she said, 'If you'd like me to come back I could do the show in Watford tonight . . .'

Bryan took her up on her offer. He told her that Jack Fever had had some sort of accident and had been to hospital for stitching. Now he was having a couple of weeks off and they'd managed to find someone else and get him trained up to play opposite her.

'He's called Andrew Alexander, he's in that new BBC lunchtime soap.'

'Fine,' she said. 'I'll drive up to Watford this afternoon.'

'You're a trouper, Kate. Listen, you are all right, are you?'

'Fine now. Fine. I'm sorry to let you and everyone down. It's just that . . . oh, God. Can I just leave it at "personal reasons"? Do you mind?'

'Okay, but I have to be sure this was a one off. You understand?'

'Of course, Bryan. Don't worry. This, um, this accident, to Jack Fever. What did he say about it?'

'Something about a vase.'

'Oh?'

'Yes, he was carrying it and he fell. Got some nasty cuts on the face apparently. He's a good-looking lad, I hope this isn't going to jeopardize his acting career.'

'Yes, that would be a shame. Poor Jack.'

So she had mustered all her energy and courage and slotted back into the company again for one final week. The company manager had obviously primed them all not to mention Kate's going AWOL, so they were icily polite to her on stage and off.

She felt even more isolated than ever. The new boy, Andrew, was fine. Unexciting, unimaginative and under the circumstances just what she needed to work with each night. Too much talent or energy would have floored her. If he was sexy she didn't notice.

After the final week of the tour she'd booked herself a holiday, determined that she would do a lot of skiing and no thinking. Not about the state of her marriage, the state of her career, her relationships with Robin, with Jack Fever, with Ben or with George. She would exercise her mind on nothing more complex than how to carve the perfect parallel turn.

Upon landing at Geneva she looked for the board with 'Fitch' written on it held up by the peak-capped chauffeur from the Hotel Anapurna. He collected her skis and bags from the carousel and swung them into the boot of a large black Audi, then whisked her along the damp roads towards Courchevel in a respectful silence. Fortunately there was a small drinks cabinet hidden behind discreet walnut doors. A few small nips of brandy helped the journey pass.

Standing at her window, looking up at the mountains towering over the resort, reflecting the pinkish hues of the setting sun, Kate knew this was exactly what she needed. A week of physical exertion and mental relaxation. She would spoil herself rotten, eat, drink and ski and forget completely about anything other than what to wear for dinner or how to correct her tendency towards shoulder swing.

She was happy to be single and anonymous in this chic crowd. The good thing about an expensive ski resort, she thought, was that everyone had class. No yobs or slobs. Nothing naff or nasty. No ski suits from C & A or accents from Essex. The right sort of people made for a better sort of time.

As soon as she hit the slopes on her first morning – well, nearer lunchtime – a sense of freedom surged through her. Like a creature staggering out into the sunlight after a season's hibernation she stretched herself literally and metaphorically, thrilling to the new but familiar sensations as the little plastic bubble swung her higher and higher up the mountains leaving her to career down as fast as she dared, the wind in her face making her eyes run and the strain on her legs bringing a delicious burning sensation in her thighs. The snow was perfect, fresh powder from the night before tended by the piste-bashers into wide, steep alleys that challenged but didn't intimidate a skier of Kate's expertise.

In her fluorescent pink and yellow all-in-one by Nevica, one-ninety skis by Rossignol, white Salomon boots and dark hair flowing free she knew she cut a dash even among the glitterati. Once she'd caught a bit of sun, too, that would really make the image complete. But she wasn't out to attract or impress. She kept her Ray-Bans firmly in place when sharing a chairlift with a stranger or sitting on a café terrace high up on the Col de Chanrossa taking a *vin chaud* and a sandwich for lunch. No eye contact, no danger. Just the elements, the mountains and the chance to be herself. What more could she want?

'*I vant to be alawn . . .*'

The voice by her ear startled her. She turned and squinted up into the bright sun, trying to decipher the face that went with the pure white ski suit now standing there, silhouetted against the clear azure sky. It was male and it was laughing gently. Why? At her? Bloody childish, she thought. Some German arsehole pissing around? Someone from the hotel?

'Sorry, Ms Fitch, did I wake you?' He actually called her 'Ms' without a trace of irony. 'I thought you were doing such a good Garbo impersonation.'

The voice was English but with a hint of something else, something friendly and familiar. Her eyes still hadn't adjusted to the light.

'How are you?' He extended a gloved hand to her.

'I'm sorry : . . I . . .' She felt mildly threatened by this tall white figure who was, as she blinked and shielded the sun with her hand, gradually coming into focus.

'Oh my God,' she said when at last the image was entirely clear. 'It's the penis!'

'The . . . ? Oh, the penis! Yes!' He laughed easily. Kate was aware of heads on a nearby table turning to listen disapprovingly.

'May I?' said Hal, waiting for Kate's 'of course' before pulling up a chair and sinking awkwardly into it, movement restricted by his ski boots. 'Sorry if I disturbed you.'

'No, no.' Seeing his face cut off by the little woollen hat and the neckline of his Ralph Lauren poloneck Kate noticed he looked just like the picture they used of him at the top of his column in the paper.

'Perfect conditions, aren't they?' he said.

'Perfect.' She thought about removing her shades but decided against it. With them on she could study his face all she liked. And she liked. He was young but had a wise and handsome head on his broad shoulders.

'I didn't mean to interrupt you. You were soaking up the sun before I arrived.'

'Well, I don't know about you but I want to be really brown by the end of the – oh . . .'

'So do I,' he said seriously.

'Sorry.'

Kate looked at his face more closely. Surprisingly fine features. Even his nose had an air of the Roman. His lips were that lovely crushed blackberry colour, thick and fleshy, the skin clear and smooth without blemishes. He looked healthy and vital. Like the cover photo for some black 'lifestyle' magazine. And much more relaxed here than she'd seen him before. He was tallish and slim. Looked as if he moved everything well. Age? Hard to be precise. Early thirties? Mature but youthful. Lucky she was *hors de combat* as far as romance was concerned.

'Anyway, never mind my hangups. I'd better leave you in peace doing your Garbo.'

He stood up and was a blurred outline between her and the yellow sun again.

'And by the way, about that address you gave me . . .'

'I think it's better I don't know what you did about it.'

'Really?'

'Yes.'

'Well, thank you for the information anyway. I wonder if you were aware how devastating it could be.'

'Oh yes, I was fully aware.'

'Do you know the . . . owner of the house in question?'

'No. We've never met.'

'I see. So why did you contact me?'

'No, Mr Brand, that wasn't part of the bargain. You don't need to know that.'

'Fair enough. Well, back to your suntan.' Perhaps he sensed her unspoken invitation. 'Unless, of course, you'd like to ski together? I mean, if you're not with someone?'

352

'No,' she said. 'I'm not with anyone. I'd like to ski with you for an afternoon, Hal.'

It was probably a mistake. He'd either be brilliant or hopeless. Oh well, she'd pretend she had to meet someone and leave him on the mountain somewhere. He could look after himself.

They took the cable car right up to the very top of La Saulire, squeezing in with a cosmopolitan crowd whose keenness on skiing was matched only by their love of posing. The air was heavy with the intoxicating aromas of Chanel and Sun-Bloc. At the summit they emerged, clanking in ungainly style down the metal steps and into the startling brightness. This was what she was here for: the sunshine so piercing it could blind, the air so clean it was a shock to the lungs. And the cold that had the power to anaesthetize.

Kate felt that familiar sense of heady fear as she saw the pistes curling and dropping away towards the distant valley. Wispy clouds clung to distant peaks like ivy around ancient statuary. There was nowhere higher to go, she was three thousand metres above the sea; this was the top of the world.

The trip down was the ultimate thrill. And she was about to share it with a stranger. The sexual parallels were unavoidable. Would they be compatible? What would their journey be like? One headlong breathless rush or a slow meander taking in the pretty diversions? Would one leave the other behind or would they cruise side by side, turning and schussing as one? The anticipation and apprehension were about equal. Not long ago she'd been thinking of Jack Fever as her partner for trips like this. She didn't even know if he ski'd; they hadn't been together long enough for her to find out. If he was a novice she'd have enjoyed teaching him that too. But he clearly didn't want her tuition any more. He had moved on to bigger things. What would she and Robin have to say to each other when they next met? They'd shared the same lover.

No, she wasn't going to think about any of that. She was just going to ski.

'It's pretty exciting, isn't it?' said Hal, stepping into his hired skis and tightening his boots for the descent. 'There's nothing like the buzz you get from skiing. Well almost nothing,' he added with an unsubtle curl of his lips. 'Would you like to lead the way?'

Well, well. A man who didn't feel his masculinity was threatened by following a woman. So much more mature than that little wanker Jack Fever. To think she'd thought she was in love with him . . . No, she wouldn't let memories of him ruin her day. Maybe Hal just wasn't very good and didn't want to be watched.

She led the way down the tricky black run deliberately keeping her speed up and weaving her way deftly through the slower skiers, not making it easy for Hal. If he wanted to ski with her he'd have to survive her pace. As they turned around the edge of the mountain and arrived in a narrow gully which needed superb control and tight turns they left the sun behind and seemed to pass into a different world, cold and unforgiving. There were patches of ice here which couldn't be avoided. Skill and confidence were needed to survive; this will test him, she thought.

He gave a yell as he negotiated some hazard and Kate heard the tell-tale sounds behind her of a bad, scraped turn. Good, she was glad he was under pressure. She needed to feel she was better than someone at something.

When she finally relented and paused for a rest she had to wait nearly a minute for him to arrive.

'Hey, fantastic!' he beamed as he stopped next to her with a short turn, showering her legs with soft powder snow. His face was wet from the exertion and alive with euphoria. 'You're a wonderful skier, way out of my class. Even the ice didn't bother you.'

'I've been skiing a lot longer than you have, young man. I started when I was eight.'

'Well, six decades' experience counts for a lot,' he

mused. For a moment Kate wasn't sure how to react. Her instinct was to tighten her lips and mount her high horse. Then she realized he was winding her up and barged him with her shoulder, trying to push him over into the snow.

'What a cheek!' she said.

'Glad you like it, shall I turn the other one?'

The rest of the day they ski'd together, varying tough red and black runs, discussing technique and congratulating each other when it was deserved. They chatted easily about themselves, swapping facts and opinions, relating anecdotes, enjoying each other's company.

For the last run of the day it was Hal's turn to choose a route and lead the way. 'Do you fancy a long, hard black?' he asked straightfaced. 'Something to stretch you?' There was only the tiniest twinkle in his eye.

'I don't think I can answer that without compromising myself,' Kate said, nearly but not quite taking up the invitation to flirt with him.

He flashed her a wide, dazzling and totally disarming grin and set off down the mountain with a very poor attempt at a yodel.

She followed close behind, not too pushed at his speed, watching the slightly feminine sway of his svelte hips as he led her down the long run called Jockeys. Too much shoulder swing and weight not far enough forward, but not bad, she thought, not bad at all. He took pleasure from his skiing too; that was, after all, the main thing. And it was infectious. His company was good for her. Never mind the flirting, that was just a silly game. He listened and didn't judge her. He also had an acute sense of irony which she rather liked. Not that he belittled her with sarcastic comments, that was George's style. No, he was simply witty in the way he deflated her pomposity. More than that, he was gentle and he was fair. Was this what they called a New Man? Who cared what they called it; she liked it. And she was enjoying herself as she hadn't done for years.

They parted with a promise to meet again at eleven the next day. He was staying in a borrowed chalet hidden somewhere among the pines. He didn't say who with and she didn't ask.

As she soaked in her bath that evening she tried to imagine what he would be doing. And who he would be doing it with. She reflected that although they had talked easily he knew a lot more about her than she did about him.

They spent the next day together. The day after that was Christmas Day, but few concessions were made to it in the resort. It was just another day to play on the perfect powder. They tested each other on their usual runs, stopped for a quick sandwich for lunch in their favourite mountain restaurant and ski'd again until the lifts closed, trying to be last off the mountain. At the end of the day's exertions they sat with a bottle of champagne and a dozen oysters on the 'Posers Terrace' as they called it, watching the fur-coat brigade pass by.

'Happy Christmas, Kate.'

'Happy Christmas, Hal. Thank you for being . . . undemanding.'

It was chilly and dark by the time they walked together down the slippery road towards Kate's hotel. She slithered over the newly-forming ice.

Hal extended his hand to her. 'Take my hand.'

'I'm a stranger in paradise. Thanks.'

He held her firmly while she got her balance.

'Look,' she said. 'If I take that path through the trees I come round by the side door. It's much easier than the road; I'll be fine.'

'Come on then.'

'You don't have to, really.'

'Do you mean you don't want me to see you home?'

'How very old-fashioned. No, I'd love you to. Thank you, Hal.' She looked at him only briefly as she felt sure her embarrassment would show on her windblown features.

Then she turned away and started up the steep path between the dark pines, their boughs bent low, heavy with the weight of frozen snow.

The air was suddenly heavy too. They walked in silence, Kate first, picking her way along the narrow path in the intermittent light of the fullish moon when the clouds let it through. The track seemed harder to follow than yesterday: last night's fresh snowfall must have obliterated familiar landmarks. Behind her she heard Hal struggling to carry their two pairs of skis but she didn't offer to help. She knew him well enough by now to know that if he needed a hand he'd ask.

She pressed on, planting her boots deep into the soft, virgin snow and hoping that any minute now they would stumble into the clearing by the Hotel Anapurna. Now and then strong shafts of moonlight burst upon them but they seemed to mock her attempts to find the track, showing up in stark clarity how impenetrable was the way ahead.

'We're obviously well off the path now,' Kate thought. 'And Hal must know it too. Why doesn't he say something instead of following mutely behind? He's just humouring me, laughing at me, waiting to revel in my inability to cope.' Even now, even here, even with someone whose company she had enjoyed so much over the week, she still felt that black, unforgiving sense of personal failure. She couldn't make a successful marriage, couldn't raise children without disaster or misery striking them, she couldn't sustain a career, couldn't keep her toy-boy amused; she couldn't even find a path among the trees.

She stopped at last in a small clearing. A branch creaked, their shoes squeaked on the snow. When she turned to Hal she was fighting the pricking behind her eyes. She almost expected a slap, which George would have administered as a matter of course, for losing the way.

'I'm sorry,' she said. 'I've got us lost. It's my fault.'

She looked up at him. The moon showed his features

clearly like a follow-spot in the theatre. His uncomprehending concern was clear. She wanted to melt against him, feel his arms around her, his forgiveness whispered into her ear.

He knew, of course. He dropped the skis to one side; they all but disappeared into deep snow. With one small step he was in front of her, he bent at once to hold her tight, wrapping himself around her and pulling her closer to his tall, strong body.

The relief and the tightness of his grip made her gasp and the gasp turned into a sob. With difficulty her breath came now; she struggled to maintain control but something about Hal's confidence reassured her that she could let go and so she did; great heaving lungfuls of air burst from her as if she had just been pulled, half-drowned, out of the sea.

It seemed as if she had been taken over by some force that Hal had released. Just his touch was enough. She was aware suddenly how much she had been wanting this from him, how right it seemed. Their skiing, their conversation and easy enjoyment of each other's presence were all a prelude to this moment. As she sobbed into his broad chest, unable to explain or excuse, he held her and encouraged her with little whispered words and sounds of reassurance.

She sniffled, aware how pathetic she was being but equally sure that with him anything was permitted, nothing taboo. She felt secure like this, a sensation that had been absent from her life for so long. Now its unexpected arrival undermined her many years of putting a brave face on abject misery. It was as if what flooded out now was a distillation of all the depression, the injustices and disappointments she'd previously been unwilling to acknowledge.

'Yes, yes, let it go. That's good.' He stroked the back of her head and rubbed her neck, seeming to empathize with her to the extent of synchronizing his breathing with hers.

'Go on, that's it . . .' And he gently drew a finger – brown on the back, beige underneath – across her face to wipe the tears from her cheeks.

Encouraged, Kate cried out loud in blind rage at the life she had pretended was enough. Now no pretence was required, Hal not only accepted her grief but positively eased it out of her, gently drawing the sting. She gripped him hard but he stood firm and didn't complain.

As her heaving chest began at last to subside Kate looked up to see his face as sad as her own. He bent, a loving parental figure, and delicately placed the softest of kisses on her wet cheek. There, there, let's kiss it better. He didn't say it but the words echoed in Kate's head. And it did make it better. She blinked into his infinitely caring brown eyes and reached up to press her lips to his in thanks for his concern.

They were full and soft and felt friendly against her own. She tasted new flavours on them, sweet and strange.

She became aware of a something wetter and stronger. It seemed natural to let his tongue ease between her own lips and insinuate itself inside her.

'No,' she thought. 'Don't let him in. He'll find his way to your heart and then he'll have control over your emotions. And you know what happens then . . .'

But her body's urges overruled her mind's ministrations. She nestled against him and felt him hard even through his ski clothes. It excited her that this handsome, exotic young man could be finding her attractive enough to be turned on. His interest validated her very existence. She was worthwhile; she was desired.

'Oh Hal, hold me tight,' she murmured, seeking protection from all the evils in the world within his strong embrace.

'Shhh, don't worry, I'm here.'

'I . . . I don't know why I'm crying. It's to do with . . . someone who was unkind to me. And I'm so . . . relieved.'

'Relieved it's over?'

'Yes.' She couldn't think straight, couldn't marshal her thoughts. 'And relieved to find you,' she whispered, afraid that even speaking it out loud would spoil it. 'I'm very lucky you're here. You're so kind, so good. So . . . pretty.'

He laughed gently, amused by the compliment. Then his soft laughter died and he spoke quietly. 'We're both lucky, Kate. Lucky to find each other like this.'

There was a question in his voice. She looked up again saw the same question in his eyes.

She wanted to say yes; she knew she ought to say no. So she said nothing, but her body language was screaming so loud it could have started an avalanche.

Hal bent her head back, cradling it in his hands, and licked her neck and throat. She'd never felt so vulnerable or so safe; chicken exposed to friendly fox.

Gazing up through the pine branches loaded with snow towards the blue-grey moonlit sky, Kate felt the pure light instilling hope in her poor worn body, refreshing it with clean, bright air. Hal undid the top of her suit and the zip on her sweater and she listened to the sounds of his warm, wet kisses as he progressed down to her breasts.

He was a master craftsman; he didn't need her course in love-making to know what turned her on. This was no exercise in trying to please her, it was the real thing. He was making and sharing love.

Kate let her arms hang loose by her sides as she enjoyed Hal's roving lips hoovering over her warm breasts and his teeth nibbling at her nipples. She shivered with pleasure and a delicate, involuntary sigh escaped her lips, a small bubble of air pushed straight up from the base of the lungs by her strong diaphragm muscle through an open, unrestricted throat.

She knew suddenly what she wanted there, to restrict and choke her. In one smooth movement she held Hal back, dropped to her knees in the snow, unzipping him from neck to groin as she fell. Ski suits were such practical items of clothing, designed for easy access.

His cock was warm and tasted good. It had a strong, male, sweaty flavour and she breathed in the new and enticing aroma of his body that mixed with the scent of the creaking trees around them.

Pines and penis, she thought. Penis and pines. Same letters, different order. Same shape, different scale. Still her brain was jumbling things around, trying to make sense of everything. She saw the end of one of his skis sticking out of the snow a few feet away. 'Head', it said. Absolutely, she thought.

With perfect technique she opened the back of her throat and swallowed him right down her gullet. Her mouth was filled with flesh and she could only just reach his balls with her tongue, moving them around in their tight sac. She loved the feeling of being stifled by him, of almost choking before releasing him in order to breathe. She grabbed his bum for purchase and pulled her head into his groin again and again, thrilling at the sensations as his cock hit the back of her throat, forcing its way deeper into her each time. His hands were on the back of her head now, sharing the rhythm and urging her on.

She could see Hal smiling. Then he started to laugh. Just a giggle at first but it became a rich, full-blooded sound.

Kate sat back and looked up at him.

'This is ridiculous,' he said. 'I don't believe we're doing this. You're outrageous.'

'I feel so wonderfully dirty!' she said. And laughed too. It felt odd to her, it wasn't something her body was used to. It was shocking to think how long it had been since she'd felt that sensation, the rocking, shuddering ripple of laughter rolling through her.

She stood up and hugged him and they laughed together. He kissed her ears and hair and still they laughed. With secret joy, not with embarrassment.

'Let's do it, Hal. Let's do it here. Now.'

'In the snow? We'll freeze to death.'

'Come on, quick before with think about it. Get down, go on.'

And she pushed him back so he fell into the shallow snow under the low branches of a mature pine. She looked down for a moment, grinning at him and savouring the sight of him spreadeagled there, a living black cross in the moonlit snow marking the place where Kate was going to have him. Like a giant game of Spot the Ball.

Swiftly she unzipped her suit, straddled him awkwardly and then squatted on to him, easily and eagerly. They both sighed at once and Kate watched as he bit his bottom lip and closed his eyes when she began to rock her hips, feeling for the first time this new person inside her, touching and igniting the most volatile parts of her body. And yet it felt that her whole life had been building up to this. To him. Here and now, in the snow. She wasn't about to defy her destiny. Hal had been sent for her; she was getting something right for once.

She ran her hands over the rippled muscles of his hard black body, at least the bits that his suit allowed her to reach. He lay semi-naked like a fruit half-peeled, its skin exposing the soft, tasty flesh. She grabbed his nipples and twisted them hard, making him wince.

'Oh Christ-all-bloody-mighty! You are – ow! – wonderful.'

'So are you, my darling,' she whispered and leaned forward to feast on his sweet lips, thrilling to different sensations as he triggered new areas inside her.

Sitting up again and bouncing higher and faster Kate put her hands behind her head. Partly to celebrate the carefree feeling of making love in the snow on a winter night in the Alps and also to arch her body backwards and keep her breasts from sagging. As she did so she clouted a bough laden precariously with several inches of crusted snow. Instantly it was disturbed the branch deposited its soggy burden in one fat mass; it hit Kate squarely on the head and then fragmented and showered over Hal's face

362

and bare chest just like the pieces of glass had over Jack.

'That'll cool your ardour,' she said, spluttering and laughing.

'I haven't got one now,' gasped Hal, brushing the freezing snow off his body.

'Ardour, ardour,' she giggled.

'That's as 'ard as it gets!'

They struggled to get up, trying to clear the cold, white lumps of compressed snow from inside their clothes and from their hair without setting off any new falls from the trees.

'I knew that would end in tears,' said Hal. 'Why couldn't you wait until we got to your hotel to ravish me?'

'Ravish? I didn't notice you struggling.'

'I didn't dare. Come here. You look dead sexy.' Half-dressed, wet and shivering they embraced in the dappled moonlight between the tall, fragrant pines. 'You are very special, Kate. An extraordinary woman. Do you know that?'

'Oh, shut up.'

They scrabbled in the snow for the skis.

'Hotels are pretty soulless places,' Kate ventured. 'How about your chalet? Could we go there? It'd be much more friendly.'

'Well, we could. If you like. It's a bit of a trek.'

'But what about . . . I mean, the others. Your friends?'

This was the question she hadn't asked all week; the thing he had skilfully avoided mentioning. Now she needed to know.

'Friend.'

'Your friend. Will he be there?'

The pause seemed longer than it actually was.

'She.'

'Oh.'

'Yes, she'll be there. Annabel will be there.'

'*Annabel.*' So that was it. Of course.

'Don't look like that.'

'I . . . I don't know what to say. I'm so embarrassed. I . . .' Kate tried to smarten her hair and zip up her suit as if to make a speedy exit from the scene. If only.

'Please. I should have said something earlier in the week. But it didn't seem relevant. We were just friends, you and I, until . . .'

Kate couldn't speak. She was shivering uncontrollably now, the cold made worse by this blow to her pride.

'Come on, we're both freezing cold,' said Hal, taking charge. She couldn't resist. 'Let's get dry and warm and have a drink. And a talk. At least a talk. Please?'

Kate nodded. What next? she thought. Just when something at last was going her way. What bloody next?

40

Dinner was at Gavvers followed by a coffee and – more likely than not – sex at Becca's house in Muswell Hill.

As they drove, their hands draped over each other's thighs, Gina stole a glance at Becca. It's true, she thought, this is a different woman from the person I first met. She's quite the independent little creature now; Gina was proud of having a hand in it. So to speak.

But what was she getting out of it? It was all very well going through this physical thing with Becca, but if she wasn't getting the information she was after and worming her way closer to her goal then what was it for? Could it really be that some of those tender things she whispered to her prim chum she actually meant? And that the gymnastic things she did to Becca in bed were not entirely devious ways to get her to spill the beans? My God, was she taking pleasure from having sex with Becca? Was it really making love? Christ, what the hell was going on here?

Gina rolled a stronger than usual joint as Becca fixed a couple of drinks in the kitchen.

'Oh, a whole weekend to devote to you,' she said, coming back with the drinks and kicking off her shoes. They were by Manolo Blahnik; a month ago they would have been from Dolcis. 'Three days without him; what bliss.'

'How do you mean?' Gina passed the joint over and sipped her drink; Becca was making them stronger now, too. Even alcohol didn't daunt her like it used to.

'The Monster's going off on one of his mystery trips tomorrow. It's only four days, but every minute without him will be wonderful.'

'Mystery trips? What does that mean?'

'Well, I know where he's going but not what for. He does this from time to time, jets off to the States or Europe and says it's for "recuperation". Ha! He couldn't do anything for the sheer enjoyment of it, there always has to be some pay-off for him. Something material or some boost to the image. But he never tells me about it; just gets me to arrange the flight and the hotel and off he goes.'

'Interesting. What do you think he's up to? Another woman?'

'Women, it would have to be. Maybe. More likely the white slave trade, knowing him.'

'Do you know him?'

'Better than he thinks.' Becca's face clouded over as something passed through her mind.

They hugged quietly, Becca dragged deep on the joint and passed it to Gina. She'd slobbered on it, she always did. Gina hated that. It was like sitting on a wet lavatory seat. Yeuch!

'Tell me about him.' She stroked Becca's hair to distract her and kissed it. Even the new style looked suburban on her. She noticed flecks of dandruff on the shoulders of the dark Yves St Laurent blouse. 'What sort of man is he?'

'Is this curiosity or for the programme?'

'The programme? Oh, yes. Well, it's both.'

'You are still thinking of making that series, aren't you?'

'Sure. If it all hangs together properly. It depends on budgets and so on.'

'Yes, of course.'

There was just enough doubt in Becca's voice to worry Gina. She snuggled down next to Becca who had now undone her blouse, ready for whatever delights Gina chose to administer. She'd really taken to this sex business; making up for lost time, obviously. She couldn't get enough, the little tart.

Not tonight, sweetheart.

Gina rested her head on Becca's slender shoulder,

keeping her head turned away in case her own mendacity should be obvious in her myopic eyes.

'So tell me about the trip.'

'Oh, it's boring. Let's talk about you for a change. We never do.'

'Hang on, honey, who's under whose wing here? As I recall it you are my project, not vice versa.'

Gina felt the weight of the small silence that grew like a mushroom into the air over their heads. Whoops. Wrong!

'A project? Is that what I am?'

Heavy backpedalling needed here, girl. Start bullshitting.

'Yes. You were. First of all.' She turned to look directly into Becca's pale blue eyes. 'That's before I started to . . . get involved. I'm sorry, perhaps that was never part of the bargain. I . . . I can't help myself. I wasn't going to tell you, but something's been happening that I . . . never meant. It's you. Your beauty and your innocence and your . . . simple goodness have just disarmed me totally. I, I think I'm falling in love with you.'

She gasped for good measure and looked away, grabbing Becca's scrawny white thigh for support. 'I'm sorry . . .' she whispered querulously.

Christ, I hope this isn't over the top.

'Oh Gina. My darling Gina.' Becca gently lifted Gina's head up to kiss her softly on the lips. Then the tip of her nose, then each eyelid and the lips again, this time pushing her mouth open and starting what was clearly intended to be a passionate sequence leading to the ultimate pleasure.

That's what she thought. Gina had work to do, information to extract.

Pushing her gently away she smiled at Becca.

'I want to give you the most stomach-wrenching orgasm you've ever had. I want to play the Choral Symphony on your g-spot.'

Becca laughed. That was a good sign. She was forgiven.

'Later on,' Gina said. 'Let's just stay like this for a while.' She moulded her body into Becca's bony frame. 'You've

367

done something to me, Bec. I don't look at anyone else these days. I only have eyes for you-hoo.'

'Silly.'

They kissed.

'You know, when I don't see you for a couple of days I'm always thinking about what you're up to. I imagine you with George King, wondering where you are, what he's saying to you. What you're wearing, imagining your smell. Wishing I was with you . . .' Gina slipped a hand inside Becca's blouse and cupped the breast she found in her hand, rolling it rhythmically in her palm. She felt as if she were about six again, modelling in plasticine. A sense of urgency seized Gina. She needed Becca. So she kneaded Becca and pressed on.

'So where's this mystery trip to?' Her hand wandered down to Becca's thighs and applied a little strategically diverting pressure.

'He's off to Bermuda.'

'Nice. Well, it's probably just to top up the tan.'

'You don't know George King.'

'So tell me.'

'Oh, the stories I could tell.' Becca sounded as if she'd gone away somewhere very distant. Gina waited for more but nothing came.

'Tell me the stories, honey.'

'No. I can't.'

'You mean you won't.'

'No, I can't. There's too much at stake. Maybe one day.'

'Sure. So, Bermuda, then? BA flight in the morning?'

'Yes.'

'Nice hotel, I expect?'

'Mm.'

'Probably the . . . um . . . that big one . . .'

'God, Gee-Gee, this joint's strong. How about that choral symphony you promised me?'

Oh God, must I?

'Come here, then, my little vaggieburger . . .'

368

As she started the inevitable process, not entirely unwillingly, Gina was desperately trying to remember where her passport was.

41

'Kit? Hello, you old sheepshagger. It's Gina, Gina Howard. Look, Kitten, I need a favour . . . Well of course you will. Because if you don't I shall give the photographs of you and a certain member of the Cabinet to one of the gutter rags . . . That's right. Bang goes any chance he might have had of the top job and your imminent knighthood is right out the window . . . On the contrary, it's you taking the Mickey that the photos show, literally . . . Well, it'd be a shame not to get your gong after thirty years on the backbenches . . .'

Gina inhaled deeply on her cheroot while her friend found his teeth and put them in. It was three in the morning and it sounded as if he had one or two gentlemen callers with him.

They'd met some years earlier at the Chelsea Flower Show when she'd been producing an OB for Radio Two. She'd shared a rough night and a bottle of tequila with a BBC colleague whose wife didn't understand him – hardly surprising as he was Italian and she was Dutch – and as she cued her presenter, Judith 'Big Hair' Chalmers, for the live interview Gina had heaved the contents of her stomach all over some prize-winning azaleas and keeled over into an ornamental pond. Amid all the horror-stricken panic about the broadcast only this red-faced, tweedily-dressed old gent with his incongruous pony-tail had seen the funny side and could be heard guffawing in the background as he dragged Gina from the water.

'God, you're a devious witch,' he said at last. 'I don't believe you'd do it, but what're you after?'

'I need some strings pulling.'

'Well that shouldn't be a problem for a woman of your low connections.'

'You're the lowest, Kit. I want to know which flight someone is on.'

'Well, my little Gremlin, ring the airline.'

'They won't tell me. Especially not at this time of the night. The person is a VIP.'

'And where is this Vip going? Somewhere nice?'

'Bermuda.'

'Very small and very wealthy. Like Adam Faith.'

'Adam who?'

'Don't be cruel, Dogsbottom. How am I supposed to help?'

'With your penchant for air stewards, surely you can arrange a free ticket for me too?'

'My God, what do you think I am?'

'A rampant old goat. And a useful one.'

'Hm. It just so happens there is a young man here who works rather inappropriately for Virgin. I had the honour of welcoming him to the MHMATC.'

'The what?'

'The Mile High Ménage à Trois Club.'

'You're making this up. Actually, knowing you, you're probably toning it down.'

'Flatteress.'

'I need to confirm that George King is on a flight to Bermuda tomorrow, I need a ticket on the same plane and I want to know which hotel he's staying at. And which room.'

'You don't want much, do you? Anything else? The whereabouts of Martin Bormann or the reasons for Andrew Lloyd Webber's success?'

'First class would be nice, but I'll settle for club.'

'I'll call you back in two shakes of a judge's joystick.'

Which turned out to be no more than ten minutes.

'All fixed, Donkeybrain. My friend here, whose name I've temporarily forgotten — *Como te llamas*, sweetie? Oh,

371

never mind — he can sort you out. I'll pass you over in a mo. Be patient, English is his second language. Body is his first. You won't like Bermuda, you know. Far too tasteful for the likes of us.'

'Kit —'

'Now then, what I want in return is an introduction to that splendid darkie your Mama's knobbing these days. Journalist fella. Wouldn't mind climbing up his chocolate channel. Yummy-bummy as my friend the archbishop would say.'

'Kit, shut up. Let me speak to your matador.'

Gina threw the highlights of her wardrobe into a bag with make-up, laptop and credit cards. With her hair still wet from the shower she took a cab to Victoria and then the Gatwick Express to the airport. At the terminal she tracked down the relevant contacts, collected her ticket — settling reluctantly for club class — and confirmed that George was on the flight, up the front of the Jumbo, of course.

In the VIP lounge Gina sat with her reviving coffee and waited for the great man to arrive. She wasn't sure of her plan of campaign yet but she knew she had seventy-two hours to do her damage from the moment he walked through the door.

Hardly a head turned when he did; nobody here would admit to being interested in anyone else's celebrity status; they were all Very Important People in their own right.

He was a lot less impressive than she'd imagined. He was hunched and rather dull-looking, like a tired business-man, his skin blotchy and grey. He had glasses on and a rather ordinary suit. His battered briefcase was the sort of thing an assistant bank manager in Eastbourne might carry on the train. She imagined a packed lunch and a telescopic umbrella inside it. Christ, what the hell was Becca thinking of, to let him run to seed like this? He was out of shape and would have to be taken in hand before things slipped too far. She saw now that Mister Television needed her as

372

much as she needed him. Right, this gave her a starting point in her plan.

She watched him devour a large cooked breakfast of bacon, mushrooms, eggs, tomatoes and what looked suspiciously like baked beans. She'd have to change all that, get him to look after his body properly. He was big – televisually speaking – now, but he could be mega if he was handled properly. Becca was too suburban, her outlook too narrow. Gina Howard would show him how things could change. He needed a new image, to move on before people got bored with the old model. Maybe humour or politics. Or his own line in casual clothes. And what about the States? Look at Oprah. Oh yes, she had great plans for George King. Together they could really do the business.

While he read the papers, from *Telegraph* to *Mirror* and everything in between, Gina kept him in her sights and skimmed through the leaflets on Bermuda which she'd grabbed from her local travel agent first thing that morning.

'Excuse me, would you like to board now?' a middle-aged ex-bimbo whispered to Gina. She walked through to the plane – the punters in Pig Class were already seated and waiting, she noticed with pleasure – and settled in. After take-off a brace of quick whiskies knocked her out; she was practically able to curl up in the seat and treat it as a single bed. Sometimes it was an advantage to be so small.

After a couple of hours' sleep she tarted herself up in the loo and strode purposefully forward into first class, smiling aggressively at the cabin staff who might otherwise have stopped her.

The wide open spaces beyond the modesty curtain amazed her. It was a haven of quiet as only the seriously wealthy can create. Only the clicking of silver cutlery on bone china broke the silence. It took a few seconds to locate George; he was slumped against the window on the left, a vacant expression on his saggy face and a vacant seat — thank God, or Kit — beside him.

Gina slipped into it as unobtrusively as she could.

'Mr King, hello. Gina Howard, from the BBC.' She picked up his hand and shook it. It was limp and moist like something recently deceased. Gina was not normally squeamish but she had to struggle not to wipe her own palm dry against her dress.

'Uh, right.'

'I'm frightfully sorry to bother you like this but when I saw you were on the same flight I just had to make contact. I'm a friend of Becca Nichols by the way and she's always singing your praises.'

'Oh, really?'

'I won't interrupt you for more than a few seconds,' she said faster as she saw his eyes search for a passing stewardess, 'but I felt I had to let you know how much I admire the work you do. Yours is simply the only show on television worth watching these days. The young kids know nothing about talk show presentation, do they? Nothing! They've only got to watch you to see the master at work. It's a very stimulating, very sexy show.'

She flashed him her most winning smile.

'Well thank you, Miss . . .'

'Howard. Gina Howard. BBC.'

'Which programme?'

'Oh, you know the bloody Corporation. Shunted around from desk to desk. You may know my work from "Avenues", "Over the Edge", "Calling the Shots", er . . .' she named some recent award-winning series, none of which she'd worked on. 'And "Runway to Rio". Amongst others.'

'You're a writer or director?'

'I like to think of myself as a freelance ideas person. Creative input's the game. Getting the team right, so the ideas flow. You must find the same thing, don't you, George? Having the right personnel around you is vital?'

'We're a very tight team. No room for hangers-on.' He considered something. 'You say you know my PA. She ever talk to you about her job?'

'Heavens, no! She doesn't discuss what is clearly confidential.'

'Hm. She tell you I was on this flight?'

'Certainly not, this is pure fluke. I'm just getting away for a few days to unwind. I do love Bermuda so. Look, we won't talk now. We've both got work to do on the flight. I just wanted to make contact . . .' she rested a hand lightly on his leg, '. . . as a fellow pro.'

'Sure.'

'I say, I wonder if we're booked into the same hotel? We could have a drink tonight if you're not too busy? Where are you staying?'

'Oh, I've a lot of meetings to attend and work to be sorted out.'

'Yes, me too. It never stops for those of us at the top of the tree, does it?'

'Oh well, perhaps we'll bump into each other again. It's been a pleasure to meet you. Goodbye.'

'Yes, I would like to bounce some ideas off you if you —'

But, as George took his eyeshade from the pocket of his shirt, a steward appeared right on cue and bent low to Gina to ask, 'May I show you back to your seat, madam?'

'Actually I was just —'

'Have a nice stay in Bermuda, Miss . . . er . . .' George gave her an antiseptic smile and pulled his eyeshade down, then lay back and reclined his seat.

'Howard,' she said as she got up. 'See you later, George.' She looked at the immaculately attired steward and wondered if he was in the MHMATC. He looked like Kit's type, but then they all did. 'Bring me a large whisky, please.'

'If you have a word with the flight attendant in economy I'm sure she'll sort that out for you, madam.'

'Club, actually.'

'Yes, madam.'

Five hours later they touched down on the tiny island in the middle of nowhere. As they passed through immigration control – a couple of desks in the airport shed – Gina tried to keep close to George. She smiled at him a couple of times as they waited in separate queues, as if they were old friends sharing the same necessary inconvenience along with all the plebs from the back of the plane. He didn't acknowledge her; had she made so little impression? She'd have to work harder at him. Tact and diplomacy were clearly called for, qualities Gina normally wouldn't recognize if they ran up her legs and hid in her knickers.

She put up with the slow questioning of the fat woman behind the desk and finally had her passport marked with the necessary stamp and the proviso that she 'must not engage in gainful occupation'. Tough, she thought, I'm intending to get myself a whole new career this weekend.

She caught up with George as he was walking towards the line of cars and their listless drivers.

'Oh, hi again. Would you like to share a cab into Hamilton?'

'Thank you but no. I really have too much luggage to share. Good afternoon.' His smile was still ostensibly polite, but it was not the crinkly one he used for the cameras.

'Where to, miss?' her driver asked.

'You see that man getting into the blue car? We're staying at the same hotel.'

'Ah, Mr Fitch, he's a regular.'

'Mr . . . ? Really? Well, follow him. But not too close.'

The Glencoe Harbour Princess comprised a central old colonial-style building in a delicate pink-painted stone and a collection of pastel-coloured cottages which were clustered around two pools amongst the pines and giant rhododendrons. The premises occupied a small promontory which looked out on one side into the vast expanses of empty, blue-green sea and on the other curled around to make a safe harbour for a dozen or so huge ocean-going yachts. Gina marvelled at the heady atmosphere and tried not to let her awe-struck jaw sag too loose. Most uncool.

Behind the desk in reception stood a tall, slender young man, coffee-coloured and with a broad, lazy smile. His short-sleeved shirt was so white and the creases so sharp he could have walked out of a soap powder commercial.

'Good evenin', can I help you?'

'Hi, I'm Gina Howard of the BBC. Look, I don't have a reservation but I'd like a room for three nights. Maybe four.'

'I'm sorry, miss, we have no rooms at short notice.'

'You don't understand, I need to stay here. It's the only hotel that will do.'

'That's very kind of you, but there are simply no rooms available. If you would like me to ring some other —'

'Listen, Larry,' she read off his name badge and lowered her voice dramatically, 'I'm here to do some business with the gentleman who's just checked in so I need to stay in the same hotel.'

'He didn't book another room.'

'No, the thing is Mr . . . Mr Fitch doesn't know about this. I want to surprise him. In a sort of romantic way, if you see what I mean . . . ?'

His face lit up with a wicked grin. 'Oh-ho! I see.'

'So I have to stay here. And, Larry, I'm prepared to pay *anything* to get a room. Or do *anything*. Do you understand?'

He understood. His big brown eyes checked around for witnesses and then he took her bag, invited her to have tea on the terrace overlooking the ocean and said he'd let her know when her room would be ready. It might take half an hour to prepare.

'Thank you so much, Larry. And you just let me know what the cost is, won't you?'

They smiled at each other and she went off for her tea.

She sipped her Lipton's Earl Grey under the most beautiful blue sky she had ever seen, unblemished by the fluff of a single cloud. Her nostrils were pleasantly assaulted by the powerful and exotic perfumes of the purple bougain-villaea and the scarlet poinciana. She couldn't believe the plants were real and she touched them to be sure. The heat also insinuated itself in her nose and mouth, making her breathe more slowly and deeply, forcing her to adapt her city pace to the simple rhythm of the island.

The other scent that hung heavy in the thick air was money. Nothing explicit, but a satisfied air of relaxed mega-bucks permeated the atmosphere.

Beyond a little garden was the beach, the sand pink and clean, the sea calm, its waves barely seeming to have the energy to rise enough to break. Perhaps they were keeping a low profile in deference to the distinguished guests. Across the bay Gina could see Hamilton, the capital, look-ing for all the world like a toy town made up of coloured blocks placed with precision by a clever child with an eye for design. She could see the spire of the cathedral thrusting proudly into the magnificently empty sky.

So what was George King doing here, on a tiny island in the middle of the Atlantic, six hundred miles from terra firma? Having a holiday without his wife? Filming some-thing? Setting up a deal about presenting a show here? Hardly. But why didn't he want Becca around?

Becca! She'd forgotten. The poor bitch would be ringing the flat in Chelsea about arranging a romantic tryst over the festive weekend. It only took a minute to find a phone.

'Hello? Becca? Hi, honey, it's Gina. How are you? All right? . . . Yes, fine. I'm in Scotland. My auntie's had a stroke and I had to rush up here . . . Near Inverness. Oh, not a bad journey . . . A couple of days, I expect. She lives by herself, you see, and there's really no one else. No, my mother's skiing in the Alps so I said I'd come up to be with her. No, they think she'll pull through but I have to be here in case things get worse . . . How are you, honey? I miss you . . . What? It's a terrible line. I said, it's a terrible line. No, you can't call me back, this is a phone box at the hospital and it doesn't take incoming calls. What's the time in London? I mean, the weather. What's the *weather* like? Is it? Here, oh, snow. Yes, lots of it. Awful driving conditions. Look, honey, I'd better go, I think the sister wants a word with me. Sorry I won't be able to see you for a few days. I'll try and call you tomorrow. Look after all your bits and pieces; keep them moist for me. 'Bye, honey, 'bye.'

God, I'm an evil pig, she thought. Still, if the gullible bitch wasn't interested in taking George in hand she would happily do the honours. Starting here, starting now.

Her room was obviously one of the staff's quarters. It was at the back of the main building, by the kitchen, small and basic. There were ornaments on the shelves, little glass animals and fluffy toys. Gina swept them up and dropped them all into a drawer.

She took a leisurely bath and dressed in a silk blouse and skirt in electric blue by Comme des Garçons. Simple snakeskin Maud Frizon sandals and a heavy gold necklace by Sandra Cronan completed the classy, sexy look. Her red hair looked even more vibrant next to the blue silk and she was glad she'd recently had it cut. Yes, she looked stunning. If only I was six inches taller, she thought again, as she did every couple of days. Her mother hadn't thought of the poor offspring when she'd gone off fucking the shortarse who was her late father. Selfish cow. Typical of her mother. Huh.

She arranged with Larry that when she went in to dinner he would show her to George's table. Men! Give them one sniff of ripe beaver and they were as malleable as putty.

On the veranda overlooking the giant yachts she had a couple of 'dark and stormies', the local aperitif, and waited for her chance to strike. She saw her prey appear, waited five minutes and then sauntered into the dining-room. Larry was now maître d' in his smartest white jacket. He gave her a wink and then, po-faced, did the honours.

'Mr Fitch, your guest has arrived,' he said and left them

379

before George could correct him. She noticed the table was already laid for two. This boy was good.

'My, my, fate is throwing us together, isn't it?' Gina beamed at him with a little shrug of her shoulderpads and sat down quickly.

'Waiter! I think there's been a misunderstanding, Miss . . .'

'Howard. But please, call me Gina. I say, let's not bother him now, he's terrifically busy and, besides, it gives us the opportunity to continue our little chat. We have so much in common, after all, being in the same business.'

'I really think –'

'Anyway, there's less chance of you being pestered by weirdos if I'm with you. Have you ordered yet?'

Dinner consisted of succulent and exotic seafood – shark, shrimp, lobster and something called wahoo which was rich and chunky – and fresh fruit that looked nothing and tasted everything. While they ate Gina burbled away about her make-believe professional life, trying to draw confidences from George, but he merely nodded and smiled, giving her nothing to chew on.

'I spoke to Becca today,' said Gina over coffee, lighting first her own cheroot and then his rather tacky Embassy cigarette with her Boodle and Dunthorne lighter. 'She's a sweet enough child in her own way. Practical but . . .'

'But?'

'What shall we say? Two prawns short of a seafood salad? Not quite alive to the potential sometimes, don't you find?'

'She's very efficient.'

'Oh, sure, efficient. But so's a lavatory brush. It does its job. But in her position someone ought to be crackling with ideas and contacts. Pulling strings and pushing on doors. Maximizing the product's potential.'

'The product?'

'Yes. You.' She exhaled smoke from the corner of her mouth and watched his face as he mulled things over. She was starting the cogs turning. That's all she was hoping for tonight.

'I think there's a lot of potential untapped in there,' she said.

'In where?'

'Within you.'

'Oh yes? What is this, some holistic crap?'

'Far from it. Pure practical pragmatism. I've been involved in some of the most interesting image-changes in recent years. The new heavy metal Kylie look, Boy George's pipe-and-slippers reincarnation, and Michael Winner the radical feminist. That was quite a challenge, I can tell you. They said it couldn't be done, but it's amazing what Joe Public will believe when it's rammed down their tube.'

'Tell me about it.'

'I suppose you'd call me an Ideas Person.'

'You said that before. Sounds like a load of wank, if you'll pardon the vernacular.'

'You have a charming turn of phrase,' Gina smiled through the grey fug. 'No, it's nothing onanistic, I assure you. This is a proven approach. Just think what you could become.'

'Become? I don't need to *become* something, I *am* something. I am Mister Television!'

'Ah yes.' She inhaled the acrid smoke and held it for a while in her lungs, then let it drift out on her breath as she spoke. 'But for how long? If you're the top banana there's only one way to go, isn't there?'

'They love me, Mr and Mrs Average of Acacia Avenue. I'm their favourite uncle, their father confessor, his best mate, her secret lover. The whole country adores me, didn't you know that? Debates are curtailed in the House because MPs want to watch my programme. I'm the biggest and the best.' He leaned forward and thrust his face at her, suddenly a different animal without the veneer of bland charm. 'George King is fucking *it!*' he hissed, his

381

hand bunched into a fist. There were beads of sweat on his forehead and Gina felt the throb of danger at seeing this beast unleashed.

'That's it!' she whispered and grabbed his arm, squeezing his white flesh with her own tiny hand. 'That's the energy you should be using, that's what'll take you up into the next league. Out of this world! That's what the public haven't seen. Give them that and there's no limit to where George King can go. Believe me.'

He seemed alarmed by his own unguarded display and quickly reassumed the look of bemused whimsy she'd seen so often on the screen.

'Well, well,' he chuckled. 'The old jet lag affects us all in different ways, doesn't it? I think it's time I turned in. Busy day tomorrow.'

'Yes, me too. Serious shopping and . . . sunbathing to do.' It wouldn't do any harm to tease him a little. One sniff of ripe beaver . . . She knocked the dregs of her coffee back and chewed the grounds.

'If I spoke out of turn, please forgive me, Mr King. Forget about what I said. You really do seem to have things nicely worked out, despite Becca. I wouldn't want to interfere.'

'What do you mean, despite?'

'Hm?' Gina was studying her coffee cup with exaggerated concern.

'You said, "despite Becca". What does that mean?'

'Did I? I'm sorry, a slip of the tongue. I'm sure she's very useful. In her way. I've found that people have to want that kind of success as much as life itself to make it happen. If they don't, they stay mediocre and are quite content. No, no, you muddle through as you are. Don't listen to my over-ambitious ravings.'

She stubbed out her cheroot and stood up. She was sure he didn't appreciate the cut of her classy outfit but she was pleased all the same to notice his bleary eyes go straight to her cleavage.

'Well, I'm going to have a quick swim and then I think

I'll hit the sack. Thank you for an interesting evening. Perhaps our paths will cross again over the next few days. If not, keep striving for new heights. And remember, you are, in my opinion, the sexiest man on British television. Goodnight, George.'

'Goodnight, er . . .'

'Oh, for fuck's sake,' she muttered under her breath. 'It's Gina, okay?'

'Right. Gina.'

'Don't get up.'

'Oh, er . . .'

As he struggled to his feet she walked away, knowing that he was watching her sashay between the tables towards the door. To give him an extra few seconds to appreciate her small but shapely physique she stopped to thank Larry for his assistance and as she left the restaurant ran her hand up the short hair at the nape of her neck in what she hoped was a gesture that said 'play your cards right and you're in here, baby'.

Yes, this might just work. He was too much the slob at the moment but there was no denying his power. And that, of course, was the ultimate aphrodisiac.

Roll on Day Two of Operation Bermuda.

42

'Imagine that! After thirty years we meet again because you start knobbing my toy-boy in the snow!'

Annabel roared with laughter, throwing her head back and showing a mouth full of large, horsy teeth.

'Sorry, m'dear. Don't look so crestfallen, not meant to belittle you. But it's a wonderful image, two of you humping away like mountain goats!'

'Not exactly like mountain goats, Annabel,' Hal added quietly. 'Sorry, Kate, I shouldn't have said anything.'

'I'd have known anyway just by looking at you. You reek of it! He said this would happen. When he met you up on the slopes t'other day. Said he had the hots for you. Didn't you, baby?'

'I don't think I used quite that expression.'

'Well, she certainly made you horny. Remember distinctly. You made some rather colourful pun on giving her some "column inches", wasn't that it?'

'I . . . I'm surprised you two have been discussing me in such . . . intimate detail.'

'Don't be offended, please.' Hal gave her a rumpled look of apology.

Kate and Annabel were sitting opposite each other on either side of the fire which Hal was now stoking, adding logs from a big basket. It crackled and hissed, adding to the heat of embarrassment Kate felt, sitting there in a borrowed bathrobe. She watched the flames dance with macabre glee as they consumed the dead wood and transformed it to ashes. She was the wood, her passion for Hal the fire that seemed so attractive but worked its way through her until she was nothing but a fine dust.

She looked up. They were both watching her, Hal with a kind of fond concern, Annabel with a hint of amusement.

'What about your bath, Brand?' She didn't look at him when she spoke. 'You'll catch your death.'

'Ah yes. Rightie-ho. See you both in a while.'

He left them to a silence into which they both relaxed.

'Tell me, m'dear, d'you feel awful?'

'I feel rather confused.'

'You wanted Hal to yourself, that it?'

'Well . . .'

'Unrealistic. You can still have him, y'know. But not exclusively. If that's what he wants, of course. I've got no hold over Hal. I wouldn't want to have. Don't want the responsibility. In a strange sort of way I suppose I love him. But love's elastic, yes? Stretches to accommodate anything; it doesn't break. If you two begin something I shan't feel threatened. If it makes Hal happier, then that enriches my life too.'

Annabel rearranged her green and gold kaftan and drained her wine glass.

'You look very bewildered, m'dear. Am I making any sense?'

'Frankly, you sound rather like a "Love is . . ." cartoon. It's rather nauseating.'

'Well, that puts me in my place, doesn't it?'

The two women looked at each other for a long time without a word. Kate was glad the years had not been kind to Lady Annabel. The traces of her youthful beauty were there, but only just. Despite the crooked teeth, the lank grey hair, the lumpy body and the clothes of an ageing drag queen, breeding would always out. It was in the spine. And the vowels.

'It's ironic, don't you think?'

'Ironic?'

'Come, now, the parallels are obvious. Just as you stole George from me as a girl, now you're attempting to spirit

385

away my current paramour's affections. You're persistent, I'll give you that, if a trifle unoriginal.'

'I had no idea Hal was here with you.'

'Although you'd seen me with him when you went to the casting for the Country Kitchen?'

'Well, I . . . I didn't know you were . . .'

'Screwing? Well we are. You thought he was here by himself?'

'People do ski alone. I am.'

'You were. You seem to have found a playmate.'

'Annabel, I'm sorry if you think I've —'

'Please, I don't want your apology. Not over Hal nor George. In fact, your theft of George could have come a little sooner, to be honest. But I live in the present, not the past. More wine?'

'Thank you.'

Annabel went to the fire where the bottle of burgundy stood and topped up their glasses.

'Do you have children, Annabel?'

'Oh my. Where have we gone to now? Yes, I do. A daughter. She was going to come on this trip. Actually she wasn't,' Annabel corrected herself. 'She was invited out of a sense of . . . what? Let's think. Not duty, I don't believe in that. Kindness, I hope. But she doesn't approve of me at the moment. And she knows I don't like her very much.'

'Ah. How old is . . . ?'

'Gina. She's twenty-nine.'

'Born, what? a couple of years after you left Cambridge.'

'Yes. I met a charming Scandinavian. Lars was very virile, it's all those birch twigs. Well, I don't have to tell you about the effect of the pines, do I? We split up shortly after the baby was born. But we'd had a lot of fun making it. I think Gina still resents me for being what is now called a "one-parent family". She suffered at school until she started saying her father was dead, then she was the form favourite. Especially with the boys. She's always known how to manipulate people. She gets that from her papa, not me.'

Annabel was standing away from Kate now, gazing out of the window at the strangely ethereal snowscape, a bluey-grey in the moonlight.

'I don't much care for the person she is at the moment,' Annabel said quietly, almost to herself. 'She's consumed with ambition. Obsessed with something that's simply not good for her. Heading into dangerous water and there's very little I can do. I'm tempted to ask your advice, Kate.'

She turned round and gazed at Kate, weighing up something in her mind. Kate couldn't quite make out her features as the room was darker now and the light was behind Annabel.

'You're either the best or the worst person in the world to ask.' She knocked back some wine, gulping it as if it were water. 'I think I'll leave it for now.'

'As you wish.'

'Tell me about George's little boy. Ben, isn't it?'

'Yes.'

'Oh, I'm not above reading the gossip columnists. Or even sleeping with them if absolutely necessary.'

'Ben is . . . a fine young man.'

'Now, why don't I believe you when you say that?'

Kate sighed and looked into her wine glass, wondering how much of herself it was healthy to reveal.

'He has the potential to be a fine young man. Yes, that's more honest. I think he finds life rather difficult at the moment.'

'Well at that age . . . I hope you've told him it gets better.'

'No. I haven't.'

'You should.'

'I don't want to lie to him.'

'Meaning?'

'Meaning, in my experience it doesn't.'

'My dear,' Annabel sat next to her and took one of

387

her hands in both of hers. 'You and George are both enormously successful.'

'George is enormously successful and I am married to him. That's not quite the same thing.'

'No. I see.'

'My career is a joke. If people do ask for me they want George King's wife. When I was young I wanted to be Peggy Ashcroft or Wendy Hiller. Now all I'm offered are parts that Lily Savage has turned down.'

'Lily who?'

'Never mind!' Kate felt the tear glands prickle into life. It was a depressingly familiar sensation.

'Oh dear, you've been badly damaged, haven't you? I don't know what George has done but I know what he's capable of. I wouldn't put anything past that old bugger. I know he's your old man and you must love him deep down.'

'The love died a long time ago. It was there once but then . . .'

'Yes, I know about your other little boy. Christopher. Do you want to talk about it?'

Kate felt oddly insulted at hearing the name from someone else's mouth; someone she hardly knew. And yet at the same time she was tempted to pour it all out, to share with another mother the grief of losing a child; the guilt she lived with, the anger over George's irresponsibility and her mistrust of Ben. Why had he let his baby brother drown? Or had he really done more than let him die, had he caused the death as George had said? When young Ben had been questioned about it he just cried and cried and refused to talk. He'd clung to Kate's skirts and hidden his face. Was he trying to hide his guilt? She would always wonder but would never know. Had Ben been more involved than had ever been proved? Didn't elder children resent the arrival of a new baby? Had Ben's childish jealousy driven him to the easy option of a gentle push in Christopher's back as he teetered on the water's edge? Was it really as horrific as George had told her? How did you say to your son, 'Did you kill my baby?'

'No, I don't want to talk about it.'

'Perhaps that's the problem.'

'Oh please, no coffee-table psychology. I don't think you're qualified to lecture me about my life.'

'No, you're right. Who the hell am I to advise, with all the cock-ups I've made?' Annabel held her glass to her generous nose and gave a loud sniff.

'I'd better go. It's late.'

'Do you want some Rescue Remedy?'

Annabel reached down for a large, shapeless carpet bag in a familiar Auntie Annabel fabric of buttercups and dandelions. She rummaged around in it and eventually found a small phial. She made Kate put out her tongue and on to it squeezed a few vital beads of clear liquid from the bottle's rubber-tipped dropper. Kate didn't argue.

'Thank you. You're being kinder to me than I deserve. After all, I seduced your boyfriend in the snow.'

'We've got a lot in common.'

'Have we?'

'Oh yes . . . the same taste in men for a start. And the image of you two doing rumpy-pumpy has given me an idea for a new fabric. I shall call it "Moonlight Shaft"!'

Kate stood up to go.

'There's a nice big spare bed up in the attic room if you want to stay,' said Annabel with an air of total indifference.

'No, I . . .'

'Do, by all means. I'll send Hal to you in the night so you can play with his tummy-banana.'

'You make it sound irresistible.'

'Well "sexual intercourse" if you prefer to be clinical. But you're more than welcome to each other; I don't have a jealous bone in my old bod. So, stay and play, if you've a mind to.'

Annabel tucked a few stray grey hairs back in their clip and they instantly fell over her eyes again.

'I'd better go,' said Kate. 'Say goodnight to Hal for me, would you? And thank him for . . . taking me seriously.'

At the door Annabel wrapped her arms around Kate and squeezed her tight.

'It'll come out all right in the end,' she said. 'It always does.'

As she walked back to her hotel Kate realized she felt better about turning down a night with Hal than she would have done about accepting. For the first time in years she experienced a warm tinge of pride.

43

Day two of 'Operation Bermuda' dawned bright, clear and unbelievably warm for December. Well, believably so in Bermuda but it was not what Gina was used to greeting when she rose from her pit in Chelsea.

Larry brought her coffee and juice and fruit and bread on a tray, explaining that it was better she wasn't seen in the dining-room at breakfast-time or questions would be asked. He told her that George had already gone out. One of the hotel taxis had taken him to an appointment at Mangrove Bay, right at the end of the island by the dock-yards. But he'd be back in the evening for an early dinner at seven.

'So you got the whole of the day to yourself, to enjoy our lovely island. Nothin' to worry about and nothin' to hurt you.' His smile was quick and broad. She wondered if he was going to demand part payment of the cost of the room, a kind of deposit, but he just grinned and wished her good luck with her mission.

After several strong black coffees and a couple of cheroots to kick start her system she dressed in a simple Armani tee-shirt and cotton shorts from Issey Miyake and walked out into the garden. A giant bush twice as tall as she was hung its white blooms over her; she picked one and stuck it camply in her hair. Breathing the pure, sweet-scented air into her lungs and contemplating the stunning vista over the exotic vegetation to the sparkling waters of Salt Kettle Harbour she thought, 'How can I be such a scheming bitch when there are views like this? My very existence defiles the beauty of this island. Oh, tough shit. Bermuda can go back to being perfect after I've left.'

Wandering on the beach she found Larry whittling a piece of wood into a grinning mask; it looked rather like him. He was wearing jeans cut off at the knee and his permanent smile.

He offered to lend her his motorcycle so she could explore. He gave her what he worryingly called a 'crash course' in how to ride it and told her not to exceed twenty miles an hour.

'It's the law. And we still have the death penalty here, miss!'

He flashed her an even wider grin of straight, white teeth. His muscled, hairless chest had a subtle sheen from the light film of perspiration the morning sun had induced. Deliberately, unselfconsciously, knowing she made him feel uncomfortable, Gina let her eyes roam over his torso, appreciating the definition of a naturally fine physique.

'Thanks, Larry. We'll add the hire charge to the room cost, shall we?'

'No extras, miss. You just drive safely. And enjoy Bermuda!'

She rode carefully down the narrow lanes until she came into Hamilton, a buzzing town of some sophistication, where she lazily attempted a little shopping. But the Bermuda shorts were hideous and mostly imported from England; she could get better in South Molton Street.

By lunchtime it was hot enough to think about sun-bathing and swimming. A woman she asked for directions said she was very brave to go to the beach as it was 'only seventy degrees'.

'Hot enough for a redhead with freckles, lady,' she said and set off to find Horseshoe Bay. It was practically deserted, just a handful of teenagers fooling around with their surfboards in the water.

Gina swam for a while, then settled down for a bit of gentle sunbathing in the dunes, letting the sun work its usual magic on the knots in her body and her brain.

She soon abandoned the god-awful bonk-busting

paperback she was trying to read and simply lay back and fell asleep.

She dreamed that George was literally King. He'd been asked to take the throne after the Queen had been run over by a speeding moped rider and Prince Charles had declined the job, preferring to run a guest house in Lytham St Anne's. Diana didn't want to jeopardize her career fronting a rock band so the nation had voted for George's face on the stamps. He'd asked Gina to be his consort, but she was nowhere near the official height for the job so two naked beefeaters were performing an operation on her legs to stretch them. It hurt like crazy but she was adamant she could put up with the agony for the sake of the job.

She woke to find the afternoon sun burning into her unprotected shins, the rest of her exposed flesh a raw pink. The surfers had gone and there was a wind blowing sand about. There was something almost unnerving about being entirely alone in such a huge expanse of empty space, exposed to the might of the elements.

She returned to her secret room, feeling like a latterday Anne Frank, doused her tender skin with natural yoghurt and cursed her Scandinavian ancestry. Why couldn't her mother have made it with a tall, dark sexy Italian, for God's sake?

She dressed for dinner in a pale green dress by Katharine Hamnett that toned well with her hair and made her look, well, if not exactly tall, not quite so short.

By quarter to seven she was in position on the terrace overlooking the harbour, where she could see all approaches to the dining-room. Despite her unfriendliest face an old American couple tried to engage her in conversation. Bobby and Martha Gornik were from Tampa, Florida, and they'd been to Britain some years before. They both agreed that their favourite parts of England had been 'Edinburrow' and Stratford-upon-Arden.

'You do history so well in Europe,' gushed Martha.

Gina managed a gracious smile.

Just then she saw George approach, shambling across the terrace in a crumpled blue cotton shirt with badly-knotted tie and ill-fitting trousers, all of dubious provenance. She went to meet him.

'Hello, had a good day? Let me buy you a drink,' she said with too much enthusiasm.

He wasn't overjoyed to see her but was too aware of his image to tell her to sod off.

'Yes. A good day's business.'

'At the docks?'

'What?' He rounded on her ferociously, clearly struggling not to bawl her out. 'How did – what the hell is your game?'

'It's no game, George.'

'Did you follow me? *Did you?*'

'Calm down, you'll have a coronary. No, I didn't follow you. I have a lot of better things to do with my time. I simply asked after your whereabouts this morning in case we might take a cup of coffee together and I was told a car had taken you down towards the end of the island where the dockyards are. Okay? I don't know what your business was but it's none of mine and I have no desire to pry. My mission is quite different.'

'Mission? What are you talking about?'

'Let's have dinner and a chat, shall we?'

'Why the hell should I buy you dinner? You might be just a little gold digger.'

'I didn't say you should buy it. Let me treat you. We'll put it on my bill.' At this rate Larry was going to be out of action for quite a while collecting his payment. 'By the way,' she lowered her voice. 'The toupee's crooked.'

George grunted in reply and went across to a quiet corner table under the broad leaves of a bushy palm and waited for her to join him. With a deft movement he restored his rug to its correct position. Gina got drinks from the bar and took them over.

'So,' he said with a wafer-thin veneer of civility. 'How was your day? Lazy, by the look of it.' He'd noticed her pink arms.

'I was in the sunshine, yes. Thinking. About you.'

'Oh yes.' He gave her an indulgent smile. 'And what conclusions did you come to?'

'Many. I was thinking about your career, you see. And where it went wrong.'

'What the hell are you talking about now, you silly bitch?'

'That's a very annoying habit, George. My name is Gina. Feel free to use it. Or "Ms Howard", but not the term you just used. How Becca let you get into this condition I can't understand.'

She looked away at the perfect sunset; so vibrant were the shades of orange and purple radiating over the grey-green sea that it could have been orchestrated by the tourist board.

'Explain. But do it fast before I call security.'

'Security? Oh, you mean my friend Larry. Well, I was thinking about the decisions that must have been taken, by you presumably, perhaps in conjunction with your agent, your wife, your researchers, Becca, or whoever. The decisions to accept certain jobs rather than others, to endorse certain products, allow certain pictures to be published, give certain interviews. Even what clothes to wear for a shoot, what questions to ask on the show, what image to present. Your whole life — the public one at least — is about making those choices, isn't it?'

'In a sense.' She could tell he was wary of her, trying to weigh up just how dangerous she could be. He didn't want to underestimate her now and regret it later. Good, she was starting to have an effect.

'All those choices make up a long chain, George. And if even one of the links was changed, the whole chain would be different. Your career would have a slightly altered perspective.'

'Does this crap have a point?'

'Are you sure the links are exactly what you want? Are you always convinced you've been advised correctly?'

'I make my own career decisions. Apart from the researchers I don't work with a whole team of advisers like an Aspel or a Wogan did.'

'Ah yes, the late Sir Terry. He was very popular.' She paused. 'For a while . . .'

'So what are you saying? My days are numbered?' He laughed.

She smiled back at him. 'Something like that.'

'You silly little girl. Do you know just how big I am? Only major sporting fixtures and royal divorces beat me. And not always then. For example, in ratings terms –'

'George, I know all the facts and figures. I've done my research. And I've done it all myself, more to the point. What I'm trying to get through to you is that, based on my objective assessment of your career over the last ten years, since you really rose to the top and have been the undisputed King of the Box, Mister Television, the House-wives' Choice . . .' – there was no harm in flattering the old bastard if that's what he wanted to hear – '. . . your formula has become, how shall I put it? Stale. Predictable. Boring. Unadventurous. Lacking the –'

'Look here, madam –'

'Oh, don't start huffing and puffing at me. I'm not on some personal vendetta, I've got no axe to grind with you. I'm simply saying that if you don't want to slip down the greasy pole again you've got to find ways to stay at the top. There are plenty of younger, better-looking, hipper guys, and women too, who would gladly replace you as the flavour of the month. Bonnie McGrath, Hal Brand, Gideon Bloom, Samira Kracjinska. What plans have you got to keep ahead of the field?'

George stared at her hard. She had an uncanny impression that he was sizing her up for a blow. Then, unexpectedly, he smiled. His thin lips didn't part but they spread across his face, his eyebrows lifted, he leaned forward and spoke.

'You've obviously gone into this in some detail. Why not give me the benefit of your wisdom?'

Gina put her drink on one side, took a deep breath and met his challenge.

'Right. Well, I think the basic problem is that your image is too cosy; it's aimed at the C2, D and E females over about forty-five years old. That's all well and good but they're also getting older at the same rate you are and your current persona isn't going to get the younger crowd interested in your show.'

'Brilliant! So I become twenty-five again?'

'Now, now. What I suggest is that you use your age in your favour. Up to a point. You don't want to be lit to emphasize all your wrinkles, but weight, gravitas, experience are things that the Gideon Blooms of this world will never have. He and his kind are airheads and bimbos. Your great advantage is that you've been around. You're a man of the world. Do you see what I mean?'

Gina was leaning forward too now, jabbing the air with a finger, trying to make him see her point. She felt she was finally getting somewhere with him. If she didn't blow this she could be in there, part of the great fame-machine.

'Not yet. I'm a man of the world? Keep talking.'

'You shouldn't just be talking to teenage soap-stars and pop singers, you're a respected elder statesman of the small screen. You have untapped potential. The power to shock, to make people think. When I saw you doing that political piece to camera — God, you were so dangerous!'

'Bland, they said. Lightweight. I showed the bastards!'

'But my point is that with the right back-up you could do that every time. You're big. You could be bigger. Add elements of the real George King, the anger, the stubbornness, to take you into a new area. There's nobody around in that field with your credentials. The pretty boys chatting and flirting with actors and sportsmen are ten a penny.

And they're all younger and sexier than you.' She looked at his loose, sagging mouth and bleary eyes. 'Am I making myself clear?'

'Oh, perfectly. Anything else?'

'Yes, plenty.'

'Oh good,' he said sarcastically.

'Conversely, although I think you should use your experience to your own advantage, we shouldn't let your age be a distraction for the viewers. Consequently the image needs a whole revamp. Brighter scripts. Clothes from Boss, Armani, Paul Smith. A new . . . er . . . hairstyle. Well, since we're being honest: a fuck-of-a-lot-better toupee. Oh, and I think you should have some minor cosmetic surgery. Just to tighten up the jawline, perhaps take away the bags under the eyes.'

She looked carefully at those ageing rheumy eyes for reaction to her onslaught, but he was giving nothing away. Was he interested? Offended? Angry? His features were as inscrutable as if he was recording all-purpose 'noddies'.

'What do you think?' she asked at last.

He gave a fruity cough and then threw the rest of his whisky down his throat. 'Since we're . . . no, since you're being honest . . . I think we should eat. Boy!'

He clicked his fingers and stood up, his chair scraping on the stone terrace. It was the ubiquitous, solicitous Larry who showed them to their table. Gina led the way, slightly wary of having the bulk of George King behind her, like a wounded rhino. Had he shrugged it off as a scratch or was he about to charge?

They ate well on conch stew, rockfish with raspberry sauce and a mixture of fresh fruit sorbets with cream and chocolate sauce. The wine was Californian but drinkable.

They didn't raise the subject of 'George King – the Image' again but chatted desultorily about Bermuda, golf, books, Gina's career. Once more she tried to prise information from him about his private life and the reasons for this trip, but again without success.

He claimed not to know what play his wife was in nor what his son was doing at all.

'We don't speak much since he ... dropped out, I believe the expression is.'

'It used to be. From?' George looked blank. 'Dropped out from where?'

'Cambridge. King's College.'

'Ah-hah. Your old college. Told you I'd done my research. Of course, that's where you knew my mother.'

'Your mother?'

'Yes, Annabel Combes-Howard. She was at Girton at about the same time. She hated it. She "dropped out", too.'

'Good God. Annabel. Yes, we were friends for a while. So you're Annabel's little girl. Imagine that.'

'Yup, that's me,' she goofed, feigning embarrassment.

'She's done well. Silly, frilly things for women.'

'Yes. Cookbooks, then fabrics and cosmetics. Everything bar the workout video. God, what a grisly thought.'

'I heard she never married.'

'That's right.'

'Your father?'

'A Norwegian papermill owner called Lars Landesmann. He died when I was less than a year old.'

'A death in the family at that age. Very traumatic.'

George reached across the table for her packet of baby cigars and took one without asking. Immediately Larry was there with a lighter for him. Gina nodded to him to light hers too. They sat puffing away in silence.

'Let's walk,' George said suddenly, his cigar clamped between yellowing teeth. Gina wondered if he'd considered having them capped, or at least whitened. Probably not. She put it on her mental checklist for later.

They walked in silence at first, George seemingly pre-occupied. Was this the prelude to a private unburdening of secret regrets? Or a discreet withdrawal from the public domain prior to a serious man-to-man discussion? Maybe he was going to invite her to his room.

They strolled across the lawn, Gina following his purposeful lead. The tree frogs' chirping was amazingly loud. And it had the urgency of angry neighbours shouting complaints. Or perhaps a warning.

He began to talk about the next day, his meetings and appointments. Gina began to think that he was accepting her presence on the edge of his life after all, that her bid for power was having its first effects. Could she work alongside Becca in the future? No, she wanted control of this man, total control.

'It's nearly midnight,' said George. 'It'll be Christmas Day soon.'

'Bah, humbug.'

'I agree. It's a load of bollocks. So, tell me about yourself, Gina.' George led the way down a flight of stone steps on to the soft sand of Alpha Beach. The wind was much stronger now and quite cool. Each wave gave a loud crash as it threw itself at their feet. 'You're a talented girl.'

'Woman. Yes, but frustrated.'

'Why so?'

'I've been in T and F too long.'

'Talks and Features.'

'Yah, at the Beeb. I need to move on. I want a challenge.'

'What sort of area?'

'I know exactly what I want to do next, I've got a very specific job in mind. But whether it comes off or not doesn't only depend on me. It's in your sort of domain; television.'

'Tell me more.'

'Well . . .' She was having to raise her voice to top the sound of the waves and the suck of the undertow. 'Perhaps not tonight. But I'll tell you tomorrow. Definitely. Where are we going?'

She'd followed him into a small bay, more of a creek really, where the surging water was forced between two steep, craggy rocks that created a narrow entrance to a tiny, almost circular beach. It was smaller than the ballroom at

Combes Hall. The moonlight had difficulty penetrating this stony dungeon, but Gina could make out a flight of steps roughly hewn into the steep rock wall. There were a couple of iron rings embedded in the rock and she remembered the tales in the guide books of smuggling and shipwrecks. This would be the ideal place for a secret rendezvous and an illicit deal.

In the half-light she couldn't quite make George out and she had to concentrate to hear him clearly, his low, slightly suburban voice sounding and resounding eerily within the little chamber.

'I love this place,' he was saying. 'It's so private, so secret. Locally they don't have a name for it because they don't admit it even exists. I like that attitude.'

'What, hypocrisy?'

Gina listened for his reply but heard nothing other than the sea. To get her bearings she reached out a hand to the rock face, flinching as she touched wet seaweed.

'I feel at home here,' George said suddenly. 'Among the rich and famous.' There was no hint of irony in his voice. His features were shrouded in gloom and she was straining to hear him over the hiss and splash of the waves as they dashed themselves to destruction.

'They tell me that Bill Cosby has just bought an estate across the bay.'

'There goes the neighbourhood!' said Gina. Again, no response. He seemed to be fiddling with something at his neck. 'No, seriously, George. Bermuda is a beautiful island. Perfect.'

'Oh, but surely you have a plan to improve on perfection. Just as you would improve me!'

This time the tone of bitterness was unmistakable.

'I . . . I hope you didn't mind my speaking out. I didn't mean . . . Look, it's very dark and getting a bit cold. Shall we go back?'

'Yes, in a minute. Gina, my dear, come over here a moment. I want you to look at this. It's fascinating.'

Without thinking, she obeyed, stumbling the few steps to him over the wet sand, her arms in front of her for protection. But it proved the very opposite.

It was a simple matter even for a man of George King's bulk and unfitness to grab her wrists, wrap his necktie around them and knot it tightly, then loop it through one of the rings in the rock wall and fasten it securely.

It was done before Gina realized what was happening. She pulled back but her wrists were tied tight to the iron ring.

'What the hell . . . ? George!'

'You stupid bitch,' he hissed at her. 'You arrogant little arsehole. You dare to sit there and tell me where I'm going wrong with my career? Christ! Who do you think you are?' She had no trouble now making out his ugly face in the dark; it was inches from her own and he screamed at her, '*Who the fuck do you think you fucking are?*'

'George. Mr King. I'm sorry. I didn't mean to offend you. It was constructive criticism. Believe me.'

'Bitch!'

'I want to work with you, George. That's the job I was talking about. That's why I came to Bermuda. It was Becca who told me you were coming here. Look, I really think I can offer you a new perspective, an objective eye on new directions, new images. How to stay ahead of the pack. I want to be part of your team, George. It was all meant in a . . . a positive way.'

'You lying little —'

'It's true!' Gina screamed above the roar of the waves, whose spray penetrated over the rocks and into the stone torture chamber. She wanted to wipe the film of sea mist from her glasses to see him better and be prepared for his next move.

'Look, George, untie me, this is ridiculous.' She heard herself sounding like a prim schoolteacher but she didn't want him to hear the creeping panic in her voice. She turned around as far as she could, scraping her bare arms on a jagged edge of wet rock. He was a vague black shape among the rest of the darkness, muttering to himself. Suddenly, too late to avoid it, she saw him lunge towards her and a dull blow from his shoe on her legs made them crumple under her. The sharp pain of the rock digging into her arm struck her at exactly the same moment that she jarred her spine on impact with the ground.

'That hurt, George!' she screamed at him, furious at the indignity and the stabbing pain. 'What the hell's happening here? Have you gone crazy?'

For a moment she couldn't hear him. Then his voice was by her ear, quiet and menacing.

'Yes. I've gone crazy. I tell you, it's going to hurt some more before I've finished with you.'

'Look, I've explained that I wanted to help you. Is that what all this is about? Just undo my hands and we can talk about it.'

'We can talk anyway. Except you won't be able to in a minute.'

'What? George . . . Mr King . . .'

The moon came from behind a rare cloud and brought a few seconds' clarity. Gina saw blood on her torn dress and noticed it was coming from a wound on her arm. She realized now that it was throbbing with real pain as she lay, twisted and half-suspended by the wrists from the iron ring. She saw George apparently fiddling with his waist as he had done with his neck.

'Does this hurt?' he shouted, his arm raised over his head like a tennis player. Then it plunged down and his leather belt smashed into her face. 'That hurts, doesn't it?' he yelled with obscene glee.

There was a long beat between the initial shock which snatched her breath away and the dawning awareness that her face stung with a pain more acute than she thought the body could bear. But the terrible leather whip crashed down again, hitting her almost in the eye. Her glasses flew off and bounced on the slimy stone beside her. And again he lashed at her, this time across her legs, the leather ripping at her soft, white flesh. She tried to tuck her legs under her, but she was weak and could feel the resistance draining from her body.

He could sense it too. While she lay, dazed from the onslaught, he pounced on her legs and wrapped the belt deftly around her ankles, pulling it through the buckle until she thought it would cut through her like a wire through cheese.

She wanted to scream, not only to summon help but to voice her outrage and express her fear. She tried but there was no strength left to fight, no energy to resist. He could do anything now.

'So I look too old, do I? Need a new image? A new toupee? Plastic fucking surgery? You jumped-up, sodding little toe-rag!' The back of his hand slapped across her face was nothing compared to the leather tongue of his belt, but after the other slashes it stung like the slice of a razor. And the salt spray ate into her wounds like acid.

Her legs were numb now, her vision blurred. She blinked and felt the sudden pang of agony somewhere behind her eyes as if her skull had been split open by his blows. It probably had. He was talking to her, more quickly now. Perhaps it was all over. Was he going to let her go?

'Let's have a look at you, girlie. Let's see how *you* can be improved.' He stood over her, ready to strike again. She was panting in pain and fear, trying not to cry or show signs of weakness. She wouldn't let the bastard see her tears.

'You're a midget, aren't you? A real short-arse. And so white. Like an ugly albino rat. Your hair's disgusting. You need a complete going over, you do!'

He bent quickly and pulled at her dress.

'No!' she shouted, surprised by the strength of her voice.

She tried to curl up and protect herself from his groping hands, but he scrabbled with her wriggling legs and grabbed them. She jerked to shake him off but he was

404

too strong; he pulled them straight and fell on to them, planting his ungainly bulk on them with such force she expected to hear them snap. Rough, cold hands were under her dress, between her legs, pulling at her pants.

'Come on, let's have a look at you. Let's see.'

'NO!' She bellowed at him, horrified. 'No, get off me!'

But she had no defence. He tore the thin cotton to gain access to her and she winced as he forced his hand between her thighs.

'YES, YES, YES! I will! I'm George fucking King and I can have you any time I like!'

He pawed at her, brutally determined. Gina screwed her eyes up and felt such a nausea in the pit of her guts she thought she was going to throw up. She couldn't breathe, couldn't move, couldn't think. Nothing made sense any more. This isn't happening, she repeated to herself. It isn't happening.

He gave a shove and suddenly was still. His hand seemed to soften.

'Oh God,' he said quietly. 'Yes . . . It's so good . . . Don't you like that? . . . You lucky little girlie . . . That's so nice. Isn't that good?'

She was breathing again now, heavily, somewhere between sobbing and gasping.

'Isn't that good? Tell me that's good!' he snapped.

'Yes, yes, it's good,' Gina managed to say.

'Has anyone ever done this to you before? Don't tell your mummy, will you? This is our special secret . . . Ooh, isn't that nice?'

And then suddenly she was empty. When she dared to open her eyes she saw him holding his hand to his face, sniffing his fingers and licking them one by one.

'You want to be part of the George King phenomenon? I'll give you part of George King . . .'

He let his trousers drop to his knees.

Oh no, not that. Please not that. She made to shout, but nothing came.

She tried with one last effort to shift her legs to fend him off but they were numb and didn't respond to the messages her muddled brain sent. Her arms were over her head, her fingers had long since lost all feeling. She could smell his body approach her and then the clouds cruelly parted again to let the moonlight illuminate the full horror of the scene. She saw his stubby brown cock jutting up almost vertically out of the slit in his underpants. The angle made it look silly, almost comical. He had his hand on it and he pushed it down as if showing it to her for her approval.

Her inspiration seemed to come from nowhere. Like a bird attracting its parent's attention she simply opened her mouth. It was enough. He gave the desired response.

'Oh, you want to taste it, do you? You little slut!'

He straddled her limp body and aimed it at her face. 'Yeh, this is what you wanted all the time. Some Christmas present, eh?'

It took only a second for her to seize her opportunity. With a single-minded tenacity and a grip she didn't know she possessed Gina clamped her teeth together on the skinny meat in her maw.

There was a scrunching sound, a hiatus of quiet and she recognized the metallic taste of blood.

She let go as soon as she heard the squeal, louder even than the roar of the wind and the waves. It could have been a stuck pig or a seagull's squawk. The shock was enough to loosen her grip.

George fell to one side of her, clutching himself in both hands and howling in pain.

Shit! You vicious –!

He was trying to find enough light to examine himself. Gina turned her head and spat the taste of him from her mouth. As she did her guts began to retch and she heaved the contents of her stomach down her chest.

'YOU EVIL BITCH!'

In her agony and shame, and in the gloomy half-light

Gina didn't see his fist coming. The full-blooded blow caught her on the left temple and slammed her head with a loud crack into the stone wall behind her. She passed out instantly.

44

'Like, what the hell are you saying, man?'

'I'm saying that things can't stay the same for ever. It's nothing too existential.'

'Aw, come on, don't get all intelligent on me.'

'No, that's a bit below the belt, isn't it?' said Ben, scrubbing at a cracked plate as he stood at the sink wrapped in a plastic apron.

'Yeh, well, speaking of below the belt – geddit, eh? eh? – how come it's all cleaning up and time for a change since you waved your willy around?'

'Well, I suppose the two things are not unrelated. Come on, Terry, lend a hand. Put all the rubbish from the table in one of those bin liners and then get the broom and give the floor a proper sweep.'

'Christ, what the hell happened to you in Germany, man? You were more fun when you used to sit on the cliffs writing crappy poems and gazing out to sea like a loony.'

'Terry!' Sue was picking at a splinter in her foot. 'I think it's a cool idea to tidy up a bit. I'll sort out those newspapers in the other room.'

She got up and picked her way between the cats that were busy on the floor with an empty tuna tin, pushing it around as they licked it clean. Ben saw Sue's hesitant, bobbing walk with new eyes now. It said that she was doomed to a life of doubt and struggle. He had cared slightly about her once, but now there was nothing he could do for her. She'd have to do it for herself or not at all.

'Wait,' he said. 'Wait.' There must have been a new tone in his voice, because even the cats' heads turned to him for a moment. Sue and Terry looked with their usual double-glazed expressions and Ben felt an urge to swing the greasy frying pan in his rubber-gloved hand into their faces and scream at them to wake up. But he knew it was already too late.

'What? Do you want to do the papers yourself?'

'Man, c'mon. I'm not into fuckin' dusting. Let's roll a spliff and chill out.'

'Oh Jesus Christ, if you could hear yourself!' Ben slammed the pan down on to the draining board and the metallic clang had possibly more effect than if he had actually hit them in the face with it. The cats abandoned the tuna tin for the safety of the other room.

'What happened to you, Terry? When did you lose your brain and the ability to think?'

'Wha'?'

'Precisely. You could have been a human being, you know.'

'Nah listen, Benny-boy, don't come the patronizing undergraduate with me.'

'That's good, that's good. An insult is good.'

'Ben, did something happen to you in Germany? When you were making the video, did they give you something?'

Sue was marginally more on the ball than Terry. But it was the wrong ball.

'Yes, they did. They gave me insight.'

'Wow. Insight. Is that like Ecstasy, man?'

'Shut up, Tez. Come on, Ben. Tell us what happened in Germany. You've really not said anything since you got back. Did it go all right?'

'I was a disaster. A total disaster.'

'You were? Why? Were the others . . . ?'

'The others were brain dead, by and large. Apart from whoever is masterminding it all and making a small fortune out of gullible wankers. No, they were the sort of people who can screw an alsatian or a sibling with the same *sang froid*.'

409

'That's weird. Screwing a sibling.'

Terry scratched his bushy beard with thick, slow fingers. 'How do you mean, Ben?'

'I couldn't deliver the goods.' He smiled at the memory of his embarrassment. Sue looked confused. 'I couldn't get a hard on.'

'Oh. But you normally . . . I mean you used to . . .'

'Hey, man.' Terry was opening his tin of dope. 'What kind of a dog is a sibling?'

'Listen. I've come to some decisions and they affect you both.'

'Is it one of those big fuckers?'

'Ssh, Tez. What decisions, Ben?'

'This cleaning up. It isn't just about the house. It's about my life. I'm spring cleaning my life.'

'Wow.'

'Well, that's . . . beautiful, Ben.' Sue smiled at him so sweetly he wanted to slap her. 'You've really thought about things, haven't you?'

'Look, being involved in that stuff has made me re-evaluate one or two things.'

'You're gonna make us all rich doing more dirty movies.'

'Not quite. If I was what they were looking for it would be all too easy to be sucked in by it.'

'Sucked off, you mean! Ha-a-a-a! Ha-a-a-a-a!' Terry's laugh reminded Ben of a vocal exercise his mother used to do when he was young. 'Hey, what d'you mean, if you were what they're looking for? What's wrong with you?' He sounded like a pimp seeing his commission about to disappear with his rejected client.

'My brain is not in my dick, is what's wrong with me. They don't want people who think. I'm going legit. I want to live here properly. Without hiding when the doorbell goes. Without stealing food to eat. Without being whispered about in the village. And without sleeping on a lumpy, bloody sofa.'

'Well, if you want to swap back again —'

'But there's two of us, man.'

'Exactly, there are two of you and only one of me. And there's one bedroom. And I'm going to sleep in it. There's one sitting-room and I'm going to sit in it. There's one bathroom and I'm going to bath in it. There's one kitchen and I'm going to, um . . .'

Sue bent down and picked up the scrawny cat that was rubbing itself obscenely against her bare legs. She held it to her face as if it were a handkerchief or a sweet-smelling bunch of flowers and muttered half-audible questions into its fur.

'What's the . . . my little . . . did you want . . . ?'

'Wait a minute. I don't get this. Where the hell are we supposed to bath and sit and –'

'Tez, I think Ben's saying he wants us to leave.'

'Well done. But there's no rush. Just be gone within the week. It's time we went our separate ways, kiddies.'

45

London. God, how she hated arriving back in this smelly, dirty, unfriendly dump. After the slopes of the Alps the delights of London seemed dubious at best. It had only been a week, but as the car climbed slowly up the hill to Hampstead through the inevitable traffic and the brown slush she marvelled at how few visible changes there were compared with the internal metamorphosis she felt she'd undergone up in the mountains. She was ready to tackle the challenges that awaited her.

What state had she left Jack Fever in? Would she be arrested for assault? Would Robin disown her? Did Ben still hate her? And what of *O Jackie*?

She'd find out soon enough.

As Alec swung the car around into their driveway she was surprised to see a small posse of people rush up to her window. She knew instantly from their seedy clothing and air of rumpled inferiority that they were reporters. The photographers were better dressed but no more civilized. She waved and nodded at them, half-hearing shouted questions but too old a hand to do more than smile.

'Alec, what's all that about, do you know?'

'Yes, Miss Fitch. I believe there's been some speculation in certain of the tabloids about Mr King.'

'Oh yes? What speculation exactly?'

'I'm not sure I should . . .'

She looked for his eyes in the rearview mirror, but he was staring resolutely forward at the long driveway as if it demanded his total concentration.

'Oh, come along, I won't blame you.'

'Very well.' He picked up a folded paper and passed it over his shoulder to her. 'I'm sorry, Miss Fitch.'

Kate took the paper. The front page screamed at her: 'King-ky George!!'

She skimmed through it quickly. Some of it was speculation, pure and simple, but a lot of the gossip was obviously carefully researched and presumably checked out by the lawyers.

Well, well, Hal had certainly followed up her lead. There was even a photograph of a blonde airhead trying to look sexy, sprawled over a bed. Was this George's mistress? This cheap little . . . floosie was the word that came to mind. She smiled as she read Hal's prose. He'd even found the space to sing her praises as the 'supremely talented but underappreciated wife, now neglected for younger, firmer flesh . . .' She wasn't sure about 'firmer'. Had he phoned his copy through after their aborted romp under the snowy pines? Or left it as a time bomb to explode while he was out of the country?

She felt both a certain pride in seeing herself discussed in a national paper — 'when will the theatre world see sense and give this woman the break she deserves?' — but also the thrill of fear at wondering how George would react when he got back from the Bahamas or wherever it was he'd gone. Kate read the article to the end. The final paragraph read: 'There has also been mounting speculation that Mr King is about to interview his wife, Kate Fitch, on his TV show. Sources close to Mr King refuse to confirm or deny it. Certainly it would be an interview that many viewers would like to see. It could be just the show to salvage his tarnished image.'

Kate handed the paper back to Alec.

'Thank you. When do you fetch Mr King from Gatwick?'

'Tomorrow afternoon, Miss Fitch.'

'That should be an interesting journey for you, Alec.'

'Aye, interesting is one word for it. Here we are, Miss Fitch. Home.'

'Sweet home. Yes.'

'This isn't going to be easy.'

'No.'

For a moment neither of them spoke, nor were they able to look each other in the eyes.

'Would you like lunch? Or a drink?'

'No. Nothing. Thank you.'

Robin sat down opposite Kate, his hands neatly symmetrical on the big oval table, his face a mixture of concentration and contrition.

'You look well,' he said without looking at her.

'Thank you.'

'Was it a good holiday?'

After the briefest of pauses Kate said, 'Excellent. Good snow and . . . I met some interesting people.'

'That's nice.'

'I had time to do a lot of thinking, too.'

'Good.'

'About my career. Or lack of it. And about . . . what happened.'

'Now then, about that —'

'Robin, we can't pretend it didn't happen. I think we should try to be honest and adult about the whole stupid business. I know it'll be embarrassing but we're just going to have to cope with that.'

'Yes. That's very sensible.'

Robin finally looked straight at her, a hint of a challenge in his gimlet eyes. 'I suppose you imagine an apology is in order.'

'No, not from you. Nor from me. I regret how things turned out, so far as I know the facts, but not my part in them.'

Kate paused and listened to a police siren wail past down in Chelsea Harbour.

'What I'm trying to say is . . . I slept with that little shit when I was feeling miserable about being married to George and about getting older and touring in a third-rate thriller and . . . I can't say he seduced me, I should have had more sense and seen what the ambitious little creep was up to. I think he was using me to get to you. Like a silly teenager I was taken in by his act. I thought he genuinely felt something for me but, as I see it now his only interest was himself. As I'm sure it always will be.'

'I think you're absolutely right, Kate.'

'You do?'

'Yes. Young Mr Fever is a scheming little tart. He'd do anything to anyone to get what he wants. He has no conscience and precious little in the way of morals. The funny thing is he won't eat French veal or tuna that isn't "dolphin friendly". He'd wash out Streisand's hankies for a part in *Yentl II*.'

'What a terrible thought.'

'Washing Streisand's hankies?'

'*Yentl II*.' She looked at the walls of Robin's conference room. Not a picture, a mirror or a photograph relieved the unrelenting white expanse.

Robin cleared his throat. 'Yes, Jack Fever was using you to get at me. He told me so.'

'What?'

'Yes. Sorry. But you're not alone. He used me too. He wanted me to represent him and he thinks his chocolate-box looks are his passport to everything he wants. So far, of course, they have been.'

Kate observed him with interest: small, neat and rather too correct in his manner. She'd always thought of him as a 'soft' person, his dubious sexuality a weakness in his character. Now she realized just how strong he was, able to show himself in all his complexity.

'So you're not . . . seeing each other?'

He smiled. 'We see each other quite a lot. But we don't go to bed together. We haven't since . . . that night. It

415

wasn't what either of us wanted. I thought it was; he pretended it was.'

'But you do see each other . . . ?'

After the briefest pause Robin looked straight at her and said, 'I represent him.'

Involuntarily Kate took a sharp breath. 'But I thought you said he was using you.'

'Yes, he's a selfish little whore. He's also a . . . useful actor. He's got a certain quality, as you told me yourself. He's watchable. And therefore marketable. And marketing is my job, after all. So I have fifteen per cent and, more to the point, control of something potentially very useful. Something that – let's be honest, as you suggested – could make an awful lot of money.'

'My God. Is that what it comes down to, Robin? Percentages?'

'Of course. Do you feel betrayed?'

'I don't know. I feel angry but I'm not sure who with.'

'You have a heart. He doesn't. That's his loss. Pity him; he'll never know loneliness, boredom, sorrow.'

'Pity him? I envy him that,' said Kate.

'No. He's shallow. That's why he'll never be a great actor. Or an even half-way decent human being.'

'But meanwhile . . .'

'Meanwhile he's just landed his first telly, a good medium-sized part in the new Alan Bleasdale for the Beeb, he's done two commercials – chocolate bars and jeans – he's had an availability for a West End musical of a Molière play and John Schlesinger is thinking of him for a small part in a mini-series he's shooting in the States.' He put down his cup. 'That's why I'm representing him.'

Kate's jaw hung open in amazement. 'There's no justice. God, I'd like to –'

She remembered she already had.

'What about . . . ? Is his face . . . ?'

'All right? That depends on how you look at it. No pun intended. He's actually scarred for life. But since he lives

416

a charmed existence wouldn't you just know that his scar is rather sexy. It runs up from his top lip, here on the left,' Robin demonstrated. 'About an inch long. It gives him a bit of a sneer, like Bogart or the young Elvis. The superficial damage can be covered by make-up for now and will disappear completely in time, but he'll always have that sexy top lip. Casting directors are starting to ask for the boy with the scar.'

'And that's a gift from me.'

Kate let a thin laugh escape her own lips. 'If I'd chopped his balls off he'd probably be a successful counter tenor by now.'

Her laugh died and she sighed deeply.

'Oh, Robin. What a mess.'

She stood up and looked out of the window. 'Right then, do we need to do any paper-signing or anything?'

'What for?'

'Well, to undo the . . . to release each other from our professional relationship.'

'Oh, I see. No, we just have to tear up a piece of paper. It's quite simple. If you want to do it now . . . ? Just a minute.' He left the room.

She felt sad to be breaking with Robin after all this time. No doubt they would promise to remain in touch and be friends, but neither of them would believe a word of it. He'd been a good agent always and a good friend when necessary for over twenty-five years. She'd have to start re-building with someone else. Was it all worth it? Just to get the occasional cameo in a telly or a Number Two tour? At this rate she'd soon be reduced to working on the fringe. Was this the time to retire gracefully?

She could hear the clatter of a keyboard and the ringing of phones in the office. Everyone was frantic: phoning and faxing and rushing and dashing about. Her life had nothing in it to make her that busy. She needed a structure; she needed a goal.

'Lili will bring our contract in.' Robin came back into

the conference room and sat down again. 'It's been a long time.'

'Yes.'

'We've done some good deals at this table.'

'Yes.'

'Not as many as you deserve. I've always felt you should have had better luck.'

'Tell me about it!'

'Perhaps a new agent will bring you that.'

'Perhaps.'

'You should be doing what Eileen Atkins is doing. Or Susannah York. Or Ju—'

'Don't say Judi Dench!'

'Sorry. Who are you going to? Which agency? We'll need to know so my angels can forward mail and so on, tie up the loose ends.'

Anyone would think somebody had died. 'I haven't decided yet. There's no rush.'

'No. Of course not.'

She knew that he knew she didn't have anyone lined up.

'Robin. There's one last thing I'd like you to do for me. If you would. If it's not compromising you, professionally.'

'Of course. If I can.'

Lili came into the conference room without knocking. She had a folder labelled 'Kate Fitch' in her hand and an expression labelled 'thrilled to bursting' on her bright, round face.

'Here we are, Robin.' She handed him the folder.

Kate felt as if she were collecting the ashes of her own career from the undertaker. She'd had a good innings but it was kinder this way; it put a stop to her many years of suffering . . .

'I thought you'd want to know,' Lili burst out suddenly. 'We've just heard from John Schlesinger's office. It's a definite yes.'

'Thank you, Lili. It can keep,' said Robin quickly.

'To play the Richard Chamberlain part as a young man. That's the lead in the first two epis—'

'Never mind now, Lili,' Robin insisted through clenched teeth.

'Oh. I'm sorry.' She obviously remembered something and began to blush. She stood there unable to speak or make a clean exit. Kate came to her rescue.

'That's Jack Fever, is it, Lili?' she asked calmly.

'Yes.'

'Well, good for him. Tell me, Lili, do you think he's sexy?'

'Well . . .' she glanced at Robin for advice but got none. 'He's . . . not exactly sexy but . . . well, yes, I suppose so.'

'Yes. I suppose so, too.' Kate smiled at her as if she'd given the right answer and then turned her back and walked away. She heard Lili leave the room.

'He's going to be big, isn't he? A young Richard Burton? Peter O'Toole?'

'No,' said Robin. 'Not that big a talent. Perhaps Michael York or Peter Firth. But we could be talking household name if we play it carefully and get the breaks.'

'You will. He will.'

'We'll see.'

Kate turned back to look at Robin. She wondered if his heart had been broken by Jack Fever too. How could she tell? His heart was so well protected from feeling anything at all.

'So,' she said too brightly. 'The contract.'

'Yes. Here it is. All we have to do is tear it up.'

'Right.'

It was on the table between them. One page of A4 paper, signed by each of them all those unhappy years ago. They both looked at it; neither of them spoke. Kate was aware of the hum of the air-conditioner. How typical of him, she thought. He even controls the air that he breathes.

The door swung open again and Lili stood there, embarrassed and awkward, a piece of paper in her hand.

'Sorry to interrupt but . . .' She shuffled forward and handed Robin the paper. Kate could see it was a fax.

'Well . . .' Robin seemed almost thrown by something, not a position he was used to. 'Well . . . I must say this is a turnup for the trousers. Well!'

'Anything I can know about?'

'Lili, I think a couple of cups of something strong. Raspberry, perhaps. Be an angel.'

'Right you are.'

'*Well.*'

'Robin, if you say "well" again I'm going to hit you. What is it?'

'It's a fax from Becca Nichols. On behalf of George. Inviting you to be a guest on his show. This Friday. Can you believe that?'

'Nothing he does surprises me any more. Angers and disgusts me, certainly. But surprises? No.'

'You'll want nothing to do with it, I imagine?'

'Robin! I want everything to do with it. I thought you had my best interests at heart? Think of the publicity. Fax them straight back and tell them yes.'

'Katie, my love —'

'It's all right, I'm a big girl now. I can cope. I shall upstage him something rotten.'

'I don't think you should antagonize him. This is the man who nearly broke your jaw a few weeks ago.'

'He's hardly likely to wallop me with millions watching, is he? He's got too much to lose.'

'But —'

'Robin, please. Just . . . say . . . yes.'

'Well, if you're sure?'

Kate nodded to him. 'Oh, our agreement. Do you still want to tear it up?'

'I didn't want to in the first place.'

'I just assumed . . . I was so unprofessional. I broke my contract, I disappeared. I also tried to kill my leading man.'

'A mere bagatelle! You silly old slug. I made a fool of

420

myself too over this beautiful, evil child. I don't want you to leave. You're practically family.'

'Then what the hell are we doing? How about we continue as before?'

'How about that? Put it there.'

Kate extended her hand.

'Shake . . .'

'Rattle . . .'

'And roll!' they said together, going through an old routine.

'And let's drink a toast,' said Kate as Lili brought in two raspberry teas. 'To Hal Brand, gentleman.'

46

London. God, she was glad to be back. Filthy, uncaring, callous, impractical London. Gina knew all its faults and loved the smelly place anyway. The taxi-driver who spouted his racist views at her and then tutted over the size of her notes when she paid the fare; the woman in the corner shop who served her while jabbering in Punjabi on the phone, the dogs who barked all night and crapped on her doorstep in the day – she loved them all. She felt safe here.

She marvelled how little things had changed in her absence. The same landmarks, the same houses, cars and people in their appointed places. Even the sky was the same dull grey as the day she'd left. The black bin liners on the pavement could have been new ones or the same as a few days earlier, before Christmas.

Just a few days. That was all that separated her from her previous incarnation. She may have thought life was bad before, frustrating and disappointing, but had she known what the last three days held in store she would willingly have settled for that rather than endure the indignities of the stone dungeon on Alpha Beach.

She skimmed through her mail and threw most of it away. Messages on the answering machine didn't excite or entice her. Gossip and boring appointments. A message from her mother who said she was off skiing with a friend and left a contact number 'in case of emergency'.

She soaked in a bath for half an hour and thought again about the events on the beach the other night. It might have been a lifetime earlier and half a world away, but the effects would never fade from her. From her mind or her body.

She looked down at it now, in the cooling water of the bath. She was hunched up, as if against the cold, hugging her knees for comfort. It didn't feel like her own flesh and blood, she wished she could disown it, give it away to a charity shop like a garment she was bored with. Slightly soiled. She felt no cleaner after the bath than before.

Her face was still sore from his blows and her wrists bore red marks where he'd tied her to the wall. Thank God Larry had come looking for her when he saw George come back alone to the hotel.

She rubbed her bruises and her fury rose once more to the surface.

The bastard! Gina was adamant that she would find a way to get even with him. To inflict on him the shame she now felt. To shaft him. To rape him. To fuck him good and proper.

When the door buzzer went Gina ignored it. There was nobody in the world she wanted to see. But the buzzer went again. And again. Wrapped in a loose silk kimono she went to answer it, to tell whoever it was to bugger off.

'Yes?'

'Gina? It's me.'

'Becca?'

'Hi. Can I come in?'

'It's kind of awkward right now. Will it keep?'

'Oh. Are you . . . entertaining?'

'No. But I . . . Oh, hang on.'

She buzzed her in through the main entrance and opened her own front door a fraction, peering out suspiciously through the vertical slit.

Warily she let Becca in and retreated to the furthest, darkest corner of the living-room, watching her carefully close the door, wipe her feet, sit on a straight-backed chair and settle herself into conversational mode, legs crossed, hands in lap, face set in a serious expression.

But when she looked, really looked at Gina, her horror was obvious.

'Lord, what happened to you? You look as if you've been beaten up.'

Gina shrugged her shoulders and eyebrows together but said nothing.

'That's terrible. What happened? Did the police — oh. You have reported it, haven't you?'

Gina shook her head.

'Oh, honey, why not? You must. Why haven't you?'

She shrugged again. How much to tell, how much to hide? She looked away from Becca's accusing, curious gaze but felt the eyes examining her damaged skin.

'What's going on, Gina?'

'Nothing.' She reached for a cheroot, her usual move in moments of stress. They both watched her hand shake as she lit it.

'Come on. You owe me that much. You weren't in Scotland, were you?'

Gina thought about it.

'Oh, I suppose it doesn't matter what you know, now. Now that I'm out of that particular game. No, you're right, I wasn't in Scotland.'

'I don't care where you were. But I think I have a right to know why you lied to me. I thought we had a relationship based on trust.'

Gina sucked hard on her cheroot, inhaled its nicotine buzz and then expelled grey smoke through the tight funnel of her lips.

'I'm afraid, Becca, you're wrong. We had — we have — a relationship based on a big, fat, juicy lie. Truth is a much overrated commodity, I find.'

Becca watched and listened, patiently waiting for more.

'Do you really want to know? It's a very nasty little story. And it affects you, in a way.'

Still Becca said nothing. She was staring at Gina, her brows low over her unblinking eyes and her mouth slightly open.

Then her eyes focused on Gina again and she whispered, so quietly that it was virtually inaudible, 'No.'

'What's that?'

'No. Oh no. Not that. Please, don't let it be that . . .'

'You want to know where I was?'

'I know. I know already. I know what happened. It all fits into place now. Oh, God, Gina. I'm so sorry. I feel responsible. How could he?'

'You know? How?'

'I just know. You went to Bermuda, didn't you? For some kind of deal with George. Something you didn't want me to know about.'

'Yeh. You're good, I'll give you that. I wanted to work for him. Take over your job and mastermind the relaunch of a new George King. I didn't know about his ego.'

'So you went with him to Bermuda.'

'Not with him. He didn't know anything about it. I gave myself three days to make him need me. I miscalculated. Badly.'

'He knocked you around for daring to suggest new ventures?'

'It was a little more than a knocking around.'

Gina broke their gaze first. The look of horror and sympathy on Becca's face would have her crying again if she didn't toughen up soon. She didn't know if she wanted to be provoked to anger or tears.

'Oh, Gina, my poor love. How could he? He tied you up and raped you? That man is pure evil; he should be put down like a rabid dog.'

'How did you know he tied me up?'

'I know this man. I've known him a long time. I know his habits.'

'You know how he rapes? That's not possible.'

'Unless . . .' Becca challenged Gina to work it out.

'Oh, holy shit. No. No! You're not serious. You?'

Becca nodded.

'Oh, Jesus effing Christ! Does he make a habit of attacking women?'

'No. Sometimes it's teenage girls.'

425

'You were a teenager? What happened?'

Becca's face showed the anguish she felt at the thought of reliving the event again after so many years. For a long time she said nothing. They sat in a weird, comfortable silence, almost like meditation. Then it all poured out.

'I was fourteen. I used to babysit for the people up the road. Mr and Mrs King. They had two little boys. Ben and Christopher. Ben was a sweet little boy. About four, I think. Little Chris was just a toddler. Lots of blond curls, like you'd draw a baby, happy smile all the time, and laughing. They were worried that Ben would be jealous of the new baby but he didn't seem to be. He was proud of little Christopher, used to show him special places like the birds' nests in the garden, the secret den they had behind the shed, things like that. They used to play together all the time, they were so happy.

'He was a bit funny, Mr King. He'd help me with my homework sometimes before they went out. He used to sit next to me at the kitchen table and lean right over me, squashing me up against the wall. I knew it was wrong because he didn't do it if Mrs King was around. I didn't like going there at first in case he was by himself, but once they'd both gone out I got on with my project or I'd play with the boys and have a really nice time. I used to think how much fun it would be when I had children myself. Ben used to say he'd come and babysit for them when he was old enough.

'The day he . . . that day, it was a warm summer's afternoon and I remember it was an English essay I had to write while I was there. "Pride goes before a fall". That was the title, I can still see it written in capital letters in my exercise book.

'He was out in the garden with the boys when I got there. I called to them all when I went through the gate. God, I can see it as if it's happening now. It's twenty years, twenty years . . .'

'I know, honey. Go on, it's good to talk.'

426

Becca composed herself and went on, speaking the words, describing the actions she'd never voiced before.

'The boys ran to me; they were holding hands. Ben helped little Christopher down the steps and I bent down to give them a kiss and a hug. Mr King came up and made some joke about him being too big for a kiss. Ben said, "No, you're not, Mummy kisses you" and we all laughed. I said I'd get myself a glass of milk and start work on my essay until he went out. Mrs King was already out, she must have been at the theatre. Inside I got my milk from the fridge but didn't have a chance to get my books out because Mr King came in and said he wanted to show me something. We went into their sitting-room and there was a new television set. It seemed ever so big and it had shiny wood all around it. He showed me the picture and there was a film on with cowboys and horses and lots of shooting. It wasn't the sort of thing we watched at home and he had it so loud. I was polite about it but I just wanted to get on with my homework. I was worried about the boys playing in the garden by themselves. I looked out of the window and I could see them by the pond. I wanted to go out to them but he said they'd be all right . . . Oh, why didn't I just call out to them, tell them to be careful or come away from the edge? Ben would have done, he was a good boy. He would have heard me, too, because the window was open. I remember the smell of the honeysuckle wafting in. That and the guns shooting on the television and the sticky heat. I was wondering how long it would be before Mr King would go out and I could get the boys sorted. But then . . .'

She stopped again, almost as if she was too weary to go through with the tale. Gina became aware of someone nearby playing music with a heavy bass beat. That selfish arsehole on the top floor, probably. If he knew what Becca was going through he'd have more consideration.

'He started to go on about how big the television was and did I like things that were big because he could show

427

me something else that was. I was young but I knew what he was talking about and I just felt embarrassed. Not afraid but ashamed. For him, that he should be trying to chat up the babysitter with his wife and children out of the way. But he went on about it and got so close to me I could feel the heat of his body and then, suddenly, he pushed me backwards and I fell on to the settee. I can see it, it was soft and green. Then he kind of jumped on top of me. He was so heavy and I shouted something as if it was all a joke but he hissed at me to shut up or else. I couldn't move. He was pulling at my clothes and I kept thinking I didn't want him to tear my school uniform because I'd have to explain the next day to my mum.

'He started to get rough and he took my tie off; it was blue and yellow stripes. He wrapped it round my wrists and then tied them to the bit where the arm of the settee met the back, there was a sort of wooden knob thing.'

'That's how you knew,' said Gina. 'He used his own tie on me, then his belt around my ankles.'

'Yes. The same. It was to stop me kicking him. Except that I was too scared to fight back. I was working for him; I did as I was told. You know me.'

'Oh, Becca, honey. You poor baby.'

'No, I should have done something, should have stopped him. I just lay there crying and asking him politely not to. Why the hell I didn't fight, I don't know.'

'You were fourteen, for Christ's sake. What did he . . . ?'

'He ripped down my knickers and did it,' said Becca slowly, almost in a whisper. 'He just stuck it in me. I remember thinking of all the ways I'd imagined my first time . . . I'd never thought of that. It hurt and I wanted to scream, but he had his hand over my mouth. It was sweaty and I hated the taste of it and the smell. His other hand was rubbing over my chest. He kept on saying how . . . Oh, I don't know. Saying stupid things all the time. He called me his "little girlie" and his "baby" and kept saying how much I was going to like it. He was bouncing

428

on me, hurting me and I couldn't breathe with my arms tied back. But the worst thing was, I didn't understand why he was doing it. It seemed so pointless.'

'Jesus.' Gina was reliving her own horror too. 'Did he . . . ? I mean, how did it finish?'

'He was sweating a lot. Drops fell on me. He called me "Beckie". I hate that, it's not my name. Suddenly he undid the tie, took his belt from round my ankles and was zipping his trousers up and telling me to get dressed. He started calling me names and that made me start to cry. I thought that was so horrible, to insult me on top of everything else. He called me a "cheap little tart" and a "fucking slut". I'd never heard anyone use the "f" word before. I can hear the exact inflection in his voice now; he sounded so angry about it, as if *I'd* forced *him* to do it. That's when we heard the screaming from the garden and he ran outside. I heard his voice shouting too and I looked out of the window. I couldn't believe what I saw.'

Gina stubbed out her cheroot and reached for another. Becca closed her eyes, took a deep breath and continued.

'He was standing there with little Christopher in his arms. He was in the pond and Christopher was limp and soaking wet, his head was hanging back and I knew at once he was dead. While Mr King had been attacking me his youngest son had fallen in the pond and drowned. Each event was bad enough in itself but together . . . that one should have resulted from the other seemed so terrible. I kept thinking, if I'd pushed him off perhaps he'd have seen Christopher by the water's edge and stopped them playing there. If I'd been stronger, braver I could have prevented my own . . . downfall and a baby's death. And now I think if I hadn't run away he'd have been brought to book then and you might have been spared the same fate.'

'Don't you dare blame yourself. It was his doing, his responsibility. Don't be a victim. Did the police ask you about the death, what you'd seen?'

'No, when I went out to help he told me to go away. Said I should tell anyone who asked that I never even got there. I just ran down the road, terrified, haunted by the picture of him standing in the pond with the dripping body in his arms. I couldn't face going home, I felt so ashamed, guilty somehow. So I ran away. Got on a bus, then a train, then I hitchhiked, slept in a bus shelter overnight and the next day got to my auntie's in Eastbourne.'

'You poor kid.'

'I had to cope with worse.'

'Worse? What, he came looking for you?'

'No. He was still with me. My period was late.'

'Oh, Jesus, no.'

'Yes. I took all my money out of the Post Office and tried to get an abortion. I had to get a doctor's permission, then talk to a social worker. They all made me feel so cheap. I finally got into a special clinic. I was sure the nurses all despised me. When it was my turn to go I was terrified. They asked about my family or friends but there was no one. I was alone. The doctor put this tube into me and sucked it out . . .'

She gasped and wiped the dampness under her eyes.

'Here, come here. You're not alone now.' Gina moved to sit next to Becca and hold her while she wept. Then she took her turn to explain about the trip to Bermuda, speaking quickly and skipping over the worst of the details.

'And you seduced me to get nearer to him?'

'Originally, yes. I'm sorry; there's no point lying to you now.'

'No. No point at all.' Becca's crumpled features were wet but she was struggling to maintain her dignity. 'You're a calculating creature, aren't you?' she said.

'It takes one to know one. There's no way I could have gone twenty years with that bottled up inside me. And working for him, too. How the hell did that come about?'

'The agency sent me on a temp job, typing and filing at a TV station. I'd been there a couple of hours and was

430

getting on well with everyone and suddenly the door opened and he walked in. I nearly screamed out loud. I blushed and stammered when they introduced me. He didn't recognize me. He was charming and witty and said he hoped I'd enjoy working there. Anyway, I kept being promoted, given more responsibility until I was working as his right-hand woman for a couple of days a week. I was doing bits of research, letters, rehearsing him, looking out archive material, you know, bits and pieces. And each day it got easier to put the past in a box and not deal with it. I'd almost justified what he'd done to me. Accepted it. Only it didn't feel as if it had been me; I'd put so much distance between me and the event that it felt as if it'd happened to someone else. My younger sister or a friend. I wondered if one day he'd look at me and remember where we'd met before but of course he didn't. He didn't think about anyone else, ever. The more closely I worked with him the more shallow his performance seemed. But I was instrumental in creating it.'

'How d'you mean?'

'I was taking over whole chunks of his life. I think even he finally acknowledged that I was pretty much indispensable to him and he offered me the position of his PA. The money was fabulous, much more than I'd ever earned, so I took it. I kept thinking I shouldn't be doing this, I should confront him, go to the police, talk to his wife. Something. But I didn't. I just kept a low profile and slaved away, eating into his life until he'd relinquished all control to me.'

'How could you see him every day, knowing what he'd done to you?'

'Some days I just wanted to pick up a knife and stick it into his back. Sometimes I was on the verge of tears, as if I was still the teenager he'd raped. I hadn't forgiven him. Don't think that. I hadn't. I haven't. And hearing about what he did to you makes me want to . . .'

'Yes?'

431

Becca's eyes were red and damp but had a bright gleam; clear in their vision of what George King deserved. Gina had never seen them like it before. She knew now she had an ally. Sweet or otherwise, revenge would be double-headed.

47

'Yes, it's true. I'm George King's mistress. We've been having an affair for many years. I love him very much, of
course. No, no, I have no ambitions in television myself, I
just want to support Georgie, to be there when he needs
me. No, I don't see the age difference as a problem; after
all, Georgie is young at heart and I've always been told
I've a wise head on youthful shoulders. Pardon? Oh no,
we can't really discuss marriage at the present but we're
ruling nothing out. We just want to be together. Thank
you, no more questions now.'

Suzi had rehearsed the answers and the clothes and even
the facial expressions in her peach-tinted mirrors until she
was word perfect. As soon as George decided the time
was right she'd be ready. Since her picture had appeared
with Hal Brand's piece she knew that time couldn't be
far off. Something was brewing. She couldn't wait to be
reluctantly exposed.

If only Georgie would contact her.

And then, the day she was thinking about breaking all
the rules and phoning him for once, he rang from his car.

'We need to talk. I'll be with you in approximately . . .
twelve minutes.'

That was it, nothing else. Typical Georgie, to the point.
She just had time to shower and dress for him in tight
scarlet sweater and the briefest black leather miniskirt she
possessed. He liked that look. Her make-up was rudimen-
tary, just the basic blusher and lots of what he called her
'cocksucker' lipstick. She didn't have time to eat any high
fibre food.

When he got to Suzi's house he sneaked in as if he feared

the presence of the press even inside the front door. He checked behind him in the street but seemed satisfied that he hadn't been followed.

'Well, Georgie honey. How's my little soldier? Does he want to play dip-dips?' She kissed him on the neck and nuzzled around his earlobe, delighted to see him after so long. But he shrugged her off and strode through the hall into her sitting-room. As she caught up with him he was pouring himself a drink from her bar.

'Jesus, how could you be so stupid? You let a reporter in here? Christ! And you let him take a sodding picture! I knew you were a half-witted moron but do me a favour. Or are you deliberately trying to sabotage my whole career? Eh, eh?'

'Oh, Georgie, I'm sorry. I didn't realize. He used a false name. And he said you'd sent him. Something about locations and you'd be really pleased when he took his report back to you.'

'Oh, for fuck's sake. You're a bleeding liability you are. I always knew you were a bad risk. I should have done something about it before now but I was too soft. I let my heart rule my head. Well, not exactly my heart, was it?'

'Georgie, don't worry. When it's all out in the open —'

'What the hell are you talking about? You're way off beam, bimbo.'

He threw his drink down his throat and slammed the glass down on the counter. 'Right, that's it. There's only one answer.'

'What, Georgie?' Was this it, the moment he decided to announce her to the public? At last . . .

'Fuck, is that right?' He was looking at her 'antique' quartz sunburst clock, the one she'd bought at a pound a week through a catalogue. 'We'll talk later. I've got to watch something.' He picked up the handset and jabbed it at the screen, stabbing button after button until he found what he was after.

Here come United on the attack again; the Spurs defence has looked very clumsy tonight although they've kept the Reds at bay so far. I wouldn't like to predict a scoreline here at White Hart Lane but nil-nil looks a safe bet.

George settled his ungainly bulk on the narrow settee and stared at the screen. Without a word he motioned to his empty glass. Suzi obediently poured some brandy into it and dropped in a couple of ice cubes.

'Georgie?'

'Not now, I need to see this.'

She gave him his drink and sat at his side. For a minute or two she watched the football, then watched him watching it. God, he was annoying at times but she loved him, God damn it.

Silently she removed his tie and unbuttoned his shirt without interrupting his viewing. He co-operated just enough by changing his glass from one hand to the other so she could tug his sleeves off and then remove his shirt. She took off his brown shoes and black socks and settled down next to him, curling up small and snuggling her head against his chest. She ran her tongue lightly over and around his left nipple. In response she felt the weight of George's arm around her shoulders and his fingers grabbed for her breast. Without taking his eyes off the screen he squeezed her flesh roughly as if performing a muscle-strengthening exercise.

They haven't taken control of midfield and their finishing's been very poor. Here's Caskey. Samways. Oh dear, oh dear!

'Georgie . . . ?'

'Hm?'

'Why do you have to watch this?'

'I'm interviewing the captain of this new combined British team for the World Cup. Giggs.'

'The paper says you're interviewing your wife this week.' There was only a hint of archness in her voice. Nothing that George would notice.

'Yes, thanks to your stu-fucking-pidity I need to be seen

435

as Mr Happily-Married again. Next week it's this bonehead ball kicker.'

'But you're not interested in football.'

'We're in transition to a different style. Not just actors; politicians, writers, sportsmen, they all get a look in now.'

'But the researchers will do all the background stuff, won't they? And come up with all the questions?'

'Yeh, but – Look, fuckwit, will you shut up and let me watch this?'

She left him in peace for a few minutes while she sipped her drink and then chewed at the small brown button of his nipple. Why do men have them? she wondered. She tried to imagine what it would be like to breastfeed a child.

Well the legs are going a bit; he's over thirty, after all.

'How old do I look?' he said suddenly. 'Ow, don't bite.'

'Sorry. What, Georgie?'

'How old do I look? Be honest.'

'How old? Well, let's see. You're a very handsome man. Very . . . telegenic.' She'd heard him use that word a lot so she knew that was safe.

'Come on, how old?'

'I should say you look . . .' The question was not whether to lie, but how much? Enough to flatter but not enough to patronize. '. . . about forty-seven?'

'Hmm.' He considered this for a while and then watched some more football.

'How do I look?'

Great long ball.

'How?'

'Yes. What do I look like? Stupid, interesting, handsome? Old . . . ?'

'You look . . . lovely to me, Georgie. All scrummy-wummy.' She tickled his hairy nipple with the tip of her tongue.

'Come on.'

That's a dream of a pass! This could be dangerous for the Spurs defence.

'No, Georgie. I love the way you look. Strong and secure and reassuring. Intelligent, distinguished; someone to look up to.'

'Avuncular.'

'Er . . . yes. Is that good?'

'Like an uncle. Someone older and wiser?'

'That's it, yes. Very . . . craggy.'

'Craggy!'

'Well, you know, like a movie star.'

'Who, for Christ's sake? George Burns?'

'I don't know him. Say like in Indiana Jones.'

'Harrison Ford?'

'Sean Connery. He played Harrison —'

'— Ford's father, yes, I know. Great.'

Schmeichel was quick off his line there; a lovely save.

'Would you like me to record the match, sweetpea? You could watch it later.'

'What for? I can watch it now.'

'I thought you wanted to talk. About . . . well, you know. Us.'

'Later.'

Bruce . . . Ince . . . Pallister . . . back to Ince.

'Well, you've been away and I want to hear all about it. Did you take any photographs?'

'Give me a break.'

'Well, what's Barbados like?'

Nice ball out to Cantona who's in a great position. This could be a real chance, he's got Giggs outside him . . .

'Bermuda. Look in the brochures.'

Yes, it's there! Giggs has done it!

'Yes! What a goal!'

Suzi stroked George's sagging grey-haired breast and thought how odd it was that little boys sucked on their mothers' teats and grew up to be big strong men who sucked on their lovers' teats just the same way.

He watched the replay of the goal and then muted the volume with the handset, pushed her off him brusquely and stomped to the little bar in the corner of the room. The padded, buttoned red plastic screamed at the predominantly pink room but neither George nor Suzi noticed.

'Georgie, sweetie, we do need to talk, don't we? About the future. You know how I feel about you.'

He sighed and poured brandy into his glass.

'That's the fucking problem, isn't it? What you feel. You feel too fucking much.'

'I can't help that. I love you.'

'Don't use that word.'

'All right, but I feel it and I can't change that.'

'For Christ's sake, that's your problem. Deal with it.' He dropped ice into his drink with a splash and gulped a mouthful down.

'But you love me too, don't you? You must do or you wouldn't keep coming to see me.'

'Listen, don't make me spell it out.'

'Spell what out?'

'Jesus Christ.'

'Georgie, please . . .'

'Don't whine, for God's sake.'

'But Georgie . . .'

'*And don't call me that!* I hate it, I fucking hate it! You make me sound like a sodding poodle.'

He turned from the bar and took two steps towards her with a look on his face so furious that Suzi thought he might do something violent. It wouldn't be the first time. She braced herself for the blow, eyes screwed tight and jaw clenched. There was a beat, and then nothing. She opened her eyes to see him staring at her with an odd, remote look. As if he'd never seen her before. Curious and objective.

He sat down in a different chair and turned his attention to the screen again. Suzi studied him warily for a few seconds, as she would a dangerous dog, and then settled quietly at his feet, pretending to watch the silent football game.

For several minutes neither of them spoke or moved. Only a branch against the window broke the silence, that and George's nasal snorts as he shifted mucus about his passages.

Suzi was still, but her mind was racing. My tongue on his breast . . . Where has he gone to? His hand on my breast . . . To live apart from George . . . A part of George . . . His child at my breast . . . ?

'You don't love her any more, do you?'

'What? Who?'

'Your wife. Or do you? Is that why she's going to be on your show?'

'Of course I don't love her, she's my wife. She's going to be on the show because it's good for my image right now. Come on, dickhead, pass the bloody thing.'

After a while Suzi looked away towards the grey view over wet roofs and sad patches of garden and said as nonchalantly as she knew how, 'So how about us, then? Is it time to tell the public?'

George groaned in disbelief. 'I don't believe this.' He turned his angry red face to her. 'You haven't any idea, have you? You've never got it into your thick skull. You really don't understand at all.'

'What?'

'"Whaaat?"' he mimicked her little-girl voice. 'You and me. Why I come to see you. "Us" as you call it. Well, there is no "us". There's you and there's me and the reason I come to see you and don't phone you and don't bring you presents and don't say "I love you" is because I don't fucking love you. I love fucking you. I want you for sex. Nothing else. Straightforward, easy, cheap, instant sex. Just fucking fucking. That's it. My cock coming in your body. Any hole, I don't care. But hearts and flowers it ain't, right? You mean nothing to me beyond what bits of your body can do for bits of mine. Is it becoming clear? Are you starting to understand how deep and meaningful our relationship is? Was. You could never interest me as

439

a person because you are thick as two short planks. You have no taste, no style and no class. You have great tits, a big mouth and a warm cunt. And that, sweetheart, is it. Geddit?'

Suzi said nothing. She gazed up at him. His face was flushed with the exertion of his speech. She could see beads of perspiration swelling on his lined brow and had to restrain herself from reaching up to wipe them away. She stared at him, replaying phrases in her mind, trying to understand. 'Just sex . . . I don't love you . . . You mean nothing to me'. No, she must have misunderstood.

His eyes were fixed almost maniacally on the flickering screen.

'Are you saying,' she started tentatively, 'that you want to have a . . . a sort of break? From each other?'

He sighed. When he spoke at last he didn't turn his head to her. 'Look, it's over.'

'It's all right, I wasn't watching it anyway.'

'*Not the fucking football!* You're history.'

'My what?'

'You're history. *You – are – history,*' he spat the words into her face. 'We're finished! Can't you understand what I'm saying?'

She frowned hard and felt her eyes dampen. She had to blink to focus properly on George's silly, angry features glaring down at her.

'But that doesn't make sense, Georgie. We . . . we've been together for so many years. It works, it's . . . it's what we do. We can't split up . . .'

'We don't have to split up because we're not together. We never were. We had sex. Great sex. That's all it was.'

'No, that's not true. I love you!'

'Tough. Get over it! And don't start crying.'

'I'm sorry, Georgie. But what . . . ? Why . . . ?'

She sniffed and wiped her eyes. Her mind was racing, thoughts lumbering on top of one another, desperate to think of a way to keep him. Why was he saying these

440

things, surely he didn't mean them? How to keep him, just a little longer? How to keep just a part of him?

'What's happened? Has something happened?'

'What's happened is you've shot your mouth off to the gutter press, peabrain. The lawyers are on to that little prick Brand, but with your help I could get ripped to shreds. My career is on the line every time I see you. And I'm not sacrificing everything just for the occasional quick fuck. It's time to call it a day. Things change.'

'I can change too. Is it something about me you don't like any more? I'll lose weight if that's it. Or dye my hair. Anything. Just tell me what to do and I'll do it, Georgie. I'll do anything for you, you know that.'

'You would, wouldn't you?'

'Yes, of course.'

'You'd have my name tattooed across your backside?'

'Yes, that would be fun! Do you want me to do that?'

'You'd let me chop your little finger off and wear it around my neck?'

'If you wanted me to, yes.'

'Christ, woman, you've got problems.' He went to fetch another drink, letting her body fall from his knees to the floor. 'Listen, I'll give you money. That'll help. Ten thousand?'

'I don't want money, Georgie. That's not what I want from you.'

'Twenty k, then?'

'Georgie –'

'All right, thirty. And you keep this place. But it's a one-off payment. I'll speak to my accountant and find out the best way to do it. Simpler all round, eh?' He ignored the drink he'd just poured and looked at her. Anyone who didn't know him would have said there was a fond look in his eyes. Then he started to pick his clothes up from the floor.

'Look, I've got to go. I'll . . . see you around.'

Even George realized how stupid that sounded.

Suzi knew she had to work fast. He was about to walk out of her life for ever. Time was against her; subtlety was out.

She stood up quickly and went to the door, blocking his exit and posing in a what she knew George would think was a tempting fashion.

'How can you say goodbye to this, Georgie? How can you resist when you know it tastes so good? Oooh, I'm wet and ready for you now. Randy for the things you do to me, baby. Don't you want to have me just once more before you go . . . ?' And for good measure she gave a little surprised whimper as some imagined frisson passed through her body. It was her Marilyn Monroe.

'Now, don't make it hard . . .'

She giggled.

'I didn't mean that.'

'But it is hard, isn't it, Georgie? I can see it is. Oh, let's play Eurotunnel just once more. And let's make this one really count.'

'No. I have to go. I've got a meeting. I . . . have . . . to go . . .'

But he didn't move and his eyes were fixed on her as she peeled the sweater over her head without comment.

Then she wriggled out of her squeaky skirt. She had nothing on underneath.

She arranged herself carefully to show off the goods to best advantage; one hand held at her cleavage, the other at her crotch, fingers rubbing against herself and disappearing from view among the blond fuzz as she moaned in convincing ecstasy. Then she cupped her plump breasts together, aiming them at him and pinching her nipples.

'Surely you're not too busy to come and stroke my fluffy bunny? Don't you want to feel my gums round your plums? Wouldn't you like to stick your hard truncheon up my love funnel?'

'Christ . . .' She saw him swallow.

'Don't you want to play with your favourite pussy?

442

Look, it's ready for you, Georgie, soft and furry. It's so warm and gentle and it tastes really sweet. Can't you imagine how good that would be? Oh Georgie, you're so big, so important. I'm almost coming thinking about how famous you are. Stick your ratings up me! *Fuck me with your fame!*'

'Oh Christ . . .'

Yes, that got to him. His hand went to his groin and he began to rub the swollen front of his trousers with the guilty glee of a teenager.

'Come on, big boy, shove your hot rod right up inside me. Pump your . . . um . . . love thingie in my . . . er . . .' God, she thought, I used to be able to go on like this for hours when I did that phone-sex job. I'm out of the habit. '. . . my juicy pussy.'

Linguistic niceties hardly mattered now. He was hooked.

In a second he was in front of her, his head buried in her soft breasts, licking, biting, smelling and groaning with pleasure. Then he dropped to the floor, both his knees cracking as he did so, and he was slurping eagerly at her crotch.

For old times' sake Suzi peeled his toupee off and flung it across the room, crying out loud 'I love you, George King!', knowing he was in no position to argue.

She performed acrobatics for him, hanging from the door frame, her legs astride his shoulders and his face thrust between her thighs. She sucked his odd little cock, pretending it was the chunkiest hunk of meat she'd ever devoured, she rode him, spanked him, sat on his face and even managed a few fruity farts. He was in heaven.

He shoved his dick into her from the front, from behind, standing up, sitting in a chair – his eyes didn't even dart to the football match on the screen – and then managed an exotic soixante-neuf with Suzi doing a handstand against the wall.

Three times she pretended to have an orgasm and three

times George came inside her, each time where she wanted him, where she needed his sperm.

The last time she was sitting astride him, working away on his tired, inflamed cock, determined to wring another few drops of life-giving fluid from his weary old body he panted, 'God, I'm gonna fuckin' miss you, bimbo.'

It wasn't exactly the sweet nothing she'd been waiting all those years to hear him whisper, but it would have to do. Besides, she had what she really wanted from him now. She hoped it would work.

She jiggled on, squeezing him dry on the inside although they were both now drenched in sweat.

Eventually, shattered by the exertion, they collapsed on the floor. For a while she lay staring at him, trying to fix his features in her mind, while he slept on the carpet, his snores buzzing like a distant machine. Then she too was asleep, dreaming of making love on a football pitch while someone commentated on her technique.

She woke up cold and aching, sucking her thumb. George was gone. Limp and useless like a sloughed snake-skin, his tie lay discarded on the floor. Screwing it into a ball she rubbed it round and round over her belly, hoping some kind of potency might be mysteriously discharged.

Then Suzi wrapped a kimono around herself, combed her hair into place with her fingers and picked up her phone.

'Hello. Is that Mr Steptoe? Harold Steptoe?' She laughed. 'It's all right, I know your game. And I'd like to play.'

48

'Two hours to go,' Kate said to herself. It was seven o'clock on Friday night and she was having difficulty keeping her nerves under control.

Robin had been wonderful, fussing round her and reassuring her all day.

'Look, lovey,' he'd said as they had tea at Fortnum and Mason's after the stressful business of choosing a new outfit for Kate. 'I want you to remember that whatever happens on the show you are —'

'What do you mean, "whatever happens"?'

'I'm just saying if there are any . . . surprises.'

'Such as what?'

'You know live television. All I'm saying is, don't be dragged down to George's level. Think class.'

The night before she'd driven up to the Hampstead mansion to talk to George about the show. It felt strange to be there, knowing that she didn't belong and yet finding it full of memories of events and chapters in her life.

He was lying on a sofa watching a video of Johnny Carson, glass of whisky and cigar in one hand, pen in the other. Around him were other, unmarked videos and more scraps of paper with scribbled notes all over them.

'Are you all right, George? You look tired.'

'I am tired. It's tough at the top.'

'Spare me the hard luck stories. I need to know about tomorrow night.'

'Yeh?'

'Well, what happens? What do you expect of me?'

'You know the routine.'

'No, George, *you* know the routine; I don't. What I need

to know is what the questions'll be so I can mug up some stories for you.'

'I don't discuss the line of questioning with the guests before the show. I like it to be as spontaneous as possible.'

'Then why do you have the questions written up on idiot boards?'

'The term is cue cards.'

'Surely you can make an exception for me? I'm your wife!'

'It doesn't feel like it.'

'What do you mean?'

'Living in rented accommodation?'

'So?'

'Bayswater. Isn't that what you said on the machine?'

'It makes sense for both of us, doesn't it? Just for the time being, while we're . . . going through a difficult patch.'

'Look, that black bastard Brand is a loose cannon. You saw what he wrote. Making up crap about me having a woman hidden away. He could just as easily insinuate that you were living with another man.'

He took a generous swig from his glass.

'Shit. You're not, are you?'

'No,' she sighed. 'Of course not. I just need a bit of space to myself.'

'Hmph.'

She noted with satisfaction how little she feared him now. Hal's comments in print had started a whisper that George was not one hundred per cent clean and he knew he needed to play everything with a straight bat for a while. She hadn't seen him frightened for many years.

'So there's no evidence they can sniff out and throw at me?'

'How do you mean, George, evidence?'

'The other man, *who is it?*' he said with a shout, as if expecting to startle a confession out of her after hours of softly-softly interrogation.

'There is no other man, George,' Kate said calmly. 'I'm

446

living there by myself and I'm not seeing anyone else, I swear.'

'No? Well, just keep your nose clean. And everything else. You know what I'd do if I found out you were messing around, taking your tabby out visiting, don't you?'

'What a disgusting expression.'

'DON'T YOU?'

'Yes, George. I know.'

She was glad to leave him to his videos and whisky. She didn't belong there any more.

Robin collected her in a taxi at seven-thirty. They travelled slowly in nose-to-tail traffic up to the studios in Camden, Robin keeping up a bright chirrup of conversation all the way, managing to find safe, uncontroversial subjects.

'What if he asks me something personal?'

'Like about the state of your marriage? Oh yes, very likely.'

'Or about work?'

'You don't know yet what your next project will be. Projects always sound much more impressive than jobs. You've got some film scripts to read which are very tempting but theatre is your first love.'

At the studios Robin led the way to the dressing-rooms. All of his starrier clients had been this way before.

'Good evening, Mr Quick' . . . 'Hello, Mr Quick' . . . 'Hi, Robin!' echoed out as they walked down a long corridor past many open doors. Nobody greeted Kate by name. What if the audience had never heard of her? What if they didn't clap when she went on? What if she wasn't funny?

'Robin, what if —'

'Just rise above it. Think class.'

Her dressing-room was number nine. Kate couldn't read any significance into that. It was small and modern and practical and soulless. She took her time, pacing herself as she would for any other performance, laying her make-up out in order, rearranging the chairs and adjusting the lampshade more to her taste. She'd had her hair fixed that morning but she checked it over now and sprayed it solid with a silent prayer of apology to the ozone layer. Hair, face, then the dress and shoes. Yes, everything looked fine. Classy.

A knock on the door was followed by the familiar appearance of Becca Nichols. Although in fact slightly less familiar now that she seemed to be changing her image. In recent weeks she'd become less mousy, more colourful.

'Hello, Miss Fitch. About time you did the show, isn't it?'

'Well, I don't know about that. I've never really qualified for the chat show circuit.'

'Have the two of you discussed the line of questioning?'

'Actually, Becca, no. He said he likes it to be spontaneous.'

'Oh. That means he doesn't usually know what's on the idiot boards until the transmission.'

Kate raised an eyebrow, not at this piece of in-house gossip but at Becca's unusual disloyalty in revealing it.

'Here. Fairly straightforward stuff.' She took a printed list from her clipboard and held it out to Kate. 'The ones in red are must-ask and the others are supplementary if time allows. Mind you, he often goes off on a completely different tack, so you sort of have to be prepared for anything with Mr King. He's a bit of a riderless horse these days. Well, you know that.'

'Quite.' She took the list and glanced at it. 'Thanks, Becca, I appreciate this.'

'Look, I'm just doing my rounds of the guests to give them the usual pep talk about relaxing and not looking at the camera and trying not to stop to think all the time. But I don't need to say any of that to an old hand like you, do I?'

But Kate noticed she'd said it anyway; clever.

'And you've seen the show enough times to know about the set and which seat to take. All that's going to be upgraded soon, according to Mr King, to reflect the change in image, but you'll find it very familiar tonight. So,' she consulted her clipboard and checked that her single earring was well anchored to her lobe; it was a skinny stickman hanging from a gibbet, a tiny noose around his broken neck. 'Just relax and have fun. I'll be back to collect you in . . . seventeen minutes.'

And the door closed behind her.

Seventeen minutes later Becca and Robin walked her down to the set, one either side of her as if they feared she might do a runner. While Becca went to minister to her boss's last-minute demands Kate was left standing in the wings ready for her cue.

'Class, class,' whispered Robin at her side.

She glimpsed George as he swanned through the studio at the head of a small phalanx of minions who had brushes, stop-watches, clipboards, headsets or other impedimenta to clarify their roles. On the stage a warm-up man was telling bad Irish jokes and getting little response. The audience hadn't come to see him. They wanted George, her George, their George, in the flesh.

Suddenly the warm-up man came past her muttering, 'Miserable bastards, someone's turned off their saline drips,' and she heard the familiar music to announce the start of the show. This was it. She felt Robin squeeze her hand.

A huge cheer, probably not even manufactured by an underling, greeted George's confident stride on to his set. He inhabited it as if it were his own sitting-room. It might as well be, he was more at home here than in Hampstead. He began his spiel with a few topical gags, which went down well. She listened to his timing and had to admit he knew how to work an audience. They obviously loved him, or the part of him they were allowed to see.

After some fairly scathing political stuff about the latest government sex scandal, he turned to a different camera and his whole demeanour changed.

'But first I want you to meet someone I've not had on the show before because I wanted to keep her all to myself. I've been told not to be so selfish so I'm thrilled skinny to share her with you tonight. She's a talented and beautiful actress as comfortable in comedy as she is in the classics. I've been lucky enough to engage her services tonight so please welcome the woman I've woken up next to for nearly thirty years – gossip writers please note – my old lady, Kate Fitch!'

She needed no push from Robin; the sound of applause drew her as a kid to Coke. She sailed on to the set almost regally and bowed deeply to the cheering audience. She didn't even notice that the floor manager was waving his arm to keep the applause going while she kissed George on both cheeks and sat in the indicated chair.

She felt all at once that this was going to be fun. And it was. George was a different man. He was the perfect host: urbane, witty, slightly flirtatious, concerned when necessary and listening to all her thespian anecdotes about forgotten lines and collapsing props as if he'd never heard an actor tell such stories before. She wasn't even aware of him looking at his cue cards with a fixed beam on his jovial face. He included the audience too, to make sure they felt involved and laughed at the right time. Once in a while he made some reference to their marriage. 'It seems silly asking you this since we've been married for about ninety-three years, but remind me . . .' Or, 'Tell the people out there who aren't family exactly when you . . .'

This fazed her a little as it brought the reality home to her. Her husband George she hated with a vengeance. He was selfish, arrogant and insensitive, but the person talking to her – 'George King' – was none of those things; he was elegance and charm personified.

All too soon it was over and he was inviting the audience's appreciation for 'my lovely wife'. In the commercial break Donny the floor manager thanked her and asked her to move to another chair. George was powdered down and someone wearing earphones came up to whisper things to him. He nodded and gave a thumbs up to someone unseen in the darkness above. He picked his nose discreetly, patted her on the thigh and said, 'Well done, old girl. Nice interview.'

Then the music came again and he was counted in by fingers under the camera for his next bit of autocue reading. He did it with such an impression of spontaneity that Kate had to check that the words really were written down for him.

'So,' he said finally, 'raise your glasses and the roof for the handsomest member of the new young generation of British stars: Jack Fever!'

No! This couldn't be true. Him, here? It was a mistake, a joke. She wanted to speak to Robin; he'd sort things out, that was his job. Wait: 'if there are any surprises', he'd said. He knew! He must have set it up. As a package deal. They wanted him and she was just the makeweight.

Kate felt humiliation burning through her, making her face tingle and her guts churn. How could Robin do this, knowing how she felt, what had happened between them both, between them all? She wanted to run, as she had before, but if Robin no longer represented a safe haven where could she hide?

She sat immobile, her features set in a fixed smile and to her horror there he was, standing on the set just yards away, waving and blowing kisses to the audience who cheered and whistled his appearance.

He looked stunning. He had skin-tight black leather trousers on, a white tee-shirt with a low-cut neck and a loose yellow jacket that might have been a Jasper Conran. His blondish hair was full and floppy, still cut in that teasing style that threatens to fall over the eyes and invites a hand to brush it back. He had a couple of days' stubble so Kate wasn't able to see the full extent of his famous scar. But he was more Beauty than Beast. Much more. His arrogance was evident in his slow walk as he almost swaggered towards them. He shook Kate's hand with no particular emotion evident and sat down, waiting for enough quiet to speak.

'I think they like you,' said George, starting a whole new cacophony of teenage lust.

'Yes. That's kind. And I haven't really done anything yet.'

'Not true, not true. You're already on our screens in a variety of things, aren't you?'

'Yes, George, that's right. I'm the boy in the jeans advert of course, the one who takes his trousers off to mend the parachute and then jumps out of the plane.'

'That looks terrifying. Did you really do that? Come on, you can tell me; I won't breathe a word to a soul.'

'Oh yes, George, I do all my own stunts.' Dramatic pause. Then Jack's face crinkled in a wry grin. 'And I tell all my own lies.'

Cute, thought Kate, very cute. Not original but it worked. She wondered if Robin had rehearsed his timing. No, he didn't need to, the boy was a natural. She sat and gazed in awed silence as he went through his paces. She remembered precisely how she'd lost her heart to him. George asked him genially about his background, his childhood and his early ambition to be a teacher.

'So how did you come to tread the boards?'

'I was just lucky to find out that acting was my thing while I was still young enough to . . . have a stab at it.' Was she imagining it or did he catch her eye as he said 'stab'?

George ran through the usual questions about making the commercials for chocolate bars and denim jeans. Was it difficult, was he making a fortune, did he think it was a fluke that might come to an end? Of course it might, Jack conceded, and if it all stopped tomorrow he'd be grateful for the good times he'd already had. The audience lapped it all up, his glamorous good looks and his level-headed modesty.

'And then I hear rumours of a mini-series in Hollywood, too. Is there no end to your good fortune?'

'Who knows, George? I could be a one night wonder, another Nick Kamen. But better looking, eh?' He laughed, tongue in cheek and pushed his mop of hair back to more cheers and applause.

'And no doubt you'll be bringing a record out one day?'

'Well, yes, there is some talk about a deal but nothing definite yet.'

'But what about the pressure of living under the bright lights all the time? Do you think you'll be able to adapt to that?'

'Now you come to mention it, it is very hot in here, isn't it?' And to wolf whistles and screams he stood up and took off his jacket, revealing his shirt to be a cotton vest that exposed his broad, tanned, muscular shoulders at the top and was cut off to show a ribbed washboard stomach below. For minutes George couldn't get a word in.

'And that's the body that goes with the brain,' he said at last to the studio audience. 'Fellahs, doesn't it make you sick?' More laughter. Jack was loving this.

'But listen, girls, let me ask you something. Wouldn't you prefer a more . . . avuncular sort of chap to spend the evening with? This young Jack Rabbit isn't the kind of chap you could fancy, is it?'

Of course they went wild, as he knew they would. So he could mutter, when the cheering died down, 'Ah well, there's no accounting for taste. Kate, could you fancy our friend Jack here?'

'Sorry?' Alarm bells were ringing in her head. Her guard had been down as she observed their banter from the sidelines.

'Do you think he's sexy?'

'Well now, I . . . er . . . that's a tricky question.' The audience laughed at her prevarication. Their interpretation was cruelly obvious.

'Come on, fair do's,' George insisted. 'Do you fancy this young man?'

'Oh . . . I . . .'

'More than she fancies you!' came a female shout from the audience. This caused much raucous laughter, but Kate saw from George's face that something had struck home.

'Well what about your looks, then, young Jacko?' he said with a hint of condescension in his voice. 'Let's talk about that for a minute. Your face and your body, which are inexplicably attractive to some of the women here tonight . . .' whistles and clapping again '. . . would you use them to further your career? Would you take off to get on? If you were offered a place on the casting couch.'

'What do you mean, "if"?' said Jack brazenly.

'So you have been?'

He shrugged his handsome shoulders and gave the naughtiest, not-quite-enigmatic smile. The audience loved it. Kate clenched her jaw in panic. Just where was this interview going?

'So, you're a bit of a prostitute, are you?' The tone of slight aggression was unmistakable. Before Jack could reply George pressed on, 'Do you think you're good-looking?'

'Oh yeh. Dead sexy.' His ironic half-smile meant he could get away with this. 'Do you, George?'

'Yes, I think you're a jolly handsome young chap.' George sounded very polite and distinctly patronizing.

'No, do you think *you're* sexy?' Jack crossed his leather-clad legs and stroked his stubble. If this was a battle of wills he was streaking ahead, leaving George struggling.

'Golly, my job isn't to be sexy,' George said, laying on the false modesty.

'But millions of women think you are,' Jack said quickly, generous to a fault. 'Don't you?' And he appealed to the audience like an old chat show pro. Some light applause and a few muted calls of 'yes' showed cruelly the extent to which Jack's sex appeal outstripped George's.

'You're very kind,' George said. 'But speaking of your looks, you had an accident, didn't you, that nearly put paid to your hopes of an acting career altogether?'

The alarm bells were there again, louder now.

'That's right. Kate, do you want to explain?'

'Explain?'

What the hell was he up to? Robin had said he was a dumb blond, but just how stupid could he be?

'About the accident that gave me the scar.'

'Er . . . no, I don't want to.'

'Well,' said Jack, 'It's just one of those silly things. I was actually backstage on *Murder in Triplicate*. I was carrying a vase of flowers to Miss Fitch's dressing-room. I think they were the ones you'd sent her, George. A huge bunch of orchids. They were in a big, heavy glass vase and I was negotiating my way along a dark corridor, holding them up like this so I could see where I was putting my feet. Suddenly, *whoomph!* Someone opened a door right into me. It smashed the vase and pushed great chunks of glass into my face.'

He told it well. The audience gasped at the impact; Kate almost believed it.

'Nasty. It must have hurt a lot.'

'Of course, but the funny thing is all I could think was "Don't make a sound", because the audience were there and the play was about to start.'

'Ah, what a pro, eh, Kate?'

'Yes, George.'

'Miss Fitch was marvellous, a real Florence Nightingale. She laid me on her couch.' There were some titters. 'Lay me down on it, I mean. She washed the glass out of the cuts and looked after me until the doctor arrived.'

'And now there's no trace of the damage.'

'Well, just a little scar, here, on my lip.' Obligingly he turned that side of his face to the camera and held it while they lined up a good close-up. She could see the shot on a monitor that glowed in the semi-darkness.

'It clearly hasn't harmed you professionally. How about privately? Plenty of girlfriends, I imagine. Are you spoken for?'

'I'm afraid my last relationship ended because of . . . shall we say, professional jealousy.'

'So he's available!' George twinkled at the rows of admirers. 'What sort of girls do you like?'

'Well, I think there's a lot to be said for the older woman.' Jack looked blatantly at Kate as he spoke, a challenging leer on his face. Predictably there were 'ooohs' from the audience. She was shocked but tried to look demure and hoped she wasn't blushing.

'Really? Well, I'm afraid this one is mine, young man.'

'Now, that's a very sexist, outmoded attitude, George.'

'Tough, little boy. How's this then: hands off my wife.' He tried to deliver his warning in a jocular tone of voice, but the embarrassment in the studio was palpable. Was George joking or not?

Kate thought that the shiver of discomfort that everyone present could surely feel, from audience to guests to floor manager, cameramen and whoever was up in the gallery, would be enough to keep George back from the brink. But she was alarmed to see the tell-tale signs of an explosion brewing. His top lip and his forehead were beaded with perspiration, his colour darkened quickly to a purplish red and his jaw jutted slightly in bulldog fashion. She was vaguely aware of people in black walking around behind the cameras whispering to each other and someone gesticulating. She was wondering how she could intervene to defuse the situation and restore the atmosphere to safe, bland jollity.

'George, dear,' she tried with her sweetest smile, 'I don't think that's —'

'Shut up, you!' He rounded on her viciously. There were one or two nervous giggles but they died before they'd really lived, subsumed into the heavy silence.

456

George screwed up his face, no longer the suave performer but turning into the monster she thought only she knew. He thrust his head forward at Jack, who still maintained his air of cool sex appeal. 'Have you got that, Mister Squeaky Clean? Hands off my wife! Right?'

Jack left a calculated pause before he spoke. Then it came, slow and deliberate without a softening smile. 'Sorry, George. I'm afraid you're too late.'

For a moment nothing happened. Nothing at all. No movement. No speech. Not even a breath. Jack Fever and George King confronted each other: youth and decay, strength and fear, the future and the past, face to face in eternal struggle.

That was the moment it could have been changed. Five seconds, no more. But nobody moved, nobody spoke.

Then it all happened at once, too fast to control. Kate became aware of the muffled sound of voices shouting loudly but dulled by soundproofing.

George snatched his earpiece out and threw it to the floor.

'Shut the fuck up! I am in control!' he shouted up towards the ceiling. Then he turned on Jack. 'What did you say, arsehole?'

Jack tried to stay laid-back and joked, 'Sorry, Kate, perhaps I shouldn't have mentioned our little fling.' He laughed stupidly.

George's fury switched to Kate. The red, sweating features veered slowly round to her. Instead of getting up and walking out Kate's in-built attitude that 'the show must go on' made her smile again and wait.

'You and him? Did you?' George's lips were wet and distorted. He heaved himself to his feet and spat as he bellowed at her, '*Did you?* Did you fuck that little jerk? DID YOU?'

He was standing, glaring down at her, a bead of sweat dripped from his chin. She looked around for support but saw only horrified faces staring back.

'Go to the break,' she heard in a stage whisper some-where behind her. 'Tell Prez they'll have to bloody well fill!'

'George,' she said, quietly, sadly. 'Everybody's looking at you.'

'I warned you!' he yelled. *'I bloody warned you!'*

'George, please. This is ridiculous.'

'YOU – FUCKING – TART!'

She thought he was turning away in disgust but although his shoulders swivelled his face was fixed on hers. She saw too late that he was winding himself up. The back of his clenched fist smashed across her face, knocking her sideways with such force that she was thrown half-way out of her chair. She heard screams now and couldn't tell if they were her own voice or other people's.

She felt no pain at first. As she straightened up in the chair she saw his arm come swinging back at her. It crashed into her face and rocked her the other way. Then a third blow hit her as he held her dress tight at her throat to keep the target still for his flailing fist.

'Tart! Cheap fucking whore! You're a disgrace to me. What about my fucking reputation? YOU WHORE!'

Amid the blows she managed through swollen, bloody lips to speak. 'You are sleaze, George. I am class.'

Unbelievably she heard a few hands clapping and a female cry from the audience. 'You tell the bastard!'

There were more shouts as he came at her again. She was ready this time and had her hands up to fend him off. She swayed back to avoid the curve of another hooked blow and then stretched out to try to push her open palm into his face, just to fend him off. But in the chaos she only caught him a glancing stroke. It dislodged his precious toupee which slid comically down over one eye.

'For Christ's sake get him off her!'

'Camera two – get a close-up of Fitch.'

'Go to the break!'

'Prez aren't ready.'

'Get off her, you bully!'

'Get out there and stop him!'

'He's gone crazy!'

'I know that, give me a close-up on two!'

Kate was vaguely aware of hands around George, men with headsets again, trying to pull him off her, but they couldn't restrain him; still his big fists reached her face. She heard the signature tune and wondered if a live audience of millions was watching this, her ultimate humiliation. Robin was there looking terrified. She saw Becca shouting into a mobile phone.

Kate tasted the blood in her mouth and tried to reach up to wipe it away. But her arm wouldn't move and the blood dribbled down her chin. Her dress would be ruined, she thought. And it was really expensive.

One last, clumsy blow landed on her nose and something cracked. She didn't care. She couldn't focus now and she felt her body give up the struggle. Slowly and in what seemed a rather dignified way she slid from the chair to the floor. She saw heavy black cables and white taped marks and a lot of feet; she could see people running about but heard no sound. She wondered what would happen next. Then blackness closed around her.

Camera two was staring down at her bloody, bruised face, quickly readjusting to bring the image into shocking focus. The director was already thinking about editing for the late news.

49

Ben surveyed his handiwork with pride. It may only have been premature spring cleaning but the symbolism of a tidy, scrubbed and polished house was not lost on him.

The chill wind was tearing through the little cottage, its windows open to welcome the icy blast. Papers skittered over the stone flags and whirled in corner eddies or wrapped themselves around chair legs until Ben came along to rescue them. The wind knocked over anything unable to stand up for itself. Or anyone.

One after another black bin liners were filled with household junk and squatted side by side at the back door. Junk that had been deemed valuable only a few days before: tattered clothes, jars of mouldy marmalade, bits of wood too damp to burn, a foul-smelling cat-litter tray, dud batteries and scraps of paper on which Ben had scrawled poetic phrases. They all went into the black plastic sacks.

The bottles of Terry's home-made beer were poured without qualms down the sink. Ben counted the bottles as he watched the pale brown liquid swirl down the plughole; there were seventeen. He was doing Terry's liver a favour.

He allowed himself a momentary pang of conscience as he wondered where Terry and Sue might be now. But even if they were homeless and arguing, which they might well be, as well as cold and broke, which they certainly were, he knew he had done the right thing. He had to take control of his life; it was time.

Terry and Sue had left the previous day, he with bad grace and she with 'no hard feelings'. They'd intended to go after breakfast; they finally made their muddled exit in the late afternoon just as it was getting dark. They'd loaded up Ben's car with their various belongings including a carrier bag of Siamese cats and driven off with a scrape of gears and no looking back. They'd promised to bring the 2CV back within a week, once they'd 'got a good gaff sussed out'.

There was a storm on the way. After so long on these cliffs Ben could almost smell it in the salty air. He hoped it would be a good blaster and looked forward to the unrelenting power of the elements tearing at the house, trying to pick it up and hurl it over the cliff edge to the rocky beach below.

As darkness fell he closed up the windows and doors and lit some candles. He felt in a mood to celebrate. To celebrate exactly what he would have been hard pressed to define, but he knew that his trip to Germany and the experiences with Boris and the others had redefined him somehow. Or at least given him an incentive for change. In that odd way that strangers press certain short-cut buttons he felt he'd opened himself more to Jo than to anyone since . . . than to anyone ever before.

He thought now about what they'd discussed over joints and sweet German wine a few weeks before. The need for space to make mistakes. The necessity of defining yourself through your actions.

'Don't slip to my level, Ben,' she'd said. 'You still have the potential to do something with your life. To be someone.'

He felt an unexpected fondness for Jo. He hoped she was all right, wherever she was, whatever new challenge she was facing. It would have been pleasant to talk some more with her, find out more about her past, share another bottle of wine and an evening of rambling conversation, but that episode was over. Never mind.

Unaware of the time Ben made himself a mug of coffee and settled down to watch some television.

He was angry to see his father going through the usual motions and then shocked when he saw who was being

461

interviewed. Disappointed too. He'd always thought one of the few good things about his mother was that she nurtured a healthy disdain for George's tiny-minded telly world and everything in it. Was she becoming part of it after all?

Still, she looked good. Glamorous and serene. And she was amusing too. Ben grudgingly acknowledged a sneaking respect for her.

Once the smarmy kid in the leather trousers came on Ben's attention began to wander. He stood at the window looking out into the night's blackness but seeing nothing. The rain splattered against the panes as if it was being thrown in bucketfuls. When he listened for it he thought he could just make out the angry crash of waves on the shingle shore. The howling of the wind had a mournful, ominous tone and Ben was grateful that he was on land, not at sea with the wild ocean beneath his boat ready to swallow any unsteady sailor.

He became aware that the sounds from the television were echoing the brewing storm outside and he turned back to watch the screen again in mounting alarm as the grisly scenario unfolded.

If he had felt powerless before in his relationship with George and Kate, nothing had prepared him for the impotence that overwhelmed him now as he saw his father lose all touch with reality and transform into a vicious brute.

'No!' Ben shouted at the screen as the first blow fell, lunging forward as if to protect his mother. 'No! Stop it! Don't touch her!'

He waited for the smooth voice to interrupt and explain that it had all been a clever joke, that nobody had been hurt and wasn't it all amusing.

But the sense of danger was evident in the camera angles, at first swooping past the terrible action and catching fuzzily glimpsed images, and then focusing and dispassionately showing every cruel blow, which was worse.

He watched as his mother's features buckled under the force of the swinging fist, one earring flying off like the top of JFK's head spinning away. The sound was not crisp and clean like on celluloid fights but dull and low-key and all the more disgusting for the knowledge that it was real. Ben's eyes didn't shift from the small screen as he stared, cold with disbelief, at the sight that he was sharing with millions of others but which hit home to him in a way it couldn't for anyone else.

Only when the beast had been controlled and Kate was lying bloody and immobile on the floor did a caption appear and a flustered female voice urge viewers to stay tuned for an extra programme of cartoon comedy which would follow shortly.

Confused and horrified, Ben gazed at the screen for several minutes after the ghastly scenes had been replaced by anodyne trailers for other programmes. He almost expected an immediate replay of highlights with freeze-frame, expert analysis and computer graphics.

As the images he'd seen replayed themselves on his inner eye he began to shake with rage and revulsion.

He dialled the Hampstead number first and got Marcella, the cook. Her English wasn't up to much but she'd seen the programme and was too distressed to talk.

'Tell them to ring me in Norfolk if they come home. Either of them. Both of them. Okay? Okay, Marcella?'

He rang the studios and couldn't get through for ages. Finally an impatient voice told him no, she couldn't put him through to George King or to Becca Nichols.

'But this is Ben King, his son. Their son. I have to speak to them, you must understand that. I need to know what the hell is going on.'

'Look. I don't know which newspaper you work for but your line is not very original. You're about the twentieth person claiming to be their son. I don't think they even have a son. Goodbye.'.

'Wait –!'

She cut him off.

'Christ!' If he hadn't let the other two borrow his car he'd be on the way to London by now. What chance of hitching? Very little. He was better off by the phone.

He rang Robin Quick's office but only got an answering machine there. He left his number and asked Robin to call with news when he could.

'Oh, Jesus Christ, what a mess. What a family. You bloody animal!'

As he shouted there was a sudden loud crack of thunder. It seemed to summon him. He released the catch on the heavy wooden door and it lurched open, flinging itself at him like a caged creature released. Ben ran outside, feeling at once the gusting east wind tugging at him, pushing him towards the crumbling cliff edge and the steep drop to the rock-strewn beach.

'Bastard!' Ben yelled into the night, staggering through the gorse bushes that littered the scrubby piece of field.

'Everything you touch you fuck up! My life. Her life. Even Christopher's. You self-centred bastard!'

He screwed up his eyes against the driving rain; it didn't matter that he couldn't see, it didn't matter where he went. If he got too near the edge of the cliffs he'd fall. So what? Who would care anyway?

His shirt was soon wet through and sticking to his cold skin, his shoes were heavy with layers of thick mud, the rain plastered his hair to his head and dripped off his nose and chin.

Still he stumbled forward, slipping to the wet ground as his feet caught in rabbit holes or tripped over tufts of thick grass. All the time he lashed out with his hands, grabbing bushes that stung or ripped his fingers, shouting into the gale that seemed to be spurring him on, encouraging him to scream his anger out.

'Mother! Mother, I'm sorry. I'm sorry I've let you down! Please don't let it be too late!'

He fell again, somewhere near the cliff path he could

tell, because the sound of the waves scraping on the shingle had a different timbre, a more immediate edge.

The water again. Always the water in times of crisis. It was as if somehow Christopher's soul had been absorbed into his own body and he was the inheritor of the dead boy's destiny.

'Mother,' he was whining now, his face in the wet grass. 'I didn't let him drown. Forgive me, it wasn't my fault. You don't know what that bastard was doing while Christopher was . . . That sick bastard! I saw what he did to her, that girl. I saw everything but I never told you. I never told anyone. I watched what Daddy did while Christopher was dying. Oh, Mummy, Mummy . . .'

'Ben?'

He heard the call, or thought he did and tried to listen. But the wind and the waves were like a white noise that made anything else virtually indistinguishable. He heard branches of trees cracking, the cry of some creature lost or in pain; it too. But no human voice. It was a bird's cry or a trick of the wind.

'Ben?'

Yes, it was there again. Louder now, questioning.

'Mother?'

It couldn't be. And yet it was.

'Ben, are you there?' It was a plaintive cry floating on the wind.

'Mother!' He struggled to his feet, looking around, peering into the gloom, desperate to see her, to run to her and hold her, feel her love and give her the love he now knew was there in him. *Please, let it be her, let her be there.*

Shapes of bushes and mounds teased him as he searched the blackness around him, shaking the rain from his eyes and pushing sodden strands of hair from his face.

'Mother?' he called, louder, anxious to make contact.

'Ben!'

Yes, there she was! Over towards the house, a distant figure silhouetted against the light that spilled from the

465

open door, making a broadening yellow fan on the ground. *She was there!*

Sliding through the soft mud, dragging his heavy legs through the gorse that scratched and tugged at him he crawled and slithered towards the cottage, calling to her so she wouldn't leave.

'I'm here! I'm coming. Wait, I'm here!'

She turned to the sound of his voice as he struggled towards her, finally seeing him and stepping back in shock as he lunged at her out of the dark.

'Jesus, what —?'

Only as he made the last few strides and saw her face in the light did he realize.

'Jo!'

'Ben. Christ, what the hell happened to you?'

'Jo. It's you!'

'You bet it is. Are you all right, kid?'

'I thought you . . .'

'You're not, are you? You look bloody awful.'

'I thought she was . . .'

'Come here.'

'I'm . . . I'm . . .'

'I said, come here.'

She grabbed him and squeezed as if to expel poisonous air from his lungs. He pressed his face into her wet hair and when he recognized her smell began to cry.

'Oh, Jo. Help me. Please.'

'I came here to ask you to help me. Will you look at the pair of us.'

'Thank God you're here. I don't know what to do. My father . . . my mother . . .'

'Sssh. Keep crying, keep crying.'

And he did.

50

The country, quite simply, went mad. Nobody seemed to have any other topic of conversation. On buses, in wine bars, over garden fences, on telephone lines and around dinner tables, George King beating up his wife was the only thing anyone wanted to discuss.

Everybody had an opinion whether they'd seen the show or not. Anyway, those who hadn't soon built up enough of a picture from the sequences shown in news reports, the grainy stills in the Sunday papers and word of mouth to be authorities on the subject.

Everyone was interviewed for their version of what had happened, from the security men at the studio to shoppers in Hampstead who had once seen Kate Fitch in the news-agents and who were encouraged to speculate from this privileged firsthand knowledge on the state of the King–Fitch marriage. One of the broadsheets ran a series of articles about how husbands coped with the discovery of their wives' affairs. Responses ranged from forgiveness to murder and everything in between. Everything, that is, except knocking them about on prime time television. This was a first.

A rival chat show — well, a coffee-morning magazine programme hosted by a Glaswegian husband and wife team — ran a three-day phone-in on people's reactions and encouraged viewers to vent their anger to the counsellor in the studio, cursing George King and detailing what they'd like to do to him. Some callers seemed more pre-occupied by the revelation of his baldness than by what he'd done to Kate. The fact that he was a 'slap-head' appar-ently either explained his violence or was explained by it.

The *Sun* — headline: '***KING HELL!!' — ran a readers' poll on the World's Most Evil Man. Easily defeated were Saddam Hussein and Adolf Hitler; George King just pipped Hannibal Lecter to the title.

Kate knew nothing of this nationwide fracas. As far as she knew she had been publicly humiliated; physically and emotionally destroyed. From her hospital bed in the private clinic in Cockfosters she was carefully shielded, by nurses taking instruction from Robin, from any paper, radio, television screen or visitor who might discuss it with her. In fact Robin himself was the only visitor, calling in twice a day with gifts and good wishes, anything Kate requested from home or Harrods but no more news than he thought she could cope with.

'You just get better, my lovey. In a few weeks you'll be fighting fit and ready to hit the big time again.'

'Oh, I don't think so,' she sighed. 'I feel so tired all the time. Weary of the struggle.'

'Now come on, that won't get the baby ironed, will it? Once the bruising's gone down and the jaw's on the mend we can get the teeth capped. And the doctors are pretty sure the nose won't look any different once it's healed. You've been a very brave girl and I'm only sorry I misjudged so horribly. I've brought you some books to read.'

He put them with the others which lay untouched on the table by her bed. The nurses had told Robin that Kate just lay in bed hour after hour, staring out of the window, picking at the food they brought her and refusing to talk when they tried to engage her in conversation.

'She'll be fine, she'll be fine,' he said to them brightly, trying to convince himself. And when he spoke to Ben he used the same phrase.

'Honestly, there's nothing you can do. She doesn't want to see anyone for a few days yet. No, not even you, I'm afraid. I'm sorry. Not until she's a little more presentable. I'll call you when she does. No, your father's not been to

468

visit and the hospital have instructions not to let him in if he tries to see her. Believe me, she'll be fine.'

Despite Robin's fierce optimism, Kate didn't feel fine. She lay in her hospital bed, nursing her broken nose, jaw, teeth and fingers, wishing the bruising would stop hurting and the swelling around her eyes would relax so she could at least see better.

But although she was saying little or nothing for hours at a time her brain was working overtime. All the while she was weighing up the pros and cons, considering the past and the present and trying to get some sense of what her future might hold.

It wasn't easy. Or pleasant. The harder she tried to pin a thought down the less point there seemed to any of it. After a few days her sadness had slumped to a state of such despair that the certainty of her worthlessness was some kind of comfort.

Knowing nothing any more other than this, Kate looked around the room and began to plan her escape.

51

George was unused to his new position of being despised and rejected. Overnight he had gone from idol to evil and he couldn't handle it.

Inside the lonely Hampstead fortress, barricaded against the microphones and telephoto lenses of the media rats out to humiliate him further, George considered his options.

He slowly became aware that he didn't have any.

Should he give an exclusive interview to one of the tabloids, appealing to red-blooded males to sympathize with his reactions at finding out that his wife had been screwing around? It didn't sound very plausible, really. His audience were the women of a certain age who were far more likely to identify with Kate than side with the cuckolded husband.

How about brazen it out, say he was proud of what he'd done and he'd do it again? No, professional suicide.

Retire gracefully? After all, he hadn't needed to earn a living for ten years. Forget it! George King was not a quitter.

So, what else?

He thought hard and long, whisky bottle clutched tightly by the neck. Restless and inelegant he prowled around his office, swiping at piles of paper, scowling at computer screens and ignoring ringing phones. None of this paraphernalia meant anything. It couldn't restore him to the top of the tree. He picked up a delicate ivory letter opener and stabbed it into the desk top; it snapped in two.

A buzz informed him that the main security gates were opening; he flicked the switches until the relevant camera's view came on the small black and white screen.

It was Becca's Volvo being steered carefully through the pack of hacks. He wouldn't have been so diligent; he'd have slammed the gas on and hoped to wing a couple as they scattered to either side.

She came in a couple of minutes later with a large cardboard box of groceries. Mostly things that could be done in the microwave. Marcella had walked out claiming that she didn't feel safe around George. He'd paid off Alec the chauffeur and told him to bugger off too. He preferred to sulk alone.

Becca took the box into the kitchen and George followed like a dog waiting to be fed. As she unpacked she tidied, putting boxes and jars away and pouring semi-solid milk down the sink.

'Put something in the mike. I'm starving.'

'Yes, Mr King.'

'You'd better show me how to use that thing one day.'

'Yes, now that . . . things have changed.' She put a plastic tray of Extra Tangy Seafood Risotto inside, bleeped some buttons and it hummed into life.

She looked at him, seeing his unshaven face, his hollow cheeks and dark-ringed, frightened eyes. He looked a wreck; worse than she'd seen him for a long time. Good, he was softened up for the attack she and Gina had planned.

He was staring into the oven, watching his food revolve, waiting for the 'ping' that told him he could eat it. He was a child.

'Oh, sweet Jesus,' he sighed deeply. 'What the hell am I going to do?'

'Do, Mr King? In what way?'

'Oh, for God's sake. What do I do now? How do I get back up there?'

'You're asking me, Mr King?'

'Yeh. You know the business. What d'you think?'

'It's not for me to say.' She busied herself again at the sink, piling greasy plates into hot water. 'I'm not paid to think.'

He laid a soft white hand on her bare arm. Goosepimples of horror rose instantly and a shiver of disgust shot right through her, but she managed not to scream or strike out. 'Look, Becca, I need your advice. I need your help, dammit.'

'You need me? Really?' She tried not to sound too smug.

'I don't know what to do. I'm damned if I'm going to roll over and play dead, but I just don't know how I should play it.'

The microwave pinged, but they both ignored it. Becca glanced at his big, sad face; she felt compromised by his proximity, threatened even by his self-pity. She thought about what she and Gina had discussed and agreed. She knew what her task was now. She moved away from him, disengaging her arm from his touch, wanting to disinfect her flesh where there'd been contact.

'I admit I've been giving it some thought. The matter of your future after the . . . after last week's show. I had thought you might not wish me to continue working for you . . . with you,' she corrected herself. Might as well make sure the fact of his dependency had sunk in. 'It could be a tough road back, Mr King, but if we pitch it right I believe it could lead to some real personal gains for you.' She lowered her voice and spoke slowly, keeping her steady eyes fixed on his bleary ones. 'The secret is your image. I think we need to change your image.'

'Oh, brilliant! Is that your master stroke? The old image was a crazed wife-beater; let's now project someone who doesn't beat up his wife! You're a fucking genius!'

'Please, listen,' Becca snapped in her schoolmarm voice. 'This is for your benefit, not mine.'

After a pause he was contrite. 'Go on.'

'When I say your image, let me explain exactly what I mean.'

And she talked about the new look she proposed. The gist of it was a new candour. He should go on television to apologize to the nation for what he'd done to Kate.

'Apologize? But she was the one fucking around!'

Becca explained that it was the only card he had left to play. Kate had cheated on him and he could trump her deceit with his honesty. Claim the moral high ground, as she put it. Then lie low for a while and wait for the public to demand his return.

'There's nobody around with your experience, Mr King, your charisma and gravitas. The public will see that once you're off their screens for a while. Then we'll be ready for the re-launch. The new, born-again George King. The King is dead, long live the King. The revamped version will be a wiser, more forgiving man. A man who can talk about the pain of life because he's been there, and the public know he's been there because they saw it happen!'

'Well . . .'

'It'll be a rebirth. A new kind of show. You won't just interview actors and writers, you'll talk to real people about their real lives, the sort of traumas we know you've been through too. A kind of "Face to Face". No studio audience, no clever sets or funny lines to camera. You talk to people about their most intimate experiences; a man who lost his limbs in the Gulf War, a child who saw his parents die on the streets of Londonderry or a woman who . . .' she turned away to reach for two glasses and poured them both shots of whisky '. . . who was raped when she was a girl.'

He took the glass she offered, knocked the drink back and held it out for more.

'Flawed people,' she said. 'Damaged people. Like yourself.'

'I like it. What's it called?'

They hadn't thought about that. ' "The George King Agenda." '

'Yeh! That gives it clout. "Did you watch 'The George King Agenda' last night?" Yes, that works.'

Becca topped up his glass.

'But the big deal here is your image.'

'Right. Serious, man of the world stuff.'

'Yes,' she said. 'But more than that. You look different. You've come through your own trauma of finding out about your wife's affair, and the trauma of being seen treating her as you did, the awful public opprobrium. Disgrace,' she added, seeing his look of incomprehension. 'You've come through your own private hell and not only survived but looking younger and fitter and even more attractive than before. With a sort of glow of worldly-wisdom and inner peace.'

She could hardly believe he was swallowing all this bull-shit. Only one more step to take him and then he'd be in the net.

'This is great. How come I look younger?'

'Plastic surgery,' she said quickly.

He considered it for a second. She held his gaze and waited. Which way would he go?

'Plastic surgery? You mean – ?'

'A tightening up of the jawline and removal of the – forgive me – bags under the eyes. To give you that fresher, more appetizing look.' Careful, she thought, don't over-cook it.

'Right.' He looked doubtful. Was he about to rumble her?

Then his features cracked into a gleeful sneer.

'Fucking terrific! I love it! You're brilliant. What are you on? Fifty k? Make it sixty! Yeh! Let's do it!'

'It shouldn't take long to set up. There are certain contingency plans that only need a go-ahead from me to start the ball rolling. You'll want total anonymity, of course.'

'Oh, shit, I hadn't thought of that.' George's face sagged even more than usual.

'Don't worry; I had.' Becca was as crisp as a hospital matron. 'What I suggest is that instead of your having to travel abroad, I could arrange for one of the world's top cosmetic surgeons to fly into London. If we look carefully we might find somewhere in the world where they haven't heard of you. Which in this instance would prove an advantage. We could have the operation done here in the strictest secrecy and the press wouldn't know a thing about it. When the bruising and swelling have gone down you could start to appear in public again, showing the new face of the new, enlightened George King. The man who is no longer afraid of facing up to anything in life, including himself.'

'You're amazing.'

'Yes. I'd need access to substantial funds, of course.'

'You can have a blank cheque. Whatever it takes. Wait, how do we find the right man?'

'Leave all that to me, Mr King.'

'But – '

'Have I ever let you down?'

He looked decidedly sheepish.

'Very well, then. Put your face in my hands.' She felt like a cross between Margaret Thatcher and Mary Poppins, a lethal combination that not even George King could resist.

Becca dialled a number on a line she knew couldn't be bugged.

'He bought it, Gina! He bought it! Everything went exactly as planned. He wants the new image.'

'Oh, baby, you're brilliant. Let's give him what he wants, then. Will you arrange the place?'

'No problem. I've spoken off the record to someone at one of the threatened hospitals. She can arrange for the relevant facilities to be made available for a couple of hours in return for a hefty donation to their fighting fund.'

'It's a good job they're all so broke. I've spoken to our man in Agadir. Mr Marjit. Or Doctor Marjit as he still calls himself, despite the court case. He was practically salivating at the thought of ten grand for a day's work. He didn't really understand the reasons for the op.'

'But – ?'

475

'It's okay. He's going to do *exactly* what we want.'

'Fantastic. George King, your nemesis awaits.'

'No second thoughts, Bec?'

'God, no. Hang on, he's coming! Got to go. Speak soon.'

Two days later, on a blustery afternoon just as the failing light heralded the imminence of evening, Becca drove the Roller out through the electronic security gates and past the knot of curious journos stamping warmth into their feet. A few pictures were taken but only from force of habit. They got nothing they could make a story from; George was well hidden in the boot. An indignity Becca enjoyed inflicting.

He was easily smuggled into the hospital and through the corridors on a trolley, his face hidden under an oxygen mask. Soon he was ready for his big moment, wrapped in a white gown, looking up at Becca as she leaned over his supine body. He was clutching his toupee, nervously folding and unfolding it.

'This is going to be straightforward, isn't it?'

'Don't worry, George. Nothing can possibly go wrong.'

He took her smile as one of reassurance but its cause was the realization that she'd called him 'George' for the first time. She was the stronger now; finally it was his turn to be the victim.

'Trust me, George, you'll be transformed.'

52

Impatiently Kate pressed the pre-set buttons on the car radio, trying to find a suitable station. Classical music seemed the most fitting accompaniment to the task in hand, but all she could get was a Strauss lollipop or atonal cacophony. No, that wouldn't do. Other stations brought thumping pop with or without inane prattle, again not right for the mood she sought to create. Then she came across a frequency where there were show tunes and film themes. That was more like it, bright and breezy. Then they played the theme from *M*A*S*H*. How depressing — that was the last thing she wanted to hear.

Or rather not the last thing she wanted to hear.

Perhaps it should be the human voice? There was 'Today in Parliament' on Radio Four and a particularly embarrassing phone-in on the subject of pets and DIY on a nearby frequency.

All right, then, silence. She tried it and her mind began to race again, throwing ideas and doubts around, plucking memories from nowhere and sending them hurtling headlong, crashing and jumbling together. No, no. It was calm and rest she wanted. To rest in peace.

She put one of her favourite cassettes on: the Mozart clarinet concerto. It was like an old friend, comfortable and yet not predictable, always stimulating. She unplugged the car phone; she didn't want to be disturbed now. This was her private time and her private business. Not even George could mess this up for her.

She was parked well off any public road, tucked up against a clump of the Heath's densest bushes so as not to make a car-shaped silhouette and risk attracting attention. The drizzle had stopped but it was still overcast and a strong wind shook the trees and gently buffeted the car. Rock-a-bye baby . . . She'd be asleep soon enough.

But first to business. She looked at what she'd written to Ben. Three paragraphs seemed pitifully inadequate as a final benediction but she'd always hated those gushy actressy types who loved the sound of their own voices and waffled on. No, she'd made her mind up to be brief. And as positive as she could be in the circumstances.

She'd told Ben she loved him even if he didn't believe her. She knew she'd made mistakes and she hoped that even if he couldn't find it in his heart to forgive her now perhaps one day he would.

'You may think,' she wrote in her neatest writing,

that this was my biggest mistake ever. If so, well, that's your prerogative. All I can say is – and I'm sorry it's such a cliché – I can't see any other way. I suppose it's a bit like playing a part. One doesn't so much commit the lines to memory as learn the motivation and the character so that given the situation at any time in the play there is only one thing that person could possibly say. In the current circumstances there's nothing else I can do but this. You see, Ben, my downfall is complete. I have been battered down by life and now beaten in both senses by your father. My public humiliation was the final insult. Nothing can resurrect me from that shame. To put it simply – I quit.

I'm actually feeling very calm about my approaching death. Looking forward to the end of the struggle. And it has been a struggle, professional and private. Most of it, it has to be said, has been your father's doing, but some has been of my own making. Believe me, Ben darling, none of it was caused by you. You brought me so much joy and I shall miss you. You

478

may miss me too, who knows? But don't feel bad if you don't.

I suppose I feel happier now than at any time I can remember, so don't worry that I was in turmoil at the end. I'm not. I hope my departure doesn't cause you too much pain. If you do cry a little, I understand. But get on with your life and be proud of everything you are; I'm proud of you and always have been. Always. No matter what took place in the past. Accidents do happen and I think I have come to accept that. Don't feel I blame you for anything. I know I was not the best mother in the world; I hope I was not the worst.

Goodbye, Ben. I love you.

The second movement had reached a particularly haunting passage and Kate had to blink her eyes dry. She'd spent too much time crying recently. She sealed the letter in an envelope, addressed it to Ben and put it in her handbag. He would probably get it in a couple of days; the police would read it first. The other letters were already written. One to Robin and one to her solicitor. And that was it, the ends neatly tied. There was nothing to be said to George. Nothing useful anyway. The days for talking to him were long past. She should have left him years ago and perhaps she'd have had a chance, but she'd missed her opportunity and been doomed to a life of compromise. Now she faced another opportunity for action; this one she was going to seize.

The music was depressing her now. She ejected the cassette in mid-cadenza, flicked the buttons again and settled this time on a pop station which was playing sixties music. Yes, that would be a pleasant way to go. 'Tears of a Clown' sang Smokey Robinson. Well, well.

She took from the carrier bag on the passenger seat the new garden hose and penknife purchased from an iron-monger's shop in St Albans with much embarrassed conversation about Friday's now notorious show. She cut off the ten feet she needed and then got out of the Mercedes to attach it. As she'd anticipated it was too thin to be wedged into the exhaust pipe so she slit the hose, forced it over the end and wrapped it carefully around with the new roll of sticky parcel tape until she was sure the seal was airtight. There could be no messing up with this; it was a one-take job. Where she jammed the other end of the hose between the passenger's window and the door frame she taped again, thoroughly, from left to right and up and down, making sure no life-preserving fresh air could get into her cosy cocoon.

She wiped her hands clean on the wet grass and sat in the driving seat, staring out into the night, the last she would see.

The body of the actress Kate Fitch was found last night in her car on Hampstead Heath. She had been asphyxiated. Police are treating her death as suspicious. She was forty-eight.

Or forty-six or fifty-one, depending on which paper you read. It always differed. What sort of billing would she get? Would she make the front page headline in the *Standard*? What about the nationals? Oh, what the hell did it matter now?

She lowered the volume on the radio – it was 'Yellow Submarine' now – and listened to find out what her final sounds of nature would be. The trees were keeping up a steady rustling, a friendly, unthreatening noise to keep her company in her last minutes.

Well, she thought, this is it. The big moment. I should have a speech prepared, something momentous to say. 'Hey, I'm speechless, I dunno what to say. Gee! Well, I'd like to thank my agent, the director, the crew . . .' No, I just want to go, to leave this life and find peace somewhere else. I suppose I could pray . . . For what? And to whom? I'm not sure if I believe in a god. Fifty-two years old – yes fifty-two, but don't print that – and I don't even know if I believe in God or not. I've really made a mess of everything, haven't I? I could have been someone, could have done something. But instead . . .

She sighed deeply. She could make out the shapes of two men in the shadows a few hundred yards away. One was dressed in leather with a cap. They came together from opposite directions, met, talked and went off into the bushes. How long would their dangerous liaison last? Ten minutes? Ten years? Would they live happily ever after or would one of them one day be in her present position?

Come on then, don't hang about. Go if you're going, don't make a mess of your exit. Leave them wanting more.

She turned the key in the ignition, the engine rumbled alarmingly into life and then settled into a quiet purr. She revved it and could immediately smell the fumes being pumped into the car. For the first time she felt a twinge of uncertainty. She had no idea how long it would take. She didn't want to be hanging around, gasping and rasping for hours, but on the other hand a few minutes to get used to her big adventure would be nice. Like the five extra minutes' acclimatization created by having the half-hour called thirty-five minutes before curtain up. It was a civilized place, the theatre. She'd miss it, even if it wouldn't miss her.

She checked her face in the rear-view mirror. God, what a mess! The cuts had been stitched and patched at the hospital but the bruising was still hideous, changing now from blue-black to a nasty yellow and brown. Practically all of her once beautiful face was swollen and spoiled. George's last gift to her. Thanks, George.

She took blusher, mascara, eyeshadow and a variety of short, fat brushes from her bag and did what repair work she could. She wanted to look her best; she'd chosen the Claude Montana outfit especially. There was no point inviting unwelcome publicity, even now.

She breathed deep on the poisonous air, welcoming its deadly effect as she took it down into her lungs. Her deep breathing and diaphragm control were standing her in fine

481

stead yet again. She felt good at last, proud of herself and her resolve, magnificent in this, her last great role. There was a touch of the twentieth-century Cleopatras about it which she welcomed. It was the nearest she'd get to the part. The unique mixture of dread and eagerness was so like the pre-show buzz of a first night that it helped her to welcome whatever the next few minutes held in store. A shame she wouldn't be able to look back with pride or tell nostalgic tales of how she felt.

Well, yes, I had a good death. I was very pleased with my performance. Dignified and understated . . .

She made sure her nail varnish hadn't been chipped and that her hair still looked good. Otherwise, she thought, I'll have to get Michi B. to refresh my make-up before the big scene.

What the hell am I rambling about? I'm raving. I must be getting high on the gases. Good.

She gulped at the air and swallowed it into her.

Well, there's nothing to keep me here now. Goodnight everyone, thank you for coming and watching the show. But now it's over . . .

Kate pressed her foot down hard and felt the powerful throb of the Merc's engine drowning the radio and accelerating her demise. She sucked hard at the deadly, sweet air. Her head was light inside but too heavy to hold up. She let it fall back and her jaw hung open. Her eyelids gently drooped as if invisible fingers pulled them closed.

Finally she felt no pain. Feeling nothing at all, she passed from life into limbo.

. . . that's in Sports Corner at half past the hour. Later, in Arts about Town our theatre correspondent Gavin Moon will be talking about tonight's dramatic announcement that the part of Jackie Onassis in the upcoming West End musical will be played by Kate Fitch. In the light of recent events, has she swung the part only because of the publicity created by certain private matters which spilled unforgettably out into the public eye? If so, *does it matter? Arts about Town on the resurgence of Kate Fitch is at the top of the hour. Now, though, here's something soft and smoochy. Let's play it for anyone who's feeling a bit lonely tonight. It's Randy Crawford. 'Some Day I'll Fly Away' . . .*

53

The moment of truth had arrived.

Three figures stood nervously in George's office, each with a different reason to be apprehensive. One was frightened the operation had gone wrong, one that it hadn't and the third worried that he wouldn't get his money and his plane back to Morocco.

'Oh, Jesus Christ, this is nerve-racking. What if it's a disaster?'

'Relax, George,' said Becca. 'This is going to be the start of the new you.'

'What was wrong with the old one?'

'Do I really need to spell it out?'

'Huh. I should never have agreed to this. It's bloody painful, you know.'

'Please, sir, try to keep still for a moment while I remove the rest of the bandages.' Dr Marjit was unwrapping the remodelled face like something in tinfoil from the barbecue. Was it done yet? How would it look?

Slowly, with infinite care and patience, he uncoiled the long white ribbons to reveal the new George King.

'Right, then, let's have a good look at you,' he said as the last of the dressings was removed.

'This is it, George, the new look.' Becca grinned at him, delighting in what she was sure was going to be a metamorphosis.

And so it was. Of a kind.

Dr Marjit studied George carefully from all angles, touching the skin gingerly and turning George's head first one way and then the other, nodding and grunting to himself, appraising his handiwork.

'What's wrong?' George asked quickly. 'What's the matter?' He could tell from their faces that his was not as planned.

'God . . .' Becca's mouth hung open. This exceeded her own expectations.

'Nothing's wrong, really, sir. Wrong would not be the word.'

'So why are you looking like that? Tell me, what does it look like?'

'God, George, it's not . . . it's not right.'

'No, no, it's a little . . . severe perhaps, you might be rather surprised, but I'm sure you will get used to it in time. I'm really jolly pleased with the result.'

'But he looks ridiculous!' Becca said with amusement, any consideration for George's feelings now blatantly discarded.

'What?! Give me a mirror!'

'No, no, Miss Nichols. Not ridiculous. The bone structure is the same, after all. We haven't changed that, although we could if you wanted us to.'

'Whadya mean "ridiculous"?'

'He looks different, certainly, but then that was the point of the exercise, was it not?'

'Give me a mirror! Ow! Why are there no fucking mirrors in here?' Shouting brought pain; pain made him shout.

George touched the raw skin under his eyes and felt for the stitches high up behind his ears where he still, mercifully, had enough of his own real hair to hide them.

The doctor – the ex-doctor – gave George a mirror. 'Bear in mind that it could be a surprise to you. I hope you won't be disappointed,' he said, but without conviction.

George held the mirror up and gazed into it. He stared and stared for almost a minute, studying the image that was thrown back at him. Then he let the heavy square of glass drop to his lap. Becca and Dr Marjit watched him and waited.

'Oh Christ,' they could just hear him say, almost as if he was beginning a very private prayer.

'George . . .'

'Oh fucking Christ. Who is that?'

'It's the new you, Mr King. What do you think?'

'No, it's not me. That's not George King.'

He stood up from his chair, holding the mirror high and looking up into it so that his face was fully lit by the fluorescent striplight. Fascinated, he again inspected the face that he saw there. It was someone who had been through a terrible accident, perhaps a fire; someone whose skin had been burned or scalded or somehow heat-shrunken like polythene film over supermarket fruit. The bones on the man's face were all too evident, straining against the red, tender skin and threatening to burst out. The eyes were ringed with purple bruising, stitches beneath them like a line of kisses at the foot of a love letter. The lower lids seemed to have been dragged down, giving the face a sleepy, uninvolved expression and showing the red capillaries that used to be hidden from view. The overall effect was of a fairly healthy corpse. Whoever the man was George didn't know him. But he felt sorry for him, he looked like a zombie after a head-on car smash.

He tried to mobilize the facial muscles to see how the new product worked. But nothing happened. He thought he was smiling; the face in the mirror registered a macabre grimace. He frowned; it hurt, but nothing showed on the other face at all. He tried his famous quizzical twinkle, the expression he was known for. Or used to be. The plastic doll he was studying came back with the look of a frightened rabbit caught in the headlight's beam.

'What do you think of your new face, eh?'

'You sodding quack,' he whispered.

'You'll get used to it, believe me. When the bruising goes down you'll really appreciate just how different you look.'

'I appreciate it. Believe me, I appreciate it! Look! Look!' He jabbed a finger at his cheek. 'That's not me, you bastard!

That's not George King!' He sprang up and grabbed Dr Marjit by his lapels, shaking him as if he wanted the other man's head to come right off. 'You fuckin' black witch doctor! Give me back my face, you incompetent Paki bastard!'

'Really, there is no need for such language.'

'*Give me back my face!*'

'Thank you, doctor,' Becca said matter-of-factly. 'You've done a wonderful job.' She took a fat envelope from her jacket pocket and handed it to him.

'What did you say to him? Wonderful?'

'I'm going to have to explain a few things, George. Oh, wait.'

Becca heard a buzz, checked a screen and let in whoever was calling. A minute later she was in the room. George turned away, furious but suddenly shy.

'Hi, Bec. Hello, George. Glad you took my advice about the facelift. So, how does the new boy look?'

'You? What are you doing here?' He talked to her without turning to face her.

'She's my partner in this deal,' said Becca, standing next to Gina defiantly. 'You don't get it, do you?'

'What?'

'You've been set up good and proper. You've been bloody shafted, Georgie-Porgie. Yeh, that's the word, isn't it? Shafted.' Gina went to him, unafraid, and reached up to turn him with a hand on his shoulder. 'Come on, let's have a butcher's.'

Slowly the great body turned, the full horror of what Dr Marjit had done gradually becoming evident.

'Oh, shit. That's terrible,' said Gina with genuine surprise. 'Really awful.' And then she laughed. At first she tittered like a naughty child in church, but then, as she caught the guilty glint in Becca's eye, roared with undisguised glee and relief.

'Shut up, bitch!' he growled.

'Are you cross, George?' Gina mocked. 'I can't tell from your face!'

A thought permeated through his brain. 'What d'you mean "shafted"?'

'Oh George, poor George. You really don't understand what this is all about, do you? Have you kept him in the dark, Bec?'

She nodded, the lieutenant now to Gina's general.

'So he doesn't know that we set it all up, that we paid our good doctor –' she looked around for him '– who seems to have done a bunk already, paid him to destroy your looks just as you've destroyed people.'

'You crazy bitches. I've never destroyed anyone.'

'No?' All humour was gone from Gina's voice now. She closed in on him threateningly, small but lethal. 'What you did to me on the beach in Bermuda was supposed to benefit me, was it? You rape me and don't expect me to retaliate? It's taken a few weeks George, but this is what you get back for your behaviour that day. You're lucky we didn't arrange for the doctor to slice your fucking balls off! He'd have done it, you know, for another grand!'

'You're mad! What happened on the beach was just . . . it was a bit of messing around.'

'Shut up, shut up!' It was Becca shouting now, intense but still just in control of herself. 'How dare you? How dare you treat Gina like that? The whole country knows now what kind of man you are. I've known what kind of sleazy animal you are for twenty years!'

'Twenty years? What are you talking about?'

'Twenty years ago, George. The day your son died. The day Christopher drowned in the garden pond. Do you remember that day? The hot summer afternoon. The day of your terrible tragedy, the papers called it. Of your wife's tragedy. Even your son Ben's. And who else? Who else suffered? Think, George. Who else was there? Come on, *think about it!*'

The tendons in Becca's neck stood out as she stared into his bleary eyes, keen to hear his response. Her lips were so tight they had almost disappeared; her back was ramrod straight and her fingers likewise, flat against the front of her thighs. She waited, head quivering almost imperceptibly, while the cogs in George's befuddled brain slowly turned.

'Who . . . else . . . was . . . there?' she ground out, her teeth clamped together. 'Your wife had gone to the theatre. Your two sons were in the garden, playing. Where were you, George King?'

'I was . . . I went inside.'

'Inside. Yes. Why?' she hurried him, an impatient teacher with a dull pupil.

'Someone came to the . . . it was the . . . she'd come . . . The babysitter . . . ?'

He stared at Becca as the truth dawned. His ghastly, ghostly features couldn't express what he was feeling, but deep in the yellow-black bruising his tiny eyes couldn't hide the gradually dawning truth.

'You?' he almost croaked. She nodded. 'No.'

'Yes.' Her voice was a whisper. 'That girl in school uniform was me. She still is me. The girl you tried to destroy then is with me every day. She's never forgotten. Never will. You don't get over something like that. So many lives completely transformed and all from your inability to control your lust. Lust for what? Power over a fourteen-year-old girl. You were pathetic that day and you still are.'

She stared at him, her chin jutting forward. He gazed back; it was impossible to tell what he was thinking.

'I've been waiting for this moment for twenty years,' she said slowly, her voice quiet and calm. 'I didn't know quite how it would be, but I always knew that one day I would see you humiliated. I can't tell you what pleasure it gives me. I hope you're in a lot of pain.'

'My face,' he said so quietly it was almost inaudible. 'Give me back my face.'

Then, in a few silent seconds, Becca watched as George

staggered a couple of steps and crumpled into an armchair. He had the pathetic air of something unable to resist the powerful drug of a tranquillizing dart.

There was a sudden scrape of keys in a lock outside, voices at the front door and Ben burst into the room.

'What's happened? Where is she? Where's −?'

He stopped, seeing Becca and Gina. Then he saw the huddled form of his father and studied him more closely.

'Robin Quick rang me. Mother's disa− What the hell happened to you?'

Jo came in behind Ben and George's hands began to flutter embarrassedly around his face, half hiding and half drawing attention to it.

'You look terrible. Are you ill?'

'This is a private office.' His voice sounded different too, muffled somehow. With evident difficulty he stood up, heaving himself out of the chair with a grunt.

'I saw what you did, you know. I saw what you did to Mother.'

'So? I'm supposed to care?'

Neither spoke nor moved. In that moment Ben knew, seeing as clearly as by fluorescent light, that he was no longer afraid of him, of the strange, sad monster standing before him, confronting him with the shell of his former personality. It had been the reputation, the image he had once held in awe. What was so great about the man? The flesh and blood on display now? Absolutely nothing. The power he'd wielded over Ben for so long dissipated completely in that precise moment like powder blown away on the wind.

'It's a facelift, isn't it? God, what a disaster. You look awful. As if your head's been boiled.'

'Thank you.' George looked away from Ben, as if unable to face the challenge his son now represented. His glazed eyes focused on Jo. He looked her up and down, twice, insultingly. Jo stood her ground, shoulders squared up to him, used to much worse from men than simple stares.

490

But it wasn't an insult that came, just a quiet observation.

'I know you.'

'Really? Well, I certainly know you, Mr King, from your television show.' She gave him a small polite smile.

'I know you from your films.' His lips moved into a kind of snarl. Ben guessed it was as close as he could get to a grin.

'You may do.'

'Yes. You're the Mother Superior with the dildo in *Nun but the Brave*.'

'Have you seen Jo's films?' Ben was mildly shocked.

'Seen them? Ha! You don't know the half of it. I've been —'

'Look. It's your mother's car.' Becca was watching the screens. She pressed some buttons and led the way out into the hall.

'Mother! Robin told me she was missing and he was worried. She discharged herself from the hospital. God, she'd better be all right or . . .'

The look he gave George was pure venom.

When Ben flung the front door open he had to pause for a moment to register quite what he was seeing. With relief he took in that his mother's Mercedes was parked there, and from the passenger door a near-naked bottom was emerging. It belonged to a man in his sixties dressed in black leather: cap with chain, waistcoat, leather boots and cowboy-type chaps that covered part of his buttocks but left white segments like crescent moons exposed. He was struggling with something on the passenger seat; Ben couldn't see what.

'Give me the hand, please,' he called as the light from the open door flooded over him. 'Quickly, if you can.'

Ben knew the voice at once.

'Klaus?'

The figure stood up and half turned. 'Ben? You? What are you —? Never mind, now. Help me to get her inside.'

491

'Mother!'

He ran down the steps and crouched at the side of the car, desperate to see her, to make contact.

'Mother, it's Ben. Are you all right? Oh, I'm sorry about . . . Mother?'

But she wasn't there. Her body was, dark bruises and stitching about the face, but it was limp and useless. As if she was drunk.

'What's happened?'

'Mother? You call her "Mother"? Kate Fitch? You are her boy? No. This I do not believe.'

'What's happened? Tell me!'

'She had a hose tube in the window. She wanted to kill herself with the fumes. I was with a new friend on the Heath. We did our business and then I saw this car with the lights off and the engine burning. I couldn't believe when I saw it was my lovely Kate.'

Ben touched her face. It was cold. Her eyes didn't seem to focus on anything and there was a dribble of spittle from the corner of her mouth.

'Lucky I know her address. She was breathing and even talking. Just nonsense. I thought the police didn't need to know so I brought her home. Oh, silly girl. She was going to be a star all over again, like the first time. She must be so sad.'

'Oh, don't let it be too late.'

Jo had moved swiftly between the two men and had laid her fingers on Kate's neck, checking for a pulse.

'Come on, B.,' she said. 'Get her inside and we'll call a doctor. Never mind feeling guilty, shift your arse.'

As they manhandled her limp body awkwardly through the hall, George emerged from his study and watched, mildly curious but unwilling to be involved, a bystander at a motorway crash.

'Doctor! Phone a doctor!' Ben shouted. George just stared back as if he was observing something on a screen.

'*Phone a bloody doctor!*' he screamed. 'For Christ's sake,

do something useful, for once!' He saw that Becca was already dialling.

They laid Kate with enormous care on a comfortable chair. Ben pulled up a stool and lifted her feet on to it. He noticed the mud on her shoes. Klaus loosened Kate's clothes at the neck and tactfully smoothed her skirt down.

'Get her on the floor!' Jo shouted, a sudden urgency in her voice.

'I think she's more comfortable –'

'On the floor, quick! She's stopped breathing.'

They pulled her down on to the carpet and Jo immediately knelt by her and bent over, listening for breath, checking for obstructions in the throat, then she tilted Kate's chin back, pinched her nose and blew into her open mouth.

Ben watched, terrified.

'No. Please. Mother . . .'

Jo continued in silence, with an almost professional dedication. She checked Kate's neck for a pulse, clenched her fists together, placed them on Kate's chest and leant on her straight arms, bouncing slightly and counting aloud. 'Ten . . . eleven . . . twelve . . .' Again she checked for breath, again she put her mouth to Kate's and again she linked her fingers and bore down.

'You. Dial nine, nine, nine. Ambulance. Never mind the publicity, we're gonna keep her alive. Ben, you take over here, like this. Hold her nose with this hand, keep her chin tipped back like this. Seal her mouth with yours and give one long, steady breath. I'll do the chest compression. Wait until I tell you.'

'But I . . . is she going to . . . ?'

'We'll keep her going until the ambulance gets here. Come on. There's a job to do, for Christ's sake stop feeling sorry for yourself.'

She showed Ben what to do. Tears streamed down his face and his whole body was drenched with sweat as he pressed his mouth to his mother's lips and forced the breath of life into her lungs.

'Oh God, let her survive!' Ben was screaming inside his head. 'I'll talk to her. I'll show her I care. Anything. *Just don't let her die.*'

She seemed half dead already. Her face was grey, her lips still had an odd blue tinge. Her skin looked thin and delicate like old parchment and was bruised a variety of colours by George and the doctors who'd patched her up.

'And breathe . . . Good. And one . . . two . . . three . . . four . . .'

He was giving her life, just as she had done to him. But he hadn't asked to be born; perhaps she didn't really want to be here. It might be kinder to let her go. No! He wouldn't. He wanted her around, needed her still to be there for him.

'Mother? It's Ben. Please don't go . . .' He stroked her hair; it was dry like summer grass.

As if in response she seemed to belch and there was a gurgle in her throat.

From Kate's open mouth came a sudden gush of brown vomit, bursting from her with amazing force and splattering over Ben and the carpet. Jo thrust her fingers between Kate's teeth and hooked out what was still in there, stringy bits of something which she wiped off on her blouse, then turned her over expertly and arranged her carefully into a sort of swastika shape.

'Thank God. She's breathing. She's going to be all right.' Jo stood up and looked around.

Gina and Becca were gazing in admiration; Klaus, in his bizarre outfit, was crying quietly like someone at the end of a fancy dress party. George was holding his new face in old hands, moaning something incomprehensible. And Ben was sitting by Kate's prostrate form, shaking violently.

'Well, g'day everyone. Nice to meet you all. My name's Jo. Now, who's going to get me a friggin' drink while I roll a spliff?'

494

54

After seeing his mother rescued from a suicide attempt and helping to pull her life back from the precipice, Ben thought the day could hold no more surprises.

He was wrong.

There was one last shock to endure.

Once Kate had been made comfortable at the hospital and sedated so she would sleep through the night Klaus, looking like a kinky chauffeur in his leathers and cap, drove Ben and Jo back to Hampstead in the Merc.

When they went inside, ignoring the small crowd of hacks who had re-formed at the gate like a recurring damp patch on a wall, they heard voices raised in anger.

'Nearly thirty years I've waited and now I have to speak out.'

'Look at my face! This is what she did to me. And this she-wolf is your daughter! Christ!'

'And why, George?' came another voice. 'Why did I? In revenge for what? Tell her what you –'

As Ben, Jo and Klaus entered the study they were confronted with three suddenly silent, still figures glaring at each other, as if posing for a sculpture.

The older of the two women, a big-jawed, grey-haired woman in her fifties, turned her head to acknowledge them.

'You're Ben, I expect. Good. Glad you're here. You should hear this too.'

'Mother!' Gina pushed her glasses up her nose.

'Annabel Combes-Howard. This is my daughter, Gina.' She spoke to no one in particular.

'Yes, yes,' said Ben, nodding at them. His mother

495

had wanted to die. Nothing else interested him. He was exhausted and just wanted to go upstairs and curl up to sleep in a big bed, his own bed in his old room. He wondered if his old bear Tedward was still around.

'Look, Mother. You can't drag me along here like a four-year-old to hear some ridiculous —'

'Gina, be quiet.'

'You stupid little bitch. What have you done? Do you know what you've done to my career?'

'Oh, I know exactly what's happened to you! And I rejoice at your downfall!'

She was clutching one of her cheroots in her tiny fist. She inhaled on it now, staring at him, unblinking, then expelled the grey smoke through the side of her mouth.

George's face was a mask of concealed emotions. His eyes were open wide but they were red-blotched and watery, his skin stretched too tightly over the bones as if he'd been prematurely embalmed. His head, bare of any toupee with all pretence now abandoned, shone with perspiration and he swayed unsteadily on his feet.

'You stupid little girl,' he whispered at Gina. 'You'll never defeat me. I can still destroy you, even looking like this. You'll wish I'd finished you off properly.'

Gina was visibly shocked by his threat. She stepped away from him and backed into Jo without noticing.

'George!' Annabel's voice echoed with generations of breeding, with centuries of being obeyed by servants. 'Listen. Both of you. All of you. This is important. More important than anything I've ever had to say before.'

'If you knew what this bastard —'

'Gina, shut up, now. I mean it. Just restrain yourself for five minutes and let me say my piece.'

She looked at them both for their agreement, then pushed some of her wild hair off her face. One strand she twirled almost girlishly round a finger.

'I don't know the right way to approach this. Thought for years how best it should be done. Indeed, if it should be done at all. Now I find myself . . . hey-ho. When you told me you'd been to Bermuda to do some work with George King – well! That and your show. Appalled, I was. So cruel. So stupid. Thought I knew you. Used to know you. But in those days I was . . . how shall I phrase it? . . . In love with you, I suppose. No, George, don't interrupt, I won't allow it!'

Her jaw was set firm and she stood with mannish hands on ample hips, equal to any challenge he could muster. He shrank back, becoming accustomed now to the taste of defeat.

'George and I knew each other at university. We had a . . . relationship. Yes, Gina, you may well look like that. But he was younger, quite the dashing man about town then. When Kate Finkenberg came along I didn't take it as a serious threat. She had no class, I thought. No breeding. But what she did have was determination. And talent. I couldn't compete with that. She was admired for her acting skills. Not just cultivated because of an accident of birth, as I was. She took him from me. Fair enough. When I failed to return for my Finals I gather it was assumed I was suffering a fit of pique at having my man stolen. Anyway, I didn't need the degree, did I? I was a member of the Great British Aristocracy so I had it made for life, of course. Well,' she took a deep breath and gave a long sigh. 'That's not why I didn't sit my Finals.'

Ben thought how pale she looked, how scrubbed-clean her face was. He could see a vein throbbing gently at her temple. She spoke quietly but firmly.

'Had to go abroad. Went to Switzerland. To a college for young ladies. Young ladies who had "made mistakes" as they called it. Where I was able to . . . to . . .'

She looked up at the ceiling, then down at the floor.

'To have the baby?' said Jo gently.

Annabel nodded.

Ben's eyes darted from Annabel to Jo to George to Gina, unable yet to work out the significance of all this. Gina looked confused but George's breathing gave notice that he was working up to a response.

'You said you were going to get rid of it,' he growled.

'I know. I couldn't. I just couldn't. I had no right.'

'So . . . ?'

'Yes, George.'

'Wait. Mother, I don't understand.' This was Gina. The ash was falling from her cigar on to the carpet now. George and Annabel both turned to look at her, different expressions in their eyes but the same meaning.

'You had a child? Before me?'

'No, darling. Not before you.'

Only then did Ben understand. Just as Gina did.

'So, you're saying he's . . . No. What about Lars? Lars Landesmann? He was a Scandinavian millowner. He was my father.'

'A total invention, I'm afraid. The photographs I found in a junk shop. No idea who they were. Your birth was a year to the day earlier than I've always told you. I'm so sorry.'

She reached a hand out but lacked the courage to make contact.

'Dear God, this is horrible. Don't you see — ?'

'I know, I know. The older you got the harder it was to break the news. You seemed happy with this Lars character as a father. It was only when you said you were going to work for —'

'No!' George moaned, incredulous. 'She's my daughter? My daughter is this cow? *Oh, no. No!*' It was the wail of defeat and disgust.

'Why do you think I called her Georgina?'

Then Gina let out a quick gasp like someone stepping under a cold shower. Jo pushed a chair behind her and helped her down into it just as her legs buckled.

'No!' George bellowed. 'NO!'

Gina was panting, struggling for breath now. Jo and Klaus moved to her, trying to calm her with voices and comforting hands. Annabel was still talking but her words were unclear. George's voice was rising and he turned one way and then the other as if there might be a way out. 'Don't,' he was muttering to nobody. 'Don't do this to me.'

Ben saw it all and heard the mounting din but understood nothing. His mother had nearly died. What were they shouting about? Why didn't they all just go away?

'You evil bastard!' Becca's voice shrieked through the air, bringing a dramatic silence. She was still and hard as a statue but her face was ugly with contempt. Through teeth bitten together in fury she whispered, *'You raped your own daughter.'*

There was silence for a second and then from George came the low, sickening cry of a man in mortal pain. Gina put her hands over her ears and her whole body began to shiver. Jo put an arm around her shoulders but she shook it off.

Ben gazed in fascination as he saw his father sway forward, then the knees bent sharply and he slumped to the floor. For a second he thought George was praying but then he saw him clutching both hands to his chest as if declaring his love. He raised his big head slowly, looking for help. He was the boxer floored, the bull stuck by the picadors' darts. His eyes seemed to be surveying them, trying to recognize a face.

'Help me,' he whispered, his voice rasping as he struggled to breathe. His face was pale with a greyish tinge and sweat was pouring off him. Still the stretched skin was inscrutable, unable to show the reality of his plight. But the fear in his eyes couldn't be mistaken.

'Pain . . . pain . . . my arms, chest . . . can't breathe . . . please . . .'

He held out a hand, it was quivering, desperate for succour. Immediately Jo sprang forward.

'Quick. He's having —'

'I know,' said Ben sharply, holding out his own arm in front of her. 'Wait.'

'But –'

'*Wait!*'

His tone of voice stopped her instantly. Six pairs of eyes watched as George collapsed forward on to the carpet.

55

'You can speak to your husband but he won't be able to reply, I'm afraid. We've got him fairly heavily sedated. It's so he won't fight the ventilator. He seems to understand what's said to him, but it's impossible to know if he'll ever recover his powers of speech and other faculties.'

The nurse's name badge was partly obscured by a fold of her uniform. Sister Pel–. Like a life cut prematurely short, thought Kate.

'He's stabilized now and we've made him as comfortable as we can given his condition. He's getting twenty-four-hour one-to-one nursing and the various machines you'll see connected to him are monitoring his heartbeat, his blood pressure and so on. So, although there's really nothing more we can do for your husband, Mrs King, he's in no immediate danger and the Intensive Care Unit is the best possible place should any complication arise.'

'Yes. Thank you,' said Kate, glancing at her watch. 'Now, if I could see him briefly? I shall only stay a few minutes.' She had an important meeting later with Mr Jungsheimer. Barney as she was now privileged to call him.

It was Barney who'd insisted on the visit in the first place and arranged for the press to hear about it.

'This is the stuff of a publicist's wet dreams, Doll Face! He beats you up, you try to top yourself, now you drag yourself from your sickbed to be at his bedside in intensive care. Honey, you're gonna upstage the show with stunts like this! And they tell me you can act too. Hey, I love it!'

'I hope you won't find it too distressing. I'll show you through. This way.'

Kate was led out of the cramped office and into the ward

itself. She held her head high, concerned to show her cool disregard for George's plight. She'd stayed away from the hospital for several days, knowing that her absence would be noted and commented on in the press. 'Kate Cool in King Crisis' said one. Another, 'Battered wife absent as shamed TV hubby fights for life', with a picture taken about four years ago of Kate smiling blandly at some media-bash.

She was aware even here at the hospital that the eyes turned towards her were looking with a new-found interest now that she was a 'star' again. This was more like it.

She kept her own eyes strictly forward, following the quick, short steps that Sister Pel– took. Condemned to a life of flat shoes, thought Kate. Who'd be a nurse?

She took Kate to a half-glass door and paused.

'Ready?'

'Hm? Yes, fine,' she said with studied insouciance.

'That's Nurse Willans.' The sister nodded through the window towards someone in the corner of the room. 'Just ask her if you need anything. I'll leave you now.' And she walked away, her footsteps pecking out a brisk rhythm as she retreated down the long corridor.

Kate stepped inside. The atmosphere was cooler here, calmer and surprisingly odour-free. There was no stench of death or smell of medication that she remembered from her own hospitalization. The machinery throbbed with relentless professional efficiency. The room had the potent quiet of a library or a church.

It was a large space but the amount of medical hardware reduced it to not much more than a strip of floor on three sides of the bed.

Kate's eyes went everywhere but at George. Clusters of small clear plastic bags of fluid hung from the stands around the top of the big bed, tubes led from them down to the body. Something that looked like a transistor radio seemed to be pumping a pale pink liquid around transparent tubing. A white box like an electric toothbrush was positioned on the other side of the bed, performing a regular but mysterious function with an almost imperceptible hiss, and a blue box of tricks with flashing green lights bleeped reassuringly in a low, friendly tone.

Kate eagerly took in useless details rather than the awful facts, busying her mind with things she couldn't possibly need but which wouldn't harm her. Words leapt out at her like key names in a script to be learned: Capnograph . . . Disposaglove . . . Graseby . . . Servo-ventilator . . .

Finally, when there was nothing else she could distract herself with, she looked down at the body in the bed.

He was staring at her. With an effort she managed not to flinch.

As she stared back her first thought was that she had come into the wrong room. This wasn't George. This was the shell of some ancient, decrepit pauper. A miserable creature on the brink of death, any dignity he'd once had removed by the tubes inserted into him. She'd been warned about the disastrous facelift but even so, this looked barely human.

'George?'

A low gurgle came from his throat and his eyes sent what she took to be a desperate plea. Kate gasped, then swallowed and tried to speak, but no words seemed suitable for the occasion. Sympathy and blame were equally out of place.

'Miss Fitch? Are you all right?' Nurse Willans was at her side, ready to do enough coping for three if necessary. Kate turned to see her big pale face full of concern.

'Yes. Yes, I'm fine. Is he . . . ? I mean, does he . . . ?'

'He can certainly hear you and probably understand you.' She raised her voice, 'Can't you, George? But the sedation keeps you a bit woozy. Doesn't it, hm?'

'All the tubes?'

'They're helping him, believe me. Would you like to know what they all do?'

'No. I just want to . . . be with him for a while.'

'Of course. I'm here if you want me.' She retreated to

her corner and Kate approached the bed. George's eyes stayed with her.

Three separate tubes entered his neck around the collar bone and two flat blue discs were stuck to his chest. Another tube entered his left nostril, held in position with a piece of tape over his top lip, and a fat ribbed tube that looked big enough to choke him extended from his open mouth via an assortment of different coloured connectors to a large blue metal machine which proclaimed itself proudly as the '900 C' model. Its front was a mass of dials and switches and changing digital displays. With an eerily regular rhythm it clicked and then sighed with a wistful note of something floating away in space. Again it did it, again and again. It could do it for ever if necessary.

The machine was breathing for George, but it wasn't a reassuring sound; its very evenness made each pump of air seem as if it might be his last, one final gasp for the breath of life.

Kate bent over and looked at him. Really looked at him. She was amazed how old and sick he was. The stretched skin of his ridiculous new face was a ruddy brown but it looked dry and friable like the greaseproof paper off a roast turkey. She could imagine taking a pinch of his cheek and feeling the flesh crumble between her fingers.

'George? Do you know who I am?'

He gurgled.

'Do you remember what you did? What you did to me?'

She felt ridiculous, talking to a dummy who might or might not understand and who certainly couldn't answer back. The expression in his eyes didn't change. Was he in there somewhere or had he already left her for another universe?

'George. This is Kate. I just want you to know, if you can understand me . . .' she moved slightly to one side to check that the eyes still moved with her '. . . that I hate you now more than I ever have.'

He gave another wet gurgle as the nurse came quickly

over, speaking with an urgent intensity but still polite.

'Mrs King, um, Miss Fitch, I really feel that you might be in danger of raising his blood pressure and his heart —'

'Did you see what he did to me? On his programme?'

'Well, yes, I did. But here in the ICU the patient is —'

'Don't you think I have a right to talk to him? To say what I feel?'

'I can't let you endanger his life.'

'I wouldn't want to. I want him to make a full recovery so that he can face the consequences of the way he's lived his life. Leave me alone with him for five minutes.'

'I really can't do that.'

'Excuse me, this isn't some poxy National Health set-up. We are paying for all this.'

'Even so —'

'I won't touch him. I couldn't bear to. And I won't touch any of your . . . machinery. You can see me through the window. I need to say one or two things to him in private. You can understand that, can't you, Carole?' Her badge was quite legible.

'If his central venous pressure or heart rate increases beyond the set parameters the alarms will sound . . .'

'And you'll have to come in and take care of him. I understand.'

'I shall be outside. I can see everything from there.'

'I know. I'm not going to harm him. I want him to live.'

The nurse cast one last professional eye over her charge and checked the flashing digits on the ventilator. Then she gave a petulant little pucker of her lips and went outside. Kate waited until she'd taken guard just beyond the door.

Alone with George again Kate sighed, more slowly than the machine keeping him alive. It clicked and breathed twice in the space of her long exhalation. She pulled the nurse's chair over to the bedside and sat. For a few minutes she just watched him. And he watched her.

'So, George,' she said quietly at last. 'It's come to this. Did you ever think it would? It's all too late for you now,

505

isn't it? I don't mean you're going to die. You might, of course, but I hope you don't. Because people may remember your smart image instead of the real, sleazy person they're just beginning to discover. Oh yes, the filth is starting to ooze out now. But there's so much more to come. Your wife-beating is just the start. What about the mistress in Kensington, the woman who's . . . hang on. I've got it here, somewhere . . .'

Kate bent to rummage in her handbag for the paper she'd bought at the stall downstairs. She opened it at the relevant page and held it up above his face so that he could see the massive headline: 'GEORGE'S BIMBO: Why I'm carrying Mister TV's lovechild.'

'It was me, of course. I put Hal Brand on to your sad little Suzi. Still, she should have a good fund of stories to tell. They'll keep her in Babygros for a while. She says she's writing a book, too. Not by herself, of course; I think Hal is going to help her with the joined-up writing. Hal's inherited the nine o'clock slot on Friday, by the way, with a new show. "The Hal Brand Agenda". He's invited me on next week to talk about – well, you can imagine. Playing Jackie. My new stardom. Yes, I'm a star now, George. Barney, that's Mister Jungsheimer to you – said it was the publicity generated by your shameful behaviour that tipped it in my favour. Otherwise it might have gone to Dame Judi. God, you do look ghastly.'

Kate smiled indulgently at him as she would to a rather dim child.

'Oh, I understand you've had some kind of professional involvement with Ben's girlfriend. You really have had your grubby little fingers in some very murky places, haven't you? Metaphorically and literally, no doubt. I'm sorry, that was cheap. It's just that I feel so damned cheerful all the time! Your Floozie Suzi says you were producing porn videos in Germany and importing them to Britain and then on to the States via Bermuda. Oh dear, oh dear. If you do pull through your life's not going to be worth

506

living anyway. The rest of it will be behind bars. Obscene publications, Customs and Excise fraud, assault. Not to mention the charge of rape. My, you've had a full life. But it's all over now, George. The game's up.'

There was another soft noise, something like a snore but from deep in George's throat and saliva bubbled from the crease of his cracked lips. Kate leaned over to stare deep into his eyes.

'Oh, George. Are you in there? Can you understand me? I do hope so. It would be awfully sad if you didn't realize how pathetic you've become. How totally your whole world has been destroyed. I do want you to *suffer*, you know. It is your turn, after all.'

The door opened. Kate didn't bother to look round, expecting the nurse to be there, ready to restrain her if she attempted to harm George.

'Hello, Mother.'

She looked up. 'Ben!'

Neither of them moved but then, imperceptibly, they each gave the other a signal that the process of forgiveness had begun. He flung himself at her as he used to once before and she hugged him with more conviction than she'd brought to any part in her career.

'Oh, that's so nice. A proper hug . . . Oh, Ben . . .'

'I'm sorry. I'm so sorry.'

'No, no. Sssh.'

'I'm glad you're here. I thought . . . we all thought we'd lost you.'

'I was being selfish. I shouldn't have done it. I was just so tired. Of being humiliated. Of all the –'

Kate turned her back to him, biting her lip, and faced the grey light outside. Leaves whisked past the window, borne on the blustery wind and carried away without a choice in where they landed. She knew exactly how that felt. If you knew you had no control you could accept that; it was believing you could influence the wind that led to disappointment.

507

'Dad?' Ben approached the bed with caution. 'Is he . . . all right? I mean, will he . . . ?'

'Yes, he might die.' Kate didn't have his qualms about saying the word. 'He could go at any time. Or he might slowly get all his faculties back. They just can't tell.'

'God.'

'They said if he'd received prompt first aid he probably wouldn't be like this.'

'I see.'

Ben gazed down at his father. Kate took the opportunity to study her son. He seemed younger, fitter than she'd expected. He was a very handsome man and she remembered how much she loved him.

'Are you all right?'

'Yes, I'm okay.'

'Don't stay if it upsets you, Benny.'

'You used to call me that when I was little.'

'Did I? I'd forgotten.'

She'd forgotten so much. She was seeing Ben as if they'd met for the first time. She was impressed. He was a strong, grown-up man, capable and intelligent. But she still saw her little boy, the one she'd never loved enough. She wanted to hug him to her and make amends for all the terrible things she'd done to him over the years. But she hardly knew him well enough to talk to him.

'All the things I've wanted to say to him.' There was a note of wonder in Ben's voice. 'All the rows I wanted to start, the fights I should have had. I could say anything now and I'd win all the arguments. But it doesn't seem worth it. I don't know if I need to now.'

'What about me?' Kate ventured, stepping closer to him. 'What about the rows you should have had with me? If there's anything we should fight about, let's not leave it until it's too late.'

'It's difficult to start after . . .' He couldn't finish but she knew.

'After not speaking for so many years. That's my fault.

And I'm sorry. I'm going to be different from now on. Well, I'm going to try. Do you think we could get to know each other a little?'

He looked at her. He seemed wary, unsure of her. 'I don't know. I hope so. You know, it's only when I saw what he did to you on that bloody programme. And then, when Klaus brought you home in the car that I . . .'

Without warning he was suddenly crying, wiping the back of his hand across his eyes and under his nose just like he had when he came home from school with a story about being bullied.

'Sorry, Mother . . .'

Kate smiled at him, feeling a rush of strength pour through her. 'No, I'm the one who should apologize. All those years I couldn't forgive you. I nursed such a grudge and couldn't put it all in the past where it belonged.'

Ben caught his sobbing breath. 'Forgive me? For what?'

'For what happened.' She paused, frightened of the dark abyss on whose edge she now teetered but knowing she had to leap, knowing it had to be confronted. 'With Christopher.'

'What do you mean, with Christopher? What have I got to be forgiven for? Wait, what do you think happened?'

He was on the alert now. Something was wrong here. Something didn't ring true.

'Oh, we don't need to go into all that again.' She gave a little flounce and pretended to study the dials and meters on a machine at George's bedside. It was a false, theatrical gesture and its hollowness annoyed Ben. He leaned forward and grabbed Kate's arm, pulling her round with a force that shocked them both.

'What do you mean "again"? Listen to me.' His jaw was firm and his teeth clenched together but his face was wet with the tears that were still flowing. 'I didn't save your life to have you ignore me now. You owe me something and I'm not afraid to demand it. You owe me the truth. In everything. You do know that, don't you?'

She couldn't meet his eyes.

'Yes. Yes, Ben, you're right.'

'You have to know this. What he did, *what he did!*' Ben pointed at the pathetic body on the bed.

'What do you mean? When?'

'That day. The day we lost Christopher. Oh, he was my friend. My best friend. If I could have saved him. If there was anything I could have done . . .'

'But George said . . .'

'What? What lies did he feed to you? *Tell me!*' Ben was gabbling, urgently now, as if everything that hadn't been said for two decades had to be fitted into the next two minutes. He was stumbling over his words in his urgency to give and get explanations.

'Did he say it was my fault? That I let him drown? Is that what he said?'

'He said . . . so many things. Different things . . . I believed him. I didn't think then that he'd lie about something like that. I was vulnerable. I just believed him. Later we couldn't talk about it at all.' Kate's face showed the doubts that were crowding into her mind.

'What? What did he say?'

'Oh God. He told me you'd been in tears, saying you were sorry. Over and over again, you said you were sorry. You'd pushed him in because Christopher was Mummy and Daddy's favourite.'

'What? No!'

'He said you . . . Oh, Ben.'

'Tell me.' He squeezed her arm and shook her, as if that would force the words out.

'He said you told him you . . . you'd . . . held him under the water until the bubbles stopped coming up.'

'*No!*'

'Tell me, quickly. Any of it? Is any of it true?'

'None of it, none of it! And I've protected him all this time. You want the truth? He was inside raping the bloody babysitter when Christopher drowned! I saw him!'

Ben turned to the immobile figure on the bed.

'*I saw you!* Did you know? You and that girl. Becca. Becca Nichols. You raped her when she was practically a child and she got her revenge by getting your precious face carved up! Isn't that *funny*? Don't you think that's FUNNY?'

'Ben, Ben. Becca was the babysitter? Are you sure?'

'You've ruined more lives than even you know about. You have no right to live!'

Ben made a sudden lunge at George, pulling plastic tubes away to get at his neck. Immediately machinery bleeped and bells rang out.

'You bastard! You said I killed Christopher! There's only one person I've ever wanted to kill and *I'm going to do it now!*'

His hands were around George's throat. The door was flung open and two blue uniforms rushed past Kate as the young nurses struggled to restrain Ben.

He didn't resist. In a moment he'd been pulled away and led from the room, choking and muttering to himself.

The sister was there, checking George and resetting machines. He looked exactly the same. Kate watched in a daze. Nothing shocked her any more. The last few weeks had been such a life-changing series of blows and revelations. She was now supposed to start rehearsals for *O Jackie*, giving her all for the stage. She'd do it, of course. She was nothing if not a pro. Now she was a star again. It was what she'd always wanted. She was more famous than George now, more loved by the public than he'd ever been. This wasn't exactly the way she'd imagined it happening, but still . . . And she was going to start talking to Ben again. Ben, who wasn't responsible for Christopher's death after all. No wonder he had hated her, feeling as he must have done the waves of hatred she'd never quite managed to disguise.

Was it all too late? Too late for the start of a new life? No. Not for Kate. Not for Ben. But too late for George, thank God. He was condemned to his self-inflicted hell.

So the babysitter was Becca? Blue movies from Germany to the States through Bermuda? There were the seeds of a good plot here, thought Kate with a hint of levity flitting over her heart like a butterfly around a summer buddleia.

Hmm. I must talk to Robin about this. It might make a mini-series. Who'd make a good Kate Fitch? I wonder if Dame Judi would be interested . . . ?